SONS AND BROTHERS

In this richly textured novel the stories
of two families — the Fessendens and the
Tolhursts — interweave through two
generations. The nation is torn by civil war,
family against family, brother against
brother, King against Parliament, faith
against faith. Warring armies devastate the
land.

Events on the wider screen are finely focused
in the characters of the three Fessenden
brothers: John, who voyages with the pilgrims
to America, Robert the hard-line Puritan, and
Isaac, who supports the Royalist cause. The
passion and tragedy of the story is played out
here. But, if the anguish of the brothers most
deeply touches the heart, it is in the character
of Anna Tolhurst that love and courage find
their clearest expression.

Sons and Brothers is ELIZABETH GIBSON's
second novel. Her first, *The Water is Wide*,
set in Northern Ireland, won her acclaim
both in the USA and in Britain. This new
novel has its roots in the stories of the
author's seventeenth-century forebears and
those of her American husband, both —
remarkably — focused on the same small
village in Kent, England, close to the town
where the Gibsons now live.

SONS AND BROTHERS

ELIZABETH GIBSON

A LION PAPERBACK

Tring • Batavia • Sydney

Copyright © 1988 Elizabeth Gibson

Published by
Lion Publishing plc
Icknield Way, Tring, Herts, England
ISBN 0 7459 1525 6
Albatross Books Pty Ltd
PO Box 320, Sutherland, NSW 2232, Australia
ISBN 0 86760 999 0

First UK edition 1988

British Library Cataloguing in Publication Data
Gibson, Elizabeth, 1949–
   Sons and brothers
   I. Title
   823′.914 [F]

   ISBN 0–7459–1525–6

Printed in Great Britain
by Cox and Wyman

To Malcolm, beloved Man of Kent
To Tony, beloved Kentish Man
And to Jim, beloved Man of Kent

One born in Africa, one born in London,
one born in America —

but all men of Kent

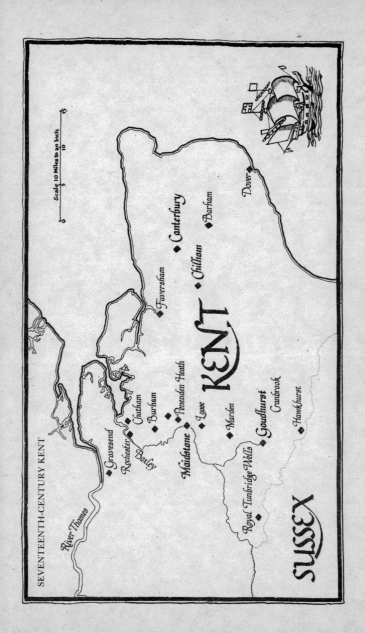

SEVENTEENTH-CENTURY KENT

Scale 10 Miles to an Inch

River Thames

Gravesend
Rochester
Chatham
Boxley
Burham
Penenden Heath
Maidstone
Looe
Marden
Royal Tunbridge Wells
Goudhurst
Cranbrook
Hawkhurst

KENT

Faversham
Chilham
Canterbury
Barham
Dover

SUSSEX

THE TOLHURSTS

Squire George (b.1570 d.1624 – Patron of Peter Longden)

George ⚭ Elizabeth (1632)
(b.1600)   (b.1610)

Anna	Henrietta	Charlotte	Eleanor	Edward
(b.1638)	(b.1640)	(b.1642)	(b.1645)	(b.1658)

THE FESSENDENS

John m Jane Triton (1621)
(b.1600)   (b.1597)

one adopted son
Nathaniel
(1638–1653)

John m ¹Ruth (1599) m ²Mary Snode (1634)
(1580–1648)   (d.1620)   (d.1659)

Robert m Patience (1634)
(b.1605)   (1612–1655)

Thomas   Nicholas   Josiah   Hannah
(1635–1654)   (b.1636)   (b.1638)   (b.1640)

Martha   Sarah   Mary   Isaac m Rebecca
(b.1606) (b.1609) (b.1611) (b.1613)   Longden (1635)
                                        (1620–1659)

Adam   Charlie   Anna   others
(b.1636)   (b.1639)   (1648–49)   who
                                    died

I

FOR GOD AND KENT

I have house and land in Kent
And if you'll love me, love me now.
Two-pence half-penny is my rent,
I cannot come every day to woo.

One time I gave thee a paper of pins,
Another time a tawdry lace;
And if thou wilt not grant me love
In truth I die before thy face.

I will put on my best white shirt
And I will wear my yellow hose
And on my head a good grey hat,
And in't stick a lovely rose.

Wherefore cease off, make no delay,
And if you'll love me, love me now;
Or else I seek some other where —
For I cannot come every day to woo.

Melismata, 1611

1

ROBERT
Chilham, Spring 1619

Through the dry, bricked vaults of the wine cellar Robert followed the voices of the kitchen wenches. The bolt of cloth under his arm had become a dead weight, and not knowing his way through the new castle, the boy was lost already. He thought resentfully, *The steward should have accompanied me*.

The cellar suddenly opened out into the wide space of the underkitchen, opened out into light, heat, and merriment. Two girls of his own age were plucking fowl, shrieking and giggling as the feathers flew in clouds round them. The cook stood at the wooden board, flour dusting her hands, her cheeks and her cap as she pounded the dough and watched the kitchen maids with tolerant amusement. Robert thought fleetingly of his mother, of her horror if she could have seen the slackness and laxity of the cook, the foolish laughter of the girls; she would never have suffered such a brawl in her own kitchen, he knew well. But neither would she have had maids to do the work for her.

He stepped forward with what he hoped was a civil bow to the cook. 'I'm come to see my lady, ma'am, and the steward bade me come here.'

The cook thumped the grain-speckled dough louder than before and ignored him, but one of the girls stopped her squealing and turned towards him. 'Did 'e, now? Well, ain't 'e the fool, then. Madam'd never deign to walk in 'ere, you may be sure of that.' With a bloodstained hand she reached to tuck a greasy tendril of hair into her cap, simpering as she did so. 'But you look like a handsome cock.' She turned to the other girl.

13

'Be 'e old enough, this lad, d'you think, Patience, for us to pluck his feathers?'

He backed away uncertainly. The smile of gratitude for their interest froze as he heard what she said.

The second girl made faint sounds of rebuke to her companion and sent him a pitying look. 'Leave off, Joan. Can't you see 'e's got something for the lady?'

The bold girl clacked her tongue, eyeing the bolt of cloth pointing towards her. 'Lackaday, I thought 'e had something for *me!*'

The thumping of the dough suddenly stopped. 'Give the lad some ale, Patience. And take that great parcel off of him afore he drops it in the flour and feathers.' The cook glanced up briefly from the pans into which she was pressing the dough. 'I'll see she gets it, don't you fret.'

Flinging a triumphant smirk over her shoulder at Joan, Patience came forward with her eyes down and offered to take the parcel from him, but he backed away. 'Nay, 'tis my father's will I give it to the lady myself.'

She fluttered her eyelashes at him so that he felt the heat rise into his face. 'Ah, poor lad. It's a heavy thing he's got.' And she bustled off to fill a tankard of ale for him.

He watched her retreating back, trying to gauge where her sympathies really lay. He liked the flattering way she had looked at him, almost as if he *were* a good-looking young fellow. He liked the way her neatly patched skirts swished over the tile floor, this way and that as her hips moved.

She returned with the ale and gave it to him. Afraid of soiling the cloth, he nervously laid the bolt down on a vacant chair. He took it with an unsteady hand; his father had recently declared that there would be no more ale in the house, that ale was a tool of Satan and that henceforth they were to drink nothing but water and milk — and he knew he would run the risk of a birching if he drank it. Still, the saucy looks of both girls stirred him to risk it, to enjoy the inevitable wait before he could see Lady Digges. He sipped the ale slowly, then, as the cook sent Joan to find her.

By the time Lady Digges came to the kitchen door, shadowed by Joan, who leered at him from behind her mistress, he was heady with the ale in an empty stomach. He felt even more provoked by Patience's insinuating looks as she now went about the business of plucking the birds with every appearance of demure coyness and innocence. He tried to rally his wits as he presented the cloth and bowed. Her ladyship welcomed him kindly, gave him a box of eggs, and seemed not to notice his agitation. At last he was free to escape from the kitchen and back through the wine cellar to the frosty out-of-doors.

He was almost out of the castle when he realized that he had been followed. A shadow darted out from behind the last keg of wine by the door, and Patience blocked his way. She had pulled off her cap so that her hair hung in loose curls round her face, and despite the smear of poultry blood across her cheek, he could see that she was pretty, and that she knew it. His throat went dry.

'What is't?' he rasped hoarsely, beginning to tremble, but nevertheless determined to show himself a man.

She twisted her shoulders and looked at him slyly. 'Cook said I might go and beg a kiss of thee, since I'd shown you kindness — '

He grinned. 'So that's your game. Well, have it, and welcome. Then let me pass, pray.' He leaned towards her, intending to escape with a brush of his mouth across her face, then to push her aside and be gone. But she took the box of eggs from him, and caught him by the arms. In his befuddled state he found his sense of space, time, and distance suddenly distorted, found that he was kissing her with a hunger he did not know himself capable of after years of cold kisses from his mother and sisters. Then he shuddered and broke free of her, a vision of his parents suddenly looming large before his eyes. 'You're naught but a harlot,' he spat.

She reached up quickly and wrenched the small falling band off his jerkin. Her eyes sparkled with laughter. 'Then I'll have a keepsake of thee.'

He tried to tear it out of her hand, but she was too quick for him, and he knew he could not follow her. He picked up the eggs, shoved the door open and fled out into the kitchen gardens and down the long walk to the front gates. There he stopped, quaking

15

inwardly, suddenly sobered by the rush of cold air and half-darkness. He must set himself to rights before he dared go home.

He had halted by the well, and now he tried to decide whether to draw water. Setting down the eggs, he leaned over the edge of the well and listened to the faint dripping below, smelt the familiar dampness and comparative warmth of it in the March frost. Then the knowledge of the long walk home and the ache of his body spurred him on. Disregarding the bite of the cold Wealden iron in his palm, he gripped the crank and forced himself to turn it. At last the winch brought the bucket to the mouth of the well. Swinging it over, he grabbed it clumsily. Water spilled out, soaking his breeches and hose. He groaned in dismay, gritting his teeth as he pictured his parents again. *Drunk,* his father would say, *and smelling of wenches.* And *You'll be starved with cold, you foolish boy,* his mother would say. *Whatever possessed you? And where is your neckband, pray?*

He bent his hands in a scoop to the water, swilled the first numbing mouthful round his tongue and teeth, and spat it out. He had to wash away the smell of ale first. Then he drank greedily, shivering. Eventually he dropped the bucket back into the well, retrieved his parcel, and went on across the village green; it was already soaked with dew.

He passed the church and gave its battlements only a half-glance flung without thought over his left shoulder. On the other side of the narrow, downhill lane ahead of him he could discern through the twilight of this spring afternoon the movements of the cottagers against the dimness of rushlights and wood fires. In the forge a smith was clanging his hammer on the anvil, the glare of the fire behind him. The banality and sameness of the scene reassured him as he walked in the shadow of the churchyard's great yew tree and long stone wall.

An old man leading a goat left the muddy alleyway between two of the Poor Row cottages just below and shuffled past Robert with only a nod at him; the man jerked irritably at the rope round its neck as the animal snorted and swerved skittishly towards the wall. An infant in one of the cottages near the bottom of the hill let out a thin, mewling cry that was answered by the screech of an owl. Absently he watched the bird flap silently towards the cloud-blurred moon.

At the end of the lane, outside the alehouse, he noticed drifting from somewhere in the woods the sweetish smell of the charcoal burners' furnace: the orange glow stained the sky above the wood to a livid, ghastly colour. His brother would have been uneasy, gabbling beside him about witches or pagan bonfires or evil spirits. John: the dreamer, the fanciful, they called him. And now John had gone to live in Leyden, in the Pilgrim Church on the Kloksteeg.

Newly resentful, Robert thought, *If I were the elder, I could be there. I'm the one should have gone. He's the elder — my father needs him, not me, to work for him. John may be no man of business, but mayhap I'm not, either. We'll not satisfy my father . . . not I, especially.* He frowned. Surely John wasn't as zealous as he was? Surely not. His letters had been full of telling details about the wool industry in Holland: the way the Dutch in Leyden wove and dressed their cloth; his own interest in the new draperies — softer, finer cloths of silk and Spanish wool dyed by clever craftsmen whose work, John said, could not be bested by Kentish dyers anywhere; the organization of the Dutch guilds; the growing respect, grudging at first, won by the Separatist church from the men of Leyden for their commercial deftness and energy. Yes, John spoke of the church there in every sentence, but more of the members' work and prosperity than of their religious life. Yes, he quoted from the sermons of Brewster and Robinson, but he wrote much more about the witness of his elders among the foreign merchants and craftsmen than about the inner workings of God in his own heart. For sure, he, not John, belonged in Holland.

A different thought stopped him. No, he was not worthy, not spiritual enough after all. He had just polluted himself at the castle — and he had enjoyed it. He would get his collar back from that wench if he was branded for it, and he would settle his account with the girl once and for all. *Patience!* What an unfit name for such a girl!

17

A thud of hooves cut across his picture of her. Unthinking, he drew back into the hedgerow. The horse was panting, in a lather; he could hear the rider's grunts as the horse's hooves struck the uneven ruts and flints of the road, and the slight creak of the saddle leather. Mantle flying, the rider drew nearer: a messenger who knew the road well, he decided, to ride so recklessly downhill in the dark. Then passed him — a sack of what might have been mail bouncing on his back, and a horn gleaming beside it in the light of the moon; the smell of oats and sweat and the stable; a splatter of mud spraying Robert's surcoat.

Robert went on, faster now. No witches or ghosts abroad, perhaps, but footpads and other rogues . . . one never knew. Muttering a hasty prayer for safety, he rounded the last curve before his cottage and searched with his eyes for the first glimpse of home.

Candles in the kitchen window. The sweet scent of bacon curing in the smokehouse, the acrid smell of tallow being rendered in one of the outshots behind the wash-house: all the familiar signs of his mother's busy, well-ordered life. He and his brothers and sisters were fortunate, he thought, to have parents who worked so hard and taught them as well as his parents had. His father was now his own master, a successful clothier who nevertheless chose not to leave his yeoman's roots — the village of his father and grandfather, both weavers. And who though he had built the timber-framed cottage where they lived — and could have built a grand Wealden hall had he wished — chose to live in simplicity, without household servants, and without all the luxuries of neighbouring gentlefolk.

Perhaps someone had heard the gate, for the studded oak door of the cottage suddenly flew open and his sister met him on the threshold.

'Robert, you're home at last. Come in, come in! Such news there is!'

He noticed her cap was slightly askew and her broadcloth skirt as dusty with flour as that of the castle cook. At thirteen she already carried herself like a young matron: as brusque and practical as her mother; and, unlike her mother, plump and comely, rapidly filling out her bodice. 'What, Martha? What is it?' He reached to tilt her cap further over one eye, for he knew it would annoy her, then turned to place his parcel on the settle by the door.

Narrowing her eyes and pursing her lips, she made a great show of straightening her cap again before hurrying down the passageway, through the buttery, and back into the kitchen. 'Now you shan't find out, you naughty child.'

'Child!' he sneered. 'And, pray, what are you?'

He was answered by three pairs of clear eyes and heads of dark curls shining in the firelight of the kitchen. Sarah, Mary, and Isaac sat side by side on stools in front of the fire. Clearly, Martha was making supper for everyone — mother for the evening.

'Where's our father?' he asked stiffly.

Martha would not look at him, resolutely stirring a thick broth in the brass pot over the fire, but she replied, all the same, 'In our mother's chamber.' She nodded towards the ceiling. 'There's much ado.'

He shifted impatiently and looked down at Sarah. 'What's ado, Sarah?'

'Our mother has the ague. She's abed.' Her serious face broke into a great smile.

Now he guessed the news. His mother never had an ague, was never one to lie abed at six of the clock in the evening . . . not unless . . . *John nineteen, himself fourteen, Martha thirteen, Sarah ten, Mary eight, Isaac six* . . . Aye, quite likely Providence had bestowed another child by now. His mother had lost a child between himself and John, and another after Isaac. And she still wanted that seventh child.

He grinned uncertainly at Sarah. 'So that's the news. Good news, aye. She's not too poorly, I hope.'

Martha gave a click of her tongue, as if resigned to his inclusion in this women's talk, and she sighed. 'Nay, weary, though . . . But there's more news, yet. As good news as the other, Mother said.'

Robert's eyes ran over the faces of his younger sisters and of Isaac.

'They know nothing more,' Martha cautioned him primly. 'And nor will you, till we sup.' She turned to

19

Sarah. 'Pray set out bread and two candlesticks, and spoons for all — on the board. And fetch me the trenchers from the cupboard. Robert, I see, is hungry, and no doubt our father, too.' She at last looked at her brother. 'Our mother told our father her news this morning — early, though 'twas after you had gone. And they did not break fast today, till now, in thanksgiving for this mercy of God.'

He frowned. 'No wonder Mother feels weak now. She will sup, I hope, at least.'

'My father said so. I doubt it not.'

Robert left the room, retrieved his box, and placed it on the bench beside the hearth. 'Eggs from the Lady Mary for our mother,' he said.

Martha swept them up without a glance and went to deposit them in the buttery. 'What, does she think our hens know not how to lay?' Her voice rose indignantly, and she clapped the buttery door shut behind her.

Robert laughed. His mother would have said the same. 'She must think so, surely, you sour little maiden.'

Behind them, Sarah moved quietly round the table with the spoons, then took a taper from the fire and lit two more brass candlesticks.

Robert went on, 'Be not ungracious. Perhaps the lady knew of our mother's state.'

'Nonsense! News travels not in the wind.'

'How knowing you are, dear sister.'

'And how discourteous you are, dear brother — ' She stopped, frowning at his jerkin. 'And where's your collar, you rascal?'

He glared back, deciding to ignore the question. 'In truth, the lady sent the eggs, besides the money she owed, as a gift of thanks. Very kind she was.' He raised his voice to a higher pitch and shed for a moment the thick Kentish accent in which the family always conversed at home. '"Give your father my thanks," said she. "The seal on his cloth, 'tis what I look for nowadays. Wool of the best. And mannerly, too, to send his son to bring it."'

His sister scoffed, though he knew she was impressed. 'Happen she might have liked it better had our father taken the bolt himself . . . had he not enough to do!'

20

'Enough of what to do?'

The elder John Fessenden had quietly opened the low door at the foot of the stairs and now stood watching Martha thoughtfully. Already flushed from the steam of the kettle, the girl flushed a deeper red and began to stammer out an answer that he stopped with a wave of his hand. 'Nay, you and Robert are full of idle talk.' He met Robert's eyes. 'What account can you give of yourself, son?'

Unaware, he licked his lips and stood straighter than before. He dreaded having to answer questions about his falling band or about the goings-on at the Castle. 'I delivered the cloth you wished, sir, and the lady was well-pleased. She bade me pay you five shillings, and gave you two dozen eggs.' He threw a quick glance at his sister.

"Twas well done.'

He went on again, gathering speed in the hope of forestalling awkward questions. 'And before that I went to my lessons, and this morning I saw to it that the weavers were paid as you bid me, and that their looms weren't idle. Abraham and David have a hundredweight of cloth — or more — ready for the fulling. David says he thinks some of the spinners lack wool. Abraham says the weavers in Loose and Maidstone wanted — '

'Never mind what Abraham says. He wouldn't know, never having been out of Chilham. But you've traversed much ground today, I see. Good lad. Is your purse safely under key?'

For a moment he panicked. *What if the wench got it off me, got more than my collar and now sits laughing at me . . . ?* He fumbled at his belt. The purse was safe. 'Nay, I forgot to put it away.'

'Then give me what you took in today, and later you'll give me a full accounting' — he fixed him with a stern stare — 'for every item. Martha, you're ready to wait on us? Come, sit up for prayers and supper, as you're bid, children.'

As the family pulled stools to the table and Martha ladled broth into bowls, Ruth Fessenden moved into the room behind her husband. Weary, as Martha had said. She did not smile as she took her place. Robert eyed her

21

through his fingers as his father prayed long and earnestly over the food. He had not seen his mother since the night before, and in just a day she seemed to have changed. Some of the force had left her, he thought. He remembered clearly her carrying the second child that had died; even more clearly, though it was when he was only eight, he remembered her being great with Isaac. She hadn't slowed her pace then. He felt strangely anxious for her. The vigorous, stern mother he'd known for fourteen years wasn't always as he had wanted her to be — but she was Mother. His mother. Fear seized him for a moment. Only for a moment. Grace over, her quietness melted quickly as she reached to chastise Isaac for dabbling his fingers in the broth. There. She was with them again: indomitable, untiring after all.

The family customarily spoke little over food; so the room fell quiet except for the crackle of the fire and the soft scraping of wooden spoons in the trenchers. From time to time Ruth met her husband's eyes, looking down the full length of the table to where he sat at the opposite end. Robert caught the glances and smiled inwardly. His mother would be all right. Pray God this child would be born strong and healthy. Pray God it would be another boy who could grow up to relieve John and himself — and later Isaac — of all the responsibility their father was slowly shifting on to them.

At last Ruth said, 'Martha, you made a good supper. Thank you.'

She bowed her head with uncharacteristic meekness. 'I had good meat and vegetables to put in it.'

Her mother sighed. 'Aye, the harvest was good last year.'

Martha smiled. 'Yes — all the fruit — remember? And the apples are fine and crisp, even the pears . . .'

Robert stared at them both, not wanting the conversation to wander far from what occupied his mind. His sister, he thought, had a fine way of talking trifles.

'What is't, Robert?' his father suddenly asked.

He looked sharply to the other end of the table, though he shouldn't have been surprised by the question; his father had an uncanny knack for sensing his moods.

22

'Something's troubling you, for all the good work of the day.'

He started guiltily, but then saw concern, not condemnation, among the lines of his father's face. 'Nothing to do with my work, sir,' he mumbled.

'What, then?'

Martha flashed him a spiteful look. *Now you'll catch it for losing your collar . . .*

He ducked her look, thrust the wench out of his mind again, and assumed an air of injury. 'There's news, I hear, and none to share it.'

'News indeed! You'll know it presently. Isaac, fetch me the Scriptures. And another candle, pray.'

Robert suppressed a moan, confronting afresh his spiritual poverty. How could the family forget prayers? His father never forgot, not even in the height of the summer — when magical daylight enticed them out-of-doors until late in the evening, when woodpigeons called, and those cutting the hay on the hillside sang until dark. Prayers: an unrelenting pattern, winter and summer. A ritual his three sisters endured in uncomplaining, even attentive silence, but one that he and Isaac fidgeted through. *Perhaps,* he thought doubtfully as his father opened the large volume to one of the Books of Moses, *Perhaps I'm not the one who should live in Leyden after all, with talk all the live-long day of God's laws and Moses' laws and sacrifice, sin, and sanctity. Not I!* But he did not yet know, either, where he'd rather be.

'Robert, you'll read to us, please,' his father said.

Taking the Bible, he swallowed hard and began at the beginning of the twenty-fourth chapter of Genesis. *The man at the well for his master, Isaac,* he thought irritably. *And a beautiful girl gives him to drink . . .* He remembered Patience again, glanced up at his father questioningly, then read on. Even as he read his mind ranged to other subjects: his sisters going to school with their mother all day, learning in the kitchen how to cipher and write, how to read aloud from the Gospel stories. His mother would be up to her elbows in flour making the week's loaves, or pickling vegetables from the garden, the benches and floor awash with vinegar. A patchwork sort of education!

23

He had started his own in the same way — as had his brother John — chanting numbers or letters in order, or verses from Scripture. John had once undertaken tongue-in-cheek to count to one-hundred-and-forty-four-thousand, as God would do at the great marriage supper of the Christ, and had memorized an entire chapter of the Book of Revelation to please his mother. But then he had teased her because she could not con the Greek alphabet besides alpha and omega. And for his pains, John had been packed off to board in Maidstone and to attend the Grammar School there as a William Lamb scholar. That was years ago now, and his parents had prospered. No longer would their children need scholarships. 'It was the right thing for John,' his mother had said. 'He wanted studiousness and discipline, and one day you'll both take over from your father. But as for you . . . no . . . you'll learn at home.'

He had not remained at home, however. The village priest had singled him out a few years after John had returned from Maidstone. There had been tutoring in elementary Latin, the Catechism, Psalter, and Bible. Only at the Prayer Book had his father balked and threatened to bring him home to lessons with his mother again. 'A popish book,' he'd grunted: words Robert still didn't fully understand. 'They chant it off as they were parrots.'

He faltered suddenly on a sentence that seemed to have no end.

His mother checked him. 'You're not minding, son.'

He read further, then listened as one by one Sarah, Mary, and Isaac recited verses they had learned that day. At last with his brother and sisters he bowed his head to his father's familiar voice pronouncing solemn invocations, petitions, and prayers for God's mercy on his own and the sins of his family. As his father prayed, Robert convinced himself he could actually see between his fingers the candles burning down inch by inch. He moved restlessly on his stool and caught a glimpse of Isaac twisting and fretting even more obviously than himself. His father's voice intoned with greater urgency than ever, suddenly punctuated by the sharp slap of flesh on flesh. His mother had pounced, and Isaac was stifling sobs in his sleeve as the prayers droned on.

They ended at last. Martha and her mother began ushering the younger ones to the upper chamber. There in the uncertain warmth creeping between the cracks of the stone chimney piece and afforded by flock bedding, by sacks of malt and corn stacked for warmth against the walls and under the lead-paned windows — there they would soon fall asleep.

Robert could no longer restrain himself. 'Father, I beg you, what is this news?'

'I see I should have told you before our devotions. You might have learned something. But no, you'd have thought of naught else, either way.' He inhaled deeply. 'The news is this: your brother John sails in April or May for England. A letter came by the post from him this evening. He's coming home with Robert Cushman and William Brewster.'

Robert sighed, 'Oh, would I could have gone with him, only to sail on a real ship across the sea and back again!'

'Hush, that's childish talk.' His father looked grave. 'Your place is here, I'm certain of it. John was called to go, as now he's called back. I don't yet know what his coming means — whether he'll stay, or go. He says changes are afoot. The Pilgrim Church is not as settled in Holland as we thought. It seems that God may call them to make a farther journey, still.'

Robert burst out, 'But where, my Father?'

Fessenden held up his hand. 'You're hot-headed and rash tonight, in a fever about everything . . . but as to why? Only the Lord knows why the Pilgrims cannot all remain in Leyden. But that they must move — that the Pilgrims know for a surety.'

'Then where should they go?'

'They've thought of the Virginia Plantation, so your brother tells us. Mr Cushman and Mr Brewster are to see some men in London at the Virginia Company. They want a patent for another venture to Virginia.'

'Then my brother has come to help them obtain it?'

'Nay, I think not.' Fessenden frowned, looking away for a moment. Watching, Robert recognized caution in

25

him, an unwillingness to say too much. 'Truth to tell . . . John is not satisfied, now, with Leyden. The ten-year truce with Spain has almost run its course, and the Pilgrims fear the Inquisition.'

Robert scoffed. 'A group of silly, superstitious old men asking them questions about God, you mean? Why be afraid? The Pilgrims walk more closely with God than any other men in Europe.'

'Bravely spoken — but spoken in ignorance.' Fessenden's face hardened. 'The Spanish Inquisition sets terror into the hearts of the Christian church in all of Holland. You cannot, being but a lad, imagine the horror and evil those men of Spain bring with them — from Satan himself.'

'But to throw away so many years of labour — ?'

His father nodded. 'Aye, but we cannot see God's purpose in all this. For John 'tis only a year . . . and other things are at work to hasten the move.' He stopped, frowning again. 'None wants to return to England. They remember too well, I suppose, what they'll face if they do — hatred at best. Forced to swear oaths that go against their consciences, and stocks and pillories and floggings if they go not against their consciences. More persecution . . . unless many things change.'

Robert was puzzled. What did his father mean? He and others who called themselves the honest folk had never suffered for their beliefs — not as far as he knew. Rumours ran rife, as always, especially in a village where the principal gentleman rode to and from London with his retinue to serve King James at Court; where one of England's greatest architects had just finished for that knight a resplendent brick castle — an edifice that had required the presence of glaziers, plasterers, stonemasons, bricklayers, carvers, carpenters, and gardeners from much further afield than Chilham. The building had gone on throughout Robert's childhood — a source of never-ending fascination for all the lads of the village; also a source of contradictory and puzzling rumours tossed about by all the gossips of the village.

His father, perhaps catching his bewildered look, continued, 'You have no idea what may happen to God's people in the next few years. We may all pray to leave

26

England! So Virginia must seem to the Pilgrims to be an answer to prayer.'

Robert digested this, still uncertain, wanting to get back on the firm ground of things he knew and understood: the Christian brothers in Leyden . . . John . . . 'And John — you say he's disappointed with his lot in Leyden?'

'He says so — but only between the lines. There's been argument between the families all along about the bringing up of children. Some are influenced by what they've seen of the Hollanders; they're not such strict parents as our own countrymen — even the God-fearing Dutch, that is. Now there are serious quarrels.'

'With the Dutch?'

'Nay, I meant among the brethren. And things are made worse by their separation.' Leaning his elbows on the board, Fessenden rested his chin on his knuckles so that his face was only inches from the candle flame. 'That's why I don't hold with being so separate, myself. It makes you too ingrown and weak in the end.'

Robert had lost the meaning again, but he listened, all the same.

'The community's so closed, you see,' Fessenden went on. 'Most of the English can speak no Dutch. In many ways the brethren are cut off, more or less. John doesn't like it any more than I would. I wasn't . . . going to tell you all this . . . but I suspect Brother Cushman's journey is providing an escape for John — an opportunity to leave without deserting.'

All evening Robert mulled over what his father had told him. As they sat working together on the day's account books he found himself distracted. What did John's return home mean for John himself? Would he come back disillusioned, full of ridicule for the church? Would he turn back on his spiritual brethren and their beliefs, setting a course towards his father, towards success in the world of the cloth industry? Or would he — with all his freshly acquired knowledge of new dyeing methods and the fashioning of new draperies — scorn his father's well-established system of business and thus anger him? Would he refuse to work as his father's factor — a post Robert himself had

27

reluctantly begun to fit into — overseeing distribution of the wool to local cottagers for spinning, weaving, and finishing? He had no idea, yet, what God would want of him. The future was clouded, hidden.

2

JOHN
Canterbury, June 1619

London lay two days' journey behind them, and Rochester almost a day behind them. Ahead stretched the almost straight chalk and gravel ribbon of Watling Street, rising and falling over the northern edge of the Downs. They had passed through Faversham already, and Boughton Street — a village familiar to John since it stood so near Chilham. But they had continued without stopping towards Canterbury, determined to reach it before nightfall. To the south, orchards gave way to sheep pastures, and they in turn gave way to sparser land; patches of heath and wild gorse still yellow with blossom. For the most part the three men enjoyed a companionable silence — all intent on walking as fast as possible and avoiding the ruts.

'I'm glad you're with us, sir,' John said, looking warmly at Brewster and unconsciously wishing Brother Cushman weren't with them.

'And I'm glad I came with ye,' Brewster asserted. He still spoke with the thick accent of the north Midlands, foreign to John even after a year in Leyden where almost all the Pilgrims hailed from Scrooby or Gainsborough or Sturton-le-Steeple — places John thought of vaguely as 'up north'. Even Brewster's Cambridge education had not softened the accent; if anything it was an endearing characteristic, something that he associated with the ringing clarity of Nonconformist preaching, something that moved him week by week as no ritual trammelled by the bounds of Acts of Uniformity could ever do.

Brewster's fingers, gripping his staff, were permanently dyed with printer's ink. He seemed as unaware of this as he was of his beaver hat and cloak, tossed on carelessly as they had left their lodgings that morning; unaware, too, that his white neckband and wristbands were now somewhat frayed, dusty with chalk and grit thrown up by passing packhorses and wagons loaded with timber and fish. But life shone in his eyes and in his voice, despite the pain and danger he faced.

John reflected as he watched Brewster that in the same circumstances he would have been joyless, tearful, and complaining. Brewster had suffered for several weeks now with a nagging pain in his stomach. Also, the King's officers were searching for him for the supposed crime of printing a seditious pamphlet. Directed against a new oath being forced by the King on Scottish Presbyterians, the godly folk and others who disagreed with rites of the established church, this pamphlet had been sent from Holland to be circulated in England, much to the King's displeasure.

'You'll be welcome indeed in Canterbury,' Cushman put in, though without warmth. 'And safer, I warrant, than in London.'

Brewster chuckled. 'Had I indeed erred in printing that pamphlet, I'd fear not to stay and face my retribution. But as long as I live, if there's truth to be declared — be it in England or Holland, or even far away in Virginia — I'll see it declared.' He shrugged. 'And, as I erred not, it matters not whether I be in London or Canterbury.' He laughed aloud.

Inwardly, John applauded. No bravado, that. Brewster spoke as he lived — forthrightly, seeing truth as something to be lived, not defended.

'Ah, Virginia,' Brewster went on. 'I hope and pray it brings our freedom. I believe it will, Brother Cushman.'

'If we be not devoured by cannibals or driven out by the smell of that wicked weed, tobacco,' Cushman muttered.

John wanted to laugh at Cushman even as a few moments before he had laughed with Brewster. Always so morose, Cushman was respected, trusted as deacon of the Pilgrim Church for the past ten years, but frequently disliked. 'Waspish,' some of the brothers and sisters called him behind his back. 'Mind lest ye step on his tail and be stung for your pains.' Still the

30

Separatists had chosen him to go with Brewster, taking their request to the London Virginia Company; they could count on him. And now, when matters were out of their own hands, as the board members of the Company had quarrelled to a deadlock in London — thus reaching no settlement for the Leyden Pilgrims — it was Cushman who had suggested that John accompany him to Canterbury. They were to lodge with the Cushman family on the Parade and to meet a man who had just sailed home from Virginia. Then John could return, if he wished, to Chilham.

Apparently having none of John's tender conscience, Brewster did laugh at Cushman. 'Come now, you're as anxious to go as the rest of us. We can't give up hope now.'

Cushman drew his mouth into a grim line. 'True. But neither can we rush ahead, foolhardy and uncircumspect.' He shook his head, forestalling protests from the others about all the obstacles that had already drawn out their attempts to obtain the necessary patent. 'I cannot help but remember what happened two years ago. We thought then that our way was sure.'

John looked questioningly at Cushman. As he did so, taking his eyes off the uneven road under their feet, he noticed out of the tail of his eye — beyond the heath — the towers of the Cathedral now only a few miles away under the evening sky. *Not far, now,* he thought in relief.

'You should explain that to our young companion,' Brewster said. Then he winked, 'Though briefly. He looks done for, poor lad.'

Cushman inhaled quickly as if meditating a sharp reply, but then tempered his expression and tone. 'You surely know some of what happened?'

John flushed. 'Little, sir.'

'Well, then.' His voice became deliberate, slightly stilted. 'Brother Carver and I went in secret to London — a little over two years ago. The church charged us with proving to the Virginia Company governors that we could ably support ourselves by fishing and trade in the Colony.' He cleared his throat. 'Also, a harder task, that though living separately in Holland, we were

31

still loyal subjects of His Majesty and obedient to the Church of England.'

'A harder task!' laughed Brewster, interrupting. 'Nay, nigh impossible.'

'Aye, even with Sir Edwin Sandys' word on our behalf to King James. But His Majesty played the tyrant with us. Referred our articles of faith to the Archbishop of yonder city for his inspection — ' his voice turned bitter with sarcasm ' — then turned on him, as well, and had us all accused of setting up a free state, defying the laws of God and England. Monstrous!'

John murmured in sympathy; he began to see what lay behind Cushman's bitterness — all the years of struggle and frustrated dreams.

'Well, never you mind, young John,' Brewster reassured. 'God will not leave us comfortless. See, Canterbury lies ahead. We're Pilgrims truly today, to go from London to Canterbury.'

'Though not to see the bleached old bones of Becket,' Cushman sneered.

Ignoring him, Brewster went on. 'I'm sure Sir Samuel will have good news for us. Perhaps within a year our church will dwell in a place where we need not fear Spanish armies or Acts of Uniformity or arrest for printing the truth — a community of God lies ahead.'

'Amen, I pray as much,' Cushman said fervently, sweeping off his hat for a moment and raising his eyes towards the sky.

'And if the Virginia Company of London stand not as our surety, then we can go to the Plymouth Company. And if not now, then soon, I believe.' Brewster smiled. 'The trade between England and the colonies is increasing. The King cannot afford to lose the revenues entailed. Sooner or later, we shall sail.' He nodded to himself, beating out the rhythm of the words with his staff. 'We shall sail.'

The three went on in silence for a while, their eyes fixed on the city walls ahead. Brewster's words of encouragement and prophecy sounded repeatedly in John's head. 'Virginia — ?' he said quietly. ''Tis the only place in America the Pilgrims may go?' He was careful not to say 'we'.

Cushman looked at him contemptuously, as he would at a child in a grammar school who had asked a foolish question.

Brewster, though, answered him patiently. 'We do not know for certain. At the moment, yes, I fear it is the only place we may go. The English settlement on the River James has prospered.'

'Tobacco,' Cushman grumbled.

'From tobacco,' Brewster acknowledged. 'But the land is vast, we understand. We need not live close neighbours to any save those we choose. And the land is rich, too. We'll learn to use it — learn from the others who've settled already. We need not plant tobacco, I'm sure.' He glanced at Cushman. 'Then if we want their help in times of plague or famine, we shall have it. And when the other settlers want help and preachers, too, then they shall have them — men unafraid to leave the comforts of Europe and preach in a heathen place.'

John could almost have predicted Cushman's response. 'Aye, unafraid, and rightly. But let's hope not unready, as well. Do not forget that of a hundred and fifty who first went to Virginia, only two score lived to see a harvest. We'll have to be better stewards than that if we're to prosper. Provisions must be laid by with far greater thought than before. And the brethren must learn to live as the ancient church lived, and share their property.'

Brewster did not reply immediately, and John guessed why. Of all the Pilgrims at Leyden, Cushman was one of only a few who believed in communal property. Had Cushman suggested or explained his convictions more gently, he might have won their ears; as it was, he had offended most of the brethren. Brewster, however, was long accustomed to Cushman's acerbity and well able to blunt the sharpness of the conversation before it injured them all. 'Aye, Brother Cushman,' he said, 'Though I can't agree with ye about sharing, necessarily, you're right about the need for careful stewarding. I'm thinking you'd be quite the man — once we secure a patent and have ourselves a stout, sound ship — to be in charge of provisions.'

Cushman first paled, then coloured. 'I'd count it an honour,' he replied with a slight smile.

John now raised his eyes from the city to the sky. Within a mile of the walls, they followed a way that led gently downhill into the Stour valley. Below the sky's china and chalk pastel, the Canterbury meadows spread out, glistening under the sun that fell almost directly behind them. The angle of the light gave the view an almost ethereal quality as fleeces of fog rose from the fields and wrapped themselves round the twin towers of Westgate. *Ethereal, yet deceiving,* John thought. The Westgate was notorious as a prison, and even from this distance he could see the loopholes where guns were mounted behind the walls. *No new Jerusalem this,* he reflected, *for all that Archbishop Abbott lives here. No heavenly city here.* And inwardly, for a moment — though he knew he might be awed by Canterbury's grandeur — he trembled to think that in leaving the Separatists he was effectively handing himself back, body and soul, to the vagaries of the Church of England as represented by Canterbury. For the godly folk — even those who could not espouse the divine right of the monarch to rule the church and set up bishops over the people — would be subject to the church as long as they feared to break away and join the Separatists. He trembled. He no longer belonged to the Separatists, nor did he belong to the Church of England, as answerable to the Archbishop and the King as a Papist to the Pope. But if he belonged only to God, how then was he to find freedom of faith in England since he would not find it, he believed now, with the Pilgrims in America?

Light was failing as they passed the watch at the Westgate and went over the Stour bridge towards the High Street. The smell of the city breweries and the candlelit clatter of late weavers at work in their cottages came to them clearly in the still air. John looked around with lively interest and forgot the rough flints and cobbles rubbing his raw, blistered feet through the leather soles of his boots. He craned his neck upwards. On the sides of St Peter's Street, as tightly together as skeins of wool in a spinner's basket, houses climbed jetty over jetty, almost tumbling over each other, to second, third, and even fourth storeys topped by gables. Vagabonds in rags stood singly on corners waiting for the unwary, while labourers in small groups jostled their way down the narrow pavements, all trying to avoid the foul and slippery gutters; weavers and victuallers, no doubt, finding their way to an alehouse. Others passed them more thoughtfully, stepping aside though the three strangers were obviously no gentlemen; occasionally John caught the low murmur of a foreign language from one of these — not the Dutch he'd grown used to in Leyden, but another tongue. *Flemish or French,* he thought. These Huguenots with their serious demeanour and skilled work in fine cloth might one day change the English cloth market entirely, reducing for ever the importance of wool! A year in Europe had convinced him of that, and he must bring all the influence he could to bear on his father's business before those changes came about.

At the Church of St Alphege, Cushman turned to Brewster. 'Sarah and I were wed here, you know.'

'Not at the Cathedral then?' Brewster asked mildly.

'Shame on you, Brother Brewster,' Cushman said with a frown. 'Your tongue is full of devilry today.'

'God forbid, but a little mirth doth shorten our way.'

'Short enough. My wife's parents live but a few yards from this place — in the precincts behind that inn there.' He pointed, and John saw a small hostelry, poorly lit from within by candles. 'The Mayflower Inn,' Cushman added. ''Tis the place appointed for our meeting with Sir Samuel tomorrow, I believe. And yonder, in the Parade, we'll find my mother, I trust.'

John almost forgot the following day that he would be saying goodbye to Brewster and Cushman within a few hours and returning to Chilham. Against their advice he left them at Widow Cushman's house in the morning and set off to see the weavers' hall and the cathedral. In the building's towering vaults of golden Caen stone the boys of the King's School were practising an anthem. The sound rose in shafts like the clustered perpendicular columns of the cathedral: in perfect harmony, blended together, smooth and polished. Again he was struck by the ethereal beauty of the place; but again,

35

too, he remembered the squalid narrowness of the lanes and alleys outside. The richness of the tapestries and the coloured glass of the windows troubled him, also. How did these speak of God: were they not gaudy trappings fit for the palace of a king, rather than for the worship of Christ, the carpenter of Galilee?

When he returned to the Cushmans' house again, Widow Cushman sent him on to the Mayflower. 'That gentleman has arrived from Gravesend,' she told him. 'You'll find my son at the inn now, and others besides, no doubt.' He hurried away, eager to listen to Captain Argall though he would probably never go to Virginia.

Before he entered the inn he realized suddenly how hungry he was. He noticed a pump on the opposite side of the road where housewives clustered to fill their buckets and jars. Squinting up at the sun he saw that noon had already passed; he ought to eat and drink, but he could hardly spend his last pennies at the hostelry. He therefore joined the crowd of womenfolk at the pump. They eyed him strangely, their talk ebbing away, but went on filling their buckets in turn before trudging dully away in bands of two or three. He waited patiently, longing to go into the inn, but also longing for water.

The women stepped forward, bent down, and worked the pump. One by one they filled their buckets, swung them up from the tiled pavement beneath, and went away. As if by common consent they made no room for John in their midst. It became a sort of game. One by one they moved away. 'Your turn, Mary.' 'Now you, Lizzie . . . Rebecca . . . May . . .' One by one they nodded to each other, yielding place to each other, but not to him; and he had no cup, either.

The splashing of the clear water on the dusty tiles and the droplets on the women's gowns began to madden him. Still, he hung back, feeling for his purse at his side and thinking, *Drink I must, but perhaps 'tis foolish not to drink at the inn after all.* Then, to his horror, his purse was missing; the leather thongs that usually held it dangled empty from his belt. He groaned aloud, turning his head quickly to see if he could discover the culprit. No cutpurse here, though; no rogue fleeing away on quick, quiet feet. No, he must have lost it as he went

36

up to the Cathedral or down again. He would have to return to Chilham with no more than the surcoat on his back. Angry with himself for not heeding Cushman's warnings, he reconciled himself to thirst and turned to cross towards the Mayflower.

'Pray wait, sir,' a woman's voice said.

He swung round quickly to face a young woman as tall as himself. Pale, slender, and pretty, she was clothed modestly in a clean cap over wheat-blonde hair and an unadorned kirtle that was laced high under her chin and tied with a loose girdle. The fabric was soft, well made, but fraying at the wide wristbands and in need of mending. She held a bucket before her, empty, two hands clenched white-knuckled around the handles.

'Forgive me, sir.' Her brows drew together.

He had to step nearer to hear her voice. She now spoke barely above a whisper. He noticed the slight smell of soap about her, and the tiny lines at the corners of her mouth and eyes. He judged her to be only a year or two older than himself. Still sore from his own lack of watchfulness, and the loss of his purse, he answered more rudely than he would usually have spoken to a woman. 'What? What do you want?'

'Nothing . . . only I saw your distress . . . and my companions' want of kindness.' Her voice was soft, free from the distinctive Kentish accent: the speech of a woman brought up in a gentleman's house, perhaps.

He glanced down at her hands again — no wedding ring — then, ashamed of his discourtesy, back at her solemn face. He thought, *She'd wear no ring anyway, if she were one of the godly folk* . . . He stammered out an apology for his sharp reply, but she shook her head.

'Nay, think nothing of it. You've been robbed, and you're a-thirst.' She turned towards the pump, now strangely deserted.

'Let me — ' he said, quickly recovering his senses. 'Pray let me fill this for you — '

'Then you may drink, too.' *She did not smile.*

'I thank you.' He worked the pump, aware now that she watched him, not brazenly, but gratefully; for the sun beating down between the houses now created a stifling heat, and beads of sweat had formed

37

on her forehead so that loose strands of hair stuck to it.

When the bucket was full she handed him a small tin cup that she had pulled from a pocket in the folds of her dress. Dipping it under the stream of water that flowed from the pump, now slowing to a trickle, he filled it and drank greedily.

'You saw the thief, perchance?' he asked when satisfied.

'No, only . . . that, as I said, the wives would give you no room.'

He nodded, handing back the cup.

'Thank you, anyway. A cup of cold water in Christ's name, this was.'

Her chin went up quickly, and he saw an answering spark in her eyes as he spoke the name of Christ.

'You're welcome.'

'Who may I say gave it me?'

She hesitated, and he knew he had presumed too far.

'Well,' he hazarded, 'I shall tell you my own name at least. John — John Fessenden of Chilham.'

'And I — ' she faltered again, looking around uncertainly as if caught as a thief herself. 'Jane Tritton, of Canterbury.'

'Farewell, Jane, of Canterbury, then.' He saluted her but found with surprise that she followed still close behind him as the crowd of the street closed about them again.

'I lodge with my kinsman, serving as one of his maids. Mr Tritton, by St George's.' Her voice was still low, but urgent now, the words rushing out.

He stopped yet again, puzzled by her forwardness and yet certain that it was uncharacteristic, born of innocence, not coquetry. 'I won't forget,' he murmured.

'God be with you, sir.'

For the last time, he steeled himself to move away from the pump square. This time, though, he saw not the sign of the Mayflower hanging over the door but the sweet face of Jane Tritton before his mind's eye. As he lifted the latch, glancing around, however, he discovered that she had gone.

If the air had been breathless and hot outside, it was worse within. The oak-panelled walls of the inn seemed to press against him, and the airless rooms were heavy with the increasingly familiar smell of Virginia tobacco. Startled, he looked round quickly. Had Cushman truly intended this as the meeting place with Argall?

He searched the room again, his eyes, blinded by the brightness of outdoors and by smoke, gradually becoming accustomed to the dimness. As he stood still on the sawdust-covered floor amid the chestnut stools, benches, and tables, wooden stairs rising into the pipe smoke to his right — he realized that the boisterous talk and laughter around him had ceased and that he was as much an object of study to the inhabitants as the inn itself was to him.

'Come here, you pretty fellow,' a woman called from one corner.

Through the haze he made out the robust figure of a girl of no more than eighteen. Smirking, she sat on the knee of a fat knight who wore his hair in lovelocks that flowed over an exaggeratedly large white ruff. He was dressed in the flamboyant fashion of Queen Elizabeth's day with bright doublet and slashed sleeves.

'Come here, pray,' she repeated, earning a cackle of laughter from all the onlookers.

'Nay, come not near that dangerous wench,' a bearded man warned him, thumping his coarse hand on the board so that the ale slopped over. 'Not unless you want the French pox.'

She raised her fist in mock fury. 'I'll see you paid for that!' Then she subsided against the willing knight in peals of laughter.

John recoiled in horror. He had expected an inn, not a bawdyhouse. 'Thank you, but you'd pay me no court if you knew I'd just lost all the money I own.'

The laughter was renewed. 'Oh, so have we all!' the knight roared drunkenly. 'To ale, and wenches. So join us, do.'

Bewildered, John backed away, thinking he would escape quickly and return to Widow Cushman's. 'Nay. I have come to the wrong place.'

Another girl sidled past him. 'The right place, you mean,' she said.

'Oh, look at him. He's one o' them Puritans,' the bearded man commented. 'No wonder he looks so serious and solemn. Faith, he is in the wrong place, as he said. Too good for the likes of common folk.'

John lifted the latch, then heard a scuffle behind him. Turning, he saw the innkeeper in a stained apron fling out of a door at the back of the room. Unceremoniously catching both the girls by the shoulders, he boxed their ears.

'Be gone, you saucy wenches, and let these gentlemen alone.' He caught John's eyes. 'Friend, if you're John Fessenden, the other gentlemen await ye. Pray, come with me.' He glowered at the other men.

John hesitated but then saw that the two women had vanished and that all the men in the room were making a close study of their ale mugs. He stepped back and followed the innkeeper up the stairs.

'I'm sorry, sir, for my daughters. 'Tis vain and idle they are, and never a fine-looking young gentleman like yourself comes a-courting, but that's no surprise, I suppose. Well-a-day, I'll get no honest sons-in-law while I'm an innkeeper, for all I may get grandchildren.' He shook his head, still plodding ahead of John, who could scarcely catch his breath before the man continued. 'You *are* John Fessenden, I warrant? For 'struth, you look like the young gentleman they bid me watch for. Your face is an honest, and your eyes be . . . ' At the top of the stairs he swung round, breathing heavily in John's face, ' . . . blue, as they did say; and you do wear the garb of the plain people. Sir, you *are* John Fessenden?'

Anxious not to be rude, but still wanting to stem the man's garrulousness, John hastily interrupted, 'John Fessenden, I am. But no gentleman. A man of Kent, like yourself.'

'But you speak like a gentleman, sir, and your garments be finely made, of better stuff than yonder foolish knight below stairs who wastes himself in here by day and year alike.' He stopped in the middle of the low corridor into which they had passed. 'Your place is here, sir, at this door.'

Automatically, John reached for his missing purse.

'Nay, the good Sir Samuel has provided all. I need not your pocket.'

Relieved, John thanked him and knocked faintly at the door.

Brewster immediately opened it. 'Welcome, John!'

He stepped in, conscious again of many eyes on his. But the looks were different this time. No mockery or ribaldry. The men within were all except one dressed like himself in dark surcoats with small white falling bands, their hair cut short and their faces sober and watchful. The man who stood apart must, John thought, be Sir Samuel Argall. He wore a small, immaculately clean ruff — nothing like the knight's ridiculous encumbrance downstairs. Above his grave eyes, neatly trimmed beard and moustache, he wore a Monmouth cap. A sword hung at his side, half concealed by his cloak. If John had expected rough, weather-worn skin reddened by sea gales, and the bow legs always attributed to sailors by envious landlubbers — he was disappointed. The man had instead about him an air of self-possessed refinement, even aloofness, a cool but not forbidding dignity. His skin was tanned but not rough, his hands sinewy but not coarse.

In turn Sir Samuel's eyes travelled over John. He stood still under their cool scrutiny, waiting for him to speak.

'Find a stool, lad. Your friends have been at their prayers till now.'

Prayers? Was Sir Samuel joking?

'For our venture,' Cushman explained.

'And for you, too,' Brewster added. 'We thought you'd fallen to some band of cut-throats by now.'

Plainly, Brewster, not Sir Samuel, was joking.

'No, sir, but a cutpurse. I fear I should have heeded your warnings.' He showed them the loose purse straps.

The men murmured in sympathy, but Brewster said, 'Well, never mind, John. We'll mend it presently. Come, we waited for you. Sir Samuel has been telling us a little of the progress in Massachusetts Bay but we wanted you to hear about the journey of the folk

41

from Amsterdam, so he has put off that part of his tale.'

John pulled up a stool next to Brewster's and looked up at Argall, whose face had taken on a pained expression.

'Like you,' Argall said, turning his head slowly to be sure of his whole audience, 'those good people were anxious to go.' His face darkened. 'But, listen well, and learn of what I'll tell you now . . . to get a sturdy ship, to sail in the spring — or better yet, the summer — and to know you're working with an honest man.' He held up his fingers, counting off the three points as he made them. 'The Amsterdam Church contracted with one Francis Blackwell. You've heard his name, perhaps?'

A few heads bowed in response.

'Aye, black indeed, his name is to me . . . he it was who was to take the last of the Ancient Church to Virginia. The ship was to sail from Gravesend, and when the emigrants saw that ship, they groaned aloud . . . ' he stopped, smiling slightly, ' . . . like the children of Israel going into captivity. That ship was never meant to carry a hundred and eighty souls. The women on the quays, both travellers and their families, fell to weeping and lamenting, every one. The men grew angry, but Blackwell determined to see them all aboard and therewithal line his pockets.' He cleared his throat. 'He lined his own coffin, instead. And others' too.'

John bit his lip. Brewster, Cushman and he had come with no inkling that Sir Samuel brought anything but good news. Argall had returned safely himself, after all. Could the crossing be as terrible as he suggested?

"Twas folly, in the first place, to leave in September. Mark well, and if you go not by July, wait until the following year. I know not, truth to tell, how any reached Virginia alive. When the ship left the estuary, even then she was low in the water, listing not a little. One of the men who reached Virginia told me he feared for their lives even in the very straits of Dover. But things grew worse. They met squalls and gales the hour they left the sight of land. The waves were mighty and the skies dark, so the master — he was Captain Maggner — lost direction. The boat went south, they thought, of its intended course, and drifted day after day. The mast cracked, and the ship wallowed in the waves, drifting aimlessly till all feared the ship would go down. The crew was worked to the marrow, and the supplies began to fail. 'Twas then that many died — the frost, the hunger, and thirst — 'twas all more than many could endure — and Maggner and Blackwell died with them.'

Argall's listeners groaned, and John with them. He found himself recoiling from the horror. He wanted to withdraw, turn away, and go back to Chilham. Surely, surely, crossing this terror of a winter ocean could not be within the will of God? Surely not within the will of God for him?

Argall had again paused. John wondered fleetingly if the man's expressive face, gestures, and habit of pausing were for dramatic effect. But as he looked at the man's eyes burning in indignation and heard the cold harshness of his voice, he doubted it.

'One hundred and eighty souls, I said,' Argall grated out, 'and a hundred and thirty perished. Buried at sea, all of them, in the tumult of the waves.'

John thought of the psalms, all of which he had memorized at his mother's insistence years before. *The floods have lifted up, O Lord, the floods have lifted up their voice; The floods lift up their waves.* He shivered.

'Fifty made landfall in March of this year of our Lord. Just before I left, they sailed in. I know not if all those fifty be alive, or how they prosper. My own crossing was smooth and easy. Three months, not six, and a hearty crew. Would I could have captained another ship to bring all safely to America — in the summer.'

The room fell dead silent. Argall stood with his head bowed and his hands clasped out of sight under his cloak. John glanced quickly at Brewster's face to see his cheeks wet with tears; but then he looked down at the wide beams of the floor. *The Lord on high is mightier than the noise of many waters, yea, than the mighty waves of the sea . . . Yet I can never go with them. I want to stay in England, trade in cloth, and get a wife.* Jane Tritton's face swam before him, the luminous eyes, blue as the Venetian glass he'd seen in Leyden. He tried to blink away her image — a chance encounter in

43

a public watering-place — but the dark oak wood floor seemed awash in swirling, luminous blue. Massachusetts Bay would have to wait this crossing.

3

JOHN
Canterbury, September 1619

John found himself blundering on through the streets
of Canterbury. Careless of his surroundings, he walked
right before a horse so that the animal reared up and
the carter flashed out with the whip, cursing both John
and the horse.

After that, shaken, he tried to gather his wits
and attend to where he was going. He spoke to
the Huguenots about the next parcels of silks that
his father intended to purchase from them, but the
conversation was halting, made slow by the lack of
a common tongue. Hence he arrived too late at the
weavers' hall and missed the master weaver he had
wanted to meet.

Now, three months since his last time at Canterbury,
he wanted only to find Jane Tritton. Not that he had
any formed idea what he would say or do when he
found her. Except her eyes, her face had faded to a
spectral memory, half dream. He remembered more
clearly, however, what she had told him. *I lodge with
my kinsman, serving as one of his maids. Mr Tritton, by
St George's.* He remembered, too, the urgent sound
of her voice as she had pressed after him in the
crowd, and the sense of certainty he'd felt about
her. *This is the way: walk ye in it.* He must find
her.

But what if she were a sorceress? What if she had
bewitched him with her brilliant eyes, convincing him
falsely of her purity and sweetness? What if — older
than he — she were wiser in the world's arts? What
if she herself had stolen his purse, then mocked him
afterwards to her friends as a fool and a gull?

45

Then he remembered the cup of cold water, the kindling in her eyes as he had spoken the name of Christ. No, surely she could not fabricate that.

The clocktower of St George's tolled the hour. He stood uncertainly at its foot and looked around in the twilight. Labourers were leaving their work for home. He panicked. Why hadn't he tried to find her at noon, in daylight? Ah, but he had done all he could in Canterbury, and he could hardly have tried to find her first. No, he would find her if the Lord willed it.

He stopped a passer-by first. 'Will you tell me, pray, where a Mr Tritton lives, somewhere hereabouts?'

The man rewarded him with a sly, derisive look. 'Nay, no such in St George's parish as I know of.' The man walked off without a backward glance.

John thought of enquiring at an alehouse next; then, however, remembering his discomfort in the Mayflower Inn, he thought better of it and turned round to face the church. *If her kinsmen be near the church, no doubt they could tell me at the rectory where Mr Tritton lives.*

Under the brick arch next to the churchyard was an iron gate and a path that led to the rectory. Having pushed open the gate, he ran up the pathway to lift the door knocker.

He was still catching his breath with nervous excitement about his nearness to Jane when she herself opened the door.

Shock, disbelief, joy — a multitude of feelings surged through him and left him hardly able to speak. Taking off his felt hat, he looked up into the same blue eyes that had looked up at him in dreams for three months. He looked up into the same face he had seen in the flesh only once and had not clearly remembered: a face he saw now was far more open, sweet, and beautiful than the one he had pictured.

The colour came and went from her cheeks as he stared up to where she stood with one hand on the lintel and the other on the door. Plainly, she remembered him, too.

Perhaps only a few seconds had passed, but to John it seemed longer before he was able to stammer out a few words. At last, he said, 'Miss Tritton,

46

I was coming here to see if I could find you. I didn't expect — '

Laughter creased the corner of her eyes. 'To find me here?'

Was she scorning him? He met her eyes doubtfully. 'No, indeed, I came to find Mr Tritton — your kinsman. I thought the rector would know where I might find him . . . ' He was lost, at sea in the blue of her eyes. She stood with the warmth and light of the hall behind her, apparently enjoying his bemusement as he stood in the damp twilight outside. But he was not to be dissuaded by her mysterious smile. See her he would, and her kinsman as well. For a moment he recovered himself, and said, 'Then, pray, let me speak with him, if he is in.' He tried to sound authoritative, more self-possessed than he felt.

His tone of voice evidently made some impression; her teasing smile gave way to anxiety, the same pleading expression he remembered at the crowded pump opposite the inn. She backed away from the doorway, hovering within.

'Then you've not . . . you've come to see my uncle?'

He ascended to the top step so that the slight advantage of his height showed. 'Nay, you know that's not it. I came to see you.' He took a deep breath, struggling to keep the fear out of his voice and to assume the same lightheartedness she had just forsaken. 'But since this is your uncle's house and he is a man of the cloth, I suppose I must see him first.'

'And what — ?' Her eyes were suddenly lambent, full of hope.

'Did you think I would forget, then?'

'Nay — yes — I know not — '

He laughed suddenly. 'Pray, let me speak with your uncle. Just use me as his visitors otherwise. 'Tis better that way.'

She hesitated, her hand to her hair in a quick gesture of self-awareness. 'Truly . . . ? Then come this way, pray.' She held the door wider so that he could pass her and enter the house. 'He's at his supper. I'll wait on him and bring him to you if he will.' Her face fell suddenly, as if she would add something — a word

47

of warning, perhaps. Instead, she left him silently in a small room that was lined with books, left him there to stare at the empty grate.

He studied the shelves · as a way to blunt the apprehension that had frozen his hands and dried his mouth. The bookshelves would yield a clue to Mr Tritton's personality and theological leanings. If he were an Arminian by persuasion, John realized with a chill of foreboding, that might suggest that Jane herself was not one of the godly folk and that her uncle would be cold towards any addresses to his niece.

Was that what he had come for, then? To pay court to a young woman he had met once in a public place? A woman he knew nothing of save — now — her address and name? What else! And if not, then for what reason had he come to search for her, and what could he say to her uncle? *Sir, I met your niece at Canterbury in the summer. Oh, confound your insolence, you young pup! What mean you, 'met my niece', pray? Or this? Sir, I beg your leave to woo Miss Tritton. Which Miss Tritton, pray? Helen is already betrothed, and Rachel is too young. Oh, no, sir, I mean your niece, Miss Jane — But that's preposterous! Our maid, why she's . . .* His mind clamped down on the last thought. Married already? Betrothed? Promised? He could not bear it.

Well, he would say whatever the Spirit prompted him to say when he had taken Mr Tritton's measure. He forced himself to look at the books. He knew hardly any of them, and could pronounce even fewer of the titles. Ovid — *Metamorphoses*. The works of Chaucer. Tottle's *Miscellany*. The plays of Ben Jonson. The works of Hooker and St Augustine and Virgil and Sir Philip Sidney . . . But there was no Bible. None of the works John had studied at Leyden. No, Mr Tritton was not one of the godly folk. An Arminian, a believer in pomp, ritual, ceremony — so what was he, John, doing here?

Absorbed in reading and thought, he had almost forgotten Jane. Suddenly the double doors opened. He swung round and saw, first, Jane — who kept her eyes carefully averted and merely murmured, 'Mr John Fessenden to see you' — then William Tritton.

The man was powerfully built with wide shoulders over which hung long, fashionably curled hair. His eyes were the same deep, Venetian blue as Jane's, but shadowed by thick eyebrows and a savage beak of a nose. But while his face conveyed shrewdness, even coldness, his dress seemed to gainsay it. Out of his top pocket protruded a crumpled kerchief: good linen, but soiled. His black clerical coat was darned and patched, his shoes shabby: the dress of a man who thought appearance of no significance whatever; the dress of a vague, otherworldly man?

'You wanted to speak with me, Mr Fessenden? I beg your pardon, but I believe we are not acquainted.' A cultured, genteel voice, deferring, yet not obsequious. And his face: watchful, perhaps even a little suspicious, the eyes darting up and down in assessment over John's plain, travel-soiled broadcloths. But the words were courteous, at least — intended, seemingly, to put him at ease. Perhaps he anticipated a new parishioner, or a man in want of a priest to read the banns and perform a wedding . . .

John collected himself. 'Thank you, sir. No, we are not acquainted. My father is John Fessenden, a clothier of Chilham. We do business with some of your Canterbury weavers.' He broke off, unsure, but then decided to press on. 'The Strangers, that is.'

'Ah —' The rector's lips curled in obvious distaste. 'Yes, strange ones indeed, foreigners who hold aloof from divine service in all of Canterbury and meet for some strange ritual of their own.' His chin went up abruptly, and John saw the expression of a man who might be proud, intolerant. 'But now — I was supping — how may I be of service to you?'

How may he be of service to me? John echoed mentally. *He asks that as if wanting to know how I may serve him!* He fidgeted with the hat in his hand. 'I'm sorry, sir, to interrupt you. Truth to tell, I've come to beg your leave to woo your niece, Miss Tritton.'

The rector turned sharply and moved towards the door. 'Have you indeed?' His voice was cold, satirical. 'Then you should never have come. Jane is but a poor simpleton. She's your senior — that I can tell by looking at your smooth face.' He paused, all inner hostility now unveiled. 'And I give her no dowry. In short, she is here

49

to serve our family since my brother died in penury for his fantastical Puritan notions of preaching to the poor and bailing them out of debtors' prison — but I need say no more. 'Twas I redeemed his debts and took his orphaned daughter as a servant. 'Twas the understanding when he died.'

John's temper rose. 'Then she's no more than a slave to you?'

The rector's face turned cruel. 'And what else would she be to a husband, pray?'

For a moment he blenched, misunderstanding the words completely. No, of course she was not married to her own uncle. No, Tritton meant something else, 'Not if she were *my* wife,' John began hotly. 'I'll have no slave, and if it's money you want to free her from her servitude and your bond, then it's money you'll have.'

The rector was apparently struck by the forcefulness of John's convictions, but only briefly, for his huge hand crashed down on the nearest shelf. Two books fell to the floor, and all the shelves shook. 'Be gone. You're an idiotic dreamer. Jane has a soft life with us. After her father's foolishness she'll want no Puritan for a mate, and she'll never marry anyway. Neither cleric, nor gentleman — nor yeoman.'

John stood his ground, narrowing his eyes. 'You say Miss Tritton's my senior, and I doubt it not. But that makes little difference. She's an honest maid, and true — that much I know. And as she's of age, she may decide.'

'Not Jane. She abides here.'

John's blood ran hot with indignation. He wanted to strike the man. A man of God? 'She *shall* decide, I say.' Immediately he knew what he must do.

He strode to the end of the room, prepared for and risking a blow from Tritton as he passed, but trusting in the thin hope that the rector might expect him to be leaving the house. He flung open the doors.

At the top of his lungs, he called out for her. 'Jane — Miss Tritton!' His voice rang up the curved staircase and through the hall.

From behind, Tritton caught his arm in a grip of shuddering brutality and twisted it backwards. 'You

50

blackguard! I'll see you whipped and pilloried for this. Get out of my house!'

Bent double under the rector's weight and the torment of the ligaments in his shoulder, John looked to another doorway at the far end of the hall and saw Jane half-concealed behind the door. Scarcely knowing her, he still knew that she was shaking in fear and anguish. He cried out for her again as Tritton began wrestling him towards the front door; then he caught sight of her over his shoulder. She had come out of hiding and was gesturing frantically to him, her left hand down in a fist, and her right arm swinging up and down at the elbow and shoulder in a movement he could make no sense of. It was just a glimpse — her arms signalling and her face pleading — then Tritton was jerking open the front door and he was teetering on the top step, no longer able to see her.

'I'll have the constables on you. What sort of a raving, ill-bred lout are you to brazen in here and shout out like — '

Beside himself, John lunged backward with his boot, but to no avail. He shouted for the last time, 'Jane I've come to — '

Tritton cut him off with a vicious twist from behind. 'What, you weakling! Think you that trembling wench'll rescue you? Nay, she's wiser than you. If she comes a step nearer she'll be beaten, and she knows it.' He hurled John down the steps. Then, hair askew, he stared down as John staggered to his feet in dull amazement.

ROBERT
Chilham, Autumn 1620

Ruth Fessenden died in childbed in early January. Never having called a midwife for the other births, she refused to allow her husband to call one this time. 'Foolish, superstitious old women,' she declared, then turned her stony face to the wall as another wave of pain swept through her body. Helpless, Fessenden knelt at the foot of the bed and cried out to God. His prayers and her pain went on for two nights; then on the third morning she gave birth to a daughter — dead. Fessenden locked the other children out of the room, for he expected his wife to rally as she had done before. White and dazed, however, she died in a violent haemorrhage that left him stricken with amazement and sorrow. She died with the same resolution and definiteness with which she had lived.

Life in the household changed. When the mother and child were laid next to the other dead children in the churchyard and the visits of mourners had ceased, Fessenden lost direction for a while. He drifted in and out of the house, in and out of the cottages of his weavers and spinners, back and forth to the staple: rudderless and crewless, John thought, as Blackwell's ship drifting in the North Atlantic the year before. Martha tried vainly for a week to take over her mother's tasks, but she was not wise enough for them and fell into hysterical anxiety each time Isaac crossed her and the supper burned or congealed. The brothers saw now how much their father had depended on their mother to be his pilot and anchor. The family listed, wallowed, but did not yet founder; John became his father's main mast, and Robert his inexperienced navigator.

Lady Dudley, hearing of Ruth's death, had called several times at the cottage with baskets of bread, cakes, and ale, and bundles of clothing for the children. Then, seeing that the family was more self-sufficient and prosperous than all the other yeomen families in the parish and not likely to sue to the poor houses for relief, she came no more. Instead, John took it upon himself to go to the castle for advice on domestic servants.

He almost expected Sir Dudley Digges to send down a steward with a rebuff for the impertinence of his questions; instead, Sir Dudley himself met him courteously in one of the ante-rooms. Genuinely moved, he offered to help in any way he could. There was no talk of the inappropriateness of a yeoman's family looking for a maid or housekeeper; instead, Sir Dudley enquired after the clothier's business and after the other children. He then recommended several young women to the Fessendens' service.

The choice rested finally on Widow Snode, a woman of thirty from Boughton Aluph. Her husband, Christopher, had once served as a falconer for Sir Dudley but had recently been killed in the German war. Childless, Mary Snode delighted in the children. Though she never neglected Fessenden and the two older sons, she devoted most of her time to the younger children. As a result they followed her round the house and the garden, never tiring of hearing her sing or instruct them, and she apparently never tiring of doing so.

Fessenden leaned increasingly on his sons for support. No longer was he suspicious of John's advice on the new textiles; no longer did he resist venture into the manufacture and sale of cloth and garments for which he himself was not entirely responsible; and no longer was Robert a mere child to be sent on trivial errands. With John, Robert had become his father's factor. While John oversaw changes in his father's business — for example the use of some foreign weavers in Canterbury for the first time, and the production of new draperies — Robert rode further and further afield on the bay mare his father had given him and took over most of the purchasing from staplers, threadmakers, and weavers. He came to love the freedom of his new job: the early morning rides to Cranbrook to a wool broker, or to Canterbury to purchase bolts of baize and flannel made to order by the Flemings, and silks from the Huguenots (though for some reason John always begged to do the Canterbury work) — or even to London to act as an agent for his father to some particularly important customer. He learned to appreciate the warmth of the Belgian flannels, the fine softness of the Huguenot silks, and the sturdy durability of English broadcloth made locally by their own weavers.

New draperies sold well for them, but so did the traditional woollens. The Fessenden seal on a bolt of cloth began to acquire greater reputation. At first, Robert was surprised. Hadn't his brother said on return from Holland that the English wool market was in decline? Hadn't

53

his father spoken grimly of the wool trade recession a thin five years before, and of the growing superiority of Dutch fabric finishing? Still — they had produced and sold more cloth in the last twelvemonth than ever before, and the weavers and fullers could hardly keep up with the demand. 'It's the mixture that gives our cloth its strength,' John maintained. 'Buy all your wool from one market and your garments may look well for a month or two, but they won't last, and they won't hold their colour. That's why you and I have to be alert all the time. We must insist on the short-staple wool fibres of our reliable fullers. But we've also to find new ways of making stronger thread out of finer wool. Softness isn't everything — yet we can't afford to ignore the new stuffs or the market's demand for them. That's the way we'll keep our trade up.'

Family councils between father and sons became common, sometimes into the late evening hours when Mary and the younger children had retired to their chambers — even when John expected to be gone to Canterbury all the next day, or Robert to one of the Cinque Ports to examine imported cloths.

They held such a council one night in the late autumn. Mary, unobtrusive as usual, had put away her mending as soon as light failed, and without so much as a goodnight had left the three men by the hearth. They heard her upstairs settling the children: the shrill demands of Sarah for another kiss, the scamper of Isaac's feet overhead as he jumped out insisting on another lullaby or prayer, and finally the creak of the bed as Mary herself put out the candle in her narrow bedroom, once a storeroom, over the front door.

Fessenden raised his eyes towards the beams. 'Widow Snode's a good woman, but those children are getting beyond themselves. Your mother . . .'

'They're happy again, Father,' John cut in. 'Let well enough alone. We should thank Providence for mother Mary.'

'Your mother would turn in her grave if she knew the goings-on.'

'Maybe, maybe not,' John murmured, while Robert threw him a quick glance. 'Mother had far too much to do when we were little. She did the work of two women.'

'Aye, we'll not replace her. No more fine bacons or hearth swept spotless every day.'

Robert nodded in vigorous agreement.

John grew bold. 'Nay, but Mary finds more time for the little ones, and they're thriving. She's grand, Father, and never a word of bothering to us. Why, if you forgot her twelve pound a year for months on end, she'd never say a word.'

'The more fool Widow Snode, then,' Fessenden grunted. 'But this is vain chatter, and you need your bed if you're to be up at daybreak. Business, Robert my lad, with you.'

Robert jerked forward, lulled before by the casual drift of the conversation. He noticed his brother's mouth turn up at the corners, as if he were party to what was to come. But then the room seemed to fall still, and his awareness of his father's brown eyes on his was heightened. He gulped, managing only a faint, 'What is't?' Something important was going to be said, he knew, and it concerned him.

'I've been pleased with all you've done for me, Robert. You've shown judgment. You've grown in confidence in your own abilities, and rightly. You're only fifteen, I know, but you're a man in my eyes now.'

He sat up, brightening with pride.

'I know how much you've wanted to work more independently. John's told me you even longed to take the place he might have had with the Pilgrims and sail on the Mayflower — ' He broke off, smiling. 'Though only Heaven knows where those souls are by now, and I'm glad you're with us, not away with them . . . But I want to give you a chance to set out on your own a bit.'

What would he say? Was he going to suggest he went to the remaining Pilgrims in Leyden or London, as his brother had done, and study for himself the ways of the European craftsmen? Or was he to set up a shop for his father — perhaps in Canterbury, where John liked to spend his time? He watched his father's face intently for a clue to the answer. It came immediately.

'You'll go to Maidstone and lodge there a while — as a trial, to see how you get on.' Fessenden glanced at John, then back at Robert. 'Your brother has a notion that Maidstone's going to become more important than it is at present; he thinks someone in the family should be there. And there are the mills at Loose to oversee — you'd be right handy for those, and that'd take a worry off me.' He leaned back, resting his palms on his knees. 'There now, what do you think of my plan?'

Robert opened his mouth and laughed breathlessly. 'Sir — I hardly know — '

'You look as winded as if you fell off a horse.'

'No — ' Robert smiled back at his brother's dry expression. 'I think I just found myself mounted on one that's galloping away with me.'

Fessenden smiled, but there was no humour in his eyes. 'A very pretty conceit, boy. But I want to know what you think, in truth. Your mother'd never forgive me if I sent you off before you were ready. Younger boys than you, though, have gone to sea and done battle, and you're wiser than most. Speak up, now.'

'I'm fair speechless.'

John prompted, 'But he's your man, aren't you, Robert?'

'Aye, Father, I'd like to do it.' He did not look at his brother.

Fessenden reached out and put a dish under the candle to catch the tallow that suddenly began to drip and spill onto the board. He began thoughtfully, 'Then let me explain. When you were just a lad — I mean about five years ago, when the trade was falling off, and we were all worried about it — there was a move afoot in London to stop all the exporting of unfinished cloth, especially cloth that went to Amsterdam. Some of the gentry thought they knew more about the trade than we do, and they said all the money was to be made in dyeing and finishing, and even though only the Dutch could do it properly, they would still insist the cloth be kept in England for finishing. John, you'll pardon me — for I know we differ here — but they forgot that the English made the best cloth in Europe.' He laughed scornfully. 'The gentry lost pride in their own weavers

56

and ranted and raved at their own dyers.' He set his mouth into a grimace. 'Treating the men that way didn't work. English wool profits didn't increase, and English dyers were no more and no less skilled than ever. They were going at it backwards. You can't change the quality of a whole bolt of cloth by finding fault with one thread in the warp, and you can't make the English wool trade the best in Europe, neither, by shunning the Dutch or by refusing to train the English craftsmen properly. So I think it's time we did something in our own little corner of the trade, time we took our best dyer and gave him some journeymen — Maidstone men — and did more of our own dyeing at Loose. What do you think?'

Robert shifted nervously. 'I know nothing of dyeing and fulling, sir.'

His father nodded. 'But you can learn. You're quick-witted enough. If your grandfather could full the cloth by trampling it with his own feet, and if I could full it with my own hands at the mill, then you can learn to do it — or at least oversee it — yourself.'

Robert watched his father carefully, containing his enthusiasm as he caught the unintended exaggeration of his father's argument. His grandfather had certainly worked in the days when fullers had laid their cloth in troughs and walked on it until it matted together in the soap and fuller's earth; but his grandfather had been a weaver, not a finisher of cloth. In the same way, his father may have been a journeyman at Loose for a short time, but there, surely, with all the modern equipment the fullers used, his father had never turned the wheels by his own effort.

'I'll learn as much as I can, sir, and willingly,' he said.

'That's right, son, I knew you would. It'll give you the chance to work even more on your own and see more of the county . . . Well, then, it's settled. You'll start on Tuesday. We'll travel to Maidstone the day after the Lord's day, and we'll see you lodged there and your horse stabled — '

'But won't it cost too much?' Robert began to frown, biting his lip, the doubts trickling back.

Fessenden's mouth twitched. 'You'll more than earn your keep.'

'But where shall I stay?'

'A wise question, lad, and I've given it much thought. I met a victualler there not long ago, an upright man once from Goudhurst. He was a landman there, but restless, and felt Providence wanted him in a town — a place where he could preach to more souls. Peter Longden by name.'

Robert frowned. 'A blackcoat, sir?'

'Nay, not a priest. But he preaches in the open air. His shop supports him now, but some squire or other helped him start, at first. He's a man of our sort, Robert — pious, God-fearing, a yeoman. He'd treat you as a son.'

Robert was pleased, though he remained silent.

'We'll go early and enquire until we find him,' his father concluded. 'Away with you now to bed. I've a word or two for John, too.'

JOHN

'I'm certain of her, sir.' John stared at the yellow-white flame of the candle and thought of Jane's hair. He had told his father everything about Jane. 'I know it sounds absurd. I know I should never have gone as far as I did, and I'm ashamed of the way I lost my temper.'

Fessenden returned his oldest son's look of despair with an answering look of compassion. 'Young blood,' he murmured. 'Hot blood.' He sighed. 'Thank God I never had to woo your mother with a pike or musket in my hand. 'Twas all arranged when we were in our cradles.' John only nodded. He saw his father's eyes mist over but did not want him to lose the thread of their conversation. 'And all this happened a year ago, you say?'

'Yes. Almost to the day.'

His father let out a small, tight laugh. 'The man was right. You're a dreamer, John, and always were.' John looked down in disappointment and shame. Was his father going to offer no more counsel than this? 'But dreams that last so long acquire a substance. And I've seen your other dreams at work this twelve-month.'

John blinked a puzzled response.

'Your plans for our draperies. Your dreams of better weavers and dyers . . .'

'Oh — those — ?'

Fessenden's hand touched John's shoulder in a rare display of pride and affection. 'Yes, those. And if those dreams prove substantial, you're not the madman he took you for; and this, too, may prove substantial.' His look suddenly became penetrating. 'You're sure she's maid, not kept woman?'

John flushed darkly. 'Never a kept woman, sir. I know it in my soul.'

'So you've seen this maid again, have you?' His father was smiling again, his face softening. 'Risked yourself to see her every time you went to Canterbury? Small wonder you journeyed there more oft this year than I in a lifetime.'

John returned the smile, relieved that his father seemed to understand. 'Aye, I've seen her several times — at a distance. But she's never seen me — until today — though I've learned her times for going in and out.' He flushed again under further scrutiny. 'I was near the Mayflower Inn again, passing the pump where I first saw her, and I suddenly thought what she meant that day when she was waving her arms at me. All this year she's waited and hoped to see me at that same place.'

'At the pump? Poor lass, with a lover too dull to know what she meant.'

John was surprised by his father's levity. Irritated, he said, ''Tis of no consequence now. No one takes account of a maid drawing water with a crowd of others and passing the time of day with a traveller who's nearby.' Inwardly he shook with excitement as he remembered it. He had wanted to throw himself at her feet and beg for forgiveness for the year that had elapsed; he had wanted to flout all that his mother had taught him about courtesy and press his mouth onto hers in the middle of the road, then and there.

'You spoke to her, then?'

John nodded. 'Aye. Told her I wanted no other, and would she consent to be my wife if we could find a way

round that dragon who lives under the nose of St George
without being vanquished — '

His father burst out laughing but instantly became
sober again. 'St George and the dragon? That's a popish,
pagan tale, son. Apt for nothing.'

'I'm sorry.'

His father heaved a deep sigh. 'But something must
be done, I see.'

'Aye, but what? I dare not endanger her. She's not as
hearty as she was, and paler.'

'You think her ill-used?'

He shook his head. 'I doubt it. Her uncle's too public
a man for that.'

'It's happened before. Blackcoats be not immune to
beating women and children.'

'Not Jane, pray God — '

'Miss Tritton, son.'

'Aye, Miss Tritton.'

'Well, I hope you're right.' His father fell silent for
a short time. Then he continued, 'And her knowledge
of God, my boy? Think you she knows aught, dwelling
in a benighted house? Could she accept our ways,
do you think?'

John's reply came back in a rush. 'Aye, I'm certain of
it. If her father was a godly — '

'Salvation's not inherited, John.'

'Nay, but . . . her face when I spoke of the Lord —
and when I told her today that we are godly folk. If she's
been with her uncle these many years, she's untaught,
maybe, but not against us.'

Fessenden shut his eyes, his brow furrowed in
thought, and John waited anxiously. 'We know too
little about Miss Tritton for my liking,' he said at
last. 'And yet there's something about what you've
told me that rings true. If I were guided by my
baser impulses, I'd say we should endeavour to talk
further with the gentleman. But I must seek the Lord
first. And John, you're young. Very young. Most
lads of your age these days aren't thinking of marriage yet.'

'I know I'm young.' He met his eyes steadily. 'But two
years ago I was not too young to go to Leyden for a year.

And now I'm not too young to work for you as any man of thirty would.'

'Nay — better.' Fessenden sighed deeply once again. "Tis true. True.' Then, tremulously, 'I'm sending Robert away, too. You knew that I planned it, and yet you said nothing to me about your hope of a wife until now? Would you have left me here alone with the children?'

John frowned, surprised at the new undertone of sadness, the sudden hint of his father's own loneliness. 'Forgive me, sir — what could I say to you until I had seen Miss Tritton again? But . . . if it should come to pass that we be wed, then . . . I'd not think of leaving here. I want to serve you. You know that. The new world — I couldn't take a wife there, not yet, anyway. And I wouldn't go there now.' He held his father's eyes with his own. 'I belong here. I want to stay here, Father . . .'

The heaviness on his father's face lifted again. 'If that be so, son, then unless the Lord counsels against it, I shall see Mr Tritton myself. It shall be done.' He smiled. 'And I'll see this paragon of sweetness and beauty, too — to be sure — before I agree to any match.'

'Sir, I'm twenty!'

'Twenty, not twenty-one.'

John made a slight noise of exasperation, but then caught a glint in his father's eye. 'You'll like her, sir. No doubt wish you'd seen her first.'

Fessenden grunted. 'Not I! What you see with the eye . . . 'tis but the appearance.' His face turned wistful again. 'No, I'll not find another like your mother.'

Masking his surge of excitement about his father's decision to help him, John tried to mirror the change in mood. 'Nay, but you ought to marry again.'

His father turned away. 'Who'd have me, pray?' He bent to stir the fire, his face hidden. 'An ageing man with six children.'

'Four now. And not old, neither.'

'Four, then.'

Slyly, John said, 'I know who'd have thee, Father.'

'Only the Lord knows that,' Fessenden scoffed. 'I'll give you counsel, John, but I'll none of yours, I thank 'ee.'

ROBERT
Loose, May 1621

Robert slowed the mare to a walk. He felt no inclination
to hurry along the Loose Road today. In the short time
it took him once a week to travel the lanes between
Maidstone and Loose he enjoyed rare moments of peace
that were generally crushed out of his life. At least out
of doors he could observe the changes in creation:
the subtle shortening of the shadows, the flutter of
nest-building birds in the high hedgerows of holly,
cobnut, ivy, bramble, elderflower, and privet; the lazy
movements of the sheep under the apple trees; the scent
of the apple blossom; the vivid uncurling of the sweet
chestnut leaves. Not that Chilham had no beauty to show
beyond its stiles and along its footpaths — but that, until
now, he'd never had the inclination to study it.

From his vantage point on horseback he could see
over some of the shorter banks into the orchards. The
clouds of blossom foamed on the trees, pink and white,
though soon to be shaken down and bruised, trampled
into disappearance. The freshness of the colours — the
arc of sky above the hedgerows, blue as the chalk moths
that flew in the summer on the Downs; the pinks and
whites of the petals and the faint green-gold spikes of
young grain — all made him think suddenly of his
brother's bride.

John had married in April. Their father had gone
to Canterbury on John's behalf more than once to
see Mr Tritton. Apparently struck by Fessenden's
forcefulness — a will equal to if very different from his
own — the Old Dragon (as John insisted on calling him,
to his father's dismay) had finally been persuaded by the
clothier to relent and release Jane to marry. Privately
John had told Robert that he doubted whether it was
their father's persistence as much as his means that had
finally won Jane away. The Fessendens, not the Trittons,
had given her a dowry.

Until the two were married Robert had given little
thought to women: a distant species who, like his
mother, worked unceasingly; or, like Mary, busy with

the children all day long; or, like his sisters, always talking or playing or interrupting the menfolk, or, like that wench in the castle, saucy and wicked. Women might be human, he decided, but not people one deliberately chose to live with for the rest of one's life. In general — creatures one might almost discount.

And yet Jane belonged in different company. He could see what had drawn his brother to her. Even in the sober blue dress and high white standing band she wore on their wedding day she looked as beautiful as a pagan princess of corn. His mouth twisted; John would not be flattered by the comparison. A pagan, indeed! But . . . that gold hair tumbling from her cap, the eyes like cornflowers in a wheatfield, her skin as perfect as the apple blossom petals before they fell. A rare beauty. He found her puzzling, a creature to idealize. Not a woman like dull Widow Snode to mend and cook and teach the children at the kitchen table . . . And yet . . . she was no faerie or enchantress, after all. He knew now after a few days at home since the wedding that Jane did as much as the widow herself to help his father and the children. Between the two women, all the work of Ruth Fessenden went on. Not, however, in a dreary, drudging way any more, but with laughter struck out like sparks in the old forge at Chilham between the eyes of the lovers.

He looked up suddenly and fancied he saw Jane's face in the apple blossom over the hedge. His jaw set hard, suddenly. He knew the taste of jealousy.

The Mayflower had reached America in November. Stories had already returned of the horrors of the journey — the stench and damp below deck, the storms that rolled and pitched the boat like flotsam in the troughs and crests of the waves, the narrow escape from disaster when one of the ship's main beams had cracked . . . Could John have endured that journey and still have survived the plague and fever that had evidently claimed many lives that the seas had not? Had they been married before, could Jane have endured that journey? No — it was unthinkable. Thank God they were both in England! He hated to imagine Jane in the dark, foul hold of a ship, flung through the waves in the grip of winds that shrieked like dead spirits escaped from hell. Thank God they had never gone to America with the Pilgrims!

But what of himself? What if Jane were his, and how would he have fared, had he fallen in with the Pilgrims — with Brewster and Carver, Winslow and Bradford — all the men his brother had spoken of? He could not imagine Massachusetts Bay, nor could he imagine himself in that settlement. Not that he had lost hope of seeing America for himself one day, but that — for now — it seemed entirely remote. As remote as Jane, he thought bitterly. He would never be anything to her but a younger brother.

Instead, life was tied to things much more concrete, present, and mundane: in Maidstone the clatter of carts, the shouts of vendors, the chiming of bells and clocks, the noise of the pretty Longden children below stairs, and the long-winded stories of Mistress Longden, his landlord's wife, about her husband's patron, the older Squire George Tolhurst; in Loose the rhythmic pounding of mallets and the splash of water in the troughs; at the staple the bleat of the sheep and the haggling of the men. All these were what made up his life now, and though they gave him no peace, they satisfied him in many ways.

The road dropped downhill now, with higher hedges and the sound of rushing water beyond them. One of his father's mills lay ahead; he could see the white-washed clapboard exterior against its background of early summer greens. Then, a few moments later, the rush of the stream could no longer be heard, replaced now by the pounding within.

Outside the mill he dismounted and led his horse into an adjacent field to crop the grass. Careful to shut the gate behind him, he climbed up the outside steps and stooped to enter the mill's low doorway. Immediately, the master fuller was beside him, knowing Robert's usual arrival time, and doubtless having expected him for some time already. His coarse apron and the sleeves of his smock were permanently bleached by the chalky earth he worked with every day. He looked at Robert warmly. 'You're here, then, son.'

Because Robert liked the man he did not resent the indulgent tone he always used. 'Aye,' he murmured. "Twas such a blithe day.'

'To be sure.' The fuller winked. 'But what would your father say if 'twere one of my apprentices getting here three hours past cock's crow?'

He was used to the teasing, but he could not laugh; after all, within the hour he would change from the son of the master to a clumsy apprentice shoulder to shoulder with the others at the trough. 'Ah, but his apprentices don't ride all the way from Maidstone for their day's work.' His voice sounded sharper than usual.

'Maidstone? Is that all, lad? I thought for certain ye'd come all the way from Chilham by now.'

Robert wanted suddenly to raise his fist to the fuller's round smug face, but he restrained himself. 'Nay, nay . . . but, come, what's ado here?'

The fuller folded his arms and sat down on a sack behind him. 'All's well. Young Ralph's a sharp one. He's learning faster than any apprentices I've given Matthew before. Or else Matthew's just a better teacher than before . . . '

Robert nodded briskly, secretly wishing (though knowing it would be impossible) that the fuller could honestly say the same of his own attempts to learn this end of the trade. He took out the note he had carried inside his surcoat bearing reminders to himself of what he was to do this day. 'And the cloth we've been bringing you? You're satisfied with the weavers' work, I hope?'

'Aye, it's been fine stuff you've got me. Your father knows a good weaver, all right.'

'And what of the earth? Have you still sufficient, my father wants to know?' His voice was growing confident.

'Come and see for yourself,' the fuller said. He lumbered off to the storeroom on the other side of the mill, carefully walking round the trap door that opened to the floor below.

Robert counted the bulging sacks of fuller's earth and made a note of the weight of soap remaining. Then, with the fuller, he examined the latest batch of finished cloth, checking it for close matting of fibres and uniform

65

colour. This was the routine he had accustomed himself to over the six months he had been his father's factor in Maidstone. At first he had felt particularly helpless and self-conscious. It was absurd for him to examine and make pronouncements about the finished work of master craftsmen! But the fuller, sensing his discomfort, had eased him into his role by showing him exactly what to look for, by teaching him (as he taught his apprentices) how to full and dye the cloth, how to make best use of the mill's equipment. Without crossing the boundary of disrespect, the fuller was able to laugh and tease Robert into competence. Now when Robert looked at the cloth he missed no flaws.

Then with the master fuller he went below to join the other apprentice lads for his weekly lesson. He feared their censure and needed their friendship far more than he did the fuller's. As — with them — he laid the cloth in the damp felting troughs, he was acutely conscious that they watched him closely — as though searching for some opportunity for ridicule. Matthew, the journeyman, was, however, intolerant of any inattention to work at all; he shouted lustily at any of his apprentices — even Robert — who dared to exchange looks and take their eyes off the cloth.

Once the cloth was laid evenly in the trough, Matthew would open a sluice which allowed the water to run over the wheel again. The mallets would turn and begin the steady pounding of the cloth as the apprentices measured careful amounts of soap and fuller's earth into the trough. Soon the splashing of the water and the slap and stamp of the mallets were all Robert was aware of until the sound ceased at last and the cloth was heaved out — now compressed — to be dyed, dried, and pressed.

By the end of such a day his back would be aching and his head still roaring with the noise of the mill. At dusk he would catch the mare and canter off to the north. He was doing what he loved; he was independent without having complete responsibility; and he was learning the path God had chosen for him: to be a clothier.

4

ROBERT
Barham Down, Summer 1625

Robert took a deep breath of sweet air: the hot, clean smell of newly cut hay from lower down, the tang of the heather and gorse that covered the hill where they sat. The fragrance renewed him, for he rarely found the opportunity nowadays to notice his surroundings. ''Tis grand to be out of Maidstone for a while,' he murmured.

His brother's wife turned to him. 'Aye, brother Robert. We're glad you're away here for a while. Especially now.' She turned her eyes towards the road down which the new king and his bride were shortly to come. Widened and smoothed for the occasion, it stretched below them like a dusty strand of undyed wool that grew larger as it climbed level with them then up again to the summit of the Downs.

John stretched out his legs. 'Never mind all this pomp,' he grunted, 'I'm thankful you've escaped the plague, my lad.'

Robert looked down. Surrounded by other local families — by men and women he had grown up with who now had children of their own, by the variegated ivories of linen shirts and smocks, wool jerkins, hats, and caps, by striped shawls brought for comfort on the uneven ground — in such serenity it was hard to contemplate the growing seediness and dissoluteness of the town he now thought of as home. The plague — absent for nine years — had returned to claim several lives already this year. His father had called him home until the pestilence subsided, and he found himself unexpectedly relieved to be back in Chilham. Here, in the beauty of the Downs — fields of ripening oats and barley below and garlands of gorse and heather above — the ugliness of the town was almost inconceivable.

He smiled uncertainly back at them both. 'Thank you. I'm glad to be here, myself.'

The pealing of bells in the village warned that the King would soon approach. A noticeable change took place in the crowd. Men stood and shaded their eyes against the glare so as to be the first to see the King. Women gathered their children onto their laps or leaned over to point out the way the royal party would approach. Robert noticed Jane watching the women with children and knew what her sad eyes expressed. He wondered fleetingly what sin she or John might be guilty of that the Lord had still bestowed no children. He moved to stand shoulder to shoulder with his brother.

'I'm hopeful England will improve,' John ventured softly to his brother.

'So may it,' Robert returned, though without conviction. His mind travelled away from Jane again and back to the sort of conversations he heard in Maidstone and at the staple every week.

'You sound doubtful, Robert.'

'Aye, I am. You've heard the tales yourself. That man Buckingham will rule as long as the King will tolerate him. I doubt Charles Stuart will prove much different from his father.'

John's eyebrows rose. 'I think he will. What I hear is that the court's a more decent place already — that none of the profanity and profligacy James Stuart tolerated is now permitted.'

'I hope 'tis true. But think you, truly, he can reverse all the years of ill his father did to godly folk?'

'You mean — ?'

'I mean the Book of Sports — an affront to any Christian. And the chains he put on men who'd preach the truth, or write or print the truth — like your friend William Brewster.'

John's face fell. 'Aye. These are hard times to follow Christ.'

'James — he was aptly named "deceiver"! If some would make a god of him for his fine Bible, they're sadly misled!' Robert shook his head.

John looked round anxiously. 'Hush, you're speaking treason, I'm sure.'

Robert only laughed. 'Nay,' he said bluntly, thrusting his thumbs in his belt with a shrug. 'Nay. 'Tis all between himself and his Maker, now. It's naught to me.'

John watched him for a moment. 'But you'll be proven wrong about his son, I trust. They say he's devout, genuinely so.'

'Devout about the right of kings to rule by God, I'm sure,' Robert said flatly.

'Come, what's the mordant in your jerkin that makes you so sour today? What know we of such things?' John searched his brother's face earnestly. 'You should have gone with the Pilgrims after all, perhaps, if you wanted none of kings.'

'Not I!'

'And you've heard, have you, of the new King's grant to the Strangers?'

Robert grinned back at him. 'How should I? I go not to Canterbury as oft as you. What is't?'

Jane looked up, but said nothing. Her blue eyes rested on each of the men in turn.

'They may keep all their rights and freedoms. His Majesty favours them.'

Robert cleared his throat. 'Good news, that, I agree.' He rubbed the wooden sole of his boot in the chalky earth of the ridge on which they stood. 'But, John, he favours the Papists, too.'

John's face clouded again, and Jane looked back to the road again uneasily. 'Aye. There's no arguing that.'

'It's that scoundrel Villiers — Buckingham — again. When the King's suit fails for a Spaniard he runs straight into the arms of a French Papist.'

'A princess.'

'But a papist, nevertheless.'

'Ah, Robert, you've been too long in the town. You talk like a bitter, worldly courtier, full of hatred and intrigue and vain politicking . . .'

'God forbid!' Robert flushed. 'But I've been there long enough with their lordships and ladyships coming in and out at assizes and the gentry talking at the markets and the staples and the inns . . . to hear what others besides myself think and know.'

'Look!' Jane scrambled to her feet dusting off her gown in haste. 'I see them coming, I'm sure.' She came to stand close beside her husband, and he put his arm round her waist.

'Aye, I see a cloud of dust . . . and banners . . . and, listen — '

'Trumpets on the wind!' a man a few feet away called out to his wife.

Robert listened intently but at first heard nothing. He could, however, see men on horseback attired in splendid cloaks. The horses moved in a slow trot with heads raised, seemingly conscious of the royal presence not far behind. As they drew nearer, beginning the climb, the whole party slackened pace. The watchers could see the horses' tossing heads, the drummers, the pipers, the infantry marching close behind with their pikes ceremonially mounted in leather slings, and the flags of the King and — notably — the flag of Kent with its white horse emblazoned over the word *invicta*. And then, in the middle of the procession, two figures mounted on horses as white as the Kentish horse, closely followed by another on a great black stallion.

Robert strained to see clearly the details of face and form, but the distance was too great.

'Do you hear the drummers, brother Robert?' Jane asked in excitement.

He frowned, puzzled. 'I hear the trumpets faintly, aye, but not the drums.'

John glanced swiftly at him. 'Yet I can hear them. How strange.'

Robert was shaking his head. ''Tis strange, indeed.' He leaned forward but caught only the low babbling of the families near them, the breeze rustling over the brush and grass. 'Well, never mind. Ah, but I would I could see their faces — ' He laughed ruefully. 'I suppose you can, brother.'

'Nay — they're too far off. There's naught wrong with your eyes, Robert.' He turned his face towards Jane. 'Jane, your eyes are bright and clear. Do you see them better than your menfolk do?'

She smiled back. Her face always lit up when John consulted her, and for a moment Robert felt the flickering of envy that had dogged him ever since the marriage. Childless though she might be, she brought more joy to John — he knew — than anyone on earth.

'His Majesty's hair is dark,' she said.

"'Tis a wig, you ninny,' John teased.

'No,' she said firmly. 'His brows are dark, and his hair is dark, too, with a wave in it. A very handsome man.'

'Prettily said, love,' John said.

'But not as handsome as you be. Never. His nose is too large and his beard too pinched for my liking.'

John squeezed her arm. 'You're a saucy wench today. Go say it to his face, pray.'

'Nay, nay. He wouldn't notice me at all. Look at his wife. All blushes and black ringlets.'

'Aye, now I see her as well as you do,' John put in. 'She's just a slip of a thing — looks no more than fifteen. Poor lass, married to England.'

'Poor lass!' Robert scoffed, becoming uneasy about the light-hearted vein of the talk. 'Her father was the King of France, and the Pope's at their beck and call. And no covering on her head — to speak of. Pity not the new Queen, John.'

'I do, though, from the bottom of my heart. And the King, to boot. The kingdom in disarray and a never-ending war in Europe, and Spain hovering like a hawk waiting for the kill, and debts, and bad harvests, and Villiers breathing down their necks . . . who'd be king?'

'Now who sounds like the cynical courtier?' Robert asked mildly.

They watched the procession reach the highest point of the road then disappear behind one of the folds of the Downs, quickening as they began to descend. The tail end of the procession — more infantry and two horseguards at the rear — disappeared from sight. Robert wondered how a man so obviously enamoured of pageantry could set to rights a country besieged by the devil himself, a country whose church called on Christ but which martyred Christians as rebels and traitors to the King. What would become of King Charles and his England?

71

5

GEORGE
Barham Down, Summer 1625

Just over the other side of the hill an enormous pavilion
had been erected for the royal party. Long canopies
extended at either end of the pavilion, and on all sides
hung the standards of the King, the new Queen, and
Kent. The scalloped edges of the tent cloth undulated
in the slight breeze, and around it moved many of the
local gentlemen. A few of their wives had accompanied
them out of curiosity, but they sat together in the shade
of one of the awnings, conversing quietly and fanning
themselves against the heat. Servants and labourers
from the village, hired for the day, hovered anxiously
within the tent, eyes agog. *A picnic*, the gentlemen had
said. *A picnic for the King?* This was no picnic. It was a
veritable banquet.

Within the pavilion tables were heaped with venison
and smoked meats; fresh breads; wheels of cheese
made by women in Canterbury, Great Maydeacon, and
Barham; two boars' heads garnished with bayleaves and
rosemary; overflowing bowls of cherries; strawberries
and raspberries; flagons of cider, butts of sack and wine,
and barrels of beer. And within the hour, most of this
would be consumed by the King and his courtiers and
by the lords and ladies waiting without. And although
(as men of Kent in the lushness of Kent's fruitfulness)
these labourers had never starved — even in the recent
famines — nevertheless they could not conceive of
so much food.

George Tolhurst was one of the many gentlemen
waiting outside the tent to pay his respects to the
King and his bride. Unlike most of the other knights,
courtiers, burgesses, and gentlemen in attendance, he

had no wife to bring with him. At twenty-five he had just buried his parents and now found himself alone — save servants and labourers — to manage his newly acquired court in Goudhurst, with its hop gardens, fruit trees, and fields of barley.

He would never have left his farm and come all the way on horseback with a groom and one manservant had not Sir Henry Oxinden of Barham invited him. All the gentry of the county were there today, or so it seemed, and those he did not know well he knew at least by name and by sight from hunting parties and from the assizes in Maidstone; he had gone to the assizes with his father for years before he had actually held responsibilities there.

He felt a little unsure of himself in this august body of men, though he could not account to himself for the feeling. The gentlemen of Kent were known for their easy familiarity with their tenants and with each other; after all, most were related to each other, and no one lorded it over another. The gentry — and the yeomen — all prided themselves on independence and freedom. They depended on each other for the perpetuation of the ancient rights and privileges of what was once the Kingdom of Kent, so there was never more than friendly rivalry among the families, and they stood together in crises. For this reason, Tolhurst was proud to be a man of Kent; still, he found himself uneasy with all the ceremony and pomp and with the company of so many older men of great experience and influence.

There was Sir Dudley Digges, for example, a friend of Sir Henry's, who had left Digges Court some time ago and built himself a fine castle at Chilham. Seventeen years older than himself — not much, perhaps, he thought, but long enough for Digges to have befriended the Archbishop of Canterbury, to have travelled as an ambassador to Russia, Holland, and Ireland, to have been imprisoned in the Fleet for his speech against the Duke of Buckingham, and to have made an enemy of a certain Bishop William Laud, who was reportedly a favourite of the new King's.

And what of Edward Dering, the son of Sir Anthony of Surrenden? Only two years older than Tolhurst, he was already well known as a King's man. Not a man — Tolhurst suspected — who blindly yielded to the whims of King James or to the demands of his son, but a man whom royalty trusted, a man who was already lieutenant of Dover Castle, who was sure to be knighted within the year.

And besides these men there were the Twysdens, Tuftons, Astleys, Sondeses, and Culpepers — all the main threads in the Kentish network of family ties. Most older than he was, all wiser . . .

Since the King had still not yet come, Tolhurst stood with Sir Dudley and Edward Dering outside the pavilion. A group of musicians inside the tent began to practise an air, and he found his foot tapping as he listened to the other men.

'What think you, sir,' Dering was asking, 'of our new monarch and his bride?'

Sir Dudley turned aside to cough into a lace-edged handkerchief, and when he looked back at Dering and Tolhurst, his eyes were full of laughter. 'It matters not what I think, gentlemen,' he said suavely. 'I serve the King, be he James or Charles.'

'Nay and so do we all, sir,' Dering replied. 'But you have been in Whitehall and Westminster these long years, and you surely —'

'"These long years",' Digges echoed with cool amusement. 'You make me sound like a hoary old kingmaker.' He ran his hand through his thick, waving hair. 'Hoary I may be . . . but no kingmaker. I'd rather be at home in Chilham to wait upon my lady and the common folk of the village, truth to tell.'

Tolhurst watched Dering's keen eyes search the older man's face in bland assessment. 'Nay, play not the country squire with us, good Sir Dudley,' Dering said playfully.

Digges' eyebrows rose. 'I knew not that I did.' He linked his arms through those of the two younger men. 'Then since you press me,' he continued, 'come, let us walk a little, and I'll put my head on the block. Do not repeat my opinions, however, for I will deny them to the death if treason's the word. I've seen enough of prison bars already to be more cautious now than I was at your age.'

74

The three men strolled round the pavilion, past an enclosed field where the horses were tethered, and up another rise in the Downs. 'In truth,' Digges began again, 'I do fear for England.' He gave a quick, grave smile: a glimpse of faltering sunlight between the dark clouds that gathered in his eyes. 'Not as our Puritan brethren fear for England with all their cant of the Antichrist at war with the Body of Christ and the great Millennium on the horizon, with Christ himself coming as their captain to blast the Papists and the Arminians to hell . . .' He drew breath, smiling faintly again. 'Not, I say, as my neighbours the John Fessendens fear for England — '

Tolhurst nodded. 'Aye, I've heard of Fessenden. The clothier who has a son in Maidstone? . . . Robert, Robin . . . or some such.'

'The very same — Robert.'

'And Robert's at lodging with some Goudhurst folk — the Longdens — people my father foolishly patronized. Peter's turned preacher — in the stocks as often as he's out, and not even able to write, let alone read the prayer book or heed the catechism . . . Fancies himself a Prynne or a Lilburne, doubtless.' He shook his head. ''Tis a scandal, such a beggar pantomiming as a man of the cloth . . .'

'You were saying?' Dering interrupted.

Tolhurst flushed with embarrassment. 'Forgive me,' he put in quickly. ''Tis a sore matter with me — that Puritan nonsense.'

'Aye, nonsense,' Digges agreed. 'Nonsense that'll soon be knocked out of their heads if Laud has his way.'

'Or if the Queen has hers,' Dering parried.

Digges pulled down the corners of his mouth and shook his head again. 'Nay, she's a poor little waif, I'm sure. The King will tolerate the Catholics more than his father, I've no doubt, but England'll not go back to the Pope in Rome. No, that's not what makes me afraid.'

Dering and Tolhurst looked at Digges, and as they did so, each caught the question in the other's eyes.

'It's this matter with Buckingham and the King, and the King and Parliament — these things I fear. Buckingham will rule, I fear, and the King, who like a little child with a spoiling uncle thinks he's getting his own will all the while, will be led from one folly to another to please his favourite. Then Parliament will rise against them, and Charles will protest they interfere in what they know not of — and we may have war.'

Tolhurst dropped his arm. 'Bleak prophecies indeed, sir.'

Dudley stood still on the grass beside them. 'Aye, bleak, but I see it coming. And we poor men of Kent will know not where our hearts should lie — with our King, who wastes the realm in his associations with dangerous men — or with the common folk His Majesty thus defrauds — or with their Parliament! Aye, we may have the worst war of all, when brother raises sword against his brother.'

His sober words hung in the silence broken at last by the faint sound of the King's trumpets in the wind.

Chilham, April 1628

George had ridden too far and too fast, and now his grey gelding was lame. Chilham was near, at last, but the long, slow climb up the Pilgrims' Way — to a haven for his horse at the forge and to food for himself at the Castle — seemed unending.

He cursed himself every step of the way for bringing no servants with him, but it had seemed a pleasant enough jaunt, at first, to set out alone with nothing but a portmanteau slung over the back of his saddle and the spring wind off the Downs in his face. And so it had been — at first. He had stayed with some distant cousins on the way . . . and had met Elizabeth.

Now that he had to walk the rest of the way to Chilham, he had plenty of leisure to think both of his reason for going to Chilham — and of Elizabeth. The two things most on his mind — one expected and the other unexpected — rivalled each other for his attention. As he marched along, occasionally whistling an air or a jig, he tried to concentrate on one or other of them. Instead, his mind wilfully swung from one to the other. If he thought of the letter from Sir Dudley that had summoned him to Chilham, he inevitably thought of another letter, arriving the same day, inviting him to spend a few days with his cousins. The coincidence was perfect, he had concluded; he could hunt with his cousins, for a day or two enjoying a respite from Tolhurst Court and the sowing of the barley; then he could go on to Chilham.

If he thought of Sir Dudley's seat in Parliament for Kent, ruminating on the influence that position was already bringing to bear in London on behalf of the county he and Sir Dudley loved so well — then inevitably he thought of Elizabeth's father, who sat in the House of Lords. *Nay, rather,* he laughed to himself, *he does not sit, but sleeps, the old fool.*

And if he thought of Dering and Twysden and Sondes and all the other young men of Kent he expected to see at the Castle, and of the earnest political discussions to which they had all been summoned, then inevitably he thought with chilling uneasiness of all the young men who came and went to his cousins' house with no other reason than to woo Elizabeth. He ground his teeth when he remembered them. The girl's father was doting and careless, he had decided. She was his darling, the only daughter among a houseful of sons, the last child of his first wife. But even as the old man doted on her, he gave her what Tolhurst considered too much freedom for a modest young woman. The men came and went, flirting and bowing and talking nonsense to his cousin. Cousin! No, hardly that — her father was his own father's second cousin, so that made them third (or fourth) cousins. No, not cousin. She was his sweetheart.

But he couldn't talk nonsense to her or curl his hair and perfume himself with pomade as some of these other gallant gentlemen did; these were not part of his nature. As she crossed and recrossed her father's great hall — her dark, reddish hair braided round her head, pearls gleaming at her throat, her waist slim beneath the embroidered bodice of her gown, and her full skirts brushing the floor — he had tormented himself with worrying and wondering about whether she actually liked these men. Was she as careless as her father, a spiteful kitten who minded not how many hearts she broke, playing without interest the same coquettish little games that so many gentle women played nowadays? God forfend it! He could not imagine that she would be as light as that, young though she was at eighteen. But could she be interested in a dull old bachelor of twenty-eight who liked to hunt, fish, dine with friends, and tramp about in the muddy fields of Tolhurst Court? A farmer — after all, that's what he was.

Only on one occasion had her father's laxity worked in his own favour. The young men had departed and the old father and step-mother had retired for the night. He had found himself unexpectedly alone with Elizabeth in the candlelit splendour of the family's dining room.

The serving maids had removed the last platters and dishes, but Elizabeth herself had shown no inclination to rise or retire, so for a blissful hour they had faced each other across the table. His eyes had never left her face. He took in the high, smooth brow revealed by the old-fashioned, simple way she dressed her hair — innocent of any Puritan cap — the wide cheek bones, the tapering oval of cheeks and chin illuminated by the golden light of the candles, the semi-circular arch of perfectly even brown eyebrows, and the greenish-blue fire of her eyes. She did not look at him directly during most of their time together, unless she was answering a question; her eyes were down, otherwise, or focused on the Dutch sideboard behind him, which was adorned with vases and china plates. So when she did look up, the colour of those eyes struck him so forcefully that he began to fidget and sweat uncomfortably and had to loosen his neckerchief.

He had felt more foolish than ever then, and more certain than ever that she must think him a country oaf with no better manners than to stare at her like a gawking yeoman in the lane. Even now, vividly remembering her expression, he felt hot with longing and excitement.

Perhaps he would have left his cousins' estate convinced of her disdain, had there not been one exchange

between them near the end of the conversation that had
left him musing in wonder and joy.

'It grows so dreary here now,' she had commented.
'My brothers are rarely here. I have little enough in
common with my step-mother.'

'Then I'm glad I came,' he had said softly. 'But you
have so much company here — surely 'tis never quiet.'

'No, I wish it were. That's not what I mean. 'Tis not
the quiet I'd mind.' She looked up briefly, blinding him
again by her eyes.

He had swallowed hard. 'Then what?'

Thoughtfully she had run her fingers round the
stem of a goblet. ''Tis the mindless prattle of my father's
acquaintances that I find so dreary.'

Relieved, and seeing her now in a different light,
he took courage to probe further. 'But they admire you
so, 'tis obvious.'

She made a noise of scorn at the back of her
throat. 'In their simpering way, yes. But I suspect
they admire my dowry more.' Her face clouded. ''Tis
unfair that a woman's naught but a ewe in the market
place to be quarrelled over according to the depth of
her fleece, poor creature ... But not all women have
empty heads bent on house and husband and infants.'
She flushed, and that flush revealed to Tolhurst more
about Elizabeth than he had dared hope or imagine.
'Some of us grew up listening to stories of good Queen
Bess — nay, *named* for her — and some of us wanted
to be as shrewd and clever as she was, or as a man
is in politics and the ways of the world.' She shook
her head. 'Instead we're mured up in our courts and
houses. waiting for the best bargain in the marriage
staple to cross our fathers' thresholds and rescue us
from one pen just to put us in another.' Her voice had
grown high, and she had looked him fully in the face
again. But there was no anger directed at him as one
of the male captors, only something ... might it have
been an appeal?

George reached out now and absently stroked the
neck of his horse. What had that look meant? And what
was it he had replied, awed by her passion and by the

79

originality and strength of her convictions? '*I've* never thought that way of women, I confess — '

'Why should you? You're unwed yourself, and free to pursue your work and your life and your opinions without troubling over the thoughts of a rebellious girl.' And she had dismissed herself with a deprecating shrug.

He had laughed then, throwing back his head and unconsciously thrusting his feet so far under the table as he leaned backwards that his feet had found hers.

He had moved them quickly, murmuring an apology, then answering her, but still feeling burned by the contact. 'Life isn't as interesting for us as you might think.'

'But London . . . Parliament . . . affairs of state . . . '

'I'm only a justice of the peace.'

'Then at least you go to Maidstone.'

'Aye, but most of my time is on the farm. I'm a yeoman, in truth. Just a yeoman with an old name, 'tis all.'

''Tis all?' Her eyebrows arched. 'Then why, if you be yeoman only, do you go to Chilham to see Sir Dudley?' She fired the question back as smartly as a musket answering the slow fire of a cannon, and he saw he was contending with a woman of quick wits, a woman as different from his dead mother as his pedigree mare was from a tinker's donkey.

He had shrugged. 'His lordship did not say.'

She gave him a piercing look. 'I don't believe you'd ride all the way from Goudhurst for naught.'

'Nor would I.' He felt ashamed, as if he'd been caught playing the same little word games he so deeply scorned in Elizabeth's wooers. 'But I cannot tell you the matter of our meeting.'

She had leaned forward. 'Would you, if you could?'

His heart had beat up fast, then, and he had longed to leap up on the table, wrest her from her seat, and feel her mouth under his own. 'Aye — ' It was all he could manage to say.

Then one of the servants had come in, Elizabeth's own maid, perhaps — an older woman — and had drawn the curtains and lifted the candle-snuffer with a meaningful look at Elizabeth. There the magical encounter had ended, now assuming the quality of a dream-vision in his mind.

Would you tell me . . . why do you go to Chilham to see his lordship? Would you, if you could? The words ran round and round in his head, repeating themselves in her honest, musical voice until they obliterated all other sensory impressions and almost all thoughts of what he was actually doing on the road to Chilham.

In fact he knew quite well why Sir Dudley had written no particulars of his meeting at the Castle. If the nature of the meeting he anticipated were discovered, he realized, there might be outcries of sedition, rebellion, and treason from certain quarters. And Sir Dudley did not have to list details for Tolhurst to know precisely what would be discussed. The theme stated three years ago on Barham Down would be played again in all its variations, now with the knowledge not of prophecy but sad hindsight.

Charles Stuart: they had met him briefly that day. The King was slight, small, and spoke haltingly, with a stammer that suggested shyness. Courteous he was — with a curious magnetism that both drew and repelled Tolhurst — and courteous he had shown himself ever since; that same quality, though, bore with it dislike and scorn for anything discourteous, for anything that smacked of commonness or coarseness. The King was fastidious, in fact. He had shunned Parliament, calling it only reluctantly and occasionally in the last three years. He had tolerated his wife's Catholic emissaries (and practices) at court and had favoured the Church of England's policy of intolerance towards all dissenters. The intolerance had magnified since Laud's appointment to the Dean of his Chapel Royal, to the Privy Council, and now to the Bishopric of London. And though Tolhurst looked down on Puritans, considering himself a high Anglican and a royalist, he still rejected the crude, extreme punishments for dissenters that were allowed by the King. He could not be uncritical, even of a king appointed by God. Yes, this meeting might well open the way for yet another rising in Kent.

Amusement creased his face. *Wat Tyler, Jack Cade.* Would the names of Dudley Digges and George Tolhurst yet be among the chronicle of Kentish rebels?

In a room bare of all ornament but candles, an oak table surrounded by stools, and heavy damask curtains pulled over the windows, George Tolhurst bent forward to listen to Sir Dudley Digges speaking from the head of the table.

'I've spoken to you all before,' the knight began. 'And we've all seen the paths the King has chosen. Buckingham has disgraced himself in France. Stade is lost. Rochelle is still unsuccoured, betrayed by Buckingham. The Exchequer has exhausted its money and its patience for four years — first for the Palatinate, and now for Rochelle. But truly — ' He shook his head grimly, his voice turning harsh, ' — for *nothing*. And now the King will use his "divine right" to imprison those who do not grant him what His Majesty calls loans, will billet men on innocent householders obliged then to put up with ill-bred ruffians who abuse their property and even commit foul murder. 'Tis not right. 'Tis *not* just. Parliament will brook no more. I will brook no more . . . and I say, we cannot brook these policies — or delays — any longer. If other counties and their men in Parliament be silent, Kent shall not.'

A few of the men nodded and murmured in agreement, and Tolhurst surveyed Sir Dudley's face in surprise. Always so mobile and sardonic, it was now impassioned and solemn.

'I represent the men of Kent, as well ye all know, and I've been persuaded by Sir Edward Coke that Parliament needs to speak more strongly. You know Coke's position well enough, I warrant — '

'Nay, Sir Dudley.' One man spoke up, but then flushed in dark embarrassment as all stared at him.

Sir Dudley inclined his head deferentially. 'Forgive me, Walter. I take the affairs of Kent with me every time I go to London. I forget sometimes that I take not the men of Kent, also.' He cleared his throat. ''Tis this. The King is God's man. That we all believe. But he's God's *lieutenant*, no more. We cannot rely on messages and promises delivered to us by word of mouth alone. We must have written confirmation of his will to change his policies. 'Tis time we present a formal petition to His Majesty.'

An older man than Digges was frowning. 'You distrust the King, then, do you — you and all yon men in Parliament?'

'Nay, rather, we distrust his ministers. And we cannot take his trust but in a parliamentary way, as Sir Edward Coke says. There must be some limit to *iure divino*. His Majesty is obliged — he must — listen. Or if not, at his peril. 'Tis time the word of Parliament regained its power.' He paused, passing a hand across his brow. 'Surely, surely you remember what happened two years ere this, when we opposed the loans forced out of Kent to support the war?'

'Aye, clearly enough,' answered one man bitterly. 'Clapped in prison, and I'm not like to forget.'

'Nor I,' Digges agreed. 'But I'll lay the King turns a deaf ear to voices from the provinces — the squires' and the justices'. But he can't do that for ever. He wants to win the war, but without Parliament, and without money — yea, without the men of Kent — he can do little there.'

A wizened man at the foot of the table nodded vigorously. 'Aye, when Spain was on our doorstep Her Majesty listened well to us. She knew right enough that if Kent stand not as bulwark, England hath no defence. But Charles, it seemeth, is less wise than his good cousin Bess.'

'True, too true.' Digges stroked his beard. 'But here's the rub. We're a free people, and thank God for that. We bow the knee to no man save the King. All well and good. This betokens, however, that we band not together or choose a leader when we have a cause. We take our rights for granted, and we take our family connections for granted, too. We scarcely think of joining together because we believe ourselves already joined. We never think of leading one another because in Kent we all be kings on our own land.' He narrowed his eyes. 'Some of that must change. That's why I called you here. God knows I'd rather be sitting by the fire or working the falcons and the hounds, but here I sit. Here you sit, and I beg your support. We must get our tenants and our yeomen on our sides also.' He waved a document of parchment on which were inscribed the tentative clauses he and Coke had discussed already with fellow members of Parliament. 'For if they be not with us, being without a cause, they'll follow the Brownists, or dreams of Eldorado on the far side of the Atlantic. Fever, plague, and despair . . . all for nothing. And the yeomen of Kent are where the power lies, verily.'

Tolhurst nodded vigorously, though he heard a few voices of dissent.

'Then tell us, Sir Dudley, what this petition will advocate, and whether we should promote it ourselves,' one man said timidly.

'Whether you should promote it yourselves,' Digges answered with a soft laugh, 'that I'll not say. 'Tis on your consciences. But we advocate naught but what is reasonable, moderate. Kent has a history of changing kings' hearts, if you recall.'

A few of the men laughed.

'Hear, then, what this petition pleads. Then let us discuss the reasons for it.' His eyes searched the room. 'Item: no man hereafter shall be compelled to make any gift, loan, benevolence, tax, or such like charge, without common consent by Act of Parliament. Item: no free man shall be imprisoned or detained without shown cause. Item: soldiers and mariners shall not be billeted upon private parties against their will. Item: commissions for proceeding by martial law shall not be issued in the future.' He stopped, looking round the intent circle of faces. 'That's all we ask, and thus far the Lords are with us.'

Immediately, loud discussion broke out, but Digges quickly quelled it. 'Listen,' he urged, as the room fell silent again. 'The Crown has taken more and more power unto itself. The bishops and the justices seem to think it their sole cause to extend and magnify the King's royal power — at the expense of all that we hold dear in our constitution, at the expense of common law, at the expense of Magna Carta itself. He creates new offences that were never offences before. He gives Buckingham a free rein in France so that the war —'

'Aye — and the marriage made to cement us to our enemies has done no good,' one man grumbled.

Digges nodded, then went on. 'And Buckingham, sent to make "peace", incenses the King of France with his indulgence with the King's wife. In short . . . unless we stand for our rights, we shall be ruled by dangerous fools. At their mercy, too, aye. And *taxed* to pay for their folly.'

The men all murmured in agreement, but the timid man spoke up tremulously again. 'Sir, what if our lands be forfeit for this petition? What if this be treason?'

All eyes turned on the master of Chilham.

'They cannot take our lands when we demand rights that are ours by the constitution of the realm, and when we do it lawfully, within Parliament. He sighed. 'And if they do — well, then — we live under tyrants, and naught that we do will be right. But if we do nothing, as Sir Edward has oft reminded me — we forfeit our substance anyway — in taxes.' He searched the faces of all men in the room. 'Who's with me, brethren?'

Tolhurst saw himself yet again as the naive country-man who knew too little about court intrigue, Crown policy, and parliamentary debates of the day. Like the others, however, he remembered painfully the 'loan' he had been obliged to make to the King only two years before. He answered Sir Dudley's raised eyebrows and questioning eyes with quick energy. 'I, for one, sir.' And then he thought of Elizabeth and knew that she would applaud his decision.

Goudhurst, 1632

For the first time since Tolhurst had met Elizabeth, no barriers divided them: no hovering maiden aunts, no perfumed suitors, no men pouring out full glasses of sack while pouring out too many words in those rare moments they had tried to be alone together. Now they lay close together in the flocked ease of the canopied oak bed at Tolhurst Court: the bed in which George himself had doubtless been conceived. The wedding festivities behind them — the heat and the crush in the family chapel, the rude country jokes that had assaulted their ears; the homely music of the shepherds' tabors, pipes, and voices; the platitudes of Elizabeth's overwise cousins and brothers; the flowing butts of claret — all these dissolved behind them now as they rested in the drugged warmth of each other's arms and explored each other's bodies.

He held her face inches from his own, shaking his head in amazement at the depth and steadiness of her eyes, the smoothness of her skin. 'I never saw,' he murmured, 'how you could love me. And now I know that you do, I curse myself for waiting all this time to make you my wife.' He shifted to cradle her head on one arm; with his free hand he pushed her tumbled hair from her face.

She moved closer to him. 'I did not know I loved you,' she said, and her voice was low. 'All I knew was that I had found a man — a sympathetic man — to whom I could talk, who wouldn't censure me for having all my wits about me.'

He threw back his head to chuckle and gave her cheek a quick pinch. 'Who wouldn't censure you anyway, since he has fewer wits.'

'Nay, 'tis not true.'

He hesitated. 'Then when was it you knew you loved me?' He knew the smile had left his face, and suddenly the room seemed terribly still, hovering on the edge of words he couldn't quite believe, truth he couldn't grasp.

Her eyes left his face and rested on the curtained windows. 'Two years ago, I think.' Then she looked back at him. 'The second — nay — third time you came to see my father.'

''Twas not to see your father, love, and you know that well enough.' He leaned over her, his hand smoothing the curves of her shoulders and breasts, his heart thudding in his ears again. ''Twas you.'

She smiled, her cheeks reddening slightly. 'And after you stayed with us — the first time, even — the men I found dreary already seemed worse. I felt insulted by them. They talk to a woman as if she's just a pretty shell, a china thing to mind lest one breaks it. Pretty, and empty.' She wrinkled her nose. 'But you were my first real friend, and you never treated me like that, and I never want you to.'

He laughed suddenly at her definiteness and sat up, leaning back against the bolster and looking down at her. 'Small hope of that, Eliza Tolhurst. I've made a woman of you, and you're a squire's wife. Worse — you're a farmer's wife.'

She reached up and pulled him down beside her again. 'So you'll make your poor little coz into a dairywoman? Like all the pretty maids of Kent who serve you already, who set their caps at you when you were a lad? You'll teach me how to shear and drive a horse and plough, will you?' Her eyes were dancing with mischief.

He gave an exaggerated shudder. 'Never!' Then he winked. 'But you shall go to the assizes with me, and help me oversee the constables and wardens and surveyors . . . and the folk hereabouts will call you good Queen Bess of Goudhurst — a shrewder judge than her husband of politics, of right and wrong.' He tightened his arms round her again, and bent his mouth to the softness of hers. What did all those civic affairs mean now he had the woman he wanted in his arms? His longing for her obliterated everything else.

She smiled again. 'Now I know why all those songs are about love. I lay the yeomen know more about it than we poor deluded gentry all puffed up with our estates and what not.' She stroked his hair, her eyes blazing steadily into his. 'And at this hour, in spite of all we've said, I care not a fig for politics or assizes or constables . . .' Her voice dropped, and her hands moved over his body, stirring his desire for her again.

'Nor I, neither.' He pushed himself up on his elbows to cover her, still dizzy with the wonder of a wife in his bed.

6

ROBERT
Chilham, March 1634

His brother Isaac stirred the fire and came to sit beside their father on the settle. Taller than his father, and broader in the shoulders than both John and himself, 'little' Isaac had become strikingly handsome with the black hair and dark eyes of all the Fessendens — save John — though his features were more even than theirs. Wherever he went nowadays — on business for his father or with his brothers — the maids turned and stared.

Robert watched him as Isaac picked up *The Plain Man's Pathway to Heaven*, which he had been reading fitfully throughout this Sabbath afternoon. *Too handsome by half for his own good*, Robert mused. He stared at him again: the thick curls of dark hair, the slight mask of freckles, the chiselled nose and chin, the sensual redness of his mouth. *Thank heaven*, he thought, *the boy is too innocent to know his own danger*. And he remembered the morning worship at the fellowship that day, when the brazen girls of the village — doubtless ill-bred wenches who served the foppish Sir Dudley at Chilham Castle — had ogled over the pews at his brother. Surely they had heard none of the sermon that day!

Then he recalled his new love, Patience, and he thanked God for her. No bold maiden was she, like the Patience of Chilham Castle! No fluttering eyelashes or faint blushes or silly talk. No lewd garments designed to tempt the unwary to their destruction . . .

He glanced quickly at Jane, sitting across the room in the windowseat with John and Mary, talking with them in low whispers he couldn't hear. Still without children, Jane had acquired none of the matronly caution in her

88

dress that he remembered in his own mother. Not that she was immodest . . . the Fessenden household would never have brooked that, he acknowledged . . . but that she seemed to have an inborn sense of artistry and design in her choice of fabrics, bodices, and skirts — and John, of course, indulged her. And Jane's still radiant beauty somehow went against Robert's grain. It was not seemly, surely, for a woman of her mature age to dress like a courtier . . . He frowned. *No, she doesn't*, he thought. *All's plain and simple, and yet* . . . He stared hard at the lines of her body beneath the materials — supple and strong from all the work she did about the house. She managed to be elegant, princess-like; even the sombre colours she preferred showed off the gold of her hair escaping from under her coif and the clear brilliance of her skin and eyes.

She caught his eyes briefly, and he dropped his down, clasping his hands round his knees in a quick gesture of guilt. It occurred to him suddenly, to his chagrin, that he was staring as lustfully at his own brother's wife as had the girls at Isaac this morning: the very girls he had condemned.

Remaining still, he shut his eyes, hoping to shut out Jane's image. Was he, too, condemned then? He tried to summon the face and form of Patience, but he could not. Was he destined thus to lust after other women — as a betrothed man, even as a married man? God forbid!

Opening his eyes, he jumped up and gave the logs in the fire a push with the fire-irons that sent a shower of sparks and soot dancing under the mantel.

'What is't, Robert?' Isaac enquired.

Robert did not hear him, so Mary Snode, sitting nearer, repeated the question more loudly.

He swung round towards the settle and caught the eyes of all the family on him: his father's and Isaac's; and, over on the windowseat, Jane's, John's, and Widow Snode's. Unlike John and Jane, he had never really liked Mary — the interloper who had tried to take his mother's place, who had spoiled his sisters and Isaac, and who now took her place in the parlour as if she were one of the family. But he had never really known her, either, having left home to spend most of his life in Maidstone, soon after the woman had arrived.

He tried to answer civilly. 'Oh . . . naught,' he mumbled, castigating himself for lying, and turning round to face the fire again.

'Where's young Patience?' John called out.

Robert repressed a sharp retort. They all did that now — this shouting at him. It was a curse to be going deaf, and only Patience understood how lonely and bitter he often felt. And, worse still, he could never be sure if his own voice was a shout or a whisper, and this uncertainty only heightened his resentment. But now he regarded his brother with what he hoped was a face of accustomed friendliness. 'She be in her chamber — ' In spite of himself, he thought suddenly of her slenderness, mentally disrobing her as he longed to do on the day of their wedding. But then he pushed the thought away, angry with himself for desecrating in his mind what he loved with all his heart. 'She's — she's reading, I believe. She says 'tis her custom on the Sabbath afternoon to read some godly book. She reads aloud with her aunt. A very edifying way to spend the day, I do believe.'

His father, looking up from the open Bible, murmured his agreement, though Robert thought uneasily that he caught a slight constraint in his father's approval.

Isaac waved his own book with a mischievous grin. 'She's right, dear brother.'

'Mock not, Isaac,' Fessenden growled.

'But it seems strange, does it not, my father,' Isaac began guilelessly, 'that she and her aunt have travelled all that way on Robert's account just to sit at books all day . . . hardly to show their faces to Robert, let alone his family.'

Robert opened his mouth to rebuke Isaac, but Mary intervened first. 'Nay, Isaac, you do overreach yourself in discourtesy to your brother.'

Robert noticed his younger brother's surprise at her sharp words, for Mary rarely corrected her beloved now and had never before taken his own part against Isaac.

90

His father joined in support of Mary. 'Have done, lad, and read your book.' He glanced at Mary, but drawing a thread through her smocking, she did not look up. "Twill soon be time for prayers and a light repast, and I'd like peace enough this day to read the word of God, if you please.'

'I'm sorry, Father,' Isaac murmured. Then he raised his voice, 'And I'm sorry, brother, for my thoughtless words.'

Robert bowed stiffly. 'I do forgive you.' He went back to his seat again; and, unwilling to look at Jane again, or at Isaac, he retrieved a devotional pamphlet he had begun reading by candlelight the evening before and tried to lose himself in the teaching it contained. Before, when he had wanted to think of his betrothed, she had eluded him. Now — when he wanted to purify his thoughts — her image would not leave him alone. Patience unhooking her bodice and discarding her petticoats; Patience in a linen shift, her hair (always tightly covered by a cap) unbound and rippling through his fingers; Patience in their bridal bed . . .

His mind stopped there, bridled by a severe conscience, and he silently bid the devil cease to trouble him. Well, thank God, they would be wed within a few weeks, and then he would not live in fancy any more but have her for himself in the flesh, as God willed man to take his maid.

Perhaps his father sensed his restlessness, for he looked up from his reading again and caught his eye. He called out, 'Nay, Robert, but you are troubled.' He stood up. 'Come with me, son. Let us walk in the garden a while.'

Fleetingly, Robert felt like a boy again, a boy who, when times of melancholy assaulted him, had sought out his mother for comfort. It had been the same then: a walk between her herb borders down beyond the outshots and the chicken run, to the rose garden. That rose garden was now Widow Snode's province, and, grudgingly, Robert admitted that she tended it with more skill, care, and devotion than his mother had ever given . . . but then, he reconsidered, his mother had borne eight children, had done by herself all the

91

churning of butter, starching of collars, smoking of meat and brewing of small ale — whereas Mary was no more than a paid servant with time on her own to play at gardening and making physic.

Wrapped in heavy wool cloaks, the two men seated themselves under the arbour — bare now of all but a few dark-red knobs that would soon burst into leaf.

'Are you not easy in your mind, Robert, about your choice of a wife? I'd thought — '

Startled, Robert interrupted sharply. 'Not easy, Father?' He gave a short laugh. 'Nay, I'm . . . I'm glad of her . . .' He struggled against self-betrayal, against revealing to his father all the base fancies that seemed to taint his relationship with her unless she was actually present. 'I'm as glad of her as I can be.' He grimaced, taking a deep breath, 'But our wedding day seems over-long away.'

If he expected censure for his eagerness, he received none. 'Ah — so that's it. And when Isaac jested with you, he touched you on the quick.'

Robert nodded. He looked down absently at the tulip leaves poking up from under the leaves and earth.

'Isaac's young, and you must forgive, as you said you did.' Fessenden paused. 'He's never known, yet, what it is to desire the love of a woman you love. Never known what it is to wait. But he will, one day.'

Robert stared at his father, wondering at the depth of feeling in his voice. 'But I fear — I cannot speak of it.' He felt the colour rising to his face.

His father laughed. 'You think I know not what you mean? You think, do you, that an old man like your father wars not against the flesh as his son does?' He spoke loudly so that Robert could hear, but his voice was gentle. 'We are all of one flesh, Robert, so hearken well. Evil is real, as well you know. But your longing for Patience is no evil. 'Tis a longing God himself has given you. Learn the difference, son. How else shall he give you fruit to her body? Fruit he commands to you both?'

'But my thoughts — I can't — ' He wanted to bare his soul to his father but stopped short. It wasn't Patience alone who aroused him. It was Jane. It was even — God forbid — the hussies in church this very day.

Fessenden put his hand on Robert's knee. 'Hush, I shall beseech the Lord in my private prayers for thee. But thou hast waited too long, perhaps, to marry. You're twenty-nine, are you not?'

Looking at the newly dug earth around the rose bushes, he sullenly said, 'Aye, twenty-nine.'

'And your brother was barely twenty-one. I told him he was too young, but now I see he wasn't. I married your mother when I was younger myself. And you've contained yourself these many years, waiting for the will of God. He cannot but bless your union, Robert.'

He looked up again, gathering fresh courage. 'Thank you. You've heartened me. I felt condemned . . . '

Fessenden smiled. 'You wonder not why I understand so well?' His eyes were warm.

'I confess — I did not expect — but it must be mortal hard to lose the woman you love, and never see her more.'

'You're thinking of your mother.'

'Of course.' He looked up sharply. 'Who else — ?'

Fessenden smiled again, a small, inscrutable smile. 'I grieved for your mother for many a year. But like you, Robert, I'm made of flesh, and bone, and blood. And God takes not away a man's longing for a bedfellow just because his wife dies.'

Robert flushed indignantly. 'Sir, you profane — '

'Nay, 'tis pride makes you think otherwise, as I have learned,' Fessenden said easily.

Robert's eyes flickered over his father's face, and the relief of the kindness he had felt from him gave way. His father was becoming altogether too soft in his judgments, too mellow. He began to mistrust the very source of his own comfort.

But his father went on, 'I was going to tell you and John this evening, in fact, that I will wed again.' He stopped, seeing the colour drain from Robert's face. ''Tis something I have peace about, and I doubt she'll

93

refuse me. With Jane and John sailing to America after all, and you to be wed, and your sisters all grown and married, there's only Isaac — ' He stopped, laying the weight on his next words, ' — and Mary Snode — left at home.'

Robert stared in shocked disbelief at his father, and some sort of unnamed resolve within him hardened against Mary.

"'Tis not right for Mary to be turned out of doors after all these years, and Isaac shall not do the work of women. Nor is it seemly for her to dwell with me and Isaac alone. I mind what evil tongues will say in the village once Jane and John set sail, and I'll not give house-room to the devil.' He smiled yet again. 'But that's not all. Yonder Mary's won a place in my heart as never I thought woman would do again.'

He was aghast. 'You'll wed *her*, Father?' Mary had cast her influence on him, then, she who had always been so lax with Isaac and the girls, who consulted Culpeper's *Herbal* more than the Scriptures.

'Aye, I will, and — like you — most gladly.' His father's eyes were slightly ironic now.

He looked back into them, thunderstruck. Was his father as weak as he was — the man who had scourged him for kissing a lass under the pagan mistletoe when he was fifteen, and again for making sheep's eyes at a new sister-in-law at Martha's wedding breakfast? Was his stern father weaker than he was? 'Sir, you amaze me altogether.'

His father leaned back so that his cloak fell open and Robert saw his fingers splayed over his knees. But then — in a gesture Robert never expected to see — he laid his finger alongside his nose and winked. 'Mind you,' he said cheerfully, 'I've not asked her yet. I'm a little forward in telling you, perhaps, so I'll thank you for your silence until she's answered me.'

Robert continued to gaze at his father in blank bewilderment. His father marrying Widow Snode? *Pray heaven she will not take him*, he thought. Anger rose, and he sought to hide it.

JOHN

'I've a few things to tend to ere morning,' Jane said.

"Tis the Sabbath, lass,' the father prompted gently, not moving from his place by the fire.

Jane looked across at Fessenden with answering warmth. 'Aye, I know it, my Father.' Except for Mary Snode and himself, all the others had now retired for the night. 'Forgive me, but what with the extra company in the house — ' She stopped, glancing at Mary with what John recognized was a hopeful look of request and mutual understanding.

Mary stood immediately. 'I'm sorry, Jane. Forgive *me*. I do forget myself.' She flushed; John saw that she deliberately averted her eyes from his father's, and their awkwardness after years in the house together amused him somewhat.

Fessenden held out a restraining hand. 'Nay, Mary, Jane will manage, for I have need of a word with thee.' He shifted and looked up. 'Son, go with your wife, or else retire, if you please.'

He stood to follow Jane, but she stopped in the doorway and smiled. 'It matters not, John, I'll be finished in a winking, and I know thou'rt tired.'

He nodded, pushing a hand through his hair. 'Aye, tomorrow'll be a weary coil.'

'Then I'll come up shortly, love,' she said.

Without a look at his father, he climbed the stairs. He knew that his father meant to speak to Mary tonight, and his heart was light with joy for them both, since he had long hoped for their match.

The little chamber upstairs was cramped: a bed raised from the floor by piles of local bricks, two straight chairs, a desk by the window at which John generally sat to do accounts, if the light had not failed, and a wash basin and ewer in the corner. As a child, John had shared this room and this bed with his brothers. But for thirteen years now it had belonged to himself and Jane. Only a few more weeks. Then they would exchange the little window for creaking ship timbers; the big bed for narrow pallets stacked one above another; their comfortable house and freedom to walk and ride the lanes of Kent for a hole under the poop deck of a ship bound for the New World.

This was no sacrifice, John reflected, sitting on the edge of the bed — but what he had longed for. What if he was exchanging the abundance of a Wealden home for the crudeness of a wattle hut in the harsh settlements of Massachusetts Bay? Yes, it was what he had longed for, after all. The other exchanges were small, and he spared them only rare moments of regret. The exchange that mattered was the one by which he was leaving behind the increasing persecution directed by the bishops and the church against all so-called Independents. In the Bay Settlement, he believed, he would find the bright light of religious freedom. Distance from the George Trittons and William Lauds of England, from the forced attendance at services that smacked more and more of the Queen's religious practices, from profanation of the Lord's Day, from the new archbishop's suppression of the God-fearing French Huguenots they knew in Canterbury . . . aye, they were longing to go.

The timing was providential in many ways. His father might be married soon, and Robert was bringing a wife home ere long; no doubt there would soon be children again to fill the house. Isaac was a grown man: strong, resourceful — no good with accounts, perhaps, but a favourite among all those with whom the Fessendens did business. And besides, some of the worst days in the Colony were over, it was said. No longer random outposts of huts in the hostile wilderness, communities and villages were now growing up all round the Bay. They would have neighbours, markets for supplies, a church and a minister already established. Thus his old hunger to cross the sea had now returned, and he was filled with the same curiosity, hope, and idealism that had once driven him to Leyden, then to Canterbury with Brewster and Cushman.

The Providence of God, he thought gratefully. *'Twas not his will for me to go then to the Colony. But had .he not bidden me to Canterbury, I would never have found my wife. And she . . .* His mind moved slowly now, heavy with an old sadness they had shared . . . *Had she conceived, as we long hoped, we might have settled here, loth to leave for our children's sakes . . .* He sighed. *Yes, God was all-wise.*

He pulled off his boots and undid his Sabbath falling bands. He did it without thinking, his mind still travelling towards the future, but now full of questions. Robert and Patience would soon uproot from Maidstone to occupy this room, taking over all his responsibilities in Chilham and Canterbury. All should be well, and yet . . .

He pictured Patience, and new misgivings needled him. What was it about her that disturbed him? She was God-fearing, pious, careful in her speech. She deferred to Mary — at least thus far — as if she had already learned of Mary's soon-to-come change of position in the household. Plainly, too, she was devoted to Robert, and he to her. *Then why this anxiety?* he asked himself uncomfortably. *The devil tempting me to doubt?* Her thin face and intense eyes appeared before him, her delicate hands and brilliant blue eyes. Briefly, he smiled — he and Robert both had a taste for women with luminous blue eyes. But without censuring himself for that thought, John realized suddenly that he found Patience — except for her eyes — very ugly. There was a pinched, tight look about her, as if she carried a grudge. Her manner to himself, Jane, and his father seemed forced, brittle, no more than mere civility.

He tried to stem his thoughts with caution. Could they expect otherwise from a poor young woman, brought up in a poorhouse, who had retained respectability by working as a spinner and occasional seamstress for her aunt in Maidstone? No wonder she was thin and fidgeted with her cap so often. No wonder after his brother and father had returned from their stroll that afternoon she had sat stolidly beside her aunt and spoken of little else but the tracts they had been reading and of the inadequacy of the preaching that morning. She had found comfort in over-zealousness, of course.

John frowned. *She's right,* he told himself, *everything she said is right.* He struggled, then, to name the cause of his unaccountable dislike of her. Was it her face? *The Lord seeth not as man seeth . . . The Lord looketh on the heart.* No, he dismissed that. Appearance had never swayed him much except — he acknowledged wryly — when he had first met Jane. But in her he had seen inner as well as outer beauty. This seemed lacking in Patience.

Irritably, he wrenched off his smock, breeches, and hose. Who was he to judge? How could he see into her heart?

He looked around the room. The candle was already burnt low. Where was Jane?

She came with a flurry a few moments after he had settled in bed. 'Just think, John,' she laughed, 'what I was witness to just now!'

'For shame!' he said mildly, sitting up again. 'Turning into a gossip, little wife?'

Her face fell, but not for long. 'Nay, but you know what's afoot, I'll lay.' Her eyes began to sparkle.

'Perhaps.' He reached up for her. 'Come, get thee to bed. 'Tis cold and lumpish without ye, and I mean to enjoy this bed while we have it.'

Laughing again, she untied her coif, unlaced her bodice, and went in her chemise to the basin. 'Sometimes, husband, I wonder about you. I'd be breeding all the time if I weren't . . .' By the candlelight he saw her eyes waver, then steady again. 'But now, seeing your father and Mary at last — I know whose son you are.'

'Jane Fessenden!'

'Aye, 'tis true. Thy father must've forgot I was off in the buttery for a time. When I came out he was standing by her with his face on fire and her hands in his. I hardly knew where to put myself.' She stopped, her face clouding. 'I fled out to the privy and then up here. Will they mind that I — '

John lay back on the flock mattress and began to laugh. 'Oh, love, would I had seen thy face, my poppet, and my father like the green lover I was with you at first. Oh, 'tis what I've hoped these many years.' He laced his fingers together. 'The Lord is a God of joy, is he not? Come, let us thank him for his mercy to our father after all these years. He's got a jewel, he has.'

They knelt together, then the candle gutted and went out. In bed again, he made love to her slowly and tenderly, then they lay still, their arms round each other in the dark.

But Jane could not sleep as now he wanted to do. 'John?'

'Aye?' He heard the sleepiness in his own voice.

'I'm glad as you are for this change for Mary. Especially now Robert marries this — Patience — ' Her tongue seemed to stick on the name. 'And now, we're away ourselves.'

Her gentle voice had jolted him more surely than a shout. He lay quite still and said cautiously, 'What can you mean, my love?'

'I feared to tell thee. I hoped you'd feel the same, or know what I meant without my saying more.'

His mouth went dry, and his voice caught as he answered, 'I often do.' He sighed. 'But this time you'd better speak your part.'

He noticed her breathing quicken. She was weighing her words, he knew, not trusting herself. ''Tis hard to say. 'Tis hard.' She took a deep, quick breath. 'But with Mary as his wife, I think our father'll be master here yet. Without her, I fear he'd fade, and Robert would command all. And lately, love, thy brother has — I cannot say.'

He put his fingers to her lips. 'Hush, I have felt it, too. He's been so silent, so turned inward.' He wanted to add, 'And too stern in his convictions, as if he'd make enemies of us all' — but he forbore.

She seemed to take courage from him. 'Aye, that's what I meant to say. And Patience is the same, only more so. Truth to tell, John, though I'll have to learn to love her as a sister, for duty commands it, I cannot like her.'

He had always relied on Jane's judgments, not about business — he would never consult her there. But about people she seldom erred. 'Nor I, but I cannot say why, though I've tried. I was thinking of them just afore you came up.'

'But *I* can see clearly why I like her not.' She dropped her voice to a whisper. "Twould offend your brother mightily if I said aught to him, and I could not.' She was shaking her head vehemently; her hair brushed against his face.

'Nor I . . . then tell me.'

She groaned. 'What good will it do for me to speak my mind? I have no wish to poison your — '

'Jane, my wise dearling, you'll never do such a thing.'

She waited so long to continue that he thought she might have drifted into sleep, but at last her voice came softly in the dark, direct, without a trace of resentment. 'It's the very thing I should most like — nay, love — her for. The reading she does. Her knowledge of the word. Her courage to dissent so openly. But instead, I find her zeal cloying. I doubt her. She was expounding this very eve on the joy of helping our Christian brothers and sisters bear burdens, but yester eve when Mary and I had the dinner still to ready and all the Sabbath food to prepare, she gave no help at all.' Jane paused, her voice changing. 'Nay, but I'm ashamed of my pettiness. She'd just come by cart all the way from Maidstone, and no doubt was a-weary.' She paused again. 'God will have to deal with me. I'm surely wrong to think thus.'

He stirred, pressing close against her. 'I think not, love. Unless I be wrong, too. You've only said what I had thought but knew not how to name.'

'John, I could not have lived here with Robert and Patience, you know.'

He did not answer immediately and consequently felt her body tense with anxiety. He searched for words to reply. 'I know . . . nor I. 'Tis better thus.' He kissed her hair, feeling her relax again. 'And Mary will look after our father. God knows his purpose for us all.'

They fell asleep at once, like children, thinking — both of them as they drifted out onto the lake of sleep — of the new land to which they would sail in only weeks.

FESSENDEN

He waited until the latch of the buttery door had fallen and until he knew by John's booted footsteps that his son was in the upper chamber. He cleared his throat and felt a new, unfamiliar warmth spreading through him. Fleetingly, he wondered if he had ever loved his first wife, for he could remember nothing of his feelings for her — save the hunger — that which Robert had spoken of — for this had never changed or left him. Now, though, his hunger had a direction, and its sharpness was tempered by a new wave of tenderness. Mary had unknowingly taught him the gifts of compassion and sympathy. Without sentiment, without laxity or godless licence, she had shown love to him and his children for the past fourteen years.

Constraint had grown up between them of late, however, and at first he had misinterpreted it. *She's forty-three,* he had said to himself, *and eager to shift for herself now Isaac's the only one left. She's restless, wanting to be gone.* It had not occurred to him, then, to question his own assessment of her apparent change of mood. Instead he found himself watching her more and more closely when they were at home together, found himself sitting by the hearth more of an evening to keep her company. If he had wondered before at the blend of cheerful goodwill and quiet usefulness in her, he wondered no more. She had always spoken more to the children than to himself, maintaining a reserve towards him that he had expected and understood. Now, though, he learned more about her and about her long-dead husband, Christopher. He learned what she thought of Thomas Jackson, the minister at Chilham's parish church, and what she thought of each of his children . . . but she had never, of course, vouchsafed an opinion on himself, and that silence piqued him.

His curiosity deepened as she seemed to begin to resist his presence in the kitchen. In private prayers he searched his heart for explanation, while she found ways to keep Isaac or Jane in the room with them after evening prayers. Again, he concluded at first that she must resent him. But in studying her closely, he found that she watched him often when he was perhaps supposed to be unaware of her eyes on him. It dawned on him, suddenly, that far from being eager to leave, she was fearful about it. It dawned on him, too, that there might be more to her dread of leaving than had met his unobservant eyes until now. It dawned on him, in fact, that there might — after all — be a woman who would want to marry an old man of fifty-four. And not out of pity for his children, either.

He watched her now. There had been a stillness about her all day, a restraining calm, as if she awaited some word or revelation from him. When she lifted her eyes from her needlework, they had been full of questions.

He was confused, bewildered, even afraid of his sudden rush of feeling for her. His confidence in the rose garden with Robert had evaporated, and with the warmth that ran through him came uncertainty.

'Mary?' His voice came a few tones lower than usual.

She folded her hands on her apron and looked away from the fire towards him. 'Aye?'

'I'm wondering — ' He bungled the question he had tried to frame in his mind all day and instead, in spite of himself, diverting their talk to another channel. ' — if ye are well pleased with Robert and his betrothed?' He swallowed, irritated with his own clumsiness. He had known her long enough. Could he not speak out and ease the strain once and for all?

A shadow fell between them as the flames died down on the last big log in the grate, and the searing pinks and oranges of the flames gave way to a faint glow.

Mary sat forward in her chair, her grey eyes finding his at last. 'I'll be sorry to see John and Jane depart. Jane's become like a daughter to me . . . But 'tis God's will, and you must make the best.'

Her words came simply, but he sensed a depth of unspoken feeling behind them. 'We'll miss them, aye,' he pressed on, 'but Patience may fill the space that Jane leaves, and Robert has been trustworthy and upright all his life. I doubt not God will bless them. I told him so this afternoon.'

Mary nodded. 'Indeed, Robert is ever the obedient son to you, as is John. Patience, though — ' she looked up, hesitating, ' — is not like Jane. And you and Robert will be hard put to it, I fear, to govern her.'

He frowned. He had been uncomfortable throughout the evening prayers, though he would not have acknowledged so, by the length of her prayers, by the words she chose, by what seemed a critical, niggardly spirit. Yet he could not have found fault with anything in particular that she had said. He shook his head. 'I hope not, Mary.'

'I have trespassed in saying so,' she began unsteadily.

'Nay, nay, Mary.' He, too, leaned forward, and his knucklebones whitened as he gripped the side of his chair. 'That's what I would say to you this very night. You've more than earned the right to speak in this house. So many years you've given us.' He surveyed the sweet roundness of her face, the gentleness of her eyes and mouth, the matronly curves of her breasts under the wool bodice and white partlett she wore, and he marvelled that he had been so blind to her for so long. 'And you might have given your beauty to a second husband long ago, but for us.'

She did not simper, but the colour rushed to her face. 'I? No, 'twas here I chose to be, and here I'll stay.' But then she stopped. 'Unless — '

He stood up and crossed in front of the fire with both hands outstretched to lift her to her feet. 'Never any "unless",' he murmured, and, holding her hands, he raised her to face him.

A rattle behind them made both of them jump as Jane opened the buttery door and hesitated on the threshold. 'Oh, pray pardon — ' Jane gathered her skirts in confusion, rushed to the back door, and was gone.

Mary laughed, suddenly, and he laughed with her, not releasing her hands. *No more of this,* his heart begged him, and he turned to face her again. 'There's no "unless",' he said thickly. 'Aye, the children have grown now, and I suppose I'll need to send Isaac to Maidstone in his brother's stead ere long. But I do not wish you to go. I've sought the Almighty, Mary, and I find it in my heart to ask if ye'll be my wife.'

Tears gathered in her eyes, surprising him. She released his left hand to wipe them away. 'I'll be thy wife, and gladly,' she said faintly. ''Tis what I've asked of God but never thought to see.'

He held her hands harder. 'I do not ask for pity of you,' he said firmly, 'nor gratitude, neither, though I'm thankful enough for all you've done, and I hope ye know it. I ask . . . because I love thee with all my heart, dear Mary.'

'And I thee,' she whispered.

He placed one hand on her waist and put his other arm around her. She was a small woman next to him, and he felt her trembling as he folded her to him. 'We'll to the church when Robert and Patience go,' he said.

She nodded.

Dumb with joy, he rocked her slightly as they stood before the fire. The warmth flowed between them, swaddling them in a cocoon of muted happiness as the fire died down to ashes and the quiet upstairs deepened to silence.

At last with a small movement she stirred against him and woke him from his daze. Looking into his face, she asked, 'Do you suppose we should wait 'til then, John?'

He started at the unaccustomed familiarity of his Christian name on her lips, and smiled. 'Oh, aye, people will gossip whatever we do, and there's the banns to be read, and the licence to be got . . .'

'Perhaps I should go away for a few weeks — if you can spare me. Now that you've declared yourself, and we're together in the house — '

He hesitated. 'I cannot spare ye, love. We may occasion gossip, but I know not where I'd send thee, anyhow.'

'What about the Castle? 'Twas Sir Dudley who brought me here. He'd give me lodging 'til we wed.'

He grimaced, so that she pulled away. 'No. You'll not go there, dear. Years ago all was well between Sir Dudley and me, but he's hardened now, like the rest of the gentry hereabouts, in the popish ways of Laud and

104

his company. I'll not see ye into his house, not even for three weeks.'

Her eyebrows rose. 'You sound like Robert — forgive me — set against all who believe not just as we do.'

"Tis not that, I hope,' he murmured. "Tis what the King and Parliament have done with men who dare to speak truth and preach the gospel — that's what I abhor, though I'll have no truck, neither, with violence and persecution, and interfering in men's consciences as even some of our own brethren do — ' He broke off, and the face of Patience that afternoon hovered before his eyes, issuing condemnation of moderate men he thought godly. 'But nor can I brook the forcing of Roman rituals down a man's throat by bishops who call themselves Laudians but flaunt themselves in splendour like papal legates.' He heard his voice rising, and stopped ruefully. 'I'm sorry, Mary, what has this to do with you?'

'I'll bide where I be, then.'

He tightened his arms round her. 'Aye, for I have need of thee, love.'

7

ROBERT
Maidstone, 1635

The first night at the Longdens' lodgings, well known to
him over years of staying there, brought an unpleasant
jolt to Robert's otherwise serene life. Marriage suited
him well: he had filled out a little, felt less restless, more
satisfied with life. Better still, though Patience had been
prudish and frigid in their bride-bed, he was rarely troubled by the lustful thoughts and desperate hunger for
the bodies of women that had bedevilled him all those
years between the provocative kiss of that other Patience
and the timorous kisses of his new wife. Patience had
accepted her new role submissively, fulfilling her duties
to him as a good Christian wife, exactly as he had known
she would. He was content.

Content, too, to have taken the absent John's place
as the eldest son of the family. He was glad that
John was happy in Massachusetts Bay, but he had
admitted to himself, too, that he was glad for his
own sake that his brother had gone. Jane had always
unsettled him. Beautiful — but barren. And children
were a reward from the Lord, he felt, to the righteous.
Jane's unrighteousness lay hidden as yet, but *he* had
found the pearl: Patience had presented him with
one child already — Thomas — and another was due
in the winter.

Trying to fall asleep without the accustomed warmth
of her back against his own to keep out the cool of this
late spring night, he had no difficulty picturing her now.
The second child had not shown itself yet — no swelling
of her body, no stirring within — but her face had
rounded and softened, and he found her more desirable
than before. *Not just a godly reader,* he thought cheerfully,

but a good breeder, please God. He reached across the bed without thinking . . . but of course she lay far off, in Chilham; she was not here.

And neither was Isaac. Where *was* that scoundrel? Carousing in one of the alehouses, perchance. A fine bedfellow he would make, no doubt, coming late up the Longdens' stairs and falling onto the bed without so much as a glance at the ewer or a search for his nightsmock.

Robert turned over in bed and groped for the tinder-box to light a candle. It was his obligation, he decided, to remain awake until Isaac returned, then to box his ears and issue some sound rebukes. His father would not do it, too soft in his old age, now wed to that easy-going Mary Snode. No, it was for him to chasten Isaac and stop his wicked, debauched ways. That was why Longden had asked one of the Grammar School masters to write him a letter, sent to him at Chilham:

> *Sir, know that your brother Isaac doth taint himself in idle sports, no longer conducting himself in the ways of righteousness. He is riotous and heeds not my words. Though I doubt not he honours his father and worketh well for him by day, I know not how long he may continue when all the while he plays by night. I beseech you call him home and upbraid him. There be another matter besides, which I fear to write here. Pray make a speedy answer, sir. I remain your servant and your friend.*

The letter was neatly written in the practised flourishes and stiff rhetoric of the teacher, clumsily signed by Peter Longden. So without telling his father what he intended to do, Robert had left the next day for Maidstone.

Here all his fears about his brother had been confirmed. Longden recounted — at first with ingratiating timidity, then with increasing boldness and savagery — how young women had flocked to Isaac for his fine looks and debonair, gallant manner.

'He's grow'd those thick black curls, you know. Looks like a swaggering cavalier. Always so civil to me, he is, but he's a sly one.' The victualler's face had darkened. 'Wooed my eldest daughter, he did, without a by-your-leave to me. I'd have been proud to see her wed to him if he'd remained as he promised at the first, but he's a blighted apple, that one. Rosy-cheeked and fair on the outside, and rotten within. The kind my customers bring back to me and I pay them back for. She swears he hath not had her maidenhead, but I . . . fear he has, and I'd thank'ee to take him away afore he sires bastards on her.' He shook his head in disgust. 'I never thought to see this day with a Fessenden in my house, and all my daughters been so chaste and sweet. I'll not have such lewd, ungodly folk above stairs no more. Your brother Fessenden'll have to shift for himself if he stays in town.'

Robert was struck silent by this news, which had been shouted to him so that he would not miss a word of it. So Isaac had discovered his handsome self! And in so doing, he had taken advantage of his relative freedom in Maidstone and had discovered women. Shame on him! Robert winced and grimaced, thinking about him, and remembered with fury the rest of his converse with Longden as darkness had fallen in the poky room, and lamps, candles, and rushlights had begun to glow without.

'He's off and away this very evening,' Longden told him loudly, 'and naught I could do to stop him save fetch him a clout on his pate with my stick, and that would make but little dint in his thick skull.' Longden shuddered. ''E's a big lad, your brother, and not the likes of you and John — not a one I care to quarrel with.'

Robert burst out, 'Oh, but he'll mind me, don't you fret!' And he thought with vicious satisfaction of the pleasure he would take in beating his brother.

'Rebukes run off him like water off a foul and slimy gutter in the High Street,' Longden added, shaking his head mournfully.

Robert stared, felt pressure building behind his eyeballs as he meditated Isaac's soon-to-fall punishment. 'Rebukes? Nay, I'll not waste my breath. I'll do with him what my good mother would have done years ago, had she lived, and what my father should have done. He'll get a beating such as he's never had.'

Longden's eyebrows curved up under his thick, oily thatch of yellowish hair with a hint of scepticism that he

108

soon veiled. 'Aye, he has it coming. Then I'll thank'ee to take 'im away for good. And I pray heaven he hath not violated my daughter. Why, even now . . . ' The man shut his eyes and screwed up his face.

Robert felt the blood rushing to his face. Anger overcame him like a red tide. 'She's off with him this very night?' The scarlet waves broke over his brain, and he thumped his fist so hard on the mantelpiece that the wood splintered at the edge. He barked out, 'Why couldn't you *stop* her, you fool?'

Longden backed away. 'I'm no fool. Devil take your ill tongue, Goodman Fessenden!'

Robert bit down on his lower lip until the blood oozed out. 'Forgive me, I spoke in haste.'

'Aye.' Longden turned away bitterly. 'Now you have children of your own you'll soon know what a coil it is to keep order even under your own roof. Especially — ' He swung round again, his voice heavy with emphasis, ' — when the devil himself puts one of his own under your roof to tempt them away from the right path.'

Robert kept silence, waiting until the man had exhausted his anger.

'But if I'm to be a shepherd of God's flock, then I *must* keep order in mine own house. The word says, "For if a man know not how to rule his own house, how shall he take care of the church of God?" Yon Isaac goes with you.'

'And if your daughter — ' Robert faltered. There was more he must say.

'Rebecca.'

'Henrietta?'

'Rebecca!'

'If Rebecca's with child?'

Longden scoffed. 'Then she'll wed a man more fitting who can foster the poor babe. I'll none of your brother for a son. Rebecca shall learn obedience of a man who's godly, a man who shall know the truth about her harlotry but stoop like Hosea to keep her as his wife, despite her wickedness.'

Remembering their talk now, Robert sat forward under the bedlinens and tried to visualize the Longden children. The eldest of them was but fourteen when he had vacated this very room to be wed to Patience, moving home to Chilham with his bride. Their young, childish faces eluded him — except one. Was she perhaps the eldest? Was that Rebecca, then?

He had noticed her always, but only because she reminded him of Jane; the same hair of flaxen gold, the same clear, sky-bright eyes, the same silvery laugh. Like Jane, the girl had been slightly built, slender. Had she grown to womanhood now, a willow beauty of fifteen or sixteen whom Isaac could not ignore? Isaac . . . the ill-disciplined Isaac, the beautiful one, the one he had always been jealous of. *Jealous?* A fearful, ugly thought! He shook his head to clear his mind, slipped out of bed, fell to his knees, and began to pray in desperation for his own cleansing and forgiveness.

He was sleeping deeply when Isaac returned, and did not wake.

When first he opened his eyes the next day, it was with the mistaken idea that Isaac had not slept in the bed at all; the bedding beside him was hardly disturbed. But as he went to the ewer in the corner to begin his toilet, he noticed a discarded jerkin that had not lain over the chairback the night before. Isaac's workboots also stood beneath the chair, old leather stained with the mud of East Lane. The lad was gone already, then, making a holiday of it. But what was he wearing on his feet?

Robert looked down at his own feet, pale and naked now on the rough boards of the room he had occupied for so long. He had never possessed more than one pair of boots, and now his younger brother was cavorting around Maidstone at dawn on May Day in a second pair of shoes! The thistles of resentment grew higher in him, and angry words that he had difficulty swallowing came to his lips. A plague on Isaac's cunning for escaping him this morning!

After Longden had presided over lengthy prayers, mainly for Isaac and Rebecca, who were caught — as he put it — in the evil enchantment of the rites of this godless day — Robert sallied out with him to find the young couple and bring due retribution upon them. He discovered, however, that Longden's purpose was wider than the mere punishment of his daughter. They were to gather up other men of their own persuasion and issue a public denouncement of the May Fair. They were the instruments, Longden believed, for the message of God to the deceived and idolatrous people who had risen so early in the day to celebrate the coming of the summer. Heartily approving Longden's sentiments, Robert offered his help, and, resentful at first because of Isaac, Longden eventually accepted it. 'Well, you're a brawny man, and middling tall. Those graceless rogues and their wanton wives will heed me if I've thee beside me. Go with me then, if thou wilt.'

Later that morning as Longden preached in the market-place and gathered a crowd of supporters, Robert's hands itched to clutch at Isaac's shirt and send him staggering backwards with a long-due blow in the face. He paid little attention to some of the men Longden was bringing into their cause. They shouted agreement with all Peter said, raising their voices in loud affirmation each time the May games were damned, and waving their cudgels. He did not notice the vengeful, bloodthirsty looks on some of the men's faces as the mayor and corporation were mentioned.

Once he caught a glimpse of himself in a warped glass that was for sale in one of the market booths — a glimpse of a man as bloodthirsty as the rest: a man he did not even recognize.

GEORGE

They had been married for almost three years. From the very beginning, Elizabeth wanted to bear his children, but none came. Then she found herself with child only to lose the unborn baby after a few weeks. Grief dampened her spirits so completely that George took her from Tolhurst Court in April, making a hurried journey by coach to St Bartholomew's Hospital to see Doctor William Harvey. The doctor examined Elizabeth closely and pronounced that he saw no reason why she could not produce a whole nursery of healthy children, especially as she was still so young. 'Just give her a little adventure now and then, my boy,' Harvey counselled privately after the examination.

'We'll go home now, my love,' George had said.

She looked at him with pleading eyes he should have known he couldn't resist. 'Nay, dear heart, pray let us not. You'll turn the horses and drive straight for Maidstone, won't you?'

'Maidstone?' he queried vaguely, having forgotten all else but Elizabeth and the poor, lost babe.

She laughed sadly. 'Aye, the quarter sessions. 'Tis the first of May in two days, remember?'

He frowned deeply, his jaws tense. 'Nay, I *had* forgot, though.'

'Please, please may I go with thee?'

He thought immediately of the plague and wished to take no chances with her. 'Never. 'Tis not safe. 'Tis not wise.' He did not tell her that though no plague deaths were reported yet for the year, only a year before forty had died. But then he began to weaken, seeing her crestfallen face and recalling her longing — since even before their marriage — to support him in all his civic responsibilities. She didn't understand, he thought with pity, how tedious most of his charges were: licences to be issued to victuallers, commissions for road repairs, bastardy orders, arrangements for paupers, fines for those who had missed divine services . . . little of it interested him. He would much rather, like Sir Dudley, follow his hounds and oversee the stringing and training of the hop bines on their poles . . . However, perhaps such a jaunt would be a small way to assuage his many worries about ship tax money, and about his wife.

So Elizabeth prevailed, and now he tried to suppress his misgivings about being in a busy town at the beginning of the plague months.

They were up earlier than usual on May Day, Elizabeth clad in glistening green taffeta and red stammel petticoats that he heartily approved in these days of dull duns, blacks, and blues that the Puritans insisted on. Her maid had dressed her hair to a perfection of red ringlets, too. She was beautiful, and she was his, her arm tucked through his own as they went slowly down the High Street.

Bright spots appeared on her cheeks as they left the Star Inn. For her, he realized, the coincidence of their return from London through the county town on this particular date was a happy one.

The rest of the town was astir just as early. Around the Bear Ringle a crowd had already gathered for the bear-baiting, and close to it — both further up the street, under the arches of the Market Cross, and also at the top of Mill Lane under the shelter of the tile-roofed Shambles — butchers, drapers, cordwainers, victuallers, mercers, and fishmongers had already set up their wares. Tolhurst exulted in the roar of activity, the shout of the crowd around the Ringle, the crowing of the cocks at the Cock Inn on East Lane, the swirling array of colour as all the women of the town — like Elizabeth — seemed to have been infected with the madness of May, the mildness of the air, and the silent withdrawal of all Puritans from the festival day. *The old days are come again,* he thought happily, remembering his father's tales of the Queen's Day celebrations in the Fair Meadow: days when the church bells rang until dusk, players and minstrels performed among the crowds, and women and children made joyful processions with candles, flowers, and fireworks.

He dismissed from his mind the burdensome thoughts of the morrow's work at the Lower Court House and of the curse of the plague, buried his nose for an instant in the pomander of sandalwood that swung by Elizabeth's girded waist, and determined to enjoy the day.

'Look, George!' she was exclaiming, 'here's the Fair Meadow. And see how many people are come!'

He took a deep breath of the damp, warm air that rolled off the Medway and over the soft, green sward of the meadow. 'Aye, 'tis a grand sight!'

They moved among the crowd, occasionally passing Elizabeth's maid, dispatched to enjoy herself at the fair with George's groom, and encouraged by a few extra pennies from his purse. In one corner of Fair Meadow, a band of mummers was performing an uproarious comedy. The jokes they bawled were lewd, the costumes patched and fantastical, but the Tolhursts stopped to watch, drawn almost against their will, and laughing helplessly. The actors danced, wagged their heads, gestured, while the bells on their caps and shoes tinkled merrily. Then, linking arms, they came to the edge of their crude wooden platform and sang a May song he had known from childhood.

> *A branch of May we bring to you*
> *As in your courts we stand.*
> *'Tis naught but a sprout,*
> *But it's well budded out*
> *By the work of the Good Lord's hand.*

As they sang, a man covered in wide, flowing hessian, his blackened face partially concealed by the rough material, capered in front of the boards. His skirts were adorned with sprigs of hawthorn, ivy, and lilac, and he caricatured the mummers' words and gestures by his own movements. High over himself he carried the carved head of a horse, which was attached to a pole and a simple lever; by working the lever from under the hessian, the man nodded the horse's head and snapped the nail-studded jaws to show off his absurdities.

'Isn't he comical?' Elizabeth called over the commotion. She was rocking back on her heels with laughter.

George, laughing too, agreed. But then he hesitated, struck by a sudden idea. 'Wait, dear Bess,' he said, 'See what the hooden horse does? Why, I remember what my nurse said when I was an unbreeched lad —

> *If a lass*
> *But kiss*
> *An Hobbyoss*
> *Upon a May Fair*
> *Be she*
> *Wife or maid*
> *Mother shall she be*
> *Within a year.*

He thrust his thumbs in his belt, feeling slightly foolish and worrying that he might have pained her by the reminder. ''Twas something of the sort,' he added lamely.

Elizabeth's laughter faltered. 'Nay, husband, I'm amazed. You're not a one to believe old tales. And I'd not kiss that old 'ooden horse for the world. Fie, shame on thee for thinking of it!' Her eyes flashed at him.

He started, chagrined by her sudden show of temper. 'Sweet, I didn't say you should do it, did I?' But then, disarmed by her hot face, and wanting to mock her, he grinned. 'I knew not I was wed to so chaste and prim a wife as that! Next you'll be telling me 'tis all superstition — ' He flung out his arm to indicate the entire fairground. ' — all of it. You little Puritan hussy!' And he slid his hand down her back and gave her a playful spank.

She leaned against him, smiling up into his face. 'And so it is. But I'm no Puritan, sweetheart. I love it, all of it.'

Satisfied, he turned his eyes back to the mummers. Their song was ended, and the hooden horse was prancing through the crowd, reaching out to grab maids and wives alike. When the horse caught one, and most were eager to be caught, squealing with delight or pretended dismay, he lapped her for a moment in his copious skirts, kissed her heartily, then set her free — red-faced — to join her husband or lover.

Elizabeth, he saw, was now staring at the middle of the fairground, her attention arrested, perhaps by the Maypole, perhaps by the colourful gypsy wagons drawn together a short distance away; she had lost interest in the hooden horse and had not noticed its nearness. George made to lead her gently away, but it was too late. Unless he offered to fight the man dressed as the horse — which would hardly accord with the good-natured spirit of the day — he would have to surrender her for a moment to the enfolding arms. And part of him — the superstitious part of him brought up in the old lore of an English country village — wanted her to be caught anyway. It would do no harm, he reasoned, and what if it worked a charm on them both and she had a baby to dandle on her knee in a year . . . ?

'Here's a pretty lady, now!' the hooden horse roared in a lusty, boozy voice, approaching her suddenly from behind and snatching her into his arms.

She let out a scream and sent George a look of helpless surprise before she disappeared into the swirling skirts. He almost felt — as well as heard — the rough, loud wetness of the man's kiss, the struggle of her hands beating, beating against him in rage. Then in a second she appeared again, her ringlets askew and one cheek smudged sooty by the man's face-paint.

He held out his arms with a look of resigned amusement. She flew into them, half-laughing, shuddering, embarrassed by all the eyes staring and mouths gaping to see a fine lady caught by a common hooden horse.

'You — you planned this,' she hissed.

He laughed indulgently. 'Nay, nay, how could I, love?'

'But thou did'st not *stop* it.'

'Again, how could I?'

'A great farmer like yourself?'

'A farmer and a gentleman, not a fighter, and — I left my cudgel at home.'

She snorted crossly, but then dissolved in laughter again, her hand shaking the sword that hung at his side. 'You're a gentleman only when it suits you,' she mocked.

He drew away. 'Look,' he said, 'see what use this fine blade would be?' He made to unsheath his sword, pulling it only half way so that he would cause no alarm to anyone. 'Rusty. Useless, I'm sure.'

She scowled. 'Then why wear it?'

'''Tis elegant, they say. Fashion dictates it, as well as these damn silly feathers.' He threw out his arms in a loose shrug and waved his hat irritably.

'Since when did fashion dictate to George Tolhurst?'

'Not often,' he conceded, weary of the sparring match she wanted with him. 'Except when I'm to town.'

She seemed to catch his change in mood, for she quietened again. 'Come, I'd like to see the rest of the fair.'

He bent to kiss her, took his neckerchief, and dabbed at the black paint on her face until it was gone. He said with a courtly bow, 'What is thy will, fair wife?'

116

She pointed ahead. 'To watch the Maypole dancers for a while. The day grows warm. Will they not crown the Queen of the May before the flowers and garlands wilt away?'

'Aye, they will surely. Look out, 'twill be you they choose, I lay.'

They ambled towards the gypsy wagons, she shaking her head vehemently. 'Not me. They'll choose a maid, not a cross old matron of five-and-twenty who shunned the kiss of the 'ooden horse.'

Before the booths of the gypsy tinkers, where men in garish clothes lounged on the steps of their wagons or bent in concentration over goodwives' broken pots; where fresh-faced gypsy women asked to have their palms crossed with silver and to tell the fortunes of credulous maidens — beyond all these stood the tall Maypole of Maidstone. Permanently planted in the Fair Meadow, it flourished each year with an array of flowers and brilliant streamers, and this year's was no different.

Clustered around the pole stood a pack of girls dressed in white smocks, full skirts, and adorned with the ribbons and flowers that befitted the day: reds, greens, and whites all mixed in bright profusion and highlighted by intricate rosettes. Beside them stood their lovers dressed in similar white slops, some smocked and others embroidered, their breeches and hose criss-crossed with leather bands, buckles, and metal bells, and their soft hats crammed with a riot of spring flowers: trailing kerria, lily-of-the-valley and violets.

Tolhurst, as much as his wife, wanted the dancing to begin, and at last a man dressed in shabby livery stepped out of the crowd, swept his hat off in a low bow, and called for the dancers and musicians. The watchers stilled, and the first beats of the tabor sounded: slow at first, a flat thud lacking the resonance of a large cavalry drum, but gradually growing in strength and speed. Soon, gitterns gave depth to the tabor, gentle strings inaudible but for the reverential hush that had fallen on the centre of the fairground. Finally, pipes began to shrill. The music interwove with itself, reeling out threads of sound that crossed and countered and pulled at each other in the perfect interlacing of a weaver's loom; the melody was of fairyland, of an older age when elves and fairies danced through flowers, blessed the growth of wheat, oats and barley, the birth of lambs and calves, and the marriage beds of brides; chased away wicked hobgoblins from the sweet, fair courts of enchantment.

The dancers loosened their ribbons and — with faces transfigured by joy — mirrored the music in their own interweaving pattern of steps. Without faltering they dipped and rose with the ribbons until a tight warp and weft of colour clung to the chestnut shaft. At last, the music changed; the dancers turned; and the ribbons gradually unfurled to their full length.

Elizabeth sighed with pleasure as the first dance ended.

'There will be more,' George murmured.

'Aye, but not yet, I think.'

He looked at the flushed faces of the dancers. Garlands were awry on the maidens' heads, and sweat plastered hair to foreheads under the brims of the men's hats. 'Perhaps you're right. Come, I'll buy thee some ribbons for thine own hair, love.' He smiled at her, delighting again in her delight, and glad that they had decided to stay in Maidstone together. Later, when they were alone again, he would see to it that the charm of the hooden horse had a chance to work. How lovely she was!

They stopped a gypsy man who carried brilliant ribbons on a tray tied round his neck.

'There, love,' he said, 'a red one for your red cheeks, a green one for your green eyes — '

'And your green fields — ' she interrupted happily.

'Aye, and a blue one for — '

'Nay, no blue. 'Tis a mournful colour.'

'No blue, then, but a bonny reddish-brown one — '
He picked through the tangle of colour on the tray while the gypsy eyed him suspiciously. ' — for the colour of your hair. And a gold one for wealth, and a white one for purity, and a purple one in honour of His Majesty . . . '

Elizabeth began to giggle. 'Fie, I didn't know,' she said, mocking his words to her of a half-hour before, 'that I had married so poetical and gallant a cavalier. I thought I married a farmer, truly I did.'

He glanced up awkwardly. Even the dark-faced gypsy was caught in the web of magic that enmeshed them both today. 'And you did,' he said. 'But we keep holiday!' He tossed a coin carelessly onto the tray, which the gypsy quickly pocketed with a sneering look of scorn at him. George knew immediately that in his excitement he had paid too much and that the gypsy thought him a fool. *Well-a-day, never mind.* ''Tis a holiday,' he repeated, 'and we shan't be gay tomorrow, I fear.'

They wandered through the crowds again, stopping at a booth to buy sweetmeats. The crowd seemed to be flowing like a river, moving with one mind towards one part of the meadow. Stretching up to see ahead, Tolhurst realized why. 'The May Queen,' he said quickly. 'They're choosing a lass over there — I lay she's one of the dancers — to be crowned. Shall we go watch?'

Elizabeth pressed against him. 'Yes, I wouldn't miss that for all the hop gardens in Goudhurst.'

He laughed at her. 'Oh, what a wager, little wife, for a wise woman to make.' All the same, he pushed forward as eagerly as she did towards the wooden structure erected near the river, until they stood as near to it as they could go in the throng.

Sprays of lily-of-the-valley and baskets of primroses, cherry blossom and forget-me-nots frothed round the stage. Above them rested a high-backed squire's chair that had been dignified for the occasion; poles were lashed to its legs so that it could later be raised up as a litter; the white horse of Kent was painted on its back, and wreaths of May blossom festooned it.

The mayor of Maidstone, Samuel Marshall, solemnly mounted the platform and stood by the decorated throne. He wore the chain and livery of his office proudly: not a tall man, but commanding attention by his clear speech. 'Ladies and gentlemen, goodwives and goodmen, men and maids all; we have a pretender queen this day, a fair lass of Maidstone, Rebecca Longden, daughter of Peter Longden, a victualler of this town, as ye all know right well.'

Frowning, Tolhurst glanced at his wife. What was there in the tone of the mayor's voice that suggested untimely impudence, even doubt as to the wisdom of the choice? Had Elizabeth felt it, too? She was standing on tiptoe, her wide eyes fixed on the mayor, but registering no concern.

The people around them were murmuring in surprise. 'Peter Longden's daughter?' they said. 'He's not of Maidstone. What can the mayor mean?'

'Lord, this'll send a pox on him and his house! How came she to be chosen?'

'She's fair, but by the Mass, she's fair.'

'Hush, that's papist talk!'

'Hold your tongue, wife, no Puritans here to hear it, are there?'

'I won't hold my tongue! You can be sure her father isn't far off — '

In a flash the significance of the name and the babble of voices around him struck home. *Peter Longden's daughter . . . daughter of the man my father sent here twenty years ago and patronized till he got himself established! And now he's a Puritan preacher!* He snorted with laughter, and this time Elizabeth did look back at him.

She whispered quickly, 'What is't, George?'

'I'll explain later, sweet. Watch, this will be worthy sport.'

A frown creased her high forehead, but before she could question him further, the mayor spoke again, this time sounding less certain but more pompous. 'God in his wisdom,' he said, 'rains fair daughters on the just and the unjust, the Laud's man and the Lilburne's man alike. What say you for this blushing maiden? Shall I crown her Queen o' the May?'

Tolhurst looked over the crowd to see a tall youth, broad-shouldered, and with striking, curly black hair, gently prompt a young girl to climb the steps to the platform. She was hanging back, biting her lip in uncertainty, one hand on the young man in a gesture of shyness. The young man prevailed, however, and raising her head high, she stepped up beside the mayor. She held a wilting nosegay of violets in her left hand, but her face was transformed now from doubt to radiant joy.

The crowd gasped in wonder at the smooth fair hair, the skin unblemished by warts, moles, or scars of the pox, at the blue eyes, the finely made body arrayed in the white bodice and full skirts of the Maypole dancers.

'Ah, but she's a fine choice, is she not?' Elizabeth asked.

His throat had gone dry, and his voice caught as he answered, 'Aye, she is, though but a child. I'll lay she's not above seventeen.' He had no memory of her; Peter Longden had left Goudhurst long ago, and George had known none of the offspring — perhaps unborn then, anyway.

'Still think they would have crowned your crabbed old wife?' she teased.

He caught a faint note of jealousy in her voice, but she had obviously misinterpreted his concentrated interest in the girl. It pained him to think that this vulnerable, pretty young maiden might be made to suffer because of her father's zeal — to suffer either at his hands or by the mockery of the crowd if any of Longden's fanatical followers stood among them.

He shuddered, but then quickly covered his misgivings and turned to Elizabeth. 'Sweet, you shall be Queen of the May for me, always.'

Sitting on her throne, Rebecca was now bowing her head to receive the crown of honeysuckle and cherry blossom. A shout went up as the mayor placed it on her head, then the musicians struck up a lilting, boisterous jig, and four young men — including, Tolhurst noticed, her own young man — lifted up the throne and carried her into the crowds followed by a line of other girls who strewed flowers left and right as they moved in procession.

Tolhurst followed the steady movement of the procession with diminishing anxiety. The sun flashed on the swords of the men in the crowd; the sky shimmered — the bruised blue colour of woad; the exultant music reverberated between the trees of the meadow and the houses at the foot of the High Street, and all was well.

He led his wife back to see if there would be more Maypole dancing. But the meadow was subtly changing; the soft haze of the warm morning had hardened to the brilliant, remorseless edge of noon, and the excitement

121

of the crowd had wilted to fatigue even as the flowers wilted. Families spread out cloaks and shawls and sat down with wineskins, bottles of ale, crusts of bread, and last year's apples. The fairground quivered in the heat and sank down under wagons, canopies, the short shade of booths; the musicians stopped, and the little Queen stepped off her throne to be once again lost among the crowd. A respite in the day.

Having no food with them, the Tolhursts returned briefly to their lodgings for luncheon. Afterwards, George endeavoured to make Elizabeth rest, but she would have none of it, demanding greedily to return to the Fair Meadow to see more of the dancing.

'Twill turn drunken as the day wears on,' he cautioned her.

'More so than my father's addle-pated hunting parties, do you suppose?' she asked brightly.

Disarmed again, he agreed to take her back, and — entranced once again by the Maypole dancers — they remained near the centre of the meadow. Every so often as the dancers whirled and skipped past them, Tolhurst caught the animated expression of that curly-headed youth as he crossed ribbons with Rebecca the Queen. He found himself curiously drawn by them both, sensing somehow — perhaps because he knew of Rebecca's Puritan family — that the two did not really belong. Their graceful bearing suggested something beyond the usual scope of the Kentish yeoman. Among the graceless yokels with their lewd looks and artificially coy girls with their sidelong glances, low-bodiced dresses and suggestive movements — among all this lusty country jollity, they stood out as if of gentle blood. The youth's garments were obviously well made — perhaps he was a rich man's servant — and Rebecca's dancing gear was made demure by a white partlett over her breasts and by skirts longer than the others wore, to cover her ankles. *Little here that her father could disapprove*, he mused.

A few shouts from the Maypole dancers, then the loud shouts of a man rang out. George stiffened in alarm. Had he not warned Elizabeth? With one hand on his useless sword and the other at his wife's waist to steer her away, he strained to see what was happening as a gang of men pressed towards the dancers, their faces dark with excitement and their fists raised. It was with only slight relief that he saw they carried cudgels rather than swords.

At the head of the men pushed a short, stocky man with tow-coloured hair and the wide, flattened features of a bull — the kind of man Tolhurst hated most. He knew the face — and the man — immediately.

'Have done with your wanton sports!' the man was shouting. He stood still now, his arms spread and his palms lifted, his men clustering behind him. 'Out upon this pagan blasphemy, for shame!'

The musicians winked and grinned at one another but kept playing. Two of the dancers, however, faltered, and at once the neat pattern of the ribbons was disrupted so that the pole swayed dangerously.

'Behold the children of darkness! They sport in the shameless daylight to worship at this foul terebinth of Baal, and God himself shakes their pole as a sign of his wrath!'

The man was screaming now, and Tolhurst saw Rebecca's face crumple, caught the look of despair that passed between the girl and her handsome partner.

ROBERT

At the Fair Meadow he saw Isaac immediately. He hadn't seen the lad for several months now, but he would have known his brother anywhere — even with lovelocks. His face illuminated with sweat and happiness, Isaac skipped in and out of the other dancers. His thick hair bobbed on his shoulders, and his huge, muscular frame was strangely graceful in movements that were entirely foreign to Robert.

Longden pressed close to his side. 'Abomination! Wicked, lustful abomination,' he shouted.

Robert reluctantly let his eyes rest on the dancing girls and murmured agreement, but as he noticed one in particular, his voice died in his throat, and his chest

123

contracted painfully. She was Longden's daughter, for sure, and as different from the other girls as velvet from hessian. *No, if she's given Isaac her maidenhead*, he thought, *then wolves go these days arrayed as tender lambs.* She was enjoying the lewd dancing, certainly — that he saw — but she danced unaware of herself; she looked at none of the other dancers but Isaac: a quick, innocent smile each time they passed. She was a maid yet.

And Isaac? There was nothing hardened in him, either. The boy was absorbed completely in the dance, not in amorous glances and coarse gestures as some of the men were . . . But suddenly Robert hardened himself against the same wily enchantment to which his brother had succumbed. Dancing itself was evil. The Maypole was the sign of crude, ancient rites of which no Christian man should have a part. Yes, Isaac must be chastened, and the girl must be separated from him before damage was done.

'Shall we wait further?' Longden hissed. 'At my signal, one and all pull down the pole and scatter the dancers.' He raised his voice to address the crowd, but the people only stared, frowned, and shifted uneasily from one foot to another. *Dull sheep in a market pen*, Robert thought with distaste, looking back at the lively dancers.

The music gained momentum, its rhythm flinging the dancers in a rainbow of colour and movement. Robert's eyes never left Rebecca, and he knew suddenly that he could not do as Longden wanted. It was his duty, because of his own brother's conduct, to save the girl, to draw her away from the wickedness to the safety of her own dwelling, to the safety of his own protection. He could not club the dancers or wrench the ribands from their hands. He could not even beat his own brother. He must get to Rebecca . . . save her from the stain of Isaac's lust . . . save Rebecca . . .

The men round him were jostling forward, crying and hallooing like Sir Dudley Digges' hounds in full pursuit across the Lees. He heard his own voice among the rest, but he hung back slightly as they pushed forward. The Maypole reeled and swayed but the musicians whistled, banged, and plucked strings louder than ever, and all but the two dancers went on with their frenzy of rising and dipping, twirling and spinning. Finally, as the music reached a wild crescendo, Longden and a few of his followers made a rush at the Maypole with hoots and shouts as wild as the music itself. They tore the ribbons from the hands of the dancers. Garlands and ribbons were flung and trampled on the grass, and with one great shove Longden sent the Maypole tottering to the ground.

A deadly hush followed. The minstrels and dancers stared at the wreck of their afternoon's May games, horrified. But the peace lasted only briefly, as once again the voice of Peter Longden thundered out, and the crowd surged forward to answer him fist for fist, cudgel for cudgel.

Robert saw the dancing girls raise their hands in fear and rush to escape the upraised cudgels. Sightlessly he saw the youths defend the girls with ill-placed harmless blows, or arms that shielded garlanded heads from the crack of chestnut-wood on shining hair. Sightlessly he watched his fellow Puritans seize the gitterns, pipes and drums and dash them on the heads of the musicians. All around him, wood splintered and snapped, women screamed, and men bellowed in fury. He was in the midst of a whirlpool, but it did not draw him down. What was happening around him was happening to someone else; he did not belong to these men of violence.

GEORGE

Elizabeth began to scream in terror beside him. He pushed and pulled her away from the brawl as fast as the crowd allowed.

'Repent, and be saved,' screamed Longden. 'Put away those lascivious, filthy ballads, those scurvy rhymes. They savour of raging sensuality! The way to heaven is steep, too narrow for men to dance in and keep revel-rout.' He paused only for an instant. 'Where is that Jezebel, my daughter?'

'There'll be broken pates, and bloodshed, in this day's work,' Tolhurst shouted over the tumult. 'Let's away quickly.'

Pandemonium erupted across the fairground. Puritans, recognizable by their sober dress, starched collars, and small ruffs, rushed in twos or threes to upset booths, tear down garlands, break the May Queen's throne, and wreak havoc wherever they might. Elizabeth stared wild-eyed at the violence and leaned more and more heavily on him, gasping as they pressed forward. In a cage by one of the gypsy wagons, a brilliantly plumed cock opened its beak, and, stirred by all the confusion, crowed raucously three times.

They reached the gates of the fairground just as the wardens and constables arrived. By now the noises behind them had risen to a furious roar, but George knew he could not lead Elizabeth straight back to the Star, so he found a bench nearby.

'We'll rest a while, my love. I'm sorry that I ever brought — '

'Nay, 'twas my doing. We shouldn't have returned.' Her face was pallid, her voice coming faintly.

ROBERT

Rebecca stood helplessly by the fallen Maypole, her face white and her hands clasped in agonized despair. She was frantically searching the brawl with her eyes. *For Isaac*, Robert thought, suddenly driven forward by his own conjecture.

Heedless of sight now, and hearing little, he narrowed all his senses on Rebecca. He was beside her before he knew he had moved forward.

'I'm Isaac's brother, Robert,' he said tersely, hardly recognizing his own choked voice. 'Mayhap you recall — I used to lodge with your father.' The words died on his lips. She had not even looked at him. 'Isaac's *brother*,' he said more urgently, and he grasped the soft warmth of her arm.

At last she registered his presence, but her eyes wandered from his face immediately. 'Aye. His brother. But where is *he*?' Her face crumpled, and tears poured down her cheeks.

Groaning, he reached his arm round her shoulders. 'Come lass, we'll find him. You must come away before you're hurt.'

She did not pull away: meek and trusting as a lamb led to its ewe in the pasture, she allowed him to lead her forward.

A fever seemed to take hold of him. The thought of Isaac with this girl became repulsive to Robert, and currents of fire seemed to invade the arm he kept tightly round her. He dared not look at her face, for he knew he would bend and pick her up, carry her in his arms away and alone. It was like a dream, a bitter-sweet and sinful dream he had dreamed repeatedly of Jane, not of Patience. And if he looked at her face, the dream would become real, and he would fall into foul sin himself. He moved forward with her as one transfixed, not even noticing the blows that glanced off his shoulders, not even noticing the shrieking crow of the cockerels or the loud screams of other women. All was Rebecca: her warmth, her terrified beauty, her fragility, her nearness. The crushed-out scent of her honeysuckle crown poisoned and maddened his senses, and his face set in the lines of a struggle that had gone on within him for half of his life.

GEORGE

He wrapped his arms round her and pulled his mouth into a grim line. *She needs not these upsets if she's to breed,* he thought, grinding his teeth savagely and looking back at the fairground. *In spite of what that doctor says . . . she's better home. Her notions of seeing 'the world' are childish, though I cannot tell her so.*

She was trembling against him. 'What will they do, the mayor and his constables? What will happen?'

He shrugged convulsively. 'Rabble such as that will not rule Maidstone, nay, nor England neither. As long as we've a king and an archbishop, weak as they may be, we'll have order here. Those men are but rogues, scum, ill-bred, unlettered — '

Elizabeth turned her face up to his in surprise. 'You sound so harsh, so unlike yourself,' she murmured.

He sighed, and his voice softened. 'Aye, you're right, sweet Bess. 'Tis just that of late they've taken too much unto themselves, those Puritans. They think they can rule because they wave a Geneva Bible, think they can stand ranting and raving in the market-place all day.' He gestured back towards the fair. 'But you have seen how loutish and indecent their carriage is; you've seen it for yourself. Indecent in the name of decency! 'Twill never do.' She was nodding slowly, and he tightened his arm round her shoulders. 'His Grace is a-weary of such fellows, and so are the judges and jurates.'

'They'll be tried and punished?' Her voice was low.

'Aye, more than likely the constables will snare their conies today.'

'And then what?'

'For preaching without licence, unlawfully, in public meeting places? Why, that alone carries the penalty of the pillory nowadays. They'll be clapped in irons tonight, at least.' He shuddered. *And mutilation for others,* he thought silently, but could not bring himself to say it. 'The sessions will be a mite more lively than of yore, I fear.' He felt the muscles in her upper arms tighten. She rarely missed his meaning, even his unspoken meaning.

'Ah, poor misled — '

'Misled, aye, and blind, who would lead others who are equally blind.' He shook himself. 'But come, let's not brood and darken this day further. Not all Puritans are canting madmen, I dare say. And 'tis warm, still, out-of-doors. Let's up to the market afore we return to the inn.'

Briefly he looked up at the gates to the meadow and saw another couple hurrying out: a young girl in white, the hem of her skirt torn and her fair hair dishevelled, her arm through that of a tall man with sinewy arms and a fierce expression on his face. She was crying, clinging to him, and with a shock Tolhurst realized that this was the May Queen, Rebecca Longden. Only shreds of her honeysuckle and cherry-blossom garland remained in her hair.

Elizabeth had loosened herself from his hold and sat forward, ready to leave the bench.

'No, wait,' he muttered. Where was Rebecca's young lover? The hawk-like menace of the other man's face disturbed him, and he felt a momentary return of the same desire to protect the Longden girl that he had felt earlier. But then he saw that she was glad to be with the man at her side. As they passed in front of the bench, he even caught some of her words. The man must be a brother, or perhaps some more temperate friend of her father's sent to extricate her from the brawl. 'Thank'ee, sir. I was so afeared . . . but Isaac . . . ' Her voice came in sobs as they passed, but there was no mistaking the relief and gratitude that mingled with the sorrow and terror, even if he could make little sense of what she said.

He studied the profile of the man before they vanished out of sight: a deep jaw, chin slightly jutting, clean-shaven, the dark hair close-cropped so that the man's ears, cheekbones, and nose were accentuated. He looked about thirty — perhaps older — and Tolhurst determined to remember him. When things calmed down he should go and see Peter Longden, try to talk him out of his foolishness, to reason with him. He could ask after Rebecca then. No doubt the girl would be well provided for — with or without her young escort.

He turned to his wife and saw that the colour was returning to her face. He promptly forgot Rebecca.

ROBERT

'No! No!' She was sobbing against his chest, struggling and weeping in a frenzy. He tore off her partlett, ripped off her petticoats, and threw her on Isaac's bed, where he held her down with one hand while he battled with his own clothes.

.She made a last convulsive effort to free herself, but he knew the house was empty now, and no one would hear her cries. 'You came to save me,' she shouted, her whole soul rising into her face, 'now you damn me as a harlot or a whore. In the name of God — '

Still dreaming, he cut off her pleading with his mouth, pinned her down with his full weight, and acted out the rest of his dreams of Jane. She was white as fuller's earth under his hands, soft and fine, pure and untried. She struggled, fought, and clawed at him, but her resistance only made him more cruel, and at last he lay spent upon her.

He did not revive until he came to consciousness of the broken helplessness of her crying, did not realize what he had done in his madness until he saw the blue lines of the veins in her neck as she turned away her agonized face in shame and despair. Now the sorrow and shame of the poor girl-child on the bed permeated the gold, white and red haze of his trance-like state, and he looked down at himself in horror: hose rolled to his ankles, breeches unbuttoned, his collar torn off, and his flaxen shirt stained with her blood. He had violated her. He had taken her maidenhead. He had sinned against her, against his brother, himself, and his wife. He had sinned against God.

He fell sideways onto the bed, away from her, drawing his knees to his chest in anguish. Sobs wracked his body, and he did not hear her leave the bed and creep away.

ISAAC

'Marry her? Are you mad? Of course I'll wed her.'

Isaac stared at his older brother, not understanding. Robert had come to call him home, away from Rebecca, and now Robert was begging him to wed her, promising to intercede with Longden. What did all this signify?

He narrowed his eyes, and suspicion grew in him. 'There's something amiss here, and I mean to find out what. Since the fair when she ran away, Rebecca's been as scared as a mouse in a sack of rye when there's a cat in the mill.' She was all he could think about, and he had to tell himself to speak loudly enough so that his brother could hear.

Robert was backing away from him, the colour draining out of his face. Isaac followed, keeping the distance between them the same, sure that Robert was tricking him. 'What's your purpose, brother?' he pressed, holding his gaze.

'Why — I — to see you content, Isaac. That's my will. I had not realized 'til I saw Rebecca what a fair lass she is and how she'd bring honour to our family — I'd thought she was naught but a — '

Isaac waved his hand angrily. 'Thou'rt babbling. Thou know'st well what she was like, from lodging here thyself.' And he thought back to yesterday's fair, the shuttle of his mind and memory passing back and forth as in a loom. 'There's deceit in thy voice.' Robert tried to smile, as if he had not heard, so Isaac roared his last complaint all the louder.

Robert's hand went up. 'Hush! Hush, dost want this whole house to hear thy voice?'

Isaac dropped his voice lower and hissed, 'Nay. But hear my voice, *thou* shalt.' Then the thread of his thinking grew tight enough to snap, and he lunged forward to grasp his brother's jerkin. 'Tell me true, if you value your life, have you been tampering with my sweet Rebecca?'

Robert's face grew livid. 'Nay, nay, I swear — '

'Swear not, you hypocrite, for I can never believe God more when men like you call on him. You're a fiend — ' And he drew his hands closer together so that he had him in a stranglehold. He would not kill him, he knew that, but he would get the truth out of him. He shook him hard. 'Speak the truth, you rogue — '

Robert's hands were flailing uselessly. 'I — I — '

Isaac shook him again, then dropped him so abruptly that he crumpled onto the floorboards and lay with his face to the floor. His body heaved, and Isaac heard sobs. 'Brother, forgive me, something came over me, I do not know — '

Isaac went cold inside and walked to the other side of the room. 'I feared this . . . This is what I knew in thee all along. Get up. Go talk to Longden. Tell him what you like, but protect my sweetheart's good name.'

Robert raised himself slowly and wiped his hand across his face so that there was a dark smear over his cheeks and nose. 'What will you do, brother?'

'Do not call me brother more.' He spat. 'I shall never go back to Chilham. When I'm wed I'll give not a fig for my father-in-law's cant or thine. And I'll not to home again. My father shall speak of me as his youngest son the tailor, not as his son the clothier, for I was meaning anyhow to quit this place and set up for myself . . . Now get out of my sight.'

He went himself, though, before Robert could gather himself together, and found Rebecca in her father's kitchen below stairs, her face swollen with crying. He took her into his arms gently, but she flinched from him. In his heart, he cursed his brother.

II

FOR KING AND KENT

King Charles anointed, by God appointed
Twenty years past to rule over this land
Is now subjected to the disaffected
Preaching rebellion with pikestaff in hand.
Shall we go down, then; desert our crown, then?
When he bids us stay, boys, why then cry 'Nay', boys.
Let us but follow; he'll scotch their base ploy.
Right on our side will always abide.
Then take no alarms, boys, down to your arms, boys,
Cast up your caps and cry,
'Vive le Roy!'

Now the king's bowmen take honest yeomen,
Put them in prison and steal their estates.
Though they be forced to go unhorsed,
And walk on foot as it pleaseth the fates.
In the King's army, no man shall harm ye.
Then come along, boys, valiant and strong, boys,
Fight for your rights which the Roundheads enjoy.
And when you come, boys, with fife and drum, boys,
Isaac himself shall cry,
'Vive le Roy!'

1

GEORGE⁻
Goudhurst, July 1642

Tolhurst grunted and settled further back in his seat.
After the commotion of Maidstone at the July assizes,
the peace of his house and gardens fell round him: a
cloak of fulled wool — soft, warm, secure. Joy rose up
in him like a spring: not the heady wine of the early days
of his marriage, but the milder ale of steady happiness,
comfort, and relative ease among the upheavals of
this hot summer.

Elizabeth sat close beside him suckling their third
child. As usual she was completely absorbed, and not
far away across the brick-paved courtyard the two
others, Anna and Henrietta, played quietly with one
of his bowling balls. They rolled it back and forth over
the bricks, chuckling, and oblivious of their parents,
their little petticoats dusty and their faces flushed
with pleasure.

He watched them absently, aware that his feelings of
satisfaction were connected as much with the farm itself
as with the fragrant nearness of his wife and the play of
his daughters. Glancing out beyond them, then, past the
well-pruned fruit trees and nut trees that flanked the
courtyard, he could see down the steps to the kitchen
gardens. Two of the maids were down among the herbs
cutting lavender, St John's wort, and foxgloves; he could
hear the snip of their shears and the babble and giggle
of their voices as they worked. Beyond them, as he well
knew, lay the lane to the stableyard on one side, and a
row of stately poplars on another.

The hop gardens. Yes, the bines were trained up
on their twine frameworks now, the extra lower leaves

pruned off, and the tops of the plants formed a 'house' of green leaves and prickling stems. He sniffed. The heavy bracts of burrs were already in bloom; the pollen blew to him in the breeze — resinous stuff that smelt like weak ale already. The bines would be ready for harvesting by the beginning of September. He shut his eyes and inhaled deeply.

The murmuring softness of the little girls' voices faded in and out of his hearing, and from somewhere in the dovecote a pair of birds crooned low in their throats. For a moment he drifted to sleep on the gentle currents of sound and smell.

Elizabeth was nudging him, at the same time lacing her bodice with one hand. The baby lay asleep in her lap now, stomach distended, arms splayed backwards, head turned aside with a thin trace of milk trickling from the corner of her mouth.

Drowsily he took in these little details. 'Oh, I'm as bad as Charlotte, dozing like a well-fed infant.' He reached over and gave the baby's stomach a light pat, and Charlotte's face puckered slightly but then relaxed again in sleep.

'Or like a doting old man,' Elizabeth teased, giving him a wink.

'An old man sated with the beauty of his wife,' he parried, opening his eyes wider at last and waking properly.

'Sated? No one will think so, not if ye keep giving me babes.'

He watched her face tenderly, heard the pride in her voice. ''Tis as we've wanted.'

'Aye, as we've wanted.' Her voice was husky.

He smiled back, but a shadow passed over him. Charlotte's birth had been long and arduous for her. He stretched out one hand and cradled the baby's head in it, leaning towards Elizabeth and with his free hand drawing her face to his own. 'Indeed, three daughters as lovely as their mother. 'Twas the magic of the hooden horse in Maidstone did the trick.' He kissed her slowly, and the shadow passed.

She pushed her hand against his shoulder and laughed at him, her head thrown back so that he could see the strong lines of her throat and shoulders. 'Nay, 'twas not! And well you know it, for Anna came not for three years after that.'

He cleared his throat. 'Oh, aye, Bess. Ever the one for thorny mathematics and logics, my lass.'

Her eyebrows arched. 'As are you, George, when you're figuring the planting and acreage, or when you're away to the assizes, fines and the like.' Her voice was serious, but he knew the barbed tail would follow soon enough. ''Tis only when you're with your wife and babes you turn into a sleepy simpleton.' She nudged him again. 'Fie, 'tis time you were down in the gardens!'

'Play the shrew, would you?' he laughed. 'It suits you not.' He stretched out his legs and leaned deliberately against her. 'Nay, I have a mind to rest this day. The assizes put me in a dreadful coil.'

The laughter in her eyes died away, and she bent away from him to stroke the baby's head. 'Forgive me. I have known it, but . . . I was afeared to ask.' Her voice turned passionate. 'Of a truth, I'm changed. I do not wish to see assizes more, nor go to London and look upon the King . . . nor any such thing. The times are ill — England is so troubled. Oh, how I long to hear thy comfort — but thou canst not give it, can ye?'

He set his mouth in a line, hating the change from lightness to earnestness. Pretence was useless; she guessed all too quickly when he was hiding from her the weight of his charges. He looked away, unwilling to let her read his face too closely.

She said, 'Nay, you cannot. I know it as well as thee. 'Tis war we'll have, and surely.'

He kept his eyes deliberately on Charlotte's peaceful face. 'It seems impossible here, does it not?' He raised his head briefly so that the sun fell full on his face, and the sound of the doves and the smell of the hops came to him again on the air.

'But 'tis foolish to pretend that it's not,' she answered.

'Aye.' He still didn't look at her. 'Sir Dudley said it years ago, and we should have heeded better then. Only pray God our own land become not a place of bloodshed.' Beside him, she shuddered, and on her lap Charlotte's arm twitched up suddenly. 'We've both seen it coming, love, since the spring.'

137

She was shaking her head. ''Tis a wicked shame when the men of a county try to bring peace between King and Parliament and then are thrown in shackles for it.'

Tolhurst thought of Dering, Twysden, Sir George Strode, and the two Richards — Lovelace and Spencer — all of whom had been imprisoned for organizing petitions to take from Kent to Westminster. He recalled that one petition had merely asked Parliament why the government could not make terms with the King, and whether the militia was to follow orders from the King or from Parliament. The petition had been prepared and presented legally, but even Judge Mallett — the reluctant Sir Thomas — had been clapped in the Tower of London for not opposing it. 'Shame?' he echoed. 'Nay, 'tis rank injustice. And Kent will not lie low under it for long.' His voice rose so abruptly that the two little girls stopped playing and turned in surprise. Henrietta, the more fearful, hid her face in her apron.

Elizabeth beckoned the girls to her knee and comforted Henrietta. 'Hush, dearling, thy father's not angry with thee.' She pushed her fingers through Anna's hair and wiped Henrietta's face. Then she turned to him again. 'You make me quake when you speak like that.'

'Ah, sorry, Bess, that I did. The goings-on have changed us all. I of all men in Kent have no desire to take sides.' He waved his hands this way and that, trying to explain the chaos to her. 'Parliament's been unjust, but so has His Majesty to Parliament. Dering was in support of Parliament until but latterly; now he sends support to the King. The County Committee supports Parliament . . . but I . . . what's an honest man to do? I'm no Lovelace to go braving Westminster with petitions — though I must sign them. Neither can I stand silent when Parliament sends an unlawful committee to sit on the Maidstone Bench, and to dispense justice in the judge's stead.'

Elizabeth frowned. 'Why would they do such a thing?'

'To frighten the knights of the shire into submission. They want no more thorns in their flesh from Kentish hawthorn hedges — ' He snorted, pleased with the conceit, ' — no more petitions I mean.'

'But I thought — '

'Aye, I mentioned it, didn't I? There was another petition.'

'You told me not the matter of it.'

He took a deep breath. 'No, but I shall. Mainy, Tufton, St Leger, Filmer — as well as Rycaut and Mr Clark, though I had scarce known either man before — sent another petition to Parliament against the ones Sir Michael Livesey had taken ere this — fawning, wretched rogue to lick the boots of Parliament!' He would have spat in contempt, but, remembering the girls leaning against their mother, forbore. 'They gave it to Augustine Skinner to take to London. All we asked — '

'We?' She was biting her lip.

'Aye, all the gentry wronged by that *committee*.' His voice sank to a sarcastic guttural. 'All we asked was for the King to get his military provisions and his ships back. We devised a plan for bringing the two sides together for a discussion, and we said that Kent, at least, is peaceful.'

'And the King knows all this?'

'He shall within a few days. Mainy, Clark, and Filmer are riding north to see His Majesty in York. He will grant them royal protection — '

'Aye,' she murmured, interrupting him, 'since his own general turns against him.'

He swung round in his seat to face her fully. 'So I have chosen sides, my love, though I see wrong in both. And all this — ' he threw out his hands to include the farm, the gardens, and the house ' — may be at risk.' He searched her face, expecting anguish and anxiety.

They did not come; instead, the Elizabeth he had first known sat beside him, her face alight and her eyes dancing. 'Perhaps. But thou did'st well to choose thus. I'm proud of thee.' Her voice was steady and clear.

He marvelled at this second change in her, and breathed more freely again. Then he bent and pushed his face into Anna's hair — she was unashamedly his favourite — and lifted her onto his knee. 'Here, poppet, give me a kiss.'

Henrietta put her thumb in her mouth and pulled on Elizabeth's skirts with her eyes alternately opening and drooping, so while Anna snuggled against him, Elizabeth took Henrietta and the baby into the house.

'It's nice when thou'rt home, Father,' Anna whispered. She found a loose piece of braided cord on the edge of his jerkin and began to twirl it round and round in her fingers.

He nodded, feeling against his cheek the silkiness of her hair, the softness of her babyish skin, and savouring the mixture of dust and warmth that rose from her thin little body. 'And I'm glad, too, love, for it seems I've had to be away too often of late. And I'm afraid I'll come back one day and find my little girls all grown into fair women who won't know their shabby, tired old father from all the other farmers hereabouts.' He looked down tenderly at her, knowing that although she didn't understand all the words he had said, she understood the feeling that lay behind them.

She in turn reached up and patted his face. 'I'll wed you, shall I, when I'm grown?'

He chuckled. 'Nay, Anna. Thou'lt find another man. A girl can't marry her own father, you know.'

'But I love thee, my father.'

'So . . . I love thee, too . . . but another will love thee more, as I have loved thy mother.'

Suddenly he could not meet his daughter's eyes any longer, nor look at the maids coming up the steps, nor at the flowers or trees. He turned his face away and screwed his eyes tight shut. What if all this be taken from us? *What if I lose my womenfolk — what then?* He clung onto Anna as if she were his last hope. The questions were unbearable, and the blessed peace of Tolhurst Court was already shattered.

He was not surprised, then, when — moments after the maids had passed by to enter the house — the kitchen door flew open again and his usually cautious, seemly manservant rushed out and almost fell headlong before him in haste.

'Sir! Sir! Rouse yourself! There's news from the Friars at Aylesford. Your wife just now received a messenger — ' The man broke into a coughing fit.

Tolhurst gently set Anna down on the bricks. 'Go in, my love, and find thy mother. No crying now, for all's well.'

She looked back at him with eyes so full of knowing

140

sorrow that he regretted immediately what he knew would be proved a lie. But a girl-child of four was not one to listen to urgent reports. Not now, not in these days, particularly.

She turned and fled into the open doors of the dining hall, her white petticoats foaming in the comparative darkness like small wave crests in blurred moonlight. His heart contracted as he watched her go, and he ached to protect her, to protect them all.

He stood to look directly at the servant. "Struth, Thomas, next time save thy news until the child's away.' But he could not remain angry for long. 'And you'd best ask of the cook some black mustard and rosewater for that cough of yours. Catch thy breath, Thom, ere you go on.'

The servant stood with his fists at his sides, opening and closing them, and the veins on his temples stood out under his flushed skin as he apparently struggled for control. At last he said, 'Sir Percival Rycaut's sent word. He's being taken to Upnor Castle, and his estate is confiscate unless he pay some vasty sum.'

'The petition — the protest, aye . . . I knew it.' He ground his teeth together, but hesitated, unwilling to say more, even before a servant he trusted. 'There was a written message?'

'Yes, sir, and your good wife has it.'

'I thank thee. Go back in now, but bid the other servants get forward in their tasks. We may have a mort of extra work here ere the week's out, I fear.'

Thomas at first did not move, then made as if to go, then stopped again. ''Twas what your lady did say, also,' he ventured.

He flapped his hands crossly. 'Aye, aye. Go now.' Then he went quickly to find Elizabeth, himself.

The nursemaid, he discovered, had now gathered the little girls into her care, and Elizabeth stood alone in the middle of the great hall, her back to the fireplace — evidently awaiting him. He saw that high colour flooded her face, and that the soft, maternal woman who had sat with him only moments before with her rounded breasts bared to the sunlight and the tug of Charlotte's hungry mouth had vanished — replaced by

141

Bess the wise woman, the Bess who had awed him from the very beginning. He became again — though he had never reason to doubt her love for him — the faltering, clumsy farmer-turned-wooer.

'Show me the message, Elizabeth.' He was surprised by the steady confidence in his own voice.

Her eyes scanned his face. "Tis ill news, husband.' Her voice was muted.

'So I understand,' he answered dryly, and he licked his lips as she passed him the paper. Sir Percival Rycaut's hand — adorned with curls and flourishes even when executed in haste — filled only a small part of the letter. He looked up at Elizabeth briefly. 'The messenger has gone?'

'Gone, and flying to warn others. He had the soldiers of Parliament on his heels. Read it, pray.'

"Tis a pity. I would have asked him where else he took his news.' He forced himself to peruse the note slowly; his heart was beating loudly under his jerkin, and panic seized him.

> Rochester is subdued, the castle taken by surprise and St Andrew's Cathedral plundered. In their fury these soldiers are bent on silencing Kent. I am to Upnor Castle under guard, all the arms and silver of my household having been taken, and I shall forfeit at least three thousand pounds. I doubt not others will suffer the same misfortune. Arm yourselves, therefore, and warn all others likewise. I know I may count on you. Beware Livesey and Sandys. PR

The letter was not sealed with the Aylesford Priory seal but he had no doubt of its origin.

Elizabeth was moving restlessly back and forth before the mantel. He watched her as her back was to him for a moment: the shapely contour of her hips, the lushness of her hair, which lay unbound on her shoulders in defiance of all Puritan execrations to the contrary. What had a woman such as she to do with the coming troubles? They were an intrusion he could not forgive or face. He drew a deep sigh, and she turned. 'Think you this is true?' he muttered, then inwardly cursed himself for the simplicity of his own question.

'Of course 'tis true,' she replied crossly.

He heard his heels click on the oak-beamed floor as he came to a sudden decision. 'Then I must gather all the men — all those able-bodied in the household and in the village — to serve us here. We cannot allow a repeat of what took place at the Friars. Parliament cannot command the King's militia to raid and sack the houses of those who serve the King! This house shall not be touched.'

She stood quite still, opposite him and only a few feet away, and her eyes locked with his. 'Nay, George, thou speak'st without thinking. 'Tis nonsense to shed thy blood for a few old pieces of plate and armour.'

'Nay, wife, 'tis thou think'st not. Dost suppose these *godly* Puritans will stop at that? Just let the fanatics and those with grudges follow after Livesey and see what shall happen! 'Twill be women and innocent babes hurt, not gold and silver and arms, if he be in command.'

The colour died from her face. 'Then you would start the war here, on this very land? You'd send out Thom and Jack? Matty and Harry and all the other simple Simons of Goudhurst against the madness and force of drunken — ?'

'Drunken? The Puritans touch not strong drink.'

'In God's name!' She stamped her foot. 'Have you forgot already what we saw in Maidstone one May Day? You *know* that is not so — '

'Then what am I to do?' He threw out his arms helplessly. 'Send out my *maids*?' If only he could undercut the deadly earnestness that had returned to her face.

She laughed without humour. 'Nay, nay! Listen, I have thought . . . We must make all appearance of knowing naught and of conducting ourselves as is our custom here. How else think you that the militia took Rochester Castle with its thick walls, unless the men were out a-harvesting?'

He nodded slowly, conceding to her but not yet following her argument.

'Perhaps if we do likewise, but first *make ready*, we shall escape the loss of too much here. Do all we can to provoke no violence, and sacrifice some things we care

143

not for, even some silver, love . . . so that the angels of death will o'erpass us.'

'But — but there is no warrant they'll not do worse here than at the Friars. You may be sure they searched before they plundered.'

Her chin went up. 'Let them! We'll hide everything we can. Let them find some of it — 'twould be unnatural for us to have no arms or powder in store — but let them miss most of it, and let us go in guise of willingness.'

'That's well to say, wife, but I'll not pretend to be a Parliament's man and perjure myself. Besides, they know already what I've signed.'

'Oh, phaw, there'll be no more petitions now, George. 'Tis far too grave for that. 'Tis war, as we've said this day.' She was smiling now, her eyes full of fervour and hope. 'And thou need'st not perjure thyself. But if thou tak'st arms thyself against them, then there's even less surety that they'll stop at plundering. You'll just force a battle then. I said, let's make all haste, take up no arms. Only be wily, cunning, and ready.'

The room fell quiet, her last words echoing faintly from the high beams of the hall. She was right, he knew suddenly.

He opened his arms to her. 'Thank God for thee, my dearling, and for thy wits. But pray God we have time — '

Her arms went round his neck, the scent of lavender from her hair against his nostrils as he swung her round once and set her down again. 'Doubt it not,' she laughed breathlessly. 'If Aylesford was taken yesterday, they'll be stopping at the Mote and West Farleigh and at Linton Place ere they ride south to Goudhurst . . . We'll have time enough.'

He nodded his head against hers. 'A goodly council of war, little Queen Bess. I elect thee my general.'

She laughed again so that he felt her warm breath on his chest. 'You'd never make a king, my love.'

'Nor ever would I. But a king's man — aye, I'll do that.'

For the rest of the day they scoured the house for arms and treasures. Leaving some in place, they concealed the rest in an old priest's hole that George doubted even Livesey's men could find. Only the steward and Elizabeth's most trusted maid were warned of what was likely to happen, and George ordered Elizabeth to clap all ale, sack, and wine under key so that no drunken, loose-tongued servant would betray them. He knew that the maids, if kept in ignorance, would brilliantly act out their proper roles of terror when the soldiers arrived. As for himself and Elizabeth, they would need all their wits to assume masks of surprise and to say nothing that would arouse suspicion or provoke violence. Before they went to bed that night, then, he carefully burned Rycaut's letter in the fireplace of the great hall. From thence he climbed the spiral back staircase to the small family chapel — scarcely used nowadays when the family was forced by Laudian injunction to attend only at St Mary's in the village. There he knelt for some time at the priedieu.

His knees seemed to grind into the threadbare cushion as he stilled himself in the chapel's chill air. A weight of sorrow and worry pressed down on his head and chest. *What will the morrow bring?*

The light flickered, and he opened his eyes to see the candle flame bent sideways by a draught from the door. Without standing, he turned sharply to see Elizabeth, another candle in hand, framed in the lancet doorway.

'Oh — 'tis thee,' he murmured. *She looks like a spirit,* he thought, *in that white shift with her hair unbound.* He said, 'Come, let's pray for peace.'

She joined him at the priedieu. ''Tis peace within as well as without I'll pray for.' She gave him an inscrutable half-smile, then shut her eyes.

He shut his too, and the two candles — his own and hers — were the last things he saw before his eyelids brought darkness. Then Anna's little face rose in his mind and obscured the darkness: the child's fair skin and angelic hair, the same look of pity and understanding stamped on her face that he had seen in the afternoon. It was for Anna that there must be peace. Unconsciously, he murmured, 'For Anna,' and felt Elizabeth's shoulder against his own.

145

'We come peaceably, sir,' Livesey said. Wearing the russet colours of his troop and the arms of a Parliamentarian, he sat on horseback above Tolhurst, the noon sun gleaming on his helmet and cuirass. 'Peaceably, unless you do some rash deed.' The hand on his sword belied his words, and the men ranged behind him sat stiffly on their horses. 'Nothing will be hurt. No one will be hurt if you obey us. Put up a fight, and you may answer with your life. Parliament's orders, sir.'

George had resolutely begun work with his men on the upper edge of the hop gardens. Some of the bines needed to be trimmed and pruned, but he wanted to be near both the house and the lane — also near to the arrival of any troops. He had worked all morning, but not steadily. Several times his hand had shaken and he had cut down healthy bines.

His men worked behind him, earthing up the small hills around the poles. He urged them on in spite of his misgivings, trying not to stint, ignoring their good-natured complaints about the morning's lack of ale against their thirst. 'Water today, and ye'll get ale a-plenty tonight' he had promised. But now Livesey and his men had come, and behind him his own men huddled, gawking at the soldiers without comprehension.

Thoughts of Kentish rights and mildly worded petitions crossed his mind; thoughts of England's constitution and the rights of Parliament crossed his mind — but he swallowed hard the sharp answer he might have given without more forethought. 'Then what's your will, gentlemen?'

'To search your property as we have others'. We know you to be a man favouring the King's cause, and Parliament looks now with disfavour and suspicion upon all such, since *His Majesty* — ' the last two words came out with venomous emphasis ' — is doing all he can to divide this nation asunder and spill its people's blood.' Livesey met his eyes. 'We'll root out any signs of sedition in this place and take your arms, sir, will ye, nill ye, and some of your goods shall go to help loyal Englishmen meet Parliament's expenses, as pleases the Lord of Hosts.'

This was too much. George felt his face grow hot in fury, and his fingers clenched hard around the hook he carried. 'Nay, we men of Kent have paid dearly enough ere this, Sir Michael. Paid with ships and money, aye, and men, too. Years ago I would have stood with you against the King. But now Parliament doth o'erreach itself against the people. So, if Parliament means verily to bring an end to the King's forced loans and ship money, let not Parliament force the men of Kent in the same way!' Livesey's mouth opened and shut like a great carp's, his eyes turning to granite. But George could go no further, for Elizabeth's warning sounded in his head again, and he drew back, muttering, 'I say, let not Parliament *force* us.' Abruptly he pushed the gate further open. 'Come, we shall *give* you what you ask.'

Livesey's soldiers murmured in surprise and, something else — was it disappointment? Tolhurst dismissed his men and marched stolidly before the troop into the stableyard.

'Ye can water and stable the horses here, if ye choose. I'll get the stable lads to wait upon ye.'

Livesey's eyebrows flickered. 'Courtesy? Either you're a turncoat, Tolhurst, or a shrewd man.' His derision disappeared, though, as he snapped orders to some of his men to guard the horses, then the rest of the party tramped into the house.

With an air of guileless absorption that surprised even George, Elizabeth sat in the parlour as they entered, her foot rocking the cradle by her chair. At the sight of the soldiers, she jumped up, her needlework in its wooden hoop clattering to the floor as she cried out.

''Tis men from London, dear,' he said wearily.

'Aye, here to search for arms, madam, by order of Parliament. Pray fetch your children and maids.' Livesey nodded to her, then to him. 'Fetch all your servants, sir, and bring them here. We want no one about as we do our task. The whole household must remain in here.'

George exchanged glances with Elizabeth, then looked back at Livesey. 'May I not accompany you, or my bailiff?' He tried to sound conciliatory.

'No, I want no trickery or mischief. My men aren't thieves, sir. You'll know what goes to the cause, I do assure you . . . Now, fetch your servants, and make haste. These men will accompany you.'

'My wife goes not alone with your men or any others. We go together, sir.'

Livesey's eyes passed over Elizabeth, and George caught her look of pained withdrawal as she pulled a partlett over her shoulders to cover the fair skin of her neck and breasts. 'Aye, with a wife like that, a wanton who shows her flesh so shamelessly, 'twould be better you went with her. And ordered her more, too! 'Tis not seemly.'

She drew up her head haughtily, and for a moment he thought she would forget her own warnings. 'When 'tis unseemly for a woman to nurse her own babes, then 'twill be unseemly to dress as I do on these hot days, Sir Michael.' Her voice was satin.

'You were *sewing*, madam.'

'Until a few moments ere ye came in, bold and unannounced, sir, I had my baby at my breast.' She gestured towards the cradle, and as if on cue, Charlotte began to whimper from within. 'In the sight of God, where be the sin in that, sir?'

'In the sight of *God* . . . nowhere . . . but, pray, cover yourself . . .' Livesey coughed and looked away.

She's bested him! George thought, glad for her.

'And see your, er, your maids . . . do likewise, even if any be . . . suckling babes.' He floundered on, and George saw amusement on Elizabeth's face, though no one else might have recognized it.

'I'll see to it,' she said blandly. 'This would be a place of miracles indeed if maids had babes to suckle — but I'll see to it, especially if I know when ye come again.'

Livesey's face darkened. 'We shall not come again, but, by God, my men shall search this nest of King's men better than the rest. 'Tis by law we're here, and by law we'll act.' His hand moved to his sword. 'Go now, and no more insolence.'

Elizabeth gave Charlotte over to the nursemaid's care, then with six dragoons in close attendance, they went first back to the hop gardens, then to the stables and outhouses, gathering men as they went. Next they descended to the kitchens and brought the cook and serving maids into the parlour with the rest of the household. The room, large as it was, began to smell of sweaty clothes, and George saw Elizabeth looking unhappily at the clods of dung on the beeswaxed floorboards and the black smears of hop resin on the chairs. Awed by their surroundings, uneasy with the soldiers, his servants sat or stood in cowed silence and waited. Elizabeth moved round opening the windows and doors.

Deciding she was safe now with the others, he mounted the wide stairway to the nursery. The nursemaid sat by an open window that overlooked the kitchen gardens, and Charlotte lay asleep on the cushions beside her. 'Soldiers are come, Nancy,' he said to her. Three of them came so close behind him into the doorway that he knew the words were in vain.

The woman nodded. She was plain, a spinster of unknown age whose temper could rarely be ruffled, except at times of childbed. Otherwise she lived placidly, moved slowly, and took the three Tolhurst children exactly as they were.

A solid old oak tree, he thought, looking thankfully at her.

'Aye, sir, I saw them ride in on their fine horses.' She screwed up the corners of her mouth. 'Be we all arrested, then?' She twitched at the lace on her cap, but her face showed frank curiosity more than anxiety.

'Nay! We've done no wrong. How then shall we be arrested?' He smiled at her impassive face, then sobered. 'But I do not want the little girls upset. The maids below are fearful enough as it is.' He bent to Henrietta, who rushed to his knees. Kissing her, he lifted her into the nurse's lap. 'You have a care of Henrietta and the babe. Let me take Anna, or she may bolt like a mare in season.' He beckoned to his oldest daughter. 'Come, love, we must away downstairs.'

Anna sidled up to him, and he knew she was puzzled by his appearance in the nursery and by the talk of soldiers. He wanted to prepare her. 'Just think, dearling,' he said, lifting her against his chest so that he could look into her soft eyes. 'Such a pother below

149

stairs! We must all sit in the parlour for a while — Anna, Henrietta, and Nancy; and Matty, Simon, Thom, and your mother . . . all of us, indeed.'

'But why, my father?' Her eyes searched his, bruised and blue-violet like the love-in-the-mist flowers that grew in the garden.

'It's a rare game, my love. These big soldiers are pretending to look for a deadly enemy. They want to play the game by themselves . . . thou'lt see . . . so we must just all sit together.' He ceased to care what Livesey's men thought of him.

Her arms tightened round his neck, and she nuzzled against his jaw. Her voice came muffled, then, as she asked, 'But — there's no deadly enemy, is there? They won't take thee away, will they?'

He rocked her as he walked back out of the door with her. 'No, pet, and no, that they won't! 'Tis all a foolish game. But my Anna will play her part like a brave, fierce lady, will she not? Come, now.' He looked over his shoulder at Nancy. 'Thou hast Charlotte, too?' The baby, he saw, was under the nursemaid's free arm, so the question was light talk to fill the silence and fear that must already be growing in the children's minds.

As they passed into the parlour, Sir Michael was pacing up and down the middle of the room without any attempt to cover his impatience. His boots clicked on the floor, and his long spurs jingled. He shouted, 'Make haste, pray!'

By the open double doors, four dragoons stood alert for any signs of rebellion. George felt his temper rising again as they entered, hot as the bodies in the sweltering room. *What right have they to disrupt my house thus?* But he fought down the anger. He wanted no carnage under his own roof, and thus far Livesey had conducted himself with fair restraint. None of his own folk was armed anyhow, and even if the household did contrive to dispose of Livesey and his men, more would come . . . more violent, certainly . . . But he was still master here, and Livesey could never take that from him. The command should come from him, therefore.

He saw to it that Henrietta and Charlotte were comfortably settled with Elizabeth and Nancy in a more airy

150

part of the room, but although he sat near them, he did not relinquish Anna. Her pliant, warm body — even, strangely, her heart beating like a wild hare's against his jacket — gave him courage. Coldly, he said, 'You may begin your search, sirs, and welcome.'

Livesey barked orders again, and, leaving more dragoons posted at the doors with orders to maintain silence within, took the others out of the room. The parlour fell quiet. Elizabeth's eyes turned on George as he strained to hear the movements that would betray the paths of the soldiers. Out in the great hall, metal clanged. *Those ancient suits of arms,* he thought. *To be melted, no doubt, for Parliament's lackeys! How dare they!* And he stiffened.

Anna must have sensed his rage. She raised her head, glanced round the room for the first time, gave a fleeting smile to her mother, then let her eyes rest on her father's. ''Tis only a foolish game, father,' she said softly.

His own comfort coming back to him from younger lips moved him. 'Aye, my lass.' He turned towards Elizabeth. 'All war's a game, is it not?' He had to speak very low.

Her eyes clouded with pain. How could she answer, *There is no war yet* — when they both knew the meaning of these forced searches and mentions of 'sedition' and 'nests of King's men'? How could she answer him?

The dragoons were above stairs now, their heavy feet marching up the long halls, curtains swishing apart, doors thudding against walls, chests splintering open . . .

'They have no keys!' Elizabeth whispered urgently.

He shook his head and answered under his breath, 'Dost suppose they'd use them, even if the steward gave them to their trust? Nay, they make a sport of the destruction they do, the rending and the bursting — I'm sure of it.'

At the door, one of Livesey's men raised his pikestaff and called for silence, but Henrietta set up a wail from Nancy's arms, and Charlotte's babyish voice soon answered.

'You've frightened the children,' Elizabeth said imperiously.

The guard rubbed his jaw uncomfortably but did not answer.

'Dolt!' Elizabeth exclaimed.

'Bess, Bess, pray — ' He started to plead with her, but immediately felt like berating the guard himself: Anna, in sympathy with her sisters, began to wriggle and push against him. Her arms flailed, and she broke away from him to the windows at the end of the room farthest from the soldiers. She scrambled up on the cushions and stood poised to jump out into the courtyard.

One of the maids lunged after her.

'Let her go!' the soldier instructed. 'She'll do no 'arm.'

Elizabeth and George rushed from their places. 'Not to thee, mayhap!' George shouted. ''Tis herself we're mindful of.'

Anna's hands had grasped the wooden frames and one of her feet was already on the sill when he caught her into his arms again. Her crying split the stifling air in the parlour, shrill with fury, and all the servants began to murmur and shuffle in pity. Then from upstairs came the unmistakable sound of shattering glass; it tinkled and rang like gold coins bouncing down the oak stairs. Loud cracks followed, as if the men were ripping up floorboards and casting them aside. Anna's crying ceased, abruptly, and Elizabeth clawed at his arms. 'Oh — what?'

He did not have to answer her. The soldiers above answered, their voices coming clearly from the beams of the floor above. 'Roman idols!' Then another crash shook some plaster from the ceiling.

The chapel, they're despoiling the chapel! The chapel where his grandfather had been wed by the family priest, where his father had prayed . . . where he and Elizabeth had knelt only hours ago and prayed for peace. The inner sanctuary of his family . . .

The remorseless zeal of Livesey's men sliced into him like a sword. Elizabeth's eyes were fixed on him, and tears started out from under her lashes. Against his chest, Anna had gone limp, beyond feeling and fear. He drew her more closely to him.

A little blue butterfly flew in through the window and settled first on his arm then, perhaps displeased with the smell of hops that hung about him, fluttered down onto Anna's hair. He caught his wife's eye; she had seen it, too. In the sunlight that flooded through the window, the tiny butterfly was blue stained glass against the rich silk of the child's hair. Its patterned wings moved up and down, speckled brown underwings appearing each time the blue sides closed together. It stayed there, luxuriating in her warmth, in the warmth of the July sunshine, though Anna — he saw — was unaware of it.

2

ROBERT
Canterbury, August 1642

Over the blurred, blue-green rim of the Downs moved a troop of horse and foot soldiers. The old hills dwarfed them: diminutive little men in buff, tan, and russet garb, their figures almost lost in the sere browns of the dried grasses, their grey and bay horses blending into the road of chalk and ragstone. Others followed on foot, pikestaffs pointing heavenward like thorns in an uncoiled crown of Calvary.

Horses and men were weary: the downward slope of the road into the city did not increase their speed; the insistent rolling of the drums had faded to half-hearted occasional taps, and no one marched in step now. The euphoria of early morning musters in Chilham and Chartham had faded to a faint memory, dulled by blistered feet, lead-heavy arms, and dry mouths. Eyes strained forward for the sight of the first welcoming inn, then withdrew uncomfortably. Livesey would brook no drunkenness, he had said. *Would to God*, some of the men were thinking, *he had not meant it!*

At the back of the troop a few men took up a song. The words died quickly in the hot wind, but the song sustained some of them and brought back fleetingly the excitement of joining a troop as renowned as that of Colonel Sandys. Their steps quickened as they sang, and the muskets slung on their backs bounced up and down.

> *The King by hark'ning to your charms*
> *Hugged our destruction in his arms,*
> > *And gates to foes did ope;*
> > *Your staff would strike his sceptre down*

Your mitre would o'ertop the crown
If you would be a pope.

But you that did so firmly stand
To bring in popery to this land
Have missed your hellish aim.
Your saints fall down
Your angels fly,
Your crosses on yourself do lie
Your craft will be your shame.

Robert Fessenden did not sing with the others, though he knew of the song. He could not be quite sure, these days, which song against Archbishop Laud was being sung. They all poured out hatred on this favourite of the King's, some in lewd words, some in angry words. But deafness shut him in now. Even the jingling of his own bridle sounded obscure and distant. He lived in a world in which sounds swished by him in soft, foaming confusion like the rush of water through the fulling troughs in the Loose mills before the hammers overwhelmed all other sound.

But the isolation deafness had dealt him rarely pained him. In fact he enjoyed the quiet of his mind: the inner whispers of God breathing the words of the Psalms into his heart. It was enough, he had found, to watch his sons — Thomas, Nicholas, and Josiah — tussling in the garden, with Hannah the baby trailing behind, a thumb in her mouth and a torn homespun following her inseparably over the green-staining grass. It did not matter to him that he could not hear what they cried out to him — only that they needed *him*. His father, meanwhile, had for several years written down all his instructions. And Patience had developed her own particular way of talking to him with exaggerated movements of her lips and hands. No, the deafness scarcely troubled him. He was content with the will of God that he live in this quiet.

He turned for a moment in his saddle and peered back over the straggling column of men. Not all were soldiers; some had joined the muster simply by laying down their scythes and quitting the fields. Even now some of them brazenly lifted flagons and bottles to their

155

lips. He swivelled forward again in disgust. *Wine-bibbers!* *Rabble,* he thought uneasily . . . and yet, could God still use them? His dream of these men as instruments of God cracked slightly, and he wavered. Should he return to Chilham?

He had made up his mind quite suddenly to follow Colonel Sandys. The muster had been announced for several days by letters nailed to posts in the village, but he had resolutely ignored them. There was work to be done, the Lord's work, especially with his two brothers gone.

John had built a house in Cambridge, in the New World, and was settled successfully as a glover. He and Jane had obviously become quite comfortable, but their wealth was stored in their house on Eliot Street, a thriving leather trade with the Indians, and glove trade with other merchants in Cambridge, Plymouth, Charlestown, and Providence. Their wealth, Robert reminded himself, was not in the Spirit, not treasure stored in heaven — as he and Patience had amassed. Nor in children, either, for John had only a foster son, Nathaniel: a child who had brought John and Jane endless woe, or so John reported in his infrequent letters. But how blessed was he himself in that way! Surely God had forgiven him that sin of lust all those years ago? It was the sin of another man, not something he connected with himself any more. Now he believed himself made new, sanctified daily by Christ. At least, he could look at his life in that way now, though at night sometimes his own hypocrisy made him bitter.

And Isaac. There was no further connection with Isaac. Not since the boy's marriage had Robert seen him. His abrupt, sullen departure had grieved their father deeply; the old man, never guessing the truth, had blamed himself for making too many demands of the lad. Robert shuddered. Those dark days were well covered by now, but his father used often to express his longing for John and Isaac. Robert had doubled his work to compensate, to prove loyalty and steadfastness to his father. He had said, 'But I shall stay, my father.' And once, Fessenden, reading aloud at the evening family prayers, had spoken of the parable

156

of the prodigal son. 'Robert is my faithful elder son,' he had said.

For a while, the venom of jealousy had lost its bite into Robert's heart. He had at last found the place he had wanted in his father's heart: he was the eldest son now, the faithful one, the prop and comfort to his father's old age.

Not so to •Mary Snode, his stepmother. But he had never wooed her, anyhow. Isaac, he knew, had occasionally written to Mary, and that threw up an additional fence between them. What if she knew, or guessed, what had passed between himself and Rebecca, himself and Isaac? *Always her pet,* he thought sourly. *I shall have vengeance on her, one day.* But Mary kept her own counsel — at least before him — of the contents of Isaac's letters. He knew only that Isaac had done as he wished and set up as a tailor in Maidstone. Rumours in Maidstone and Loose declared that Rebecca's father, Brother Longden, had turned soft in the head. No doubt the young couple lived untroubled by the affairs of either the Longdens or the Fessendens. And just as well. Robert wanted no reminders of the past, no dredging up of what God had washed away. There were enough reminders, as it was.

Yes, there was work to be done for his father. Why, then, had his father urged him to the muster after all? He frowned, shifting in the saddle, glancing to the walls of Canterbury not far ahead. Had his father sensed his restlessness? He had never quite lost the conviction that the Lord had some higher calling for him than inspection of the mills, supervision of the weavers, spinners, fullers, and dyers. And if only he could discover that calling . . . at last he could then turn his back on the past and on the torment that had wracked him. Lust had sometimes driven him half mad: first for Jane, then for his poor sweet wife Patience, then for Rebecca. Without knowing the cause, his father certainly sensed this tension. Was this why he had sent him with Colonel Sandys today?

He drew breath heavily. Perhaps this journey to Canterbury was all intended. Perhaps he would discover some higher purpose there. He had tried to hide the fact from his father, but the general demand for wool was definitely falling off. Merchants now chose to buy from larger manufacturers who owned not cottage workers but highly organized mills where almost all the work was done in one place. The wool trade had fallen off twenty years before because of the wars in Europe; and now the English cloth, in comparison with that of the cunning foreign weavers, was no longer the best. The family's trade, however, had in those years somewhat increased, mainly because of John's undertakings with the Flemish and Huguenot weavers — the Strangers — in Canterbury. But he was not sure that the Fessenden trade could survive a war in England now. *A war, that's what it is,* he told himself excitedly.

Charles Stuart, it was said, had raised his standard in Nottingham only a few days ago. Lovelace, Tolhurst, Astley, Dering, and Culpeper were among many prominent men of Kent who had declared themselves King's men and had sent their support to Nottingham. Kent, Robert surmised, would, like the rest of the country, be torn in half by war — as violently as a piece of cloth torn by a tailor before the stitching begins. But he knew on which side of the cloth he belonged: not with the garish, fluttering standard in Nottingham, where the King's supporters would pay for their errors, but with the dusty, bedraggled standards of these men. The true men of Kent, flawed as they might be, marched and rode in this column. And they rode for the Lord of Hosts, not for the papist King or for the would-be pope, Laud. But for God. His chest swelled with pride.

One of Sandys' soldiers, a man who had kept up unflaggingly even over the steepest tracks on the Downs, suddenly collapsed beside Robert's horse. His musket clanged as it struck flint, but his body made only a dull thud. Robert, however, heard nothing — only saw the body crumple.

His reveries dissolved, and he flung himself from the saddle and loosened the cap on his water-bottle. His horse ambled away to crop the grass, and he knelt quickly, stretching out the water. The man's mottled face was averted, his mouth gaping and his eyes black with terror and unknowing.

'Rouse thyself, man,' Robert urged. 'You'll ride my horse to Canterbury.'

A strange, choked sound escaped the man's throat, and two dirty hands reached up and clamped themselves on Robert's falling-band collar. Dismayed, he leant forward to try to make sense of what the man was trying to say, then twisted backwards away from the stench of sweat and filth. The collar ripped away from his jerkin with a searing, angry sound that even he could hear. Then the man's eyes became glazed, fixed desperately on Robert's face as death rode over him. For a second Robert saw the screaming mouth and stricken eyes of Rebecca, but the image dissolved. With the grip of death, this man was pulling him down, not fighting him away as Rebecca had done.

He cried out himself now, overtaken with disgust, horror, and pity. But beside them the line moved past as if nothing had happened. The horses' and men's movements seemed monotonous, unmitigating, especially to Robert, for whom they moved in silence. He hated their dull purposefulness, suddenly. And he hated the dying man, too.

At last another horseman stopped, one Robert knew. Looking up, he said blankly, 'He's dead.'

'Then God 'a mercy on the wretch,' the other shouted back.

Remembering himself, Robert pulled off his felt hat. Together they lifted the first casualty of Colonel Sandys' war on superstition and idolatry in Canterbury over the back of Robert's horse. The corpse slumped, not stiff yet, and the horse snorted and shied away.

Robert rejoined the column, on foot now, and leading his horse. There would be time, later, to find out who the man was and send word to his widow. His pride had melted, replaced by a vague feeling of foreboding.

In Canterbury Sandys set guards on the cathedral and on the houses of the dean and chapter. The townspeople rushed about in confusion until assured that no harm would come to them.

Robert's efficient arrangements for a pious burial of the dead man had attracted Sir Michael Livesey's notice,

159

and early on Saturday morning he was summoned to Livesey's lodging. Informed that he was deaf, Livesey shouted throughout their conversation.

'Few of my men are as well educated or skilled as yourself, Goodman Fessenden,' he roared. 'I need your support. You're not a soldier, I know, but you think like a soldier, I suspect. I want you dressed like one, in the colours of this troop, and I shall provide a helmet and cuirass myself. I shall need you with me. We must needs pay a little visit this day upon Mr Bargrave, he who calls himself "Dean".' Livesey bowed his head deferentially. 'Will you do me the honour of accompanying me? We have the Lord's work to do this day.'

Robert hesitated, asked Livesey to repeat some of what he had said, and strained to hear. Something struck a chord in him. *The Lord's work.* Yes, this was all as God had planned. *'All things work together to them that love God . . .'* He flushed with pleasure and put aside all thoughts of flattery. Of course he was better educated than most of the men in the troop! Who else but he could thus be singled out? Yes, it was all the doing of Providence. He smiled back at Sir Michael.

'Aye, sir, I should be honoured.'

Livesey's broad hand struck the table. 'Good.' He shook Robert's hand earnestly. 'Have you broken fast yet?' The man was miming eating, his hands flying to his mouth and down to an imaginary trencher.

'Nay,' Robert faltered, but then he remembered he was addressed by another godly man. 'Nay, I was at my prayers when your servant came.'

Livesey's eyes opened slightly wider, his eyebrows flickering. 'Quite so,' he murmured. Then he raised his voice again for Robert's benefit. 'Well, then, I'll see if I can stir the wenches of this idle place to bring us vittles for the day's work. You'll join me, I hope.'

It was a command, not an invitation, and Robert gladly complied. He was attracted by Livesey's direct manner, pleased with the man's understanding of his deafness, pleased that the deafness did not — here at least — exclude him from honour and usefulness.

The two men breakfasted on bread, oatcakes, and small ale. The ale surprised Robert — the Fessenden

160

household had consumed no ale for years — but he made no remark about it and enjoyed the lift in his spirits that a second tankard gave him.

Immediately after the meal, one of Livesey's attendants came with a cuirass, breastplate, buff coat, bucket boots and helmet for Robert. Gladly shedding his dusty white jerkin and high-tongued boots in favour of what was now the unofficial Parliamentarian dress, Robert tried to temper the renewal of excitement he felt. It would not be enough, he thought, merely to be in the good graces of Livesey and to look like a soldier of Colonel Sandys: he must win their respect by loyalty, zeal, and courage.

Livesey took him with a small troop of dragoons to the deanery. There they demanded the keys of the cathedral so that they could sequester all the gunpowder, ammunition, and arms known to be stored there.

His stomach tightened as he watched the great wooden doors of Christ Church swing open before them. If the people of Canterbury thought to turn their cathedral into a magazine or fortress ready for war between King and Parliament, they were mistaken. It was his hand that had turned the key in the enormous lock, his hand that had made way for soldiers to carry away the means of victory from the rebellious, godless men of Canterbury who dared call themselves men in divine office!

And now they were joined by others in Canterbury who were of his own persuasion: who thought Laud the Antichrist and the interior of the cathedral a hellish room for Rome. In the crush of men in the church precincts, Livesey introduced him to Richard Culmer, rector of St Stephen's, and a supporter of Sandys. Robert took Culmer's measure quickly — tall, crow-like in his black robes and loose sleeves, his face fierce with the same determination and zeal he knew in himself. He smiled faintly, but then they were separated in the crowd.

The relative darkness and arching height of the great church checked for a moment his enthusiasm. Briefly he felt again the same wavering he had known more than once on the road to Canterbury. Had not John — his

161

godly brother John — spoken in wonder and delight about Christ Church? *Aye, but John was then besotted with a daughter of the neighbouring parish,* he thought sourly. How could he make right judgments then? Did not all the world look fair when Jane looked kindly on?

The soldiers in Sandys' troop were jostling in impatience at his back, more and more of them entering the vaulted doorway behind him. He heard a low murmuring in his ears and saw that they were shouting angrily, pointing at statues, windows, and tapestries.

Idols, he thought. And suddenly he was swept forward among them. He found his sword raised and felt himself swell with rage. He shouted, too, and surged forward. By his side again, Culmer waved his sword in equal frenzy, the sleeves of his gabardine falling back to reveal huge, knotted muscles such as Robert had never seen on a minister of God before. He felt as if he were shoulder to shoulder with St Paul himself in his war against unrighteousness.

The confusion was short-lived; one of Sandys' men discharged a round of shot. Robert heard it plainly. The sound echoed round the pillars and ceilings; it silenced and stilled the troops.

Livesey mounted into the canopied pulpit. 'Our orders are to destroy all such idols as do disgrace this shrine. Without fear of judgment ye may destroy it all. This place has become naught but a stable for idols, and the filth and abomination within it are ours to sweep away, as God will sweep all away on Judgment Day.'

Robert could not catch more than a few of his words, even though he had quickly learned to read Livesey's expressive face. But he had known in advance what the officer would say, and he knew what his own part would be.

With Culmer, forgetting all his doubts again, he mounted the steps to the communion table. Together they overturned it with a crash. A few of the soldiers pressed behind them and tore down the velvet cloth that hung before it. Robert saw one of them with fire in his eyes — a great Samson of a man from some East Kent farm — rip the cloth in two between meaty hands and throw it down the steps.

Others began attacking the intricate wooden screen of the tabernacle. They pushed and pounded it with their pikes so that it cracked, crumbled, and fell in splinters to the stone floor. Robert heard little of the rending sound of the ancient wood, nor the shouts of the men in their lust for destruction, but he saw it all, and his heart filled with high joy. They were angels administering God's wrath to a wicked whore posing as a bride of Christ.

Livesey was directing some of the men up the narrow tower staircase to the organ loft. Beside Robert, his chest still heaving from the effort of upending the altar-table, Culmer touched his sleeve and pointed as the last man ascended the steps. 'Come!' he shouted. 'Let us break this abomination that it sound no more.'

The two men ran after the others. Robert's breath came as fast as Culmer's now. In the gallery they wrenched the pipes from their places. Culmer roared in a voice so loud that again Robert was able to hear, 'Cast them down!'

The pipes dropped from their hands to the pavement below the gallery. The larger pipes could not be moved, but some of the men tore up the service books and stuffed the loose pages into the mouths of the pipes. Robert turned over benches and stools looking for more books, while Culmer broke open the singing men's cupboards and put his sword to their surplices. Around them the broken idols mounted up: bent pipes, shredded books, ripped surplices.

Robert stopped to catch his breath. Exhilarated, he leaned over the edge of the gallery and looked into the quire. The devastation below matched that above; organ pipes hurled by men beside and behind them rained down, and an arras that ran the length of the quire was hanging in tatters now. He called Culmer to his side.

'Look, brother. They despoil that blasphemous tapestry some say portrays the life of Christ.'

Culmer nodded vigorously and shouted directly into his ear, 'Aye, 'tis work well done. Hark, how the organs go! Mark what music we may dance to!'

A soldier below them bellowed in a frenzy, 'Here be Christ!' Robert could scarcely hear Culmer now, but he

163

saw the soldier point with his sword to a faded image, an untouched part of the arras. Then the man suddenly fell on it, slashing and cutting until the whole tapestry descended in ribbons around his head and a great cheer went up from below.

With the arras down and the service books strewn throughout the quire, the men turned to look for other objects for their hatred. Watching them, Culmer shouted something that Robert could not hear, then ran breakneck down the spiral stairs to the quire. Robert followed, unsure — though only for a moment — what was expected.

Culmer had rescued the Bible from its elaborate lectern. Balancing the heavy volume in the crook of one of his strong arms, he was waving in his other a sword. Was he exhorting Colonel Sandys' men to be mindful of the Word of God, and to purify God's house? Why else were they rooting out these signs of popery and of Laud's wicked reign?

Several men swarmed to the empty lectern. Robert joined them in slashing and pushing at the rails and seats near the lectern. Carvings split, and the brazen eagle appointed like an idol of Assyria to hold up the Holy Scriptures was thrown with a clang to the granite flags beneath. Satisfied, they then looked to Culmer for further guidance.

Robert took command, suddenly. Several times during the morning he had noticed the windows, so lofty and inaccessible that perhaps no one had given them consideration. And yet, he thought, they housed some of the most blasphemous idols of all: Mary enthroned above the moon and stars as spouse of God, St George, Thomas à Becket in full regalia ... Surely those windows should be broken, too?

He flew up the steps beside Culmer. He raised his voice as loudly as he would have raised it in the weavers' hall over the clatter of the looms.

'Men of Kent! Hear me, I pray you.' They stilled for a moment, and Robert caught Culmer's nod of approval. 'Hear me. though I who am deaf cannot hear you.' The deafness no longer mattered. It was a mark of distinction, almost, a claim on others' attention when he most needed it. He saw that they were listening and grew bolder. 'Are those glassy idols sacrosanct, then, brothers?' He waved his arms towards some of the windows. Culmer followed his gestures with rapt attention. 'No, I say! And who shall gainsay me?'

'Wait!' One of Sandys' soldiers, a seasoned soldier — by his clean sword, mahogany skin, and frayed cuffs — pushed forward and stood before Robert. 'Colonel Sandys has given orders that the windows be not touched. 'Twould cost blood.'

Robert could not hear him, so Culmer answered in his stead, 'If 'tis no shame to drive out statues and effigies in this place, then 'tis no shame to destroy the windows. They be the fruits of idolatry; they be the occasion of idolatry. See how the men and women of Canterbury worship their Diana?' He pointed to several of the windows in which Mary was pictured, and a great groan went up from the few cathedral officers who had dared remain in the building. But Culmer's voice rose to a fearful crescendo over the other noise, 'Let us do as God bids, not as Caesar bids. Proud Becket shall see his glassy bones upon the pavement yet. A ladder! Ho, fetch a ladder.'

In wonder, Robert heard that last command, but the men could find no ladders tall enough to reach the windows, and all of them wandered about shouting. He expected at any moment that Sandys himself would reappear and marshall his men for the next march. They were due in Dover by nightfall . . . Fear gripped him again, for he did not want to cross Sandys. *I must decide — now,* he told himself.

Almost forgetting that the present hubbub had been stirred by himself in the beginning, he separated himself from Culmer and the rabble and moved aside to an arched porch that led to steps and side aisles on two sides and to the cloisters on the third. He wanted time for reflection, and this place was empty of soldiers.

He had roused Culmer, that was certain, though the man was already hot in his zeal and might well have recollected the windows himself. But Culmer was a Canterbury man, committed to staying in the city in support of the other godly folk, and in defiance of all

165

who would exalt Archbishop Laud and bring Rome to rule in England again. *But I cannot,* he thought, *remain in Canterbury to work with Culmer.* Parliament's army offered much greater hope, a much higher calling, than the small work he could do here, drifting in and out of Chilham and always burdened with the affairs of the dwindling cloth trade. But if he stayed faithful to the new army for the length of the war . . . then there would be the hope of glory and advancement, the respect of men and the praise and adoration of women . . .

Culmer sat in one pan of the scales, and Livesey and Sandys in the other. The weightier pan trembled and descended, and Robert made his choice. He would serve the Parliamentary army against the King for as long as the war lasted, and he would set aside for now all cares for his father, for the cloth trade, for his family, and for what went on in Canterbury. God's wider kingdom was more important. *'Whoever he be of you that forsaketh not all that he hath, he cannot be my disciple.'* He reminded himself of the verse his mother had so often quoted at his bedside. Well, if John could not obey, and if Isaac had chosen the fleshpots, it was for him to answer the call to righteousness.

He turned and walked deliberately past Culmer and his followers. A ladder had been found, at last — a city ladder some sixty steps high. Culmer himself was mounting the rungs, and a hush had fallen as even the most careless of soldiers had refused to make the climb.

'Have a care, reverend sir!' one called.

I would not venture so high, Robert thought with a shiver, pausing for a moment, in spite of himself.

'Thou'lt break thy neck!' shouted a man who stood right beside Robert wringing his hands helplessly as he watched the spectacle.

Robert looked scornfully at this representative of pomp and popery. 'Nay, he's on his Father's business.'

The cleric covered his ears in horror and rushed away from Robert, but Robert only laughed harshly and turned on his heel again. Behind him the glass tinkled down as blow after blow of the pike in Culmer's hand shattered the window.

Walking purposefully to find Livesey and Sandys, Robert heard none of it.

He found his new masters outside the precincts with a group of young dragoons who were dressed as he was. One by one the young men took aim at the statue of Christ that stood in a niche above the cathedral gate. A cheer went up each time the musket fire hit the stonework.

Robert surveyed the scene with cheerful satisfaction. He had made the right choice, and within hours he and the other soldiers would cross Barham Downs. The broken organ pipes would whistle merrily in the mouths of the soldiers, and the torn pages of the service books would be rolled and smoked in pipes all the way to Dover.

3

GEORGE
Canterbury, Christmas 1647

Something about this couple reminded George of
Maidstone. The little spark of memory smouldered at
the back of his mind but would not ignite. Where had
he seen the man? He towered above his wife: wide shoulders, thick, curling black hair, a generous mouth and
freckled cheeks ruddy from the wind. His clothes were
immaculately made, and he held himself proudly, yet
clearly the man was not wealthy — else he would have
sent a servant to look after the little market booth.

Beside this giant of a yeoman the wife was dwarfed,
though she again seemed significant in his eyes as that
flicker trembled in his brain. *I know these people. But
when, where, how?*

The woman looked up at him but then withdrew
her eyes in haste. He saw fear in them and noticed
her twisting her hands under her shawl. She was
not dressed warmly enough for the day, he thought,
though she was wrapped in her husband's jerkin. She
could not have been older than her husband, yet her
beauty had obviously faded, and she looked dowdy and
wan beside him. Two boys chased each other round the
booth — dark and vigorous like their father.

He glanced at Elizabeth. Her eyes were directed
towards the discernible bulge under the woman's loose
garments, His throat constricted for a moment. After
the hopeless years of waiting for a living child, Bess
had finally proved more than fruitful — nay, lush as
his cherry trees in her generosity. One daughter had
followed another in rapid succession . . . but this poor
woman did not look well. She was too frail by half to be
breeding again.

His eyes moved back to the man's face. For a reason he couldn't explain to himself, he almost expected to see cruelty and lust, but instead he saw tenderness. The yeoman seemed not to have noticed him at all but was watching his wife anxiously. Before he and Bess passed on, the man caught his wife to him and bent to say something softly in her ear. Her face lit up as she murmured an inaudible reply. Yes, she had been beautiful once, and the memory crackled again, taunting him, but still slipping away.

ISAAC

Isaac drew Rebecca close to him. Even the closely stitched sheepskin jerkin and woollen hose he wore were not proof against the wind, and she was shaking from the cold, too, her own garments even more useless than his own.

He took off his jerkin, lapped her in it, and bent down. 'Thou'lt need warm covers on the bed this night, my darling.'

She looked up, smiling. In the cold her eyes were red-rimmed and watery, but the azure of her eyes wasn't dulled by the grey day. She was still his pale princess. 'Aye, and I will.' She groaned, 'Ah, but I would we could be home this night!'

'And I, dear love. But it cannot be.' He tightened his arm more closely.

A gentleman passed the stall with his family. He moved with a slight faltering in his steps, but the wife was stately, her red hair parted and braided cleverly across her head. She was tall, and he saw that her cloak was made of fine Spanish wool. He noticed, however, that the man cared less for his own appearance; his boots were muddy and his cuffs frayed. They were country folk, then.

The man was no taller than his wife, stout around the middle, his fair hair thinning slightly. Isaac noticed his face: it was watchful, kindly; he had observed Rebecca's pinched face and blue lips and his eyes had dropped quickly — but not rudely — to her belly.

He shut his eyes briefly, wishing the gentleman away, and then opened them to look at Rebecca again. He saw the terrified, haunted expression that crossed her face whenever a man ran his eyes over her, and he clenched his teeth. The man meant no harm; he saw that immediately. And what man could avoid a second glance at Rebecca, especially now she was with child? But as for *Robert . . . damn Robert.*

He bent down again. 'All's well, my dear. See? The mistress likes our wares.'

Rebecca answered him with a reproachful stare, waiting until the family had passed. A string of three little girls followed their parents: fur muffs and wool surcoats.

'Aye,' she said, 'but not enough to buy.' Her voice was bitter.

'Wait. They will. Thou'lt see.'

GEORGE

George guided Elizabeth farther along the road. ''Tis strange, love, but I swear I've seen those two before.'

'The tailor and his wife?' She looked up quickly. 'The little woman breeding?'

'Aye. He was a tailor, was he? I had scarcely noticed what was on his stall.'

She curled her lip. 'Nay, and I should have known it. Ever an eye for the breeder.'

He scoffed. ''Twas not that, and you know it.' He turned briefly to ensure that Anna, Henrietta, and Charlotte were still close behind. They had left their fourth daughter, Eleanor, asleep in the hostelry, watched over by Nancy. 'Nay, but I'm sure I've seen those two before.'

'Mayhap, and very likely.' Elizabeth stopped and turned back for a moment. ''Tis a small kingdom we dwell in. Perhaps you have tried them, seen them at the assizes.'

He shook his head. 'Nay, 'twas not that. And yet I know I've seen them in Maidstone, somehow.'

'Where else but the assizes, then?'

He shook his head again. ''Tis no matter. I'll come back later and enquire of them. They look like plain people — Puritans I mean.'

She flung her head back quickly. 'Puritans? And he with that great forest of curls on his poll? Never!' She stopped a few stalls away from the tailor's and made a decisive movement with her hand. 'Anna, make haste, do! Bring thy sisters along — ' She dropped her voice. 'Husband, I'd like to get some gewgaws for the girls . . . aye, I know we've not much to spend on trifles now. But there's so little pleasure for the children nowadays.'

George's face fell. Elizabeth wasn't complaining, but lately he had suffered on her account. These days it was rare for them to make a holiday from Tolhurst Court at all, let alone buy trinkets for the girls. Parliament had reduced the estate now; they had lived meagrely in one of the wings of the house ever since George had returned from Marston Moor nursing a leg wound. And they had sent many of their servants from their doors: the men whistling merrily to join the 'cavilly men', and the maids weeping bitterly at the prospect of returning to families impoverished by war.

Through all this, Elizabeth had held steady. She had comforted the household and proved a better steward than the man he had dismissed. But her resolution and strength had lately begun to waver, and he wanted earnestly to restore to her some of the freedom from care, and gaiety, that had been quenched by years of worry.

Business for the county courts had brought him to Faversham just before Christmas. With little to tend to at home but the milking of a few dairy cows, he had decided suddenly to take the family with him. Leaving Tolhurst Court with Matty, one of his older servants, he had removed the family — muffled in shawls and with hot bricks at their feet in the coach — first to Faversham, then to Canterbury.

Elizabeth, he hoped, would revel in the bustle of the great city. He wanted to see the colour return to her

171

cheeks and hear the laughter in her voice again. With money he had safely hidden in a pot since before the troops had ransacked the house, he had endeavoured to spoil her. They had the best chambers in the inn and ate from the best board below. While she had been uneasy with this profligacy, asking anxiously how they could possibly afford it, the little girls had blossomed in the unfamiliar surroundings, renewing their parents with their round-eyed wonder and glee.

He looked fondly at Elizabeth as Anna caught his hand, reaching them again with the two younger girls. He leaned to whisper over Anna's heads, "'Tis ribbons you want for them, is it?'

'No — I — '

'Just say it, dearling. They shall have whate'er you desire for them.'

Her eyes melted, and her face softened. 'I know I've been womanish and fretful about our purses . . . '

'Nay, just careful, my lass.'

She drew her brows together. 'Fretful, 'tis true. I say it myself. But as I see all these goodly things, and I think how few delights we've had, I can't help — '

'Nay, nor I. But listen. I've had some gold put by that I never told thee of. So, if you please, no more words about money. Ask what you will.' He stole a quick look at Anna, but her eyes were averted and her face expressionless.

Light broke on Elizabeth's face so that his innards twisted and turned over. After all these years she could still make him feel this way. Desire, tenderness — they flooded him in an instant. Why should the wars take everything away? Elizabeth, Anna, and the others — they were all he needed.

'Then, George, I'll beg some woollen jackets for the girls — those the tailor had. They were fine indeed, and not the drab colours we are wont to see nowadays.'

He hesitated, looking back briefly with a tug of jealousy. Had she looked warmly at the tailor? He frowned. 'Not green, I hope.'

Her chin went up. He knew she had always loved this colour best, though she could not wear it now

172

because the Puritans said it smacked of witchcraft. 'And if 'twere?'

'Then I'd say thee nay, sweetheart.' He sighed. No, it was the clothes she wanted, not the handsome young man.

Her face crinkled, and he recognized that flare of high spirits he had not seen for months. '"Ask what you will"?' she repeated.

He gritted his teeth. 'Save *green* jackets.'

She laughed naughtily. 'Nay, but they were *scarlet*.'

'*Scarlet!* Oh, dear heart, we cannot —'

'Aye.' She pursed her lips. 'The colour of wicked women. Of course, my love, how right you are.' Her eyes were dancing. 'Then I'll have to settle for blue, I suppose. There were blue ones, you know.'

'A sober blue?' He pictured the dismal colour worn by most elderly folk nowadays, and felt strangely disappointed.

The corners of her mouth twitched, and Anna gazed up in bemusement from one to the other. 'Nay, they were light blue, the colour of the little blue butterflies thou see'st up on the Downs of a summer's day. A novel colour indeed. Can we afford — ?'

His mind finished her sentence immediately, and he cut her off. 'No more discourse of our purse, I said. We can, and we shall.' He bent to Anna. 'A surprise for you girls, my sweeting. Wait and see!'

ISAAC

Rebecca shifted her weight from one foot to the other and sighed. 'Forgive me. I'm ever complaining and peevish.'

'Peevish! Nay, we're all starving with cold, and thou'rt a-breeding.' He gestured to the older child. 'Adam, here's a penny. Fetch thy mother some mulled ale over yonder. Quick about it, lad.'

Rebecca smiled again. 'Ye're always kind.'

'For I love thee, love thee, little honey.' He nuzzled her hair with his mouth, then let his eyes wander to the family that had just passed. They had stopped again near the top of the market, the wife talking quickly to her husband as the three girls clustered around them, jumping and clapping their hands against the cold.

Three daughters! Aye, some men were lucky. He had sewn little garments for a daughter every time Rebecca had been with child. She had borne two daughters dead, and now — after this one — she would bear no more, boys or girls. It was too much grief. He had promised himself he would live chastely with her from henceforth. He could stand her suffering no longer, and his two sons were good, healthy lads.

The stall was set out with apparel for babes and children, as well as frocks, surcoats, jerkins, petticoats, and breeches. He prided himself on the fine intricacy and durability of his stitching, in his knowledge of the best cloth, and in the unusual designs. But most of all he loved the soft, decorative work necessary for little girls' clothes.

It made him ache to see that gentleman with three daughters. Not that he begrudged the man his good fortune. About his brother John's age, perhaps . . . late in life for so young a progeny.

Three daughters. It was the oldest who caught his eye. She hadn't the natural high colour and regal air of her mother, but she had inherited the rich, golden-red hair and slender body. She hadn't the high spirits of the middle daughter — and certainly not of his own son Charlie — but her watchful devotion towards her father moved him.

Oh, Christ, for a daughter like that! Unthinkingly, he moved his hand lightly over Rebecca's belly, but she flinched and pulled away. The cord of closeness was snapped.

'*Don't*, Isaac.'

His hands fell to his sides. 'Forgive me, I was . . . oh, thinking of this babe of ours.'

She followed to where his gaze had been fixed. 'Aye, a girl, God willing.' She touched his arm softly; her hand was blue. 'I know, love, what thou thought'st.'

174

'Then why spurn me?' He reached for her gloves and pushed her hands into them.

'I didn't mean to. Thou'rt always kind. I'm sorry, I just said so ere this, didn't I? Peevish, as I said; I cannot help myself.'

He shook his head. 'Nay — but here's Adam. Put thy lips to this, sweetheart. 'Twill warm thee.' He held up the frothing mug, then watched, frowning, as she began to sip the brew. She was right. Their journey to Canterbury had been futile. Only Adam and Charlie had enjoyed themselves, and the cost of the journey had by far exceeded their takings. A mistake he would not make again: to come to a town where he was more or less a stranger. It was a risk anyhow. What if his father or Robert — no doubt like other Puritans at business as usual despite Christmass — had come to Canterbury? No, that was more than he cared to think of.

He looked at Adam. 'Son? I think we'll not stay here for the close of the marketing. Thy mother's a-weary, and we've made a poor showing of it.'

The child's face fell, and he bit his lip.

'Aye, I know. Thou'd like to stay. But 'tis a holiday, and we've had enough. Thou'll help me put it away now, pray.'

Charlie pinched his elbow. 'I'll help, my father! Let me.'

Isaac caught the look of anxiety in Rebecca's eyes as the two boys vied for his attention. *'Tis naught to fret about,* he signalled silently.

'Ye'll both help, then. Charlie, fetch the sack.' He reached for Adam's shoulder, but the older boy had stiffened.

'Look, my father. Those men mean harm.'

Voices were raised, and a mob advanced among the booths. Rebecca moaned, falling against him in despair. He caught her to him, anger mounting inside. *Could there be no peace? Not even on Christmass tide? What was their cause this time? What brawl now, on the Nativity of the Lord and in the city of great Christ Church?*

He barked orders to the two boys. They leaped about as he passed them armfuls of clothing, but he did not release Rebecca. Not for the first time,

175

he gave thanks for his own vigour: he would need it today.

'Hurry, Charlie, Adam!' He snatched another bundle of clothes and pushed it into one child's arms.

Rebecca began to cry and wring her hands.

His fury boiled over. 'Adam, guard thy mother, dost hear?'

The boy nodded stolidly, seizing her round her swollen waist more for his own protection than for her own. She sank down on one of the sacks behind the stall and wept, the two boys fussing and cossetting her, beginning to cry themselves.

GEORGE

They had just turned when Tolhurst noticed a band of yeomen approaching the booth nearest the edge of the market-place. Some of the men were armed with staves, their faces menacing, but he could not be seriously alarmed when he saw their long hair and bright clothes. None of Livesey's men, these — but King's men. All the same, his grip on Elizabeth's arm tightened, and he stopped. Without thinking, he gathered the three girls close to him.

'There's something ill ado, sweetheart,' he said, loudly enough only for her ears.

Her gaze was fixed directly ahead, and she licked her lips. 'Aye, I see it. But we'll not let it spoil our festival, George? We've waited too long for this — '

'Perhaps, but let's bide a moment. We can watch the tailor lest he shuts up shop, can we not?' He drew her away, and the girls followed closely. Then he reached for his old sword, but the scabbard and sword were missing; he had long ago given up pretence of wanting to use a sword. His only weapon now, he had once joked to Elizabeth, was his plough-share.

Anna's fingers gripped tightly on the loose folds of his breeches. He looked down and met her eyes.

'What's amiss, my father?' Her voice was low and hollow.

Letting go of his wife, he bent down and pulled the child roughly into his arms. 'I don't know, poppet. Nothing, perhaps, but we'd better move on.'

He guided his family to the steps of the Saracen's Head Inn, so that they had a better view of the market. It was better to be cautious . . .

He looked first at the tailor and his wife. The woman shrank against her husband, and the two boys were clearing the stall, frantically filling sacks, sobbing with terror. The mob's voices came clearly over the frosty air, threatening and jeering. 'We'll break your pate and beat your brains out unless you close up here. 'Tis a holiday!'

George saw that one of them held a football behind his back, and another carried a goodwife's basket overflowing with holly and mistletoe. The bizarre mixture of their ugly words and clownish appearance struck him almost as funny, but the laughter did not come. The yeomen had plainly come from the alehouse, and blood might be spilled.

''Tis not a holiday,' cried a Puritan merchant from nearer to where the family stood. ''Tis an idolatrous festival, not the Sabbath. No plum pottage, and no nativity pies. Market shall be kept open this day as any other.'

'Aye, and so it shall,' a rich and compelling voice shouted from right beside George. He jerked around to see a tall man in the dark, sober clothes of a Puritan minister move to the top of the steps.

'Culmer! 'Tis that dog Culmer!' The fever of the mob rose again, and they seemed to forget the stallholders.

'Sir, you would do well to quit this place afore they set on you,' George said urgently.

Cold eyes turned on him, spurning him. 'Nay, these scoundrels shall feel the pinch of iron on their ankles ere this day's out. Shame on you, sir, for a gentleman, to favour — '

George felt the colour rise into his face.

'Stop, husband!' Elizabeth begged.

His hands dropped to his sides, and he looked at the man Culmer with his teeth clenched. 'I favour *no* rash or

177

violent men. Neither violent in deed, nor in word. You stir the rabble with your words. Shame on *you*, sir.'

'Culmer, step down if ye dare,' the men taunted. They stood at the bottom of the steps now, ranged round.

Over their heads, George saw that all the merchants were now rushing to stow their goods into barrows and sacks. He found Anna's arms pressed round his waist and her soft strawberry-roan hair buried in his jerkin. She shook like a hop bine in the autumn winds. Henrietta began to shriek for her mama to pick her up, but Charlotte was flushed and eager to see what would happen. She kept crying for sweetmeats from the stall. He began to curse himself for bringing them out. Why, oh why had he not left them all with Nancy?

'We'll hang up the green at the Saracen's, shall we, gentlefolk?' one of the men bawled. 'Holly, and mistletoe, and bay, as at thy country alehouses. Nothing to pay, and "welcome gentlemen".'

The others laughed raucously, and the footballer hurled his pig's bladder into the air and kicked it up as it fell again.

'Kick him down, the knave!'

'Aye, kick Culmer down.'

'Stone him, he's one of Weldon's bedfellows.'

George wavered. He wanted no part of either side, but he couldn't remain where he stood. 'Make way, sirs,' he shouted, feigning a hearty smile. 'Wassail to ye all. Make way for the goodwife and children, pray.'

The men parted. They were not interested in the Tolhursts. Surrounding Culmer like hounds round a quarry they had scented for miles, they parted but then came together again. He saw them raise their staffs.

Sickness seized him. Could he leave even a hated Puritan minister to the mercy of cut-throats — even royalist cut-throats?

'Elizabeth, make haste and take these children to the inn. Dost hear?'

'But the jackets — ?'

He stamped his foot irritably. 'Come, come. This be no place for women and children. Do as I bid, and make haste.'

But Anna began to cling even more tightly. 'Please — oh, pray, my father, stay not here — '

He clenched his teeth again and with an effort unhooked her from him. 'Do as thou'rt bid, daughter. Go with thy mother. She needs thee. Go ye all to Nancy and wait till I come back.'

Behind them the shouts grew ugly. Forcibly he pushed the womenfolk along the cobbles, past the stalls, and away.

And now for Culmer, to help —

But Culmer was gone. He leapt off the steps with a sword swashing left and right, running with his black gabardine flapping like a monstrous crow's wings. The mob followed, hounds again, their throats full of revenge.

George's chest tightened, and fear closed on the pit of his stomach. In all the noise of the shouts and crash of the staves, another mob of men ran across his mind: Cromwell's men. Three years ago he had fought under the Invicta flag with Mainy, Filmer, and Twysden in the name of the King. Marston Moor: far from his dearlings, camping under the June and July stars at night, and marching and waiting by day. Watching the enemy range themselves — like a hideous, invincible machine — against the army of the King. He saw them now, Cromwell's men in their dull colours surging towards him. Voices in full cry, mowing down men in the ugliest harvest of all: a fierce July wind blasting a field of Prince Rupert's prime grain. The bitter, bitter taste of a battle lost, a battle in which he had fought only on the fringes: fearful, wanting to flee, afraid for Elizabeth and his daughters . . .

The bitterness of that and other battles, the longing for home — they peopled his memory now. He had escaped from the army without disgrace when a musket wound had festered and laid him low. But now the war had caught up with him again, this time on Kentish soil.

He saw them scoop mud and filth out of the gutter and send it after Culmer. For a moment, his sympathy shifting, he wanted to join the chase. What right had Culmer to say the stalls should open or close? Was Culmer judge and jurate here? Was his ally Sir Anthony

179

Weldon of the Parliament County Committee to declare laws for the spoiling of Christ's mass?

But what right had the mob, either, to pitch Culmer into the gutter as they did now? The man's starched white ruff was caked with filth, one side of his face smeared with it. George saw him open his mouth in protest, heard staffs strike against his back as he wallowed and struggled to stand. Was this murder, then, and was he party to it as a silent witness?

The shouts of rage turned suddenly to cruel laughter as Culmer tottered onto a dry pavement.

'Baptized in foul muck, ye are, Culmer.'

'Foul enough for the devil himself.'

'See how we use the man who would spear Christ in the gate and knock out windows in his church.'

'Tooth for tooth!' someone else screamed.

The minister's replies were lost in the uproar, and then, whimsically, the mob careened round, forgetting Culmer. George rushed forward as the men fell on the stalls and threw the remaining merchandise to the cobbles and gutter.

This time he could not hesitate, especially seeing the terror of the pale, wispy-haired woman — the tailor's wife.

She screamed high and shrill, her face white. He heard a grating, rending sound and saw the tailor stoop by the corner of the table, the blood pooling in his neck and face as he wrestled with someone unseen under the stall. Then the tailor straightened, and the table tipped violently to one side.

The tailor held one leg of the table above his head, the nails protruding.

'Let me defend you also!' George shouted, but the tailor did not hear, and he felt more foolish than ever.

Imitating, he bent to wrench off another leg. He tasted bile in his mouth. A Tolhurst defending a roundhead tailor (or was he?) against a mob of King's men at Christmass. Strange days!

The tailor now saw his intention and shouldered him aside. 'Here, take this.' And he snapped off a second leg as easily as a twig. Long, irrelevant thoughts skeined through George's mind. *A tailor? This man? Never!*

But the tailor was shouting suddenly above the mob. The men had closed in but were cowed by the makeshift clubs and by the tailor's height. The shouting dwindled. No one else came to their rescue, and the street was deserted now — no Culmer, no merchants, none to buy their wares: just a crowd of grimy men of Kent carrying staffs, a football, and holly. Country fools, more so even than himself. A parody of himself.

'Lay not a hand on me or mine,' the tailor warned. The man's dark brows were fierce, and his eyes blazed.

The man with the holly basket stepped backwards, grinning absurdly. 'We meant no 'arm, I do warrant 'ee, sirs.'

"Twas a sport, 'tis all.' The man holding the pig's bladder dropped and kicked it over the cobbles until it rolled into the mire and disappeared. The tailor's two dark-haired sons wistfully watched it sink.

The tailor drew his wife close but did not for one moment loosen his hold on the table leg. "Tis well, for though I'm selling my wares here, I'm one of your own.'

'And I,' George found himself saying unexpectedly, gathering courage.

Mouths opened.

'Aye.' The tailor's voice grew bitter. 'Can ye not see I'm but a tailor with a family to feed? Think ye I *want* to spend my holiday in commerce like some prating, busy Puritan?'

George gaped at him, wanting to laugh, but afraid.

'He's a knave. He will trick us,' one of the ruffians said.

'Nay, I speak the truth,' the tailor answered. 'I'm not of Canterbury, as ye should know, but Maidstone. I knew of no mayor's ordinances either for or against.'

'He'll trick us,' one man hissed again. 'Turn 'is table o'er.'

'Hush, 'tis turned already. 'E turned it by 'imself.'

'Aye, so he did,' George agreed quickly.

The tailor gave him a grateful look. 'I'd rather sport as ye do, though not with strong drink. But see, my wife's a-breeding again. Ye'll not touch a woman that's with child, I warrant.' Uneasily, he looked both at his wife and back at George.

'Look at 'is 'air.'

'He's one of His Majesty's own.'

Others backed away, and George marvelled at the man's power over the crowd, at the slavish, dog-like faces of the men standing round them.

'Then peace to ye, tailor, and no offence,' ventured one man in the crowd, nodding also at George.

The staves were lowered.

'And peace to ye all this Christmass tide,' the tailor answered. He, too, lowered his weapon.

George hesitated, then took a step forward. The men backed away, and the woman began to weep more quietly, her shoulders heaving.

'Hush, mother,' one of the boys said. 'All's well now.'

ISAAC

Rebecca's sobs had subsided, strangely at odds with the festive mood of the inn. An enormous log burned in the hearth, and holly and mistletoe festooned the sills and shelves all round the room. Adam and Charlie sat close to their mother by the fire, she stroking their dark hair in the firelight, and they leaning against her, at peace now. Mugs of steaming cider and ale stood before them all, and in the next room several families were singing carols in defiance of all Puritan ordinances against profane, lewd songs.

He looked around the room, some dim memory stirring in his mind. Had there not been Christmasses years ago before his father and brother had become so strict and his tight-lipped first mother had died? Or had he only heard stories at Mother Mary Snode's knees of years and times before his own memory?

His eyes began to sting. This was another age. England was in winter, a winter that had lasted many years. Only in isolated corners such as this, where they could pay to keep their servants silent, did men dare to flout Parliament's laws and celebrate Christmass. And Canterbury had seen enough violence for one day. The fierce temper of the filthy Puritan minister, and the fierce faces of the king's men . . . he wanted neither of them.

The gentleman who had stood with him in the market watched him guardedly but seemed at a loss for words now that they actually faced each other across a board. He felt he must address him, somehow, but fences had come up between them: he a yeoman, and this man a knight or gentleman of the shire — a man with three daughters, and a queenly wife who wore Spanish wool.

'Sir, I thank you. Rebecca — ' He pointed hastily, in embarrassment, with his thumb. 'She does thank thee, also. We owe a debt, and I don't even know your name.'

'Tolhurst. George Tolhurst.'

Isaac remembered his cap and whipped it off, bowing his head. 'Then, thank you, Mr Tolhurst, sir.'

'George Tolhurst,' the other repeated gently, the skin of his cheeks flushing darkly. 'You may — '

Isaac saw that the gentleman was even more awkward than himself. He wished the conversation over. But Tolhurst had insisted on providing lodging for them, helping them carry their goods to the inn where he himself was lodged with his family, stabling his donkey, and setting ale and fruit puddings before them. Adam, Charlie — even Rebecca — had eaten greedily and then retired to the chimney corner. And now he was left to talk to a stranger to whom he owed perhaps not only his own life, but that of the unborn baby's. Who could tell whether the crowd would have dispersed had he stood alone against them?

'You may — ' Tolhurst began again.

'Nay, sir, I care not to be familiar. But how can I repay you?'

'Don't think of it.'

Isaac's mind moved quickly. 'You wanted something from my table, did you not?'

Tolhurst's eyebrows rose. 'My wife — she — that is — ' And he stammered into silence.

Isaac felt compelled to take the lead. 'For your wife, perchance?'

The other man looked down, rubbing his hands over his thighs. The breeches were worn, Isaac noticed uncomfortably. And now the poor man was saddled with debts for another family as well as his own.

'For your daughters then?'

Tolhurst seemed relieved. 'Aye, my daughters.' A small frown flickered across his brow. 'But how did —'

'Your daughters are fair, sir.'

'You flatter me.'

'Nay, you know they are.'

Tolhurst smiled and after a moment said, 'As any father knows his own are.' And he nodded towards Adam and Charlie.

'I noticed your little girls in the market-place.'

'Aye, that's kind of you.' Tolhurst's resolve seemed to rise, suddenly.

'*Kind!*' Isaac shook his head. Was the man a simpleton?

'Yes, as I said . . . And you noticed my wife, too. Everyone does. She was talking to me of your blue jackets. I would have bought them all. We have four daughters. The youngest shall need something of her own one day, instead of cast-off clouts from the elder ones, though she be but a little hazelnut now. And we saw that thy work will last.'

Isaac barely heard the compliment. '*Four* daughters?'

'Aye.' Tolhurst flushed again. 'God has not ordained boys for us, like yours.'

'Nor girls for us.' Isaac looked down at the shadowed sawdust floor. 'Well, never mind, sir. He knows what's best, I'm sure.' The words came of themselves, surprising him. How long was it since he had spoken of God naturally or with any warmth?

Tolhurst was nodding slowly. 'Then you'll let me buy your blue jackets? 'Twill be a surprise for my wife.'

'Buy them? Nay, ye shall have all four. Choose what you will.'

Tolhurst stood up abruptly and held out his hand. He had hardly touched the tankard before him. 'I'll pay thee something, for sure. And the landlord's to give your account to me, as I said. He knows it.'

Isaac took his hand and shook it. 'I'll send Adam to you in the morn, afore we go.'

Tolhurst hesitated. 'You — your name? You have not given it me.'

Isaac suddenly felt on his guard. His father's name was far too well known. But then he relaxed. The name was common enough in all the county.

'Fessenden, sir. Fessenden.'

Tolhurst let his hand drop. 'Of Chilham — John or Robert, is it not?'

Isaac looked away, his jaw tightening. 'Nay, of Maidstone, as I told the men out there.' He cleared his throat, still grateful, but longing to be left alone with his family in the public parlour where they could keep the rest of Christmass without this stranger's kindly inquisitiveness.

Tolhurst was looking at him oddly, frowning slightly, but not saying more. 'Aye, well, Master Fessenden, God rest ye all this night.' He nodded towards Rebecca and the boys. 'You've earned good rest, indeed. And ye've two bold sons.'

Isaac stood and bowed slightly. 'And you have brave womenfolk, sir.' He could still picture the oldest girl: her steady eyes like violets and her hair that warm colour of russet homespun.

4

JOHN
Cambridge, The New World, June 1648

John gripped the arms of the chair. Some folks had
to be tied down, the man confided cheerfully. That
news did not make him feel any better, but he had
refused the restraining bands gruffly. 'I'll bear it,
thank 'ee.'

Later he was not as sure. The drum of pain began
to beat in his head — softly at first. He shifted in the
chair, his mouth stretched wide to admit the other man's
fingers and the black pincers. The tooth seemed as
embedded and firm as a piece of granite in the hillside,
and he groaned.

'Aye, 'tis a stubborn.' The same cheerful voice,
sanguine about the pain of another.

Now the drum beat louder. The pincers ground and
twisted against the enamel of the tooth. He screwed his
eyes shut and tasted his own blood. Neither pain would
last long now: the immediate, wrenching pain, and the
more chronic, dull ache that had left his face swollen on
one side for several days until at last Jane's pleas that he
have the tooth removed had availed.

The man's fingers were turning, pulling inside his
mouth, sure of their work. The tooth tore away from the
gum, and with it came the taste of more blood and pus,
sharp and foul on his tongue.

'Aah — nasty, that one.' The barber was holding the
tooth triumphantly between the pincers right in front of
John's eyes as he opened them. 'Here. Thou'd best rub
salt in't and take a syrup of poppy seeds and mithridate,
or hyssop and vinegar.'

John felt the side of his face. It was bruised and tender, but at least the tooth was out. 'Aye.' He turned to lean over the edge of the chair, and spat into the sawdust on the floor. It was too much effort, suddenly, to add any more courteous words.

The man proffered a block of salt. John broke off a fragment, crumbled it between his forefinger and thumb, and reached gingerly inside his mouth. More pain now, but different. The salt was clean on his tongue. It made his spittle run, and he spat again. Then he pushed a small wad of poppy leaves into his mouth. He had been carrying them in his pocket all week to make the pain bearable.

The man stood expectantly. Behind him a child waited with his mother, scuffing the sawdust with his foot, pale in the face and sullen.

John dropped a coin into the man's hand and reached to touch the boy's shoulder. 'Thou'lt feel better soon, lad.' His voice sounded strange, the voice slightly slurred by his swollen lips and cheek.

The boy scowled at him, unconvinced.

"Tis kind of you to say so, Goodman Fessenden,' the mother said, and she pushed the child forward.

John turned in haste. He did not want to witness the suffering of the child. What if it were Nathaniel bound to the chair and crying piteously?

'Wait, sir, for a bandage. 'Twould take the swelling down sooner.'

John stopped on the threshold, his hand going up to his face again. 'You have a bandage, then?'

The man pulled a linen cloth from a cabinet beside the chair and tore off a long strip. 'Aye, I'll tie it on.'

John paused. All of Cambridge would know he'd lost a tooth. But the taste of pus returned to him. 'Very well. Tie it on.'

The man wound the cloth under and around John's jaw and tied it on top of his head. The pressure on his cheek eased the ache. He replaced his beaver, frowning. What an absurd sight he must look now!

'Come, John, 'tis thy turn.'

He swung round abruptly at the woman's word, but she was speaking to the unhappy child, and without more ado he slipped out.

He was glad to see the street was empty now, especially as he found himself on Winthrop Street, close to where he and Jane had lodged when they first came to Cambridge. He would prefer to meet no one he knew this morning. But at this hour the men were about their work, the children at their lessons, and the womenfolk within — spinning and baking.

Another house was going up further along the street, not far from where they now lived, and he could hear the men driving the pegs into the walls to hang the clapboards. The sound brought back to him the sight of the peg-and-tile roof of his family home in Chilham, and for a moment he wished himself back in the Old World.

His gum still throbbed, but he fancied the swelling had already subsided. Reaching into his pocket, he found another fragment of the salt block, crumbled it, and dabbed it gently into the empty socket in his mouth. He winced, but he felt relief. Jane had been wise to urge him to the barber.

For a moment he doffed his hat and stood quite still at the edge of the road. Ahead of him the *tchack, tchack* of the hammer went on, and above him the blustery clouds — unusual for early June — churned and rolled from the east. 'Great sovereign Lord,' he murmured, 'I thank thee for Jane.' Immediately, he remembered her as he had first seen her in Canterbury all those years ago. In his eyes, she was as fine and beautiful as ever, with her eyes like soft blue wool and her hair like smooth, bleached linen . . . But he called himself back to the prayer. 'And for thy provision of health to us both.' Winter after winter he and Jane had been spared the agues and fevers that ravaged the settlements of Cambridge and Charlestown. Summer after summer the bloody flux had stolen away children and their parents: but this, too, they had been spared. People came to Jane of an evening, sometimes, to consult about their ailments. She comforted them but claimed no knowledge, and for this he was glad.

'And for our safety, Lord,' he added, bowing his head, no longer looking at the sky. Behind the darkness of his eyelids, he saw Nathaniel again, and he began to frown.

Once again he replaced the beaver, now walking more slowly, his face thoughtful. That child had brought them nothing but trouble, had been an affliction to them both from the first day. What was the Lord teaching them? Was he chastening them for presuming to gainsay his 'no' to their prayers for children by taking the child of others into their home? *No, surely not.* He sighed, wishing himself wiser.

Nathaniel was orphaned four winters after they had arrived in Cambridge. The child had been born to poor unfortunates on a ship from Plymouth. Weakened by fever and the months at sea, the mother had died after landfall, soon followed by the father. Jane heard of the infant and begged John to let her bring him home. At last, he had thought, he might have a son, rather than an apprentice, to take over his business when he yielded up his spirit to Christ's keeping: another to make and sell fine leather or wool gloves — for the cloth trade lay years behind him now, left to Robert and his father.

The child was sickly, though, and needed a wet-nurse. Jane had found one close by on Winthrop Street, and soon Nathaniel thrived and came home to them. They had given him their own name. But he was a noisy, fractious, greedy child, and their lives had changed from that day on. Now ten, he had disgraced them repeatedly in their congregation, calling the Reverend Thomas Shepard a fool to his face, and lying to him. John loved the child, nevertheless, and yearned for him to love God in his turn.

He pushed open the nail-studded door of their home and stepped down into the kitchen. Jane had gathered a handful of flowers from the pasture behind the house: blue chicory, spindly buttercups, and some white, three-petalled flowers he did not recognize. She had arranged them carefully in a brass pot; they provided the only colour in the otherwise plain room. *Dear woman!*

Smelling yeast, he looked into the dough-box. She had been baking. A mound of dough was ballooning within. He shut the lid hastily, aware of her silent but definite disapproval. *It'll fall, husband.* Then he clicked his tongue, impatient with himself. By this time in the morning he had usually stitched one glove and — even in June — sold a pair or two. What was he doing at home? He stood still again, to remember. *Ah — I wanted to write a note to brother Robert.*

He stepped to the sideboard to open the secret drawer where he kept a roll of paper. The stuff was harder to come by in the New World, and he hoarded it away from Nathaniel's marauding fingers.

A piece of slate Jane always kept on the shelf above caught his eye. *To the apoth* she had written; her writing was childish but clear. He smiled. Always she anticipated what he needed, what would relieve him or give him pleasure.

At the table he spread out the paper, sharpened a quill, and began to write. No letter had come from his father in Chilham since one sent in the previous autumn — a letter that had not reached him until March. Now he feared that something was amiss. He had sought God's comfort about it but had found no repose. If his father had fallen ill, why had not Robert sent word by the next ship out of Gravesend? Or if Robert and Patience — or the family trade — had come to grief, why had not his father written to him? Could the northern battles and bloodshed they all heard word of in the New World have spread south — even to Kent? Had the King been captured and all England come at last into Parliament's hands? He furrowed his brow as he dipped the quill into the inkhorn. He was glad to be in the Lord's new land, glad to have left the persecution of England, but he could never turn his back on his kin, and he must know what was happening in Kent.

Forgetting his tooth, he bit down hard on his thumb, then cried out. Pain shot up the side of his jaw and across his scalp. He groaned and screwed his eyes tight shut, but the pain passed instantly, serving only as a reminder that he must use more salt and poppy leaves.

To my dear brother, greetings. I trust thou and thy
household be safe in Christ's care, but I have heard
naught. Kindly send word, straightway. And is our father
well yet? Make haste to answer me, pray. We continue
safely here and by the Lord's grace do prosper —

He grimaced, mentally adding 'Aye, save for Nathaniel,'
but then went on:

I do meet the ships as they enter the harbour, or send my
boy to do so. Remember us in thy prayers. Thy faithful
brother and servant, John.

He dried the ink with sand, cut the top off the paper,
and sealed the letter.

Outside he saw no sign of his wife or of the child;
they must have gone out just before his return. He
would send his apprentice down to the harbour and
would return to work himself.

In the shop behind their house he found no apprentice, either. A piece of leather lay on the bench ready to
be cut, but the apprentice had done no more than open
and peg it, stretching it for the cutting. The rascal had
discovered his master's absence and gone off; he was as
untrustworthy as Nathaniel!

John gritted his teeth, then winced. 'I'll beat that
lad,' he muttered aloud. But he knew he would relent
at the last and let him off. He always did. And the town
wardens would do that unpleasant work for him — and
more besides — if the lad were caught rolling in the
pasture again with one of the selectmen's daughters . . .
Now the day was wasted.

Irritably, he stopped to use more salt, then strode
out and down Eliot Street. He covered the two-mile
walk to the harbour in a short time. There was always
some novel sight along the way: new houses going up,
or perhaps a church. The settlement was growing, and
with it his excitement about the New World. He had
been a freeman of Cambridge for seven years now,
and proudly so. Some of his fellow freemen had
even muttered about seeing him into the office of
selectman — but that could happen, he reflected, only
as God willed it.

191

Down by the wharves, two ships lay at anchor, great wooden shells rising and falling with the swell. The rigging creaked in the breeze, and at the edge of the wharves the water smelled foul and brackish where it was trapped, almost stagnant, between ship and shore. He looked at the more battered of the two with satisfaction. Yes, surely that one had just sailed from the Old World. This time he would know for certain if there was no word from his father. He shouldn't have trusted his apprentice; perchance there had been letters before; he should have come to the ship himself, as now.

Inquiring of several seamen as he approached the jetty where the ships lay, he discovered that his conjecture was right. The master of this ship was Matthew Rolvenden, they said, recently returned from Gravesend and Plymouth. He quickened his pace, smiling slightly. Not only a fellow countryman, but a fellow man of Kent. Surely there would be some news now . . .

He found a lad to lead him to Rolvenden. The narrow steps and galleys smelled stifling and close as he went below, but the master's cabin was surprisingly clean and orderly: instruments of navigation set in their places, the books tied onto their shelves, and a hammock rolled and tied in one corner of the ceiling. The lad stood aside for John to enter. He ducked, too tall to stand upright anywhere on board, and pulled off his hat again.

The master, bowed over open books and charts, did not look up. John took in quickly the thick mane of grizzled, straggling beard, the stained jerkin around the man's wide shoulders.

'Master Rolvenden, sir?'

'Aye.' Still the master did not look up.

'The name's Fessenden, once of Chilham, and I think you may have a letter for me.'

'Fessenden, ye say?' The master's head came up, and John saw that one of his eyes was missing, the empty socket a raw, purplish dent in his face. 'Fessenden?'

John was startled by the ugly face squinting to examine him. 'I have a letter for you to take, too, but first — I am, as I did say — one of your own

192

countrymen.' He turned the rim of his beaver uneasily in his hand, not liking the scrutiny.

'*Once*,' the other repeated laconically. But then the master pushed aside his stool, reached to some hatches behind him, and lifted one of the flaps. 'Aye, Goodman Fessenden, I've a message for ye. Addressed to Eliot Street in Cambridge.'

'That's right.' His heart began to pound.

The master cocked his head on one side. 'It'll cost thee.'

John paid him and took the letter. He recognized the Fessenden seal on the outside and bowed. 'I'm grateful, sir.'

''Twas one Robert Fessenden did give it me.' The man looked curious, still watching with his one eye.

'Thank you. 'Tis one of my brothers. Fair sailing, I hope?'

'Aye, could ha'e been worser.'

'Godspeed, then, Master Rolvenden.'

The man sneered. 'Good *luck* t'ye, Fessenden. What's a man o' Kent doing on these shores?'

John stopped, still stooping to duck the doorframe. He felt an unfamiliar lump in his throat. 'Sometimes, I know not, truly, but the Lord — '

The master threw back his head and cackled. 'Ha! A more honester Puritan I ne'er met ere this!'

John scowled and went up on deck again, through the bulwark hatch, and over the gangplank to the jetty. As he stepped over the slight gap, the ship yawed, nearly sending him into the water; he realized how easily he had forgotten the continual surge and roll of the sea. Still clutching the two letters, he hurried to the bottom of the thoroughfare by the harbour and sat down on a capstan.

His fingers damp with sweat, he broke his father's seal and unfolded the letter. Irrelevantly, he remembered that he had not given his own letter to Master Rolvenden. But the ship would not be sailing again yet, and this letter from Robert would doubtless require another reply.

He looked at the top of the paper, where his brother had written 'March 1648', then read on.

Brother: the news is ill. Our father hath departed this life, and I have buried him with our dear mother in Chilham. I bear all at home, when I am not to the wars, for Isaac will not and should not return. Mary Snode is sent to Isaac at mine own behest, for Patience and I cannot have her. Our trade is fallen off, thanks to the villainy of the lords, nobles, and servants of Charles Stuart. Greetings to thy wife. Your servant, Robert.

He folded the letter. His eyes stung, and he turned his face to the eastern horizon, to where far off from Cambridge the sea curved and blended with the clouds. He wept. Kent was far away. He would never see his father again.

He leant forward, removed his hat, and covered his face with the back of his hand. He remained still, weeping, for a long time.

Then it came to him that the seagulls were still circling and screaming overhead and that the water was still slapping and swashing against the harbour wall and under the jetties. He remembered soon the words of the psalmist: *Deep calleth unto deep at the noise of thy waterspouts, and all thy billows are gone over me. Yet the Lord will command his lovingkindness in the daytime, and in the night his song shall be with me, and my prayer unto the God of my life.* Then he sat up again slowly and opened his eyes. Striking away the tears, and confident of his father's entry into the New Jerusalem, he began to think of his brothers. His mind moved painfully, and he let his head droop.

Why had Robert sent Mother Mary away from Chilham? Mary had mothered them all, had even kept faith with the absent Isaac. And, apart from their father, only Mary had written to Jane all these years; no letter from Robert — until now.

Puzzled, he tried to recall Robert's demeanour towards their step-mother. He realized he couldn't recollect Robert's ever seeking her out or speaking to her unless it was necessary. But then, he reflected, his brother was a man of few words anyhow, hardly speaking even to his brothers. And to give Robert his due: since he had gone deaf, the effort of discourse, John had concluded years ago, must be great.

194

He wondered now what sort of a father Robert was to his children. Mary would have loved and cosseted them, just as she had fussed over Isaac, but he could not imagine Robert or Patience tolerating Mary's gentle, soft ways with children — certainly not now his father was gone. Perhaps that had been the rub between them. Thomas, Nicholas, and Josiah must be growing up apace — please God not as delinquent as Nathaniel — but no doubt they tried him sorely, like any boys. Aye, perhaps the children had added unwittingly to the strife.

And what of Isaac? That generous, joyous child had probably not changed as a young man. John could still not believe the news of the May Day brawl or of the hasty marriage to Rebecca Longden, news that had reached him from his father. In fact, there were many questions and doubts in his mind about those years in his family's history. Jane had always said that there was something strange about the resolute silence (except from Mother Mary) about Isaac once he had settled permanently in Maidstone. Isaac — had he been banished, or had he chosen to be? And it had grieved John that his younger brother had never sent news to him directly. Any news had come through Mary, and now Mary, too, was banished to Maidstone. *I must pray for them all*, he thought, *and pray that Mary writes me.*

He reread Robert's letter and broke the seal on the one he had just written. It was useless now; he would have to write another.

Lifting his head again and staring out across the water, he straightened his back. His father had raised three sons (and three daughters) and had greatly built up the Kentish cloth trade. He had served the Lord all his life and had lived to be an old man. What more could a man expect?

It occurred to him that had he remained in Kent, it would have fallen to him to try to rebuild the local wool trade; the war between King and Parliament could not go on for ever. He was relieved now that this was Robert's lot, not his.

No, his lot — under Providence — was to work for the establishment of a godly city on a new hill beyond the ocean. To bring up Nathaniel in the knowledge and fear of the Lord. To care for Jane.

Suddenly he longed for his wife. Stifling the renewed urge to weep, he turned back up the steps and went to find her.

The pain in his jaw reasserted itself even through the grief for his father and the uneasy thoughts of Mary, Robert, Isaac, and Nathaniel. It was a reminder, however, that he was alive, though his father was now dead.

5

GEORGE
Goudhurst, 9 May 1648

Elizabeth clung to his sleeves. Her wide brows were
straight and low over her eyes as she looked up at him;
in the darkness, her eyes gleamed in the uncertain light
from the lantern she held.

'I must go, love,' he murmured. Beside him, the mare
shifted, grazing her hooves on the bricked courtyard,
her saddle leather creaking. In the shadows of the
stable, one of his servants waited at a distance with
another horse.

'George, I'm afraid,' she begged. 'I dread thy going
away, especially now.'

'Now?'

'The war — the King's rebels riding through. And
Parliament's men.' She shuddered.

'The King's rebels?' He smiled faintly. 'Bess, and
pray what dost think I am? Thou'rt married to one,
thyself.'

'A very gentle one, though. And not a notorious
scoundrel like some of them.'

'Gentle to thee, aye,' he said grimly. 'And no doubt
the other "rebels" are gentle to their own womenfolk,
too. But you have naught to fear, sweetheart. All Kent
will rise ere long.'

She shrugged and sighed. 'Perhaps!' Then she
frowned again. 'But tell me again how long thou'lt
be gone.'

He put his foot into the iron and swung himself
up onto the mare. She skittered sideways away from
Elizabeth, dancing over the bricks and shaking her
head until the bridle and bit jingled. George reined her
in and leaned forward against the mane to steady her.

The old wound in his leg was aching. 'I cannot say, you know I cannot.'

'But the trials could go on for weeks.'

He pressed his hand against the bags he had strapped onto the back of the saddle. 'Aye, they could. Thou'lt have Matty and young Edmund to look after thee, and the girls to look to — ' he dropped his voice ' — and you know where I've hidden the little extra gold I've had . . . ? Aye, you'll do well, my love.' He saw her eyes fill with tears as she shook her head, so he bent to put his hand under her chin. 'What's this? Tears? You're not a-breeding again, surely?'

She shook her head again and wiped them away on the back of her wrist, laughing a little. 'No . . . but, George — I don't understand why the committee chose thee — of all people — to sit at Canterbury. Why? Everyone knows you support the King.'

He narrowed his eyes. 'No, Bess, you know not what you say. You're privy to what I think, but there be few others I can trust — except Mainy and one or two besides. And we've lain low for years. The Kent Committee hardly knows who I am now — just another justice who's caused no harm, while some are so hot-blooded — '

'Aye, Lovelace and his fellows — '

'Hush, sweetheart.' He turned in the saddle. 'Mainy is Lovelace's cousin. They both love the King — and we never know who may overhear us.' He pinched her cheeks. 'And when did you last see a Roundhead here? Hmm?'

She stiffened. 'Pray God I never shall!'

'But *when*? Think now.' It suddenly became important for her to remember, and for him to press her to be calmer. In the last few months she had seemed less able to think clearly, less able to concentrate on anything except himself and the children.

She puckered her forehead and dipped the lamp so that the flame danced madly and the shadows wavered over her face. 'Not since the beginning, 'tis true. Five years? Or is it six?'

He felt his advantage and pressed it further. 'And why, pray?'

Her head went back again. 'Because we paid them off when they took so much of our substance?'

Violently, he wrenched his hand away from her face. 'No — never! Never! Is that what you thought?'

'George — ' Her voice broke. 'These may be our last moments, and we're quarrelling. I'm too *tired*.'

He hoisted his right leg back over the horse's tail and dropped down beside her again, full of remorse. 'Forgive me! I'm sick with worry myself, but trying to put a brave face on't. But truly . . . thou dost not need fear the Roundheads here, nor King's men, neither. Since we did as we were bid — or so Livesey thought — by him all those years ago, we've been left alone, haven't we? And yet, none of the King's men who are privy to my thinking doubts me.' He reached out to her and pulled her head against his chest. More than anything, he wanted her to believe him. More than anything, he wanted to believe himself.

'Left alone, you say? Left *alone*, aye,' she answered bitterly, her voice muffled by his jerkin, 'alone, but poor.'

He tightened his hold of her shoulders. 'Nay, even that's not true. Look.' He bent and took the lantern from her hand and held it up towards the back of the house. 'They can force us to shut half this place — as we've done — to pay our rents to the County Committee, and to grow barley for their troops . . . but this is still ours, and one day the King will be out from captivity in Carisbrooke Castle, and all shall be restored.'

Canterbury, 10 May 1648

The Town Hall chamber was stuffy. George nodded, jerked awake, and nodded again. The County Committee had decreed that they would settle routine matters first, and he found them as dull as the county assizes at Maidstone. He resolved to say little and to keep his seat in the middle bench of the hall, saving his tongue for when he might have need of it later. But as the parliamentarian justice droned on, he found himself increasingly sleepy.

His drowsiness was short-lived. The arrogant, snapping voice of Sir Anthony Weldon cut the air again and again, and more than once he caught sight of Michael Livesey in his place at the hall doors, moving in the shadows like a malignant snake. *Pray God I be not recognized,* he thought, but then gave thanks that his hair was scarcer than it had been in earlier days. And as he looked around he was not the only one still faithful to His Majesty King Charles.

He realized, too, that he had come a long journey since his first, timorous stand against Livesey six summers before. He would be less afraid, now, to contend with Livesey than he had been then.

The sergeants — Wilde and Creswell — stood near the justice. As the introduction ended, George's eyes came wide open, and he searched the room. He caught the eyes of several others, men he knew to be Cavaliers, far more bold and outspoken than he had been in recent years but — like himself — silent for the present. They were men who had lost land and houses and still stood for the King.

And what had he done, he suddenly asked himself angrily. Little in comparison, except for an inglorious skirmish on Marston Moor, when he had been wounded, then dragged into the tent to have a musket ball cut out of his thigh and the wound salved and bound; little except an even more inglorious confrontation with the vulgar fellows of Canterbury last Christmass. And little indeed in comparison with the men the Cavaliers had called martyrs for Kent — those who had languished in Leeds Castle since the riots and now awaited trial . . .

His eyes roamed over the crowded hall. Was it his imagination, or were other eyes kindling? There was a slight stir as men adjusted their jerkins or shifted on the benches.

George disliked Sergeant Wilde instantly. As all the accused were penned in the dock, the man's opening remarks about the Christmass rioters sounded bloodthirsty. Had he not witnessed some of the struggles himself? Were these men — some of whom were guilty of merely playing football or hanging holly at their doors — the vicious criminals Wilde reported them to be?

Listening, he began to scowl. But then laughter broke out as Creswell stood to close the charge. The sergeant shuffled apprehensively, darted a look at Wilde, and proclaimed, 'God save the King!'

The words were customary but had not echoed in Canterbury halls for years. Moderates and Cavaliers broke into laughter, but Parliament's men rose with a shout of fury.

Livesey ran from his post at the door. 'Troops! Send for ten companies this very hour!'

Wilde raised his mace and called for silence, but the laughter spread, turning to mocking and jeering. Some of the prisoners began to laugh and call, 'A King, God save His Majesty!'

Weldon rose at the front of the hall. 'Ye make mirth?' he screamed over the din, and his jowls trembled. 'A comedy of solemn justice! We shall adjourn.'

'Never!' cried one Cavalier, rising to face him.

Wilde advanced upon the man, threatening him, and — watching hopelessly — George knew he might soon be watching tragedy, not comedy.

'Sergeant Creswell! Sergeant Creswell!' Wilde appealed to his colleague.

All around the room, men slowly lowered themselves to the benches, and attention was riveted on the two sergeants.

'Brother Wilde, I am doing as law bids, and that you know.' Creswell's voice was low in the still hall.

'Fool! Old laws made void — ' Wilde's voice was harsh, ' — when Charles Stuart saw and heard the key turn in the door of his Carisbrooke prison.'

The murmuring began again, and George sat forward, fascinated, though his heart still raced with anxiety.

Wilde went on, 'There be a statute, the Statute of Twenty-five . . . it makes plain our right to arrest and hang the dissident Kentish gentlemen and rogues in this place. Under law of King Edward III, Livesey should bar the doors and hold all fast within.'

George rose, among many this time. He felt the blood rushing to his face. Around him, men were hallooing and cursing, and his voice joined theirs. A few other men rushed out, their faces drained and panicked.

'Nay — ' Creswell held up his mace and drew himself up. 'We durst not apply this statute. These men are not guilty of levying war on their king — as the statute intends. They are in no way guilty of such — but if we continue in this vein, sir, we may like to be hanged by your fine statute ourselves. So say no more of Edward III's laws, pray.'

George grinned, and flashed a look at Weldon. The committee man's face was a sculpture of grim fury, but Weldon could not argue with Creswell. Wilde, too, was silenced, and everyone seemed suddenly aware of a break in the tension, for many leaned back. For a few moments the case against the rioters proceeded, but George felt a crushing indignation. This was no impartial commission. Only Creswell seemed honest, resolved to play fair. And what of the jury?

He counted them off mentally, most of the faces known to him: men of old families ... Edward Dering's son, Oxinden, Harfleete, Hobday, Thornhill, Broadnax ... and almost all — he knew — loyal to Charles. His mouth twisted. *Oh, what a thorn in the side of the commissioners this jury might prove!* Weldon would be bested at last.

George lifted a mug of ale to his lips. It was years since he had sat down of an evening at a city inn — except last Christmass with that extraordinary tailor fellow. The homely Star and Eagle, next to St Mary's in Goudhurst, was hardly a city inn, and not since he and Elizabeth had wed had he felt any desire — or had any freedom — to while away the evening hours over slow mugs of Kentish ale at the inn.

Beside him, Mainy and Filmer flashed him quick-silver smiles, and all around the men's voices rose and fell in excitement.

'The House wanted a verdict ... Weldon'll have those jurors' heads on a platter yet ... '

'Nay, the man's stark mad. Who'll stand with him?'

202

'"Twas contempt of Parliament.'

Laughter followed. '"Twas better than any play I ever saw of Mr Shakespeare's!'

'Will Shakespeare's? He's long dead, fool.'

'Aye, dead, and his playhouses with him, God rest 'em all.' One of the Cavaliers crossed himself. 'Why talk of Shakespeare's comicry now, when we can watch our own, without fear of being clapped in prison for't!'

'I'm not so sure,' a timid man rejoined. 'We may yet join those poor souls in Leeds.'

The others jeered, and George pitied the man, who promptly stood to leave.

'Let him go!' one of the Cavaliers shouted with a toss of his head. 'We need no cowards here.'

Young Edward Hales of Tunstall leaned forward. He was more richly dressed than any present. 'There'll be no talk of cowards.' The laughter died away; Hales was one of the few they would all listen to. 'Let every man prove his valour. Then we'll see who be the cowards.'

George winced inwardly and exchanged glances with Mainy, but Mainy quickly looked back at Hales, and George found himself strongly drawn by the young blue eyes and flushed, eager face. Would this be the man to lead Kent in yet another rebellion — this time against Parliament?

'Edward Hales is right.' The dark-skinned man beside Hales spoke for the first time. He was not a man George recognized.

'And who be you, sir, that we should heed your affirmation?' one dissenter asked.

All eyes turned on Hales and on his companion, and Hales spoke up, 'Forgive me, gentlemen, squires . . . Roger L'Estrange is here among us. I have awaited his coming many months now. And he may serve us.'

A babble of voices ensued, and George frowned. L'Estrange was a pamphleteer known all over the east of England, but the man was from Norfolk, not Kent.

'How may he serve us, Child Edward?' another man shouted scornfully.

L'Estrange stood. 'I'm willing to draft you a petition. Settle once and for all the just deserts and rights of King and Parliament — and Kent. What say you?'

203

A few of the men jeered; others cheered. George merely groaned. Another petition! Lord, this game had gone on twenty years!

'Go back to Norfolk, L'Estrange,' one man said sourly. 'What good have any of our petitions done us?'

'Nay!' Suddenly George was on his feet, surprising even himself, his mind changed altogether by the other man's loutishness. 'Let's not be so proud we cannot take aid when it's offered.'

'But on what surety?'

Edward Hales stood, too. 'On mine, sir. On mine. You have my word. This man is our ally. Norfolk stands with Kent and with the King.'

'Then where is Norfolk?'

'Here!' L'Estrange spat, jamming his fist onto the table so that tankards pitched and rolled to the floor.

George jumped in alarm, but then gained courage from the renewed stillness and from Mainy's eager look of encouragement.

'Norfolk? Nottingham? Kent? What does it signify what we call ourselves if we be for the king? And what better time to frame a petition than now, when we are all hot, when we are all here and ready?'

'And when I can supply all the arms we need to go in a muster to Westminster,' Hales put in.

The sceptic sneered again. 'Thou'rt naught but a boy — still smooth on the cheeks! To Westminster, pray? And all of London standing trembling under Parliament's shadows? Phaw! Get back to thy nursery!'

L'Estrange glowered across the table at this opponent. 'And get you back to your churchyard, old man. We don't want old blood for this petition. This one's signed in blood — *young* blood.'

George's heart was beating high with excitement. Hales and L'Estrange, he saw, were pitted against only one vocal man. The others — including Filmer and Mainy — were silent. He wanted to divert the argument. Young blood? His blood was young no longer, but it was rising.

He sat down abruptly. 'I believe we should listen to Edward and to Master L'Estrange. Let's hear him out, at least. Kent's never been as resolute, as united as now. Let's hear them out, I say.'

Almost all the men in the room murmured in agreement.

'Very well,' the sceptic allowed, 'but let Hales speak, not this *foreigner,* pray.' And he, too, sat down.

L'Estrange's mouth twisted, but then he turned to Hales. 'Go on, sir.'

While the others sat down again, Hales remained standing. 'I will speak, then, if't be your will. But I shall speak for Roger L'Estrange, also ... The jurors returned *ignoramus,* and the Committee has foundered. I appeal to ye as others have done before, since our fathers were delivered from the laws of the Conqueror, and as they and we have prospered in this fair county — to remember the rebels and think of His Majesty over all else. It cannot be the will of God that our king be 'prisoned in the Isle of Wight. We must demand our rights, and his. Parliament's grown fat by stealing, arrogant by its uncivil army, partial in its laws ... 'tis time to put an end to it, and stop once and for all the villainous taxes levied on us all, or else — '

'Fine words! Fine words!' the sceptic cut Hales off, but then seemed to lose his resolve. 'Very well, Master Hales, Master L'Estrange — begin.' He leaned forward. 'For God's sake let us write this thing and be done wi't.'

Smelling victory, George nodded, smiling at Mainy and even at the sceptic. 'Aye, let's write, and then let's gather men and signatures.'

'And away to Westminster,' Mainy murmured.

'Blackheath,' L'Estrange said. 'We should meet at Blackheath.'

'Aye — and call men from all of Kent to sign,' Hales agreed. 'Young Dering — you can get your cousins, those of Charing and Egerton ... and Thanet can bring in the northern villages ... and there's Barham, and Romney, and St Augustine's ... '

George felt the smile growing on his own face, and Filmer smiled back at him.

What would Sir Dudley Digges have thought this time?

Burham Heath, 30 May 1648

He had scarcely thought of Elizabeth in the frenzied
hours since the petitioners had begun to assemble.
The Earl of Thanet had defected, but some of the
Canterbury Parliamentarians had been persuaded by
the Cavaliers to join the petitioners. By now, George
thought, running his eye over the tents, bundles,
supplies, and horses that indicated the presence of the
absent king's army — by now there must be ten thousand men at least. He and Filmer, along with some of the
other seasoned soldiers, had spent the first few days with
the charge of collecting arms from the nearby houses
without giving offence to the inhabitants. Remembering
Livesey clearly and bitterly, he had done the job unwill-
ingly. Now all they could do was wait until the muster
was over and they could move on to Blackheath.

But the strain was still almost visible. L'Estrange,
Hales, and the Earl of Norwich (now appointed General)
argued hourly with some of the older men about the
wisdom of inviting support from Essex, Norfolk, and
even from men who had fled to France. Commands and
counter-commands issued and reissued from one tent
after another as one gentleman after another claimed
his prerogative to govern his own men as he saw fit.
Meanwhile some of the horsemen were hedged in at
Sittingbourne, and others — grown impatient with long
indecision — had deserted or laid down their arms at
the urging of itinerant Parliamentarians. All was tumult,
rumour, and counter-rumour.

L'Estrange passed the tent that George, Mainy, and
Filmer shared. 'The Earl wants not two days of giving
the King his crown again,' he shouted cheerfully, reining
back his horse only briefly.

Filmer snorted. 'I doubt it, Roger. 'Tis the work of
weeks, not days, much as I wish otherwise.'

'Ill-favoured wretch you are, Filmer,' L'Estrange
mocked. 'Have ye not heard of the ships that left

Parliament's service and seized a half dozen of the coastal forts — or more? 'Twill be Carisbrooke next, I warrant you. I'm defying Fairfax to keep his men in Blackheath. They'll come to us, no doubt.'

A few young men not far away began to sing roisterously:

> *May you unconquered still remain,*
> *Tread down the common foe,*
> *And help the King to the crown.*
> *May ages after say*
> *This noble Kent*
> *Gave the greatest blow*
> *To that cursed Parliament!*

George saw Filmer turn with a faint smile towards the singers.

'Dost think we'll truly be champions of Church and Crown, George?' Filmer made a dismissive wave of his hand as L'Estrange moved away.

George shook his head and sighed. He longed for L'Estrange to be right. 'Nay, I fear not.' He stood up and stretched stiffly. The ground where they had been sitting was damp from rain that morning, and he was weary of waiting, weary of mud, weary of cleaning again the musket he knew he would never use. The wound in his leg was aching again, too. 'Dover's still in Parliament's hands,' he said. 'That doesn't augur well. Fairfax is well organized, while the Earl of Norwich — ' He stopped, hesitant, unsure whether he could voice his doubts, even to Filmer.

Mainy joined them at the opening of the tent. 'Aye, the Earl of Norwich . . . ' His voice was low, full of laughter.

' — Is like to be a sound man,' Filmer said brightly, but his smile was forced. 'Son-in-law of Birling Manor — Abergavenny, you know — hardly a foreigner, George.'

The word 'foreigner' was beginning to grate on George. 'What does it matter whether he was born in Kent, or no?' he muttered irritably. 'We can only be concerned — ' He stopped. Others nearby were staring, and he had unwittingly raised his voice. 'What our care should be is that he be able to exercise his office.'

Mainy and Filmer stared at him; then Mainy said, 'He's as apt as any man who's had no experience of war. He's all frolic and pleasant humour . . . I know not who else is to lead us, but I've little faith in Norwich.'

Filmer nodded slowly. 'There is no one else. But you may be right. We must be on our guard. The men of Kent — we know we can count on them, but the others . . . '

Mainy's mouth puckered in distaste. ''Tis not that the Earl's from out of Kent, friends. 'Tis what I said before — all fun and frolic. Why, I heard this hour that he'd a smuggler as a captain. What sort of a general will he make? Is he the match of Fairfax, think ye?'

'Of course not,' George laughed. 'The Earl of Norwich will make a laughing stock of himself if he seeks to buy off Fairfax's soldiers with money we poor wretches have none of!' He rested the musket against his leg and wiped his hands on a rag. 'Fairfax is too shrewd. He's not in charge of Parliament's men for naught, and he did not chose Oliver Cromwell as his second for naught, either. He knows what he's about, that man. But as for our Norfolk — I'm not so sure.'

Filmer stared back at him gloomily, and Mainy simply nodded. He looked back at them for a moment, retrieved his musket, opened the breech, and sighted down the barrel to make sure it was clean.

He could see a circular patch of blue sky. He remained motionless for a moment, the musket pointing at the sky and the blue circle his only lodestone.

Elizabeth could see that same sky, he reflected. And was she looking up, like him now, only a few miles away, praying for him, perhaps? What would she say? *Thou'rt not in Norfolk's hands, sweetheart, whate'er befalls. Thou'rt in God's.*

He put the musket down, suddenly, and found Mainy and Filmer watching him.

'Clean?' Filmer inquired caustically.

George turned back into the tent and murmured, 'Aye, clean.'

6

ROBERT
East Malling Heath, 31 May 1648

Some of the men had gone with Colonel Gibbon to Rochester and Dover, but. Robert preferred to remain in the column where he was best known: under Oliver Cromwell. They had marched all day from Wrotham through the Downs to Meopham and at last to East Malling, where they were now camped in thick hazel woods. General Fairfax's scouts had seen the King's rebels encamped on Burham Heath, but although the local villagers had fled as Parliament's army of seven thousand had swung south of Maidstone, the enemy seemed unaware that Fairfax was so close.

Battle was imminent now. There was no question in Robert's mind as he lay awake, thinking, thinking. He was wrapped in the ragged bedding he had not carried to battle during the last three years of relative peace.

From the first word that had come to Chilham a week before, he had known that he must rejoin his fellows under Fairfax. Friends of the King were rising all over the county; if he did not stand with Cromwell and Fairfax, who would? But parting from Patience and the children had been sadder than usual because he had been more fearful. It was common knowledge that the Royalists outnumbered them this time, and most were fighting on home ground. So she had wept sorely, standing at the door of the house with Josiah and Nicholas ranged stalwartly on either side of her.

Thomas was swinging carelessly on the gate as he left, playing foolishly — Robert had said — at making a drawbridge. Hannah, timid and shy as ever, held tightly onto Nicholas and gazed up with sloe-eyed awe at his buff coat and helmet.

He passed Thomas, cuffed him on the ear, then stood in the lane beyond the gate to look back at them all. Thomas was shouting as usual, his mouth open and laughing, but as usual Robert could not hear him. He caught Nicholas' eye for a moment. His second son's face was stern and veiled, and Robert knew that it was duty, not love, that kept the child close to his mother now. Nicholas, he knew, had never cared for his mother as much as Thomas did, though Nicholas could be trusted. Thomas, however, was the oldest, and should take that part.

'Go to thy mother, son,' he ordered sharply, turning to face Thomas again. 'Thou'rt the oldest and must provide now.'

Thomas leapt off the gate, landed in the mud, then wiped off his hands on his hose. He signed to his father that he was sorry. Robert reopened the gate, reached for the boy, and held him close. Thomas meant no harm; he was thoughtless, that was all, Robert decided.

Over Thomas' wavy hair he caught Nicholas' eye for the second time; then he released his eldest son and watched him bound to Patience's side. Thomas hesitated at the step, gave Nicholas and Hannah an unceremonious push, then put his arm round his mother.

'And thou, Nicholas,' Robert said, resting his hands on the gate and staring at the mute family tableau only a short distance away, 'thou, my second son, art charged to keep the peace in this house while I am gone. See that Thomas and Josiah do not drive thy mother witless with vain argument. And see that no one oppress thy sister.'

Robert nodded to Hannah and, in a rare rush of tenderness for his daughter, suddenly went back and picked her up. 'Hannah, love, be kind and obedient to thy mother, as thou always art.' She nodded back, and her eyes filled with tears. Some of Patience's fear had transferred to her. 'The Lord of Hosts is watching over us all, Hannah.'

The child nodded back wordlessly and slipped down to catch hold of Nicholas again. Robert searched for Josiah, who was sulking. 'Josiah? Thou must apply thyself to thy books, dost hear? Nicholas is a man in booklearning already, and there's naught but a year or two between ye. When I come back, I'll diligently examine thee myself.' He stopped, his eyes finding his wife's again. Her small mouth was trembling, but her jaw was set tight. How well he knew that resolve!

'Patience, wife, be of good cheer. We'll see these rascals into prison, then it's home again, and peace under God and Parliament for ever.'

She held his eyes a moment longer without answering, but he knew by now that although she had never said she loved him, she would stand loyal no matter what the outcome of the battles ahead. She would also rule the household wisely in his absence.

He'd kept her face in his mind as he swung his pack over the horse's back. Then he set off down the lane with his eyes alert for fellow Parliamentarians he had arranged to journey with. He could not look back now.

Lying now with the rough fabric against his face, he found it hard to picture Patience. She was always elusive when he was away, and he felt suddenly horribly alone and empty.

He hunched forward and tried to pray, but the Lord seemed far away, too. He lay down again and shut his eyes. His father had left a failing business, taken away by the Lord. His brother John was master of a thriving trade but was far away on a shore almost as distant as his father's, with only an ingrate foster-child to be his heir. His other brother Isaac was . . . ah, yes, giving roof to old Mother Snode. *And Rebecca, oh, Christ, was she still as beautiful?*

Moaning, he turned on his side and opened his eyes to blot out the girl he remembered as clearly from May Day all those years ago as if he had seen her on this May Day. Forgiveness — had the Lord granted him that? He was less certain now than he had been before.

He was filled with gnawing doubt. The deafness had worsened — if it were possible — in the last few years. Now even the soft swishing sounds were gone. Stony silence defined his world. He could speak, but even his own voice was lost, and he wondered often if the words still formed themselves correctly or if his speech was as clumsy as he often suspected.

211

Deafness . . . death . . . the disintegration of his family and his trade . . . was anything left? He sighed and looked up at the sky. *The Lord of Hosts is with us,* he thought slowly, *The God of Jacob is our refuge*. And he repeated the words over and over until he fell asleep.

Maidstone, 1 June 1648

Under lowering clouds, the parliamentarian cavalry advanced north from Loose. Robert thought only passingly of his boyhood days riding the same lanes to oversee his father's fullers and millers. The world had seemed lighter then, he thought, remembering clouds of apple blossom, and hedges white with cow-parsley. But it was already June, and the fruit trees had lost their blossoms and leafed out thickly. The lanes were awash with leaves: the yellow-green of the beech leaves, the uncurling of scalloped oak leaves, and the thin grace of long, trailing willow twigs. Only the chestnuts and hawthorn were flowering still: the chestnuts holding up cerise and white candles in the gathering dark, and the hawthorn drenching the air with over-heavy pink-and-white sweetness.

He looked up at the clouds. Strange: it could not be later than seven o' the clock, yet the sky was as black as at dusk. Then he looked at the men riding beside him. They rode in silence now, but only a few minutes ago Livesey had passed through the ranks with the word that the enemy was divided: some to Rochester, some still left at Burham Heath, some to the high ground of Kits Koty, and only two thousand in the city itself.

'They've thrown up barricades on Stone Street,' Livesey had shouted, signing to Robert until Robert had understood what he was saying. 'There's only Mainy and Dudley to lead them. The fool Earl of Norwich has fled to Rochester — in a fright, and no wonder!'

Maidstone is ours, Robert thought gleefully. He could easily imagine the colonels of the King's fragmented army calling first for an advance, then for a retreat.

212

Indecisive, foolish, irresolute men! The battle would be over in no time. Fairfax, though stiff with gout today and complaining loudly of their damp quarters on East Malling Heath — would lead them to victory and see the Royalist rebels and scoundrels to prison in Leeds and Westernhanger Castles.

Large raindrops began to plash onto the leaves overhead. Then the rain began to drum on his helmet; he could feel rather than hear the slight vibration of the raindrops on the metal. And he could certainly feel the coldness of the drops that slid down his neck and under his wide collar; he shivered and hunched his shoulders against it. The air was grey with water; the rain bounced off the summer-hardened road and soon swirled in brown eddies round the horses' hooves.

Then, ahead of the column, he saw the first mound of earthworks raised hastily in place by the Royalists. Enemy troops were drawn up on either side of the road and beyond the earthworks. He could see the red standards of the King hanging limp and discoloured in the downpour.

The horses quickened pace; Fairfax must have given his command. In turn, his own heart quickened. The skirmishes at the bridge over the Loose Stream had been insignificant, and until now he had not come close enough to a Royalist even to raise his musket for the aim.

Somewhere a cannon went off. He could not hear it, but he felt the thudding burst of air strike his breastbone. He pressed forward, even as he saw some of his fellows flee in panic. *Deserters.* They would be caught and shot unless they turned again . . .

Fairfax's cavalry advanced on the barricades. Muskets fired on both sides, the flowers of flame and smoke blossoming all around Robert as the men fired them. Still the horses pressed forward.

Beyond the earthworks, some of the King's men scattered. In the open way they left, Robert could see — even through the rain — the blurred outlines of the houses and shops at the base of Stone Street. They looked different now, however, for all were barred with logs and planks of wood, and defended by musketeers.

Robert's horse laid its ears back and faltered in the noise and confusion. He had to remind himself that the poor animal could hear, while he could not. But it must go forward, so he dug his spurs into the soft flesh, shortened the reins, and pushed forward with the rest.

A great blast from one of the cannons on the top of the hill ahead split the air. The ball slit a furrow through the men only a few feet away, and for the first time, sickness gripped Robert's throat. But he dared not pause to look at the carnage beside him: only to move forward, forward.

His horse veered sharply to one side, snapping the reins, and dodging back through the cavalry in panic. The animal knew his own fear, then. Frantically he reached to catch the leather thongs in his hand, but the horse turned again and flung its head and neck back so forcefully that Robert looped backwards over the tail and found himself surrounded by the legs of several horses, in danger of a trampling.

The other horses snorted, shied, and reared up, but his own lashed out with its hind hooves and then disappeared in the tumult.

Dazed, Robert remained where he was. Hands reached down to pull him up; faces and mouths moved in words and gestures he could not understand. He frowned. *What's happening?* He felt strangely drowsy, and somewhere in his body a pain nagged at him, but he could not decide where.

One of his fellows was urging him up, so he staggered forward clutching his musket and bandolier. The houses and shops swayed as another cannon ball ripped down the hill.

Then suddenly, for the first time in years, the world came clear to Robert. The rain eased briefly, and he could see the standards on both sides quite distinctly. He could also hear quite clearly the roar of the men, the echoing clap of musket fire, the neighing of the horses. He lifted his arms into the rain in frenzied joy.

'I can hear! Livesey! I can hear! Great God of Hosts! I can hear!'

'Out of the way, fool.'

Men surged past him, faces intent, muskets and pikes raised. This was no place to pause. The cavalry had passed him now, and he was among the foot soldiers.

The cannon roared again and belched smoke over the top of King's High Town. All Robert's fear had gone. Laughing, screaming with delight, he ran forward among the pikemen. 'The cannons have given back my ears! I can hear!'

No one listened, but the running men had slowed, and just in front of him his fellow Parliamentarians were fighting the enemy hand to hand. Orders were shouted from both sides, and from cracks in the barred windows came intermittent musket fire and showers of broken pottery. This was a new kind of battle, he thought, fought with new rules. No open battlefield and ordered charges. This was man to man, Kent fighting Kent in its own county town.

'For God . . . !' a Royalist shrieked, bearing down on him out of the crowd with an absurd broadsword raised ready to club him down.

Still laughing, Robert aimed straight at the man's open mouth and saw him drop to the gutter in a gush of blood. The man's cry still echoed in his head, and for a moment another wave of horror squeezed his innards, but . . . by God! he had *heard* the man as well as seen him.

' . . . King Charles, and Kent,' other Royalists were crying.

Maddened shouting broke out all round him, instantly making him dizzy again. The buff and red coats merged, crossed, and separated. Which was the enemy? He paused, half knowing the danger he was in, half denying it, and steadying himself on a doorpost.

Then out of the rabble stepped a Goliath of a man, or so it seemed. The man had lost his hat, but the thick black curls waving onto his broad shoulders proclaimed him unmistakably a King's man. Around them both, bottles and crockery rained down from the jettied windows above, and the rain still fell in black curtains.

'Traitor!' roared the giant, 'Cromwell's fool.' His face was harsh, and he raised a thick wooden club in his hands to strike.

215

Trembling, Robert felt for his helmet, leaped to one side, and raised his musket again. But then he lost his balance, and the houses, sky, and rainwashed street turned a somersault as the other man struck the musket from his hands. He staggered up again immediately and stood defenceless, but still aware that though he might die, he could hear his enemy's voice.

'Fool, thyself, then kill me,' he challenged. Nothing mattered now. 'Your King will be dead ere long.'

The other man came forward, his eyes slits, his breathing hard. He reached out and wrenched Robert's helmet backward so that the leather chinpiece broke, his collar was ripped, and he was almost choked. Unthinking, Robert reached forward for the other man's throat, but then the stranger's face changed and he felt himself abruptly dropped.

'*You* — '

Robert stared back, uncomprehending. Was he not to die after all?

'*Robert* — ?'

Suddenly he knew the other man. He saw his own death in the other man's eyes before he knew death, also.

ISAAC

Isaac dealt death with one unerring blow to the other man's head. Then he stooped for a moment to make sure he had made no mistake. Yes, the severe mouth and beak-like nose were the same, but the open, horrified, dark eyes were like none he had ever seen, and he recoiled.

He turned, then, and fought his way up the hill. No one challenged him. The troops were still stuffing the ordnance with cannonballs, powder, and rags. He dodged among them and in all the panic and darkness no one heeded him as he scrambled over the huge earthworks.

Outside the Crown Inn on the lower end of the High Street he stopped and retched violently. For two days he had not eaten, and the wrenching spasms of his stomach twisted him with pain and soured his mouth. *I have killed my own brother. My own brother . . . my own . . .* The words corroded his mind and burned as bitterly as the acid in his mouth. But he could not dwell on Robert's death now. As long as the battle raged on Gabriel's Hill, and as long as darkness cloaked the town, he would have a chance of escape. No, he could not think of his brother now, only of reaching safety; he had seen enough of death for a lifetime.

He began to run towards the river. He heard the ragged, frantic sound of his own breathing as well as the musket fire and shouts of battle behind him. How was he to escape now? All the bridges were held by Cromwell and Fairfax, and he knew that to stay in the town or go back down Stone Street was certain death. He could not even hide in his shop; that would never be safe, either. And the battle was all over for him, anyway. *I have killed my own brother . . .*

On the edge of the Fair Meadow he hesitated again. The expanse of shadowed grass and trees looked eerily quiet. Roundheads might well be hiding there to ambush the unwary. But no, they had come up from Loose, funnelled into Stone Street and Gabriel's Hill where the King's men waited. There was no reason why he should be caught here.

On the bank of the river he shed his boots and jerkin and dropped the club he had clasped unconsciously all the way up Gabriel's Hill. If only he could cross here, then again near Wateringbury, he might be able to reach Rebecca and the children without meeting the enemy soldiers who were spread out all over the southern edges of Maidstone, Loose, and East Farleigh.

He looked down at the black water. With all the rain it was angry and swollen. No, he could not swim; it was foolish to think so. He reclaimed his clothes and went back a little way and sat under a linden tree with his back pressed against the bulbous trunk, the rain dripping unevenly from the branches and leaves above.

The familiarity of the sound steadied him, and the noise of the siege had faded somewhat in the watery night. From up in the market-place the courthouse

217

clock chimed ten, answered then by All Saints and St Faith's Chapel.

He put his head on his knees and wept. It was the second time this year he had wept. When their third living child — born only a few weeks ago — had died, he had cried then, too, after years without tears. He had wept for Rebecca's loss — for she had longed for the little girl child who had died, as others had died before. But he had wept, too, for the unnamed child herself, buried now in St Mary's churchyard in Goudhurst.

Goudhurst. It was a long way to Goudhurst. But he had taken Mary his stepmother, Adam, Charlie, and Rebecca to Goudhurst for safety some time ago, to her cousin's house. He must somehow find his way there from the Fair Meadow.

And he wept here also for the silent dancers who years before had skipped and laughed on Fair Meadow under the same sky, then sunny, that now spouted rain on his bare head.

Thirteen years. He shut his eyes tightly, caught his breath, and pushed away the scalding grief. The day he had fallen in love with Rebecca, and the very same day Robert had stolen her from him. *Stolen.* The word was right and fair. Robert had stolen not only her maidenhead; he had stolen her joy, her laughter — even her beauty. Ever afterwards she had been thin and cowering as a hungry rabbit in the winter woods around Chilham. Always cold, always fearful. Robert had stolen her from him, and the girl who skipped on Fair Meadow under the May sunshine was buried as it were at her father's old house near the Shambles. Another Rebecca lived on as his wife: a Rebecca he loved as much but who was no laughing Queen of the May garlanded with honeysuckle and cherry blossom.

He clamped his teeth hard together. *This was all Robert's doing.* But then he remembered Robert's last look of horror again, remembered that the man he had killed was his own brother. The tears burned his eyelids, and bitterness rose into his mouth again.

The cannons roared from the High Town. Were they still fighting? How long would the battle drag on? How long would he be safe here?

Pushing himself forward painfully, he lurched onto his knees, intending to stand and walk again, though did not yet know where. But as soon as his knees touched the yielding softness of the sodden grass, he bowed his head down and found himself praying.

For years, angry with Providence, he had spoken few words to God. The God he had known as a child was the hateful, fierce God of Robert and — at times — of his father. But now he was talking to the God of his stepmother Mary: the loving God who forgave and understood and called him his son. Could this Almighty God forgive even murder? He shuddered.

But I did not know 'twas Robert until — I did not know — O, Lord —

He crouched down further, the rain running forward on his neck and up into his thick hair. Then a picture came into his mind of the thin, sharp-faced woman, Patience, whom Robert had wed. They had borne children, he knew, for Mary had spoken lovingly of them all: Thomas, Nicholas, Josiah, Hannah. *Little ones, fatherless ones. I promise thee, O God, that I shall care for them . . .*

He scrambled up and wiped the mud off his hands onto his breeches. His own sons would be fatherless if he did not find a way back to Goudhurst. He strode towards the Medway again.

On the bank he paused to listen. Thinly through the rain he heard the shout of men's voices and the crackle of musket fire. He could not go back.

He threw his jerkin aside but held his boots aloft. *I must swim with these boots, somehow, please God.* But he knew they would fill with water and sink, so he tied them upside-down inside his belt. Then he plunged into the water.

The cold rush of it took away his breath. He rose to the surface, gasping. Immediately a swell surged up and slapped him under again. He thrashed blindly, surfaced again, and struck out for the far bank, praying he would not flounder into quicksand or marsh on the other side. Around him the water pulled and swirled; every lift of his arms begged desperate effort. The boots turned over and were filling with water.

219

Their weight began to pull him down. He wrestled with his belt, slipped under the water again, then managed to wrench it off. Instantly the boots disappeared in the flood, and he was buoyed up with a renewed freedom and energy.

In the dark he strained to see the far bank. It seemed nowhere near. Was the water sending him downstream to Allington? He flailed wildly in a sudden panic, but then his bare feet touched sand and he propelled himself forward with his last strength.

His head struck a wooden surface. More in surprise than by choice, he reached up and found himself bobbing madly with his hand on a craft moored by the edge. Pulling himself hand over hand around the prow of the small vessel, he found the mooring rope and held on tightly to its twisted and swollen fibres. Never had a rope offered so much security. Never had he thanked God as he did now.

On the leeside of the boat he floated in the rising and falling water with his feet grazing the river bottom. His heart clamoured and his teeth chattered with excitement and cold, but he knew that neither Roundheads nor King's men would catch him now; he could regain his breath and make his way back in the dark.

He hung in the water for several minutes until he felt calm again; then he heaved himself up onto the bank by the rope and sat dripping by the capstan. His body felt unutterably heavy and spent. For a moment he leaned sideways. Sleep was a cordial he longed to sip, but he could not risk discovery by daylight on the edge of a river. He must walk to Goudhurst and evade the Roundheads all the way.

On his feet, he swayed, braced his feet against the capstan, and turned his face towards the south-west. There would be a climb up into the Weald, but he must ford the river again and skirt round Linton in case Fairfax's reserves were camped there. He could perhaps reach Goudhurst by dawn if he moved with stealth.

The rain had stopped. Maidstone and the fighting, dying men lay miles behind, a world away from the fragrant, drenched orchards and lush fields of the Weald where he walked now.

An overpowering need for sleep sapped his ability to think and move. He stopped at a gateway and leaned against it. His head immediately dropped forward, but his chin jarred on the top bar and brought him harshly awake. He shook himself and trudged on, but within moments he knew he could go no further; he must find a hedgerow or hovel and curl up in it — damp or not — for the sleep of his life.

The gate, he thought dully. *I'll go back to the gate.* He turned, hauled himself over it and stumbled down the long, banked-up rows of earth between the hop poles. The wet earth squeezed up between his toes but felt soft and kind after the rough stones of the road he had followed for some miles. Somewhere in this hop garden would be a hut where the farmer sheltered or kept his balls of twine, or somewhere a stack of hop poles he could set round him as a hiding place . . .

Above him the moon floated between the ragged rain-clouds; it was pale, swollen and waterlogged as a pig's bladder football on the end of a jester's stick-and-bells. It gave meagre light in the blanketing darkness, but it gave comfort. He lifted his face to it and went forward again until he came to the end of a row. For an instant he thought of following the ditch a few rows to one side since he had walked down the central row — the row where he would most likely be discovered — but he was too weary now to take those last steps, and so he sank down where he stood. Insensible to the cold raindrops that clung to the leaves around him, he dropped into the long furrow of sleep.

He might have been asleep for a moment or for an hour — he did not know how long — when a violent tug on his bare foot sent him bolt upright and shouting in terror.

'Don't move! Don't move or thou'rt a dead rat!'

The farmer. In the dark? Something cold and hard was piercing his side, right against his ribs. He froze.

'Thy name? What art thou?' The voice was a command, sharp and peremptory.

221

Isaac's body was now twisted into an awkward posture. He wanted to shift but dared not. In the dizziness of a sudden awakening his head hardly seemed to belong to his own body, and the voice issuing from the darkness — equally disembodied — seemed unreal.

The cold point twisted against his skin. 'Answer me, you scoundrel!'

This time as the other man's voice rose shrilly, Isaac heard something else: fear. 'I'm but a tailor . . . of Maid — of Goudhurst, sir . . .' He heard the same fear in his own voice, and was surprised.

'A tailor! Then what in — ?' The voice stopped, and the sharp metal moved away.

In spite of himself, Isaac smiled. Was the man a simpleton? Would he believe anything he was told? He murmured, 'Aye, I was caught in Maidstone against my will . . .'

'Maidstone? Then what art thou, I say? Speak, or thou'lt taste this musket.'

'You'd slay an unarmed, unshod man, sir? Fie, for shame.'

'But I cannot see thee . . .'

Isaac quickly drew up his legs. 'Then may I stand, sir?'

Back came the tip of the musket in his ribs. 'Nay. Stay where thou'rt, *and tell me thy name.*'

'Fessenden, sir.'

The other man let out a hoarse cry. 'Fessenden? Of Chilham?'

Something in this exchange of words was familiar. Isaac struggled with the memory but lost it. 'Nay, that was my father. He's dead, sir. Died a four month ago.'

'Of Maidstone then . . . and Robert's thy name?'

Isaac felt a convulsion run through his body and found his face contorting in anguish, 'Nay, 'twas my brother . . . died this very night fighting . . . for Lord Fairfax.'

The musket dropped suddenly, the stock ringing against a large pebble on the edge of the ditch. Then Isaac heard a clumsy movement as the other man dropped down beside him. The man's breathing quickened, and his face came so close to Isaac's that he could feel the breath on his face. 'Then you are Isaac Fessenden?

Of course . . . the *tailor* Isaac . . . but I did not think you were of Fairfax's persuasion.'

Isaac's fear had left him. He shifted so that his body was straight again. 'I'm not, sir. I'm for His Majesty.'

'Ah —' The other man's breath expelled faintly. 'That's good.' Then he gave a shaky laugh. 'But I mistook thee for a Roundhead! Nearly killed thee — Master Fessenden — do you remember that riotous day last Christmass in Canterbury?'

Somewhere in the top of a tree a nightingale rolled out its song. Isaac searched the darkness with his eyes; the light was coming, and he wanted to look this strange, foolish man in the face. 'Of course,' he answered guardedly.

'And George Tolhurst, to whom you gave the little blue coats?'

His own breathing quickened. 'Tolhurst? Yes, of course I remember.' And wasn't there a squire Tolhurst in the village of Goudhurst he'd never seen? Could this be the same man?

There was a moment's silence except for the breeze rising in the hop leaves. ''Tis I, George Tolhurst, for His Majesty likewise.'

At dawn, reassured by each other's company and by their distance from the town, the two men went across country under the inverted, pale green bowl of the sky. They exchanged stories, and Isaac discovered that George had fled along with Mainy when the outcome of the pitched battle became apparent. The Royalists had been driven all the way into St Faith's churchyard.

'Many of us fled,' Tolhurst admitted. 'We have wives and children, and the King wasn't coming to our aid. We must wait for his pleasure or his end, I suppose . . . but I lost my horse and some of my friends, for we were all scattered. Hales, L'Estrange . . . they fled, too, though I know not whither. Brockman is killed, and Norwich retreated to Greenwich . . .'

In return Isaac related his own tale, and as light shortened the shadows of the hop poles around them, he saw the sadness lengthen on his companion's face.

'Your own brother, Master Fessenden?'

223

'Yes, sir.'

'Ah, poor lad,' Tolhurst sighed. 'You must tell me of all this — if you will.'

'Yes, sir, I shall.'

Tolhurst stopped and faced him. 'Hold, you may be a yeoman by birth and have lost your boots. But though I'm a gentleman farmer, I've lost my horse — which is a good deal worse, I lay. And under the King we are brother soldiers, and under God — brothers.' He blinked, and Isaac began to smile at his dancing eyes; clearly the man was rarely given to such long speeches. 'So have done with this "sir", pray.'

Isaac laughed. What a strange, affectionate man he was! 'So I shall, then — George.'

They went on in silence for a while, Tolhurst limping slightly. Isaac limped, too, for his feet were cut now, even through the calloused skin, and beginning to make every step painful. He could not help wincing, but then to distract himself began telling Tolhurst about his brother — even about Robert's betrayal of Rebecca. Now that his brother was dead, he reasoned — and here was a man he knew without doubt could be trusted — it gave him relief to tell another what had happened.

Tolhurst murmured in sympathy, asked a few pointed questions, and listened carefully. 'You cannot condemn yourself,' he said at last. 'Until the helmet came off, you didn't know who the man was, and cannot therefore be blamed. No man alive would have done other than you did, Isaac.'

Isaac felt his throat swell as if he would cry again in response to such generous and spontaneous pity. Embarrassed, he stopped, picked two ferns from the hedgerow, and busied himself soothing his feet with the leaves so that he would not have to look into Tolhurst's face. He could not bear to think of Robert any more.

The other man, perhaps knowing his humiliation and revulsion, kept walking, though more slowly, his steps still faltering. 'But why came you to Maidstone? You said you were caught there. Surely you did not go to the muster in Penenden Heath or Burham Heath?'

Isaac quickly shook his head. 'Nay, I knew nothing of what was ado until I came to Loose this morning . . . no, last morning . . . ' He rubbed his eyes and crinkled his brow. 'Lord, I know not even what day it is. I was about my business — nothing untoward — fetching cloth at the mills there. Lo and behold the whole village was astir with word of Fairfax's coming.'

'And you joined the King's men?'

Isaac shuddered and started walking again. 'I've had no great love for Cromwell — no, not even when those idle Royalists would attack my stall in Canterbury last Christmasstide. But I'm a family man, and my father was of the godly folk, and I never thought to fight with any man . . . until my brother turned against me, against Rebecca. Then I hardened my heart against him and against all his kith and kin among the Puritans, wanted none o' them. I'm for the King, through and through.' He thought of his stepmother, suddenly. 'There be only one Puritan I trust — ' Then of John, to whom he ought to have written when their father died. 'Or mayhap, two.'

Tolhurst's brows rose in inquiry.

'Aye, my father's second wife, Mary. She lives with us now that Father's gone. And my brother John, though I've naught to do with him these years, as he's away to the New World.' He was abreast of George again.

'And your goodwife? And the boys? And your stepmother . . . ?'

'In Goudhurst for the while. My wife's family lived there once. They're safely lodged with cousins until the war in Kent subsides.'

George looked surprised. 'I'm taken quite aback. I did not hear of it. But this is good news! We shall be neighbours!'

'For a short while.' Isaac looked down, frowning, uneasy with the other man's warm appraisal and reluctant to give away his own uncertainties. 'But it cannot be for long, sir.' He felt that Tolhurst's apparent liking for him could not possibly last; gentlemen — even farmers — simply did not speak this way to yeomen.

'*George.*'

'Not for long, George,' he repeated ruefully, but then he smiled again; Tolhurst's grin was contagious. 'I have my shop in Maidstone.'

The other man shook his head. 'You'd be safer in Goudhurst for now. So would your sons. There's no telling how long Parliament's folly and the King's imprisonment will endure.'

Isaac scoffed, 'No, but your Goudhurst tailors won't welcome another, and I have built up my trade. I cannot but return when there is peace again. I have too many to feed now.'

George looked troubled. 'I'd be glad to serve thee in any way I could.'

They went on side by side, their eyes fixed on the climb ahead to the sleeping village of Goudhurst.

Goudhurst

A small, thin child sitting in a window-seat by the front door saw them — or one of them at least. Isaac saw her throw down her handwork, disappear from the window, then fling herself out of the front door. She ran wildly down the brick path towards them. Her hair, he noticed, was a golden-red cloud around her head; the breeze blew it back as she ran under the early morning light, and her cheeks were pink as chestnut flowers.

'Father! Father!'

She had not properly seen him, and Isaac's throat tightened painfully again as he saw the look of intense love and longing on the girl-child's face. What did he know of little girls?

George bent down, squatting on his haunches, as his daughter flew into his arms. Standing a few paces behind them, Isaac could see the breadth of this man's back, the ridges of muscle across his shoulders. *Whatever else Tolhurst is*, he thought, *the man is no weakling or coward because he loves his family more than battle*. It was an irrelevant, unexpected thought slipping between the leaves of his mind: there and gone.

George rose painfully, still holding his daughter, and for the first time Isaac noticed that one of his legs was positioned oddly. Had the man been injured?

226

'Thou'rt looking at my Marston Moor leg,' Tolhurst said wryly, following the gaze.

'Aye, forgive me . . .'

'Musket fire. 'Twas messy. But I was lucky to get out alive at all, I suppose. So many were cut down, and it rarely troubles me.' The dazed, bemused smile Isaac had seen on his face as he stood up had gone now, replaced by the distant stare of memory. Then the eyes focused again. 'However, Isaac Fessenden, enough of war for this day. And thou'rt uneasy thyself, I see, on those poor torn feet. Come, my wife will dress them for thee ere — '

'Nay.' Isaac backed off. George was hospitable, but he did not belong at Tolhurst Court. The little girl's cool, direct eyes told him as much. *Go away. I want my father to myself.* And the thought of her tall, queenly mother bathing his feet — no, it was not possible.

'Indeed, you shall stay. Your way lies another mile or more, does it not? And we'd not suffer even a beggar to go from our gate with feet as cut as thine.' George's hand came out to him. 'Pray, be not proud.'

Not knowing why, Isaac let his eyes go to the little girl's face again.

Her eyes dropped, and the colour in her face deepened. She bobbed a curtsy, and Isaac suddenly wanted to laugh at this formidable little piece of womanhood. 'Please stay, sir, as my father wills it and you are his friend.'

George clapped his hands together and chuckled. 'Well spoken, my Anna.'

Isaac looked from one to the other, wooed by their unabashed courting. George: solid, almost bovine in the stoutness of his body, grinning amiably at him with pleasure and — something else? — relief, perhaps, that the Kentish war, though lost, was over. Anna: slight, her coppery hair around violet eyes and faintly freckled, pink skin. How beautiful she would be as a woman!

His own sons passed before his eyes: Adam and Charlie, both about her age; and Robert's, though he had never seen them — Thomas the rascal, Nicholas the scholar, Josiah . . . they must be only a little older. Lucky the young men of Kent growing up to court so fair a maid as Anna Tolhurst! Especially if in time to come a yeoman might court a gentlewoman!

'Very well,' he answered them at last. 'I thank you.'

'Then my wife shall wait upon thee,' George said.

Anna looked at him timidly, her eyes scanning his face, muddy clothes, and bloodied feet. He wondered uneasily how he appeared to her.

III

MAN AND MAID

'Madam I will give to you the keys of Canterbury,
And all the bells of London Town shall ring to make
us merry —
If you will be my love, my one and only dear,
And walk along with me everywhere.'

'Sir, I'll not accept from you the keys of Canterbury
Nor all the bells in London Town to ring and make
us merry.
And I won't be your love, your one and only dear,
Nor walk along with you everywhere.'

'Then Madam I will give to you a pair of boots of cork.
One was made in London, the other made in York.
And I will be your love . . .'

'Sir, I'll not accept from you a pair of boots of cork,
Though one was made in London and the other
made in York,
And I won't be your love . . .'

'Then Madam I will give to you a little silver bell,
To ring for all your servants and make them serve
you well,
And I will be your love . . .'

'Sir, I'll not accept from you a little silver bell,
To ring for all my servants and make them serve
me well,
And I won't be your love . . .'

'Then Madam I will give to you a handsome oaken chest,
Enwrought with gold and silver, and jewels of the best,
And I will be your love . . .'

'Sir, I'll not accept from you a handsome oaken chest,
Enwrought with gold and silver and jewels of the best,
        And I won't be your love . . . '

'Then Madam I will give to thee the embroidered
                silken gown,
With nine yards a-dropping and a-training on the
                ground.
        And I will be thy love, thy one and only dear,
        And walk along with thee everywhere.'

'Then, Sir, I will accept from thee the embroidered
                silken gown,
With nine yards a-dropping and a-training on the
                ground.
        And I will be thy love, thy one and only dear,
        And walk along with thee everywhere.'

1

JOHN
Cambridge, The New World, Autumn 1653

The green light of early Boston twilight capped the houses and cottages of Eliot Street. In the scullery, Jane Fessenden was scouring the bowls and tankards they had used at supper time, and in the kitchen John sat hunched over the table. He was reading the Scriptures, poring over the Book of Amos as the light failed around him. He was too tired to get up and light the candle.

The clatter of trenchers ceased, and Jane stepped back into the room behind him, wiping her hands on her apron. He looked up for her quick smile. She was bending now to find her sewing in the basket by the chimney.

'Thou'lt go as blind as Robert was deaf, if thou dost not light a candle, husband,' she murmured reproachfully. 'And so shall I, what's more.'

'Light it for me, pray, Jane. I'm weary altogether.' He glanced over at Nathaniel, who had flung himself on the settle and now lay there, his face puckered into a disagreeable scowl. John straightened his back and cleared his throat. 'Up, Nathaniel, lazy boy, when thy mother enters the room.'

The boy's only concession was to swing his legs to the floor and sit forward with his elbows on his knees. 'What do you wish me to do, Father?'

The words were polite enough, but the boy grunted rather than asked, and John's irritation mounted. He motioned to Jane to sit beside him, then looked back at Nathaniel. 'Thy mother's toiled all day and still has sewing to do. You can light candles, at least.'

Nathaniel's eyelids slid half-shut, and John saw his jaws tighten. 'Aye, Father, I shall.' And he took a taper from the chimneypiece, lit it in the fire, and brought it to the candles.

John watched his sullen expression with a strange mixture of pride, anguish, and doubt. Nathaniel had grown tall, with a thick, muscled body and large hands that could nevertheless stretch and sew wool and leather deftly. *Could.* But John's anguish arose because of the boy's strong-willed and careless behaviour. If he did not have his way, he sulked, worked slowly, and was rude to those who traded at the tanyard and the shop. What kind of future did the family have in this, its only American son? The lad was only young, true, but by now he should be trustworthy, upright, and diligent.

Nathaniel was none of these things, John knew. He sighed. 'Thou'rt waiting to speak with us, perchance, son?'

Nathaniel's hand stopped over the last candle so that the flame licked up the taper to his fingers. He gave John a cold stare and did not seem to notice the flame. 'No, Father.'

'Foolish boy,' Jane said in a low voice. She bent forward and blew out the spill. 'Thou'lt hurt thyself. And thy speech is discourteous. Amend it, pray . . . Come, you may join us as we read.'

Again, John looked at Nathaniel's face and saw hostility in his eyes before the lids came down and veiled it. He remembered, suddenly, the family Bible readings in Chilham. How impatient had his younger brothers been to hear the closing 'amen' from their father! He frowned slightly, looking back at the closing pages of Amos before him. Could he condemn Nathaniel for the same impatience?

Nathaniel paused by the fire and dropped the last piece of taper into the grate. They kept only a low fire at this time of year, for the coldest weather was still a month away.

'Well, will you join us, or no?'

The boy seemed to have stiffened. He was silent, his eyes leaping first to Jane, then to himself. 'If I have a choice, no.'

232

Jane's head went up sharply so that John felt the bench beneath them shift slightly on its legs. '*A choice*, Nathaniel?' she said mildly. 'Why, of course you must choose.'

'But choose to read, that's what you mean, is't not?'

'Thou'rt an insolent pup, Nathaniel! No, that's not what thy mother means, at all. You must choose now. Thou'rt old enough.' He caught his lower lip hard under his teeth to bite back other words. He doubted that even now — after years of gentle teaching and example — the lad understood.

A triumphant smirk glittered in Nathaniel's eyes. 'Then I'll be off . . . nay . . . *forgive me*.' He bowed to Jane. 'Pray excuse me, Mother, but my brethren bade me meet them on the Common, and I promised I'd come there by seven o' the clock.' He reached up for his surcoat where it hung behind the door.

John knew that Jane longed to ask why the boys of the fellowship were meeting on the Common in the dark, but that she wouldn't. He slowly eased himself up and faced Nathaniel. *At least I am still the taller.* 'For what purpose, pray, Nathaniel?'

The lad swung open the door and laughed bitterly. 'To make *choices*, Father. I bid you good night.'

The room was silent for only a moment, then John groaned. 'Much as it pains me, that boy shall feel the rod for this.'

Jane's face fell, and she swallowed so loudly that he was afraid she would break into weeping.

'We've been too soft with that hot-blooded youth. And now we live to regret it.'

'Will he go a-wenching, think you? Is that what he intends?' She shivered.

'I'll not wait long to see.'

'But thou must rest. Thou'lt not go out in the dark, surely, when evil is abroad?'

'Jane! Jane!' He smoothed back the thinning grey hair only half-covered by her cap. 'We must trust God, who is abroad day and night.' He pointed to the cupboard by the door. 'See, he left the lantern. Were he truly going to the Common, he would have taken it. He'll be off somewhere else. And I'll take the

233

lantern myself . . . But shall we continue the word of God to Amos?'

Jane moved to the bench opposite him. Her face was lined now, though the skin on her cheekbones was still taut, and many of those lines were drawn by laughter. He still loved her as she smiled back at him. 'Aye, read on, John.'

He cleared his throat. 'I was in the seventh chapter.'

'The visions?'

'Indeed.' And he began to read, slowly and low at first, but he heard his voice gathering in power: '"Thus he showed me, and behold, the Lord stood upon a wall made by a plumbline, with a plumbline in his hand. And the Lord said unto me, Amos, what seest thou? And I said, A plumbline. Then said the Lord, Behold, I will set a plumbline in the midst of my people Israel: I will not again pass by them any more: And the high places of Isaac shall be desolate and the sanctuaries of Israel shall be laid waste; and I will rise against the house of Jeroboam with the sword."'

The words filled the room, hovered and hung heavy in the air around them. He stopped and glanced at Jane, whose head was now bowed, her eyes obscured by the curving edge of her cap. Then he looked back at the yellowing page and continued into the next chapter. '"And the songs of the temple shall be howlings in that day, saith the Lord God . . ."'

A minute sound from Jane's lips arrested him. In amusement he looked to see if she had hiccoughed, but her hand was over her eyes now and her mouth was oddly contorted. She was crying, after all, almost choking to hold back the sobs.

'For shame, love,' he reproved her gently. 'What ails thee, now?' And he stretched out his hand toward hers, stroking the chapped skin and murmuring softly.

In answer she let out a gulping wail.

'Ah, don't, sweetheart —' He levered himself up and came round to kneel beside her. Pulling her head roughly against his shoulder, he repeated the words 'Don't, don't . . . what is't?' several times before he could make sense of her reply.

234

'Nathaniel, 'tis Nathaniel,' she finally cried. Her eyes were streaming with tears that he tried to wipe away. 'I foresee the Lord's judgment on him, too. All his wild ways. I know things about him I dursn't tell even thee — '

'What things?' He grasped her wrists and shook them. 'Why didst thou not tell me?' He was surprised at the anger in his voice. '*What* things?' he demanded again.

His wife's hurt, tear-swollen face reproached him, but she answered directly this time. 'He's told me of a maid he means to wed when thou hast loosed him from his apprenticeship. A maid he said thou'd not approve, though I know little enough of her.'

'*What* maid?' He let her go and stood up. 'Wed? Phaw! 'Tis utter nonsense. I'll whip sense into that boy if it's the last breath I draw doing it. Fifteen! Apprenticed! And he's got a wench!'

She reached out a restraining hand. 'Nay, John, wait, thou wast but twenty thyself — '

He turned away furiously and bit down on his lip. Dimly he realized that he had never been so angry. The emotion drained and frightened him; he did not want to be mastered by it. He drew a long, unsteady breath and relaxed a little. 'Aye — but — '

Jane looked up anxiously. 'Thou wast far wiser than Nathaniel.'

He shrugged. 'Wise in choosing thee, aye, but not in other ways, mayhap . . . ' He frowned at her. 'But do you know this maid?'

Jane's eyes slid away from him. 'By name only. She's Owen's daughter — serves at the ordinary.'

He ground his teeth together and reached for the lantern. 'I might have known as much! She's unlikely a maid, drawing ale in that abhorrent place . . . I'll fetch him out for lying and wenching, so I will.'

The lantern shed only a feeble pool of light on the cobbles below his feet, and every time the salty wind gusted up from the harbour, the light wavered and shuddered. John clutched its swinging handle tightly and beat the ground firmly with his staff to make sure of his way.

235

He passed a drunken couple asleep in a doorway. The long forms of their outstretched legs and the tangle of skirts caught his eye only just in time to save him from falling headlong over them. He drew back for a second, hearing the sharp intake of his own breath. Holding the lantern quite near their faces he could see that they were young — the lad scarcely older than Nathaniel. But their cheeks were ingrained with grime, hollowed out under the cheekbones. The girl was snoring, and the sharp smell of sour ale rose to his nostrils. He sighed heavily. Could this be happening in the New World already? Homelessness, hunger . . . ?

He went on more slowly now. The alleyway stank of vomit and cats so that his gorge rose as he groped his way forward. He regretted not having gone the longer way over the Common, especially since Nathaniel might have gone to the Common after all — though he still doubted it.

A gust of fresh air heralded the end of the alley and the more open area of the square where he expected to find the boy. A few flickering candles in draughty windows showed up faintly the uneven outlines of the crude hovels that had been built only a few months before. Other lanterns bobbed round him in the darkness, but they were veiled, and he felt strongly the presence of evil, stealth, and men who would not want to be known to walk abroad in this part of the town at night. Not that he was afraid to be known himself, as he was very soon.

'Goodnight t'ye, Goodman Fessenden.' The voice was civil but seemed to come out of nowhere, somewhat slurred.

He held his lantern aloft and searched the darkness with his eyes. 'Goodnight, friend,' he answered hesitantly.

'Aye, John, ye've naught to fear.' The voice broke into a cackle. ''Tis only poor Gronwort, thy neighbour from Sussex.'

John saw appearing out of the darkness the vacant, witless face of the man they all called 'Gronwort o' Bedlam' — though the name had become affixed to the man more through pity than scorn. He had

236

seen his wife washed overboard on a gale in the great sea crossing and had lost his wits on the same day. Everyone in Cambridge was kind to him, giving him bread and simple tasks in the summer, and a bed in the outhouse or stable in the winter. And now here he was wandering in the darkness with no lantern.

'Alas, poor fellow,' John said gently, and took his arm. 'Ye should be in bed long ere this.' Voices rose in the ordinary — curses and shouting and the sound of splintering furniture that made his stomach churn with anxiety.

'And ye also,' the other replied, so quickly that John almost doubted the tales of Gronwort's weak wits were true.

John held the lantern higher again. 'I'm looking for my boy, Nathaniel. Hast thou seen him? You know him, don't you?' Gronwort had scythed down a field of tall grass for him earlier in the year, and for part of the day had worked with Nathaniel. But would he remember?

Gronwort's tongue lolled out of his mouth, wet and pink like a dog's. He rubbed his hands together. 'Aye, I do.'

John shook his arm with slight impatience. 'Then have you seen him? Pray tell me.'

'I'm thirsty, John Fessenden.'

'Ah, you'd like — '

'A jug of ale, sir.'

John dropped his arm. 'I don't buy ale, Gronwort. Ye'll have to excuse me.'

'And leave me maundering in the dark, neighbour?'

John hesitated, trapped by his own pity and by his concern for Nathaniel. But he would have to go into the brawling ordinary, anyhow, if he wanted to find the boy, for he was now convinced Nathaniel must have gone there. So he reached slowly into his pocket and drew out a coin. 'Here, friend. This will buy you what you want. And will you look for Nathaniel within, and report to me?'

Gronwort took the coin and stumbled away without answering, but John knew the man had understood and

Gronwort took the coin and stumbled away without answering, but John knew the man had understood and would, even in his beclouded state, seek out Nathaniel. Then he remembered. 'Wait, Gronwort!'

'What is't?' The disembodied voice again, now further away, towards the orange lamps of the ordinary — annoyed now.

'Do not tell him, pray, that you seek him. And have a care. The place is ill.'

Gronwort cackled again and slapped his sides in glee; John heard the thwack of his hands on rags and flesh, then another mirthless cackle and a burst of song:

> *Back and sides go bare, go bare,*
> *Both foot and hand go cold.*
> *For sure I think, have I good drink,*
> *No man can do me harm, boys,*
> *No man can do me harm —*

The ordinary door creaked open, and Gronwort vanished within.

John waited, growing cold, and doubted his own wisdom. If Nathaniel were not in the ordinary, he had lost time and money both. And if he were in the ordinary — he shifted unhappily from one foot to the other — he might have to search the place himself, after all.

He leaned his back against the side of a hovel and prepared for a long wait. He found himself praying, no longer afraid, but sorry, longing for the souls of benighted men who hid their faces without — and hurried within — the ordinary to carouse the night away and wake in the filth and squalor of an alleyway in the bleak morning. He remembered the couple he had seen, too, and prayed for their souls, as well. Then he lost account of time, and ceased to notice the noise of the square.

It seemed to him as his senses withdrew that Cambridge was no longer the haven of light, peace, and freedom he and Jane had envisaged. Cambridge was not the city on the hill they had sought. The realization weighed on his mind as he recollected his early dreams among the brethren in Leyden. Things had soured there, too.

It wasn't only the square that seemed dark; suddenly all life seemed oppressive, wearying, and dark as the harbour under massing north-easterly storm clouds. First his father had died, and his own brother Robert had sent Mary away. Then, soon afterwards, Robert had died fighting for Cromwell in Maidstone . . . six years ago, now. A wasted life, he thought. Mad Englishmen! Could they never be content unless spilling one another's blood! And now Isaac had turned sullen, rarely sending news. Mary — faithful Mother Mary — had written that he was exhausted with working to feed his own as well as Robert's family; that Isaac openly argued with Patience each time they met; and that he now claimed allegiance with some of the more outspoken of the Cavaliers, including a certain Squire George Tolhurst, of Goudhurst. All this, she said, troubled everyone, even the gentle Rebecca. Mary had also written to him — though not so often recently — that Isaac sometimes suffered days of black melancholy. On these occasions he would shut himself up; she had heard him grieving — she had written more than once. Only a ride with the donkey-cart to see the mysterious Squire Tolhurst would avail.

Was Isaac perhaps unwisely entangled with another woman?

John put his hand on his brow, wanting to wipe away all the questions. His father . . . Robert . . . Isaac . . . Nathaniel . . . the young couple in the alley-way . . . would none of them find the peace he wanted?

A man and woman muffled in heavy cloaks brushed past him and pulled the door of the ordinary shut behind them.

Peace . . . silence . . . there was silence now. In the dark the lanterns had stopped bobbing. Even the ordinary lay quiet with no one coming or going through the door. Just heavy silence. He stiffened. It was a silence heavier and more fearful than the tumult before. He must know where Nathaniel was!

'A bowl, fetch a bowl!' a woman's voice within cried out.

He walked over and lifted the latch of the door. By the guttering candlelight, he could not immediately discern the faces within. The place reeked of Virginia tobacco, rancid tallow, and ale. He stood still, his head light with anxiety, his eyes straining. *Nathaniel?*

A face pressed close to his in the haze of smoke: distorted, ugly, gibbering . . . it was Gronwort's. Tears made greasy furrows down the man's cheeks, and a groaning cry bubbled out of his mouth. The devil-may-care song of a half-hour before hung between them in mockery —

> *For sure I think, have I good drink,*
> *No man can do me harm, boys . . .*

Other men crowded round, hands gesticulating, shoulders shrugging. The air hummed with confused voices as in a choking nightmare. John wrestled with the fear and darkness around him and called out, 'God 'a mercy! Where be my son?' He grasped Gronwort's collar and shook him, terrified now. He wanted to strike the man out of his babbling folly, but even as he shook him and saw the eyes widen in fear, he relented and checked himself. *Is poor, crazed Gronwort at fault?* Nay, he was only playing messenger.

Abruptly, John released him. The men caught Gronwort as he staggered backwards, his crying redoubled. John felt his heart go cold, chilled by the disorder and dirt in the room. 'Will no one speak to me save this poor wretch?'

'Goodman Fessenden — are you not?'

Ah, a sane voice, though gruff. 'Aye, and looking for my son, if any know of him.' He looked round accusingly, his eyes resting on the tall, rough man who had spoken. A sailor by the look of him: weathered, with great knotty hands and only one fierce, clear eye. The other was missing. Vaguely familiar, somehow.

'I know naught of thy son, Fessenden,' the sailor said harshly. 'But I lay there be a lad here in sore trouble.'

'It *is* young Fessenden,' another murmured.

Then the crowd of men parted to let him through. The sailor led him by the arm to the back of the ordinary. Gronwort followed closely, his arms waving wildly and the loud lament continuing, but John hardly noticed him now. Though the ordinary was not large, he felt as they traversed the few steps through the crowd as if they were walking down a long, tree-tangled Wealden pathway in the dark: fearful, narrow . . . he longed for light at the end.

Instead, someone lay on a cushioned settle with his head in the lap of a buxom middle-aged woman whose hood was thrown back, though she still wore a cloak. He formed an impression quickly: she was decently and modestly dressed with a neat cap and a high-necked dress: a godly matron, by her looks . . . then why was she in this den of wickedness? She was bent over with a sop in her hand, wiping the battered face that was so close to her own. A bowl of water close to her feet was red with blood, and her cloak was splattered by it. She seemed to be whispering comfort.

He stared in disbelief and dismay. Nathaniel? Was he dead? No, the lad was sorely injured. Trembling, he rushed forward and fell to his knees by the woman.

'What ails thee, Nathaniel?' His voice came out in a strangled cry; he scarcely knew it. The swollen eyelids flickered but did not open. John reached for the boy's shoulders to shake and revive him. Surely this was some nightmare?

'Nay, doan't thou tooch the puir lad, sir,' the woman begged him. Her speech was thick with a north-country accent he did not know. "E's been a-brawling, this wild boy, so 'e 'as.'

'But 'tis my boy!'

The woman continued stroking Nathaniel's face and wiping away the blood. He stared at her, half bewitched, half angry. Who was she to cradle his own son? Ah, but Nathaniel was not his son.

'Then pray, sir, pray as ye've ne'er prayed to this day. Beseech the Almickel tae spare the puir laddie, for he be nigh untae death.'

Behind him the circle of onlookers shifted uneasily. Hats and caps came off, and the men in the corner stopped gaming to watch. John felt a thrill run through

241

his veins so that his skin pricked and the hair on his arms stood on end. Would God perform a miracle in this hellish place?

He poured out prayer after prayer. The words flowed out like the minister's preaching on the Sabbath. If Nathaniel heard, and if the onlookers understood, they gave no sign. Nathaniel's life passed before his eyes: the wailing babe handed to him after the shipwreck; the laughing, carefree child who skipped off from lessons and his work in the tanyard and shop; the sullen, ugly youth who had left so rudely this evening. And as he prayed, he kept his eyes on Nathaniel's face, alarmed to see that the blood was still flowing fast from the wound on his temple. Could the woman not staunch it?

His prayers died on his lips, and he wrenched the kerchief off his neck and pressed it hard over the wound. 'Why, why, Nathaniel?' he begged.

The boy's eyes opened for a moment, but they were unseeing. Yet he seemed to hear, trying to answer at last.

'"Twas a fight o'er some lassie,' the woman interposed mournfully. 'A worthless, scur'lous minx.'

John pressed harder with the kerchief. The blood seemed to be slowing down. But the boy's face had turned ashen, the lips blue. John hardly took in the woman's words.

'The other lad's gang awa' by noo, nae doot.'

This he heard. 'Away?' John leapt angrily to his feet. 'Did none arrest him?'

The men stared at him like dumb, foolish sheep.

'Did none — ?'

'None!' the sailor suddenly spat out. 'For 'twas this boy that struck the first blow. Unjustly done, too, as all here will tell thee.'

The others murmured in assent, and John looked round, horrified. Then he looked back at Nathaniel. The boy was open-eyed again, one hand raised. But his face was full of terror. Then a thin stream of blood trickled out of his mouth. The eyes rolled backwards, and the hand dropped.

John bowed his head and wept.

Madam — he wrote painfully to Patience —

Nathaniel my foster-boy has died. I pray thee, send my brother's son Thomas to me, if that ye can spare him. But if, since he be the eldest, you had rather send Nicholas or Josiah, I pray thee do so. I trust Isaac our brother still cares for thee and thine, as would I, were we dwelling still on your shores. My greetings to thee, sister, and to Isaac's family also. May God keep ye all.
Your kinsman,
John

Sighing heavily, he sealed the document with the same familiar seal his father had used on bolts of Fessenden cloth in Chilham forty years before, and he addressed it to Widow Patience Fessenden of Chilham. The letter would go out on *The Venturer* at the next tide.

ISAAC
Maidstone, March 1655

Isaac pushed the needle in and out of the cloth, his fingers moving fast, but his mind moving faster. The rebels would see him handsomely rewarded, George had assured him, if he joined the new rising for the King. And as he sat at work above the shop, Isaac wondered how else they would survive the year. Patience had died of a fit soon after the news of her son Thomas had come from the Bay Colony by way of Dartford: Thomas had been lost at sea. A foolish accident, the captain had reported. Foolish and unnecessary. The young boy, bent on showing his mettle to the other sailor lads, had climbed the mizzen-mast in high seas. The waves had come up and snatched him. Like Nathaniel, the boy was gone. He would never serve John in Cambridge.

Isaac had gone by cart to Chilham to fetch Nicholas, Josiah, and Hannah to Maidstone. Nicholas was a steady, clever lad, a boy who would work hard. Isaac liked and trusted him, as he would never have trusted Thomas, for Nicholas could be relied upon. The boy had cherished and comforted his sister Hannah as she grieved for her mother and brother, but then Mother Mary and Rebecca won all their hearts, and the sorrow was eased.

But how was he to feed so large a family? Mary ate little and worked hard, even as an old woman, but Rebecca was breeding yet again and could do little . . .

He sighed. *Breeding again.* He could not leave her alone! It shamed him, but he could *not.* She had borne yet another girl who had lived, in Goudhurst seven years before. He had named her Anna, for George's child, but the baby had died with King Charles in the harsh winter of 1649. Died — like the rest of them. And since then, every babe had been stillborn. He did not expect otherwise . . .

And there were Adam and Charlie, his own sons — big, hungry lads now, as well as Robert's sons and his niece Hannah . . . So many to feed! Ah well, no more than penance for Robert's death.

If only John had stayed in Chilham! Perhaps they would all now be living off the fruits of the Fessenden woollens. But no; too much had changed; there had been bad harvests for six years. The war had destroyed the roots of trade in England, and the old cloths were no longer in demand. Parliament had spoken against unnamed 'ills' in the wool trade; created ordinances to forbid the export of wool; and encouraged only the largest wool masters to produce. Cromwell, once so plain in russets and homespuns, now affected the dress of French courtiers and smiled upon his daughters decked like princesses in silken finery. *The turncoat! I'm glad I'll none of him!*

And many followed after Cromwell. The clothes Isaac sewed for the gentlefolk nearby were of finer stuff than his father had ever dreamed of. Ah well, as long as he still had cloth to sew, and people still wanted clothes to wear, he would find a living somehow. Adam was good with a needle, too, and Rebecca, when she felt well enough —

But he needed more money than they could earn, and he would never go begging or send Robert's children to the poor house.

George's proposal was tempting indeed. He could overlook the fact that all the Cavalier plots in Kent had failed thus far. This one would be different. The plot of 1654 was wild and ill-advised, right under the nose of Cromwell's favourite, Governor Thomas Kelsey. But though the Governor of Kent was watchful now because of it, George was convinced that the King's men stood a better chance this time. Tolhurst and his Cavalier friends had asked Isaac, then, to serve as a captain of their infantry, and they had promised him a rich recompense.

"Tis thy bearing and height, Isaac,' George had said warmly. 'You're a King David in the frame of a Goliath. Come now, Kent has need of thee.'

'I wonder at you, George,' Isaac had said easily. The two of them had walked together around the leafless orchard one Sabbath afternoon. 'Thou wert ever a man of peace.'

'And still am,' George agreed. 'But how can we live quietly as long as kings are beheaded in our own realm and houses are plundered and men like you must feed two or three families at once?'

'Aye, and the Committee allows lawlessness.'

'Then, Isaac, the risings *must* continue.'

'I'm glad Nicholas, my nephew, cannot hear thee!'

'He's a canting Puritan, is he?'

Isaac would not have accepted harsh words, even of Robert's children, from anyone but George Tolhurst. He laughed bitterly. 'Yes — yet, no. Not in the mould of his mother. There's a fineness about him — I cannot describe — I like the boy. He and Josiah know not what to make of me, I lay, for I'm so unlike their mother and father. But Nicholas is only eighteen. Unformed yet. He'll change — if he needs to.' He spread his palms and dismissed the boy. 'That's for God to dispose, not me.'

They stopped under a few dead brown hops that had been left to dry and die in the wind since last autumn: hops that would, George had said superstitiously, assure the growth of new plants this spring.

'For God, aye, thank goodness! But, Isaac, to the matter at hand. Have you considered?'

245

'Yes,' Isaac murmured, 'but not for long enough. And I must talk to Rebecca. You understand?'

'Aye. Of course you must.'

'If aught went against me and I were killed, or imprisoned, Rebecca would surely die. Robert's girl Hannah is but a little thing, scarcely as old as thy Henrietta. Could I leave her in the care of four green boys and a woman too old to do — '

'And could I leave my womenfolk even in the care of my wife?'

That was the question that had stayed longest and most painfully in Isaac's mind. George was willing to sacrifice his life and risk everything in a rebellion, even though Elizabeth, too, had been unwell with a mysterious flux that kept her indisposed whenever Isaac came to Goudhurst.

And now as he finished a seam and nimbly turned the garment inside out, he weighed the consequences of pledging himself to yet another rebellion.

Rebecca's eyes widened. 'Surely, sweetheart, you cannot go again?'

He saw that she was frightened, and his resolve weakened. They sat in the light of a single candle in the kitchen. Above them the rest of the family slept the long winter night; only Mary sat by the fire with them, her chin on her sunken breast, her cheeks sucking in and out with her faint breathing.

He had waited for a quiet moment to talk with Rebecca, intending to tell her that indeed he must stand beside Tolhurst and with the Cavalier rebels. But she would not listen.

'You cannot, love,' she repeated. Her face was drawn, and her hands turned and twisted on her small lap. Above her knees, another coming child curved its back toward him. He leaned forward and stirred the fire, not daring to meet her gaze. *Live, child, live,* he prayed silently.

He cleared his throat at last. 'I was talking with George just last Lord's day. The men of Kent need me.'

She laughed sadly. 'Need you to rot in Leeds or Westernhanger — or worse, since thou'rt not "gentle-folk"? Aye, they surely need thee, Isaac, but not as *we* need thee. Pray, do not join them, love. The Cavaliers are rash, wild young fellows. I cannot believe George Tolhurst thinks otherwise.' She stopped, and he saw on her face a struggle that went on deeper within. 'But — but — if you must — '

He looked up quickly as her voice died. She did not weep easily, unless she was afraid, but when she did weep, the tears were his undoing. 'Nay,' he murmured, 'I doubt you can spare me . . . ' He sighed. 'But I feel as torn asunder as an old smock. George pressed me so — '

'And flattered thee, no doubt.' She was smiling slightly, but he knew she was uneasy with his friend George, and he had accepted that long ago. He sighed, again, shifting on his stool. 'But 'tis such a pity, wife. The king over the water is to land with his court ere long.'

'So they say.'

'And the plot is well arranged and cannot fail.'

This time she did not answer. She didn't have to, for he knew her thoughts. *Yes, so thou hast said before.*

He shrugged and dismissed the rising. 'Well-a-day, Rebecca. So be't. I'll not leave Maidstone but bide here, safe I hope.' He watched her face soften and relax a little. 'Anyway, dearling, the babe's nigh now, and I'd rather be at hand.'

Then he retreated into silence, staring absently at the fire, and Rebecca took up a calico coif she was sewing for a gentlewoman on East Street. Isaac could not bear the thought of sewing more; his eyes were tired after a day of close stitching on red stammel petticoats. And he wanted to work out in his mind what he would say to George about the captaincy.

For a moment he debated deceit. What if he were to go to Canterbury or Chilham for cloth and be gone a day or two? Rebecca would never know — unless he died or were shut up in prison. But he rejected this idea at once. He had never lied to her before, and would not now. Perhaps Providence was using Rebecca to warn him. His angel . . .

Rebecca caught his eye and then went on with her sewing. He stood up, suddenly hungry and thirsty. But it was not food he wanted; Mary had served them an ample stew that night, the result of a neighbour's gift of a chicken. No, he was unaccountably and deeply thirsty — as he had not been for years — for God.

'Where's the Bible?' he asked gruffly. In spite of Mary's gentle reproof and Nicholas' open disapproval, he had not read it aloud to his family of an evening for so long that he could not remember where it was kept.

Mary stirred, blinking her eyes. 'The Bible, Isaac? Is that what you want?' She made as if to rise, but she was weary and slow these days.

'Nay, Mother,' he restrained her, 'I'll fetch it myself.'

"Tis in my chamber, Isaac.' Mary's old face was rueful. 'On the shelf, under my *Herbal.* Mind you don't wake Hannah.'

He laughed. 'Fie, you thief, Mother Mary!'

Rebecca laughed, too, and he felt a wave of love for them both. 'Then may I fetch it down, fair ladies?'

'By all means.' Mary adjusted her shoulders, sitting more upright. 'Will it please thee read aloud?'

He looked uncertainly at her. 'Aye, I shall.'

In a moment he was settled again with the heavy book open at Psalm 42 and a candle at his elbow.

'"As the hart panteth after the water brooks, so panteth my soul after thee, O God. My soul thirsteth for God, for the living God. When shall I come and appear before God? . . ."'

At the end of the psalm he fell silent.

He had dreamed the night before of a deer. In his dream he had been running from an unseen foe through a dense wood that looked uncannily like the hop garden where he had met George again all that time ago. But instead of meeting George, he had run face-to-face with a reddish-brown doe. She had stopped with her hooves in a dried watercourse, her head jerking up, her eyes wild. Then he became pursuer and she the pursued, bounding over the thickets and brambles and bines until — in the quirk of all dreams — she vanished.

Sitting now in the quiet of his own house, he felt loss and hunger. What did the deer mean? Not given often nowadays to melancholic ramblings, he hardly knew how to answer the puzzle, but he bowed his head anyway and sought God.

Warmth began to fill him. He felt flooded by a calm and completeness he had not known for seven years. If it were right for him to join the rebels and rise against Parliament, nothing would impede him. If it were not, God would make that clear.

His hands still covering his face, he smiled slightly. So long since he had thought in this way — of God as his guide and shelter. God had too long been his adversary, the One pitted against his will and desires. But Mary knew — though she had lost both the men she loved, and now her grandchild Thomas — that God was no man's adversary. And John knew, though he had lost his foster son — that God was not his adversary.

Had Robert known that — bent on proving himself righteous before man and God, though both knew otherwise? Had Robert known that God was not his adversary? *Hush,* an inner voice bade him. *That is the Almighty's concern. Hush.*

'Hush!' Mary's cracked voice roused him suddenly. Had he fallen asleep? 'Hark, do you not hear — ?'

'Footsteps on the path,' Rebecca said anxiously.

Isaac stretched and yawned lazily. 'Naught to fret about.'

Someone pounded on the door. 'Open, friend!'

''Tis Kelsey's men come for thee, dearling.' Rebecca dropped her sewing and jumped up. A spool of thread unravelled on the floor at her feet, and Isaac saw her stiffen like a weft thread ready to snap.

'Nay!' he laughed, and he pulled back the lock and the doorpin.

A stranger stood on the threshold muffled against the cold. Isaac caught the stink of horse-sweat on his clothes. *A messenger* — but he was alone.

'From George Tolhurst,' the man said breathlessly.

Behind them Rebecca sat down again. She was still fearful; he knew it without even turning round.

'Come in, then,' Isaac beckoned. 'Have you a seal or letter about you?'

The messenger stepped in and threw back his cloak. Isaac recognized one of George's older servants. 'Aye, a letter from the Squire.' He pulled a folded paper out of his jerkin.

'Fetch ale and a bite of bread for this man, Rebecca,' Isaac murmured absently. He had already begun to scan the letter. 'Sit you down — Matty, is it? — and eat, will you?'

George wrote awkwardly. He should have asked Elizabeth, more accomplished in the art, to pen the letter. The words were blotted, the script running over invisible downs and dales in the paper. The flourishes looked absurd.

> *Friend: Penruddock's Rising sall not bee. Sir John, Edward Hales, and Thos. Culpeper bee all arrested, and the magazine is disclosed — and all is lost. Tufton is to the Tower. I sall lie low, not being charged. Howbeit I may even be called to sit at the assizes when they be tried. A foolish spectackle indeed!*
> *Thy servant,*
> *GT*

Isaac looked up at Matthew. 'You know the import of this letter?'

The servant stared back with bulging eyes and fat cheeks. He was stuffing himself with half a cottage loaf Rebecca had set before him. Isaac laughed at him. His voice sounded oddly merry in the still, tightly woven room.

Mary leaned forward in her chair. 'For sure he knows, son, whate'er it be.'

Isaac smiled vaguely back at her. His eyes returned to the servant's. 'Then . . . say naught of this to anyone.'

The man swallowed noisily, stammering, 'No, not no one, neither, sir, but . . .'

'But?'

'My master bade me take this word to others in Maidstone, besides your good self. You must let me go, I pray.'

'Go then, and peace be with thee, old Matty.'

Standing at the open door, Isaac watched Matthew's dark cloak blend into the darkness of Mill Street. In a moment he heard the clatter of hooves on the cobbles, and the man was gone. At least for now, he would not stand for Kent.

2

NICHOLAS
Maidstone, August 1656

My cousin Adam, he thought, *is a dullard.* Of course he
would never have said that to anyone, except his brother
Thomas — if Thomas had lived. Different as they were,
he could always tell Thomas what was on his mind. But
not Adam and Charlie (though they were his age), and
not even his brother Josiah.

It was easier for him to talk to Isaac than to anyone
except his grandmother Mary or his sister Hannah. And
though he loved Hannah, she hardly counted.

It was curious how he had drawn closer to his uncle.
Isaac only occasionally read the Bible and acknowledged
God, and Nicholas guessed that belief was barely more
than a hollow shell to him. Isaac, he knew, had no
sympathy for everything his own parents had stood for.
But death makes strange bedfellows, he thought, and now
here were Robert Fessenden's children in the family
and care of royalist Isaac — the uncle rarely mentioned
in the Chilham household; the uncle he had scarcely
known existed until the great dark-haired pillar of a
man had come to offer help to his mother, and finally
to fetch them to Maidstone and close the house when
his mother died. Isaac: sometimes withdrawn and fierce,
sometimes full of merry laughter and joy . . . the uncle
he had come to respect and love.

He was merry today. He seemed carefree, Nicholas
thought, glancing sideways as they walked along East
Street on the Sabbath afternoon. It had been raining
all morning and the road was pitted with evil-smelling
brown pools. But Isaac had put on a clean jerkin in

honour of his friend and had talked in excitement all the way up the High Street.

Nicholas caught the excitement, too, wondering at this paragon of kindness and goodness they were soon to meet, and at his inclusion in the jaunt. There was nothing untoward about Adam's going: he was Isaac's older son, after all. But for him to go — !

Adam plodded silently beside him. He rarely spoke, and when he did was neither courteous nor churlish. At home he watched over his mother with the ferocity of a terrier, but otherwise showed no strong emotion.

How different he knew himself to be! He could see why Adam and Charlie petted and loved their mother; she was such a frail, gentle woman — but he had never felt so protective of his own mother. And for most of his childhood, his father had been away either on errands for the cloth trade or off to war. Isaac, however, was always nearby, either at home or in the shop. And he wanted to be.

He glanced at Adam again, then at Isaac. Had Adam noticed what a risk his father was taking on the Sabbath afternoon? For Isaac was whistling 'A Kentish Man I'm Proud to Be' as clearly and saucily as could be. It was enough to set one's teeth on edge! He knew the words well enough from the brazen boys at the grammar school who sang it deliberately under their masters' notice in the Corpus Christi Yard, usually earning a cuff for their wickedness . . .

All the same, he couldn't stop smiling in delight at his uncle's roguish behaviour, and at Adam's dogged indifference. It was as if Adam noticed nothing. Was that because all his care was to work? Because already he was finished with his tailor's apprenticeship? Perhaps — for his cousin cared nothing for learning, as he himself had grown to care. But — *no*. Nicholas inwardly stopped himself. Who was he to accuse his cousin of dull-wittedness? *Not all the important learning of this world falls between the covers of a book,* his grandmother Mary had said when he was little.

He often remembered these words. He had heard her say them again, in fact, since he and Josiah and Hannah had all been reunited with her early the year before. But he was not sure, yet, whether he quite believed her. He had read and reread *Eikon Basilike*, morbidly preoccupying himself with the death of the tyrant Charles Stuart. His mother had long ago forbidden the book and twice had tried to burn it, but he had secreted it in a cubby hole in his chamber. Isaac had read it now, and they had argued over it, his uncle vehemently taking the part of the dead tyrant.

Nicholas had revelled in the debate, though they could never agree, and Adam had sat by open-mouthed as the discussion became more heated. Now he wanted Isaac to read John Milton's rebuttal of the book, *Eikonoklastes*; he was certain his uncle's wavering faith would be strengthened, and that he would view the King differently. But they would only argue again . . .

'Would that we had ten pound a year to send thee away to Cambridge, Nicholas, to make a gentleman scholar of thee the way we ought,' Mary had once said.

Now he sighed. Small hope of that! Instead, since he was no hand with a needle like his cousin, he was out early on messages and business for his uncle: usually delivering garments and collecting payments for the work. His time for books was snatched on the Sabbath or occasionally at home of an evening if there were candles enough in the house for him to read by after dark. He sighed again.

The whistling stopped. 'A sad sigh, nephew Nicholas.' Isaac's dark eyes twinkled at him, a question in them.

Adam made a grunt of acknowledgment and continued walking at the same pace, only now a few steps ahead. Nicholas fell in beside Isaac.

'Not sad. I was musing on books, 'tis all.'

'Ah, indeed.' His uncle's face was warm; the corners of his mouth turned up in his mobile, expressive face. 'And what was the end of thy musing?'

'That I want no end to books.'

Isaac laughed.

'And does Sir George — does he care for learning?'

Isaac threw back his head. '*Sir George*? .Oh, fie, he won't know what to do with thee if you talk to him thus. He'll not brook a title. Squire George . . . George the Farmer . . . those names suit him better.

And as for books? Not a straw does he care, I'm sure. His wife's the one for books, I warrant. Or was, anyhow.'

All this was very puzzling. 'But is he not a justice of the peace in this county? How can he make laws if he cannot con his books?'

'Oh, he can con his books well enough. He did it as a lad, you may be certain. But justices pay little heed to *books*, I fear. That's for the clerks of the town . . . but thou'lt see for thyself in a moment.' He reached forward to touch Adam's shoulder. 'See, Adam? There's where we stop. He's lodged at the inn there.'

They crossed the highway cautiously. Although this far from the market-place the streets were more wholesome, still the men did not want to dirty their best clothes in the mud.

A stout, ruddy-faced man with sparse, flaxen hair stood under the arch of the courtyard looking up and down the lane. Nicholas only half observed the man, wondering with increasing curiosity about his uncle's friend. But then Isaac made a small exclamation and flashed him a smile before loping ahead towards the archway.

The stranger saw him coming and stepped forward. 'Isaac!'

'George! My dear George!' Isaac was crying excitedly. The two men were gripping each other's hands and staring hard at each other.

Nicholas stopped dead. Something was wrong. Was this well-fed countryman George Tolhurst, justice of the shire? Surely not. He could not be, could never be George Tolhurst. Tolhurst was a dashing prince of a man with curling lovelocks and soulful eyes: the coolly imperious look of a Charles Stuart or a Richard Lovelace. Someone he would not like but would admire. This was surely not the Royalist who had rescued his uncle from the hop garden after the battle, who had taken him home to Goudhurst and washed his feet like the Good Lord Himself. *This* man George Tolhurst? He wanted to laugh. It was too impossible!

'Adam, Nicholas! Don't stand there wool-gathering and gawping. Come hither.'

His uncle had turned now and summoned them to follow into the inn. Adam went on without a word, but as Nicholas followed, his eyes fixed on Tolhurst's wide back and uneven gait, his head spun as he tried to adjust his ideas of what his uncle's friend was like. He knew he must hide his surprise from Isaac, and perhaps he had already failed in that uncomfortable deception, for his uncle kept glancing over his shoulder — while they passed through the flagged entrance corridor — looking anxious, as if he had been indiscreet.

This fellow . . . red-cheeked, broad, a slight limp as he moved . . . why, he was scarce more than a bumpkin!

Once again, as the four men settled in a small, low-ceilinged parlour at the back of the inn, Nicholas reproved himself. The man was kindly — that was clear. He called for ale from the taproom for them all, though it was strictly forbidden on the Sabbath, then sat staring at Isaac without saying a word, a happy grin splitting his wide face. Adam, meanwhile, sat looking at his boots. Nicholas watched them all, intrigued, but wishing he had someone else to speak to about it all.

At last Isaac introduced Adam and Nicholas to Sir George. There was a moment's confusion as Tolhurst mistook him for Isaac's own son. Adam wasn't in the least offended — something that surprised Nicholas — but what surprised him more was that Sir George seemed to be scrutinizing him as if he *were* Isaac's son.

'He's like to his father, is he?' Tolhurst said to Isaac after a long stare in his direction. He did not look rudely, only with a puzzled curiosity.

His uncle paled. 'Nay, see for thyself.'

Tolhurst grunted. 'He looks like a son of thine own, I'd say.'

Isaac just smiled in return, and Nicholas' heart lifted. For all their differences of opinion, he would have been proud to have Isaac as a father.

Tolhurst then dropped his voice with a searching look at Isaac, and said, 'May we speak freely, friend, when — ?'

Nicholas stood up, his face flushing in indignation. 'Of course you may, sir.' The heat carried into his voice.

Isaac looked dismayed by the outburst, the muscles in his face tensing. 'Be seated, nephew, and do not take offence. George — yes, his father was a Parliamentary man, as you rightly know. And Nicholas is a godly fellow, too. But he's our friend. Say on.'

Nicholas subsided into his seat but did not feel at ease. They spoke as if he were not in the room, or as if he were a hunting dog whose pedigree had to be wrangled over before he could lie in the master's hall. He resolved that he would not like Tolhurst if the man were so suspicious and hasty in judgment.

A maid brought ale into the parlour at that moment, and everyone's spirits rose.

'Fetch my daughter from her chamber, wilt'ou?' Tolhurst asked the maid. He put a halfpenny into her hand, and Nicholas wondered at this largesse, too.

Dropping a curtsy, the maid withdrew. Isaac leaned back in his seat and drank deeply of the ale; the Fessendens rarely drank it these days — not for any scruples, but because Rebecca had been unlucky in her last two years of brewing. The ale was frothy and redolent of last year's best hops. Nicholas, not used to it, had nevertheless learned to like it. Adam drank deeply, too, and caught Nicholas' eyes over the top of the tankard: the first spark of life all afternoon.

'You brought your daughter?' Isaac was saying.

'Yes, Anna . . . dost remember?'

Isaac nodded. 'Of course I remember. The eldest, and like her mother.'

'A comely maid, yes, and like Elizabeth, yes — fair to look upon . . . as she was before her illness, poor wife . . . but Anna's not like her in other ways.' Sir George looked over at him. 'She'll make good company for your two lads as we talk a while.'

Nicholas was irritated. He did not want to be condemned to the company of a fat, spoiled country girl when he could listen to the men's converse. And Adam was no fit company for anyone today, either.

'How go the petty sessions, George?' his uncle asked.

'Oh, dull, compared to the assizes last year past, that is.'

Isaac's eyebrows rose quizzically.

257

''Tis all petty nonsense bent to send a man to sleep. Breach of the Sabbath. How many strokes of the birch should such-and-such a one have for the wickedness of playing the viol on the Sabbath in a public house . . .'

'Thou must be hard put to't not to laugh, thyself.'

George set his tankard on the table. 'Oh, I often am. Little men amusing themselves by making big rules. Petty sessions? No, 'tis a *trial* — for me, I mean.'

'And there are more inns closing, I hear.'

'Indeed. "Dens of sedition and iniquity".'

''Tis a wonder this one's open, then,' Nicholas interposed. Then, seeing his uncle's face, instantly regretted the words and hung his head.

Tolhurst seemed not to hear. 'The usual run of cony-catchers, gamesters, drunkards, and players. Vagabonds and gamblers, I understand, must be stopped ere they dupe the poor . . . but drunkards, poor souls, I feel sorry for 'em. Who has not drunk too much at least once in his life? And strolling players — what harm in them, unless they've gulled the poor with all their mummeries? All they do is dwell in their own giddy fantasies. I like a good "George and the Turkish Knight" myself, or a fine side of Morris.' He laughed lustily. 'Instead, I'm supposed to see 'em into the stocks.'

'You whited sepulchre,' Isaac teased.

Nicholas watched this interchange with bemusement.

'Ah — quoting Scripture at me, are you now, you rogue?' There was a smile on Tolhurst's face.

'But how can you sit there imposing Puritan laws when you don't believe them yourself?'

'Because it's best if I'm thought a conformist, Isaac. Best for my family, and best for Kent. At least you know there's *one* honest King's man in the courts, Isaac. There I'd be, and few now to connect me with rebellions or Charles Stuart.'

Nicholas' mouth dropped. This man was a turncoat! Whose side did he really serve, and who was tricking whom? And why did Isaac therefore trust him? He shook his head.

He noticed then, that a young girl had come in. How long she had been in the room, he did not know. *Tolhurst's girl?*

258

She sat in the corner only a few feet away, her needlework in her lap and her eyes down so that all he could see of her face was a broad brow and straight nose. Adam sat staring at her, his colour heightened and his hands folding and unfolding on his knees as he watched her sew. She was no fat country maid.

Nicholas looked again at her. She was beautiful. Her hair shone red-gold in the afternoon light, and her skin was as pale as milk. He could not help staring.

'Not like that, if you please, mistress — ' Adam said softly, standing up and gesturing towards her sewing. 'You'll prick yourself and bloody the linen with the needle that way about.'

Nicholas wanted to laugh at his cousin's concern for the stitching. For himself, he could not take his eyes off her face.

She looked up at Adam, ignoring Nicholas altogether. The eyes were a pale blue-violet, soft as fading bluebells in the chestnut woods around his Chilham home. 'Will I now?' she said vaguely. 'And what would you know, young sir?'

Adam was covered with confusion, and from the other side of the room came talk and laughter Nicholas only half heard now.

'" — an abhorrent feast to be stamped out lest England fall again to popery, he said."'

'Oh, no! 'Tis Canterbury all over again, George. "Dost thou think, because thou art virtuous, there shall be no more cakes and ale?"'

George was laughing at Isaac, and somehow these words were familiar to Nicholas. He could not place them right away . . .

'Will Shakespeare,' Isaac laughed back. 'Sir Toby Belch, I think. Probably the only quotation I remember from my schooling, save the Bible.'

George only shrugged. Nicholas was surprised his uncle could quote Shakespeare, but he quickly forgot again and looked back at Adam and the daughter. His cousin was kneeling at her feet now, one hand holding the needle and the other grasping her sewing. She was bending forward to see what he was doing, so that their

259

heads were almost touching: Adam's dark and curling like his father's, and hers soft and fine.

He felt a strange pang. She had not even acknowledged him. He watched Adam in annoyance, divided again between wanting to win the girl's attention and wanting to take part in the men's discourse. He had not come out with his uncle to chatter about fine stitching!

'You mentioned last year, George?'

'Aye, surely you were in Maidstone a twelvemonth ago?'

Isaac frowned. 'Yes, as far as I remember.'

'And the name of Sondes — that means something, does it not?' Tolhurst sipped his ale noisily.

'Sondes . . . Sondes . . . was he not the sheriff?'

'The very one. They took his house away — Lees Court — in all the sequestrations . . . though he's done better than many at restoring his fortunes, except in one regard, poor soul.'

'And that?'

Nicholas lost interest in Adam and Anna again. The men's conversation was more fascinating by the minute.

Tolhurst bent forward to answer, 'His own son Freeman — last year it was — slew his own brother.'

Nicholas saw Isaac flinch as if he had been struck. Tolhurst, too, seemed afraid he had blundered, for he began to stammer. 'Isaac, no . . . pardon me, this was an affair of the heart.'

His uncle made an inarticulate, guttural sound in his throat but seemed unable to reply.

'Very ugly, it was. Jealousy. Killed him with a cleaver and dagger while he slept at home.'

Isaac shuddered, and Nicholas caught an anxious, hunted look as it passed between the two men: a message his uncle had flashed out silently and the other man had understood. A warning.

'They were both in love with the same woman,' Tolhurst said slowly. 'Their father couldn't tame Freeman.' He looked down. 'The assizes tamed him. Saddest case I ever sat on. He was hung at Penenden a year ago this month.'

The room fell silent again. Adam was watching his father now, the needlework having slipped from his hands. Anna had left off watching his stitching and was looking up. Her eyes were fixed on Nicholas', seeing him for the first time.

He looked back at her. She was as frightened, he saw, as he was. At the same time he felt angry. How could anyone love a woman enough to kill his own brother?

'Both in love with the same woman,' George mused again in a sad voice.

Anna's eyes held his, wavering now. Her forehead puckered into a slight frown.

'Don't be foolish, lad,' Isaac said gently. 'What would we have to offer?'

Nicholas clenched his teeth tightly. 'And Adam? I suppose Adam's already spoken for her?'

Isaac shook his head as though befuddled with ale. 'Adam? Nay, he's not got a mind for maidens yet a while. And just as well. Nicholas, dear nephew, thou'rt being rash and hasty. You must not think of it.'

'Because I am a Parliament's man?' He knew his voice was bitter.

Isaac shook his head, impatiently this time. 'Nay — no — that's naught. But thou'rt a yeoman.'

'And is not Sir George, at heart?'

Isaac smiled sadly. 'At heart, yes. But he would never hear of it. If thou hast a mind for wooing, Nicholas, you must woo elsewhere.' He rubbed his brow with a tired expression. 'Again I say: Anna Tolhurst is her father's oldest. She'll marry a fine gentleman, and when King Charles returns she'll be a great lady, perhaps at court. Her mother is as tall and fine as a princess. Not for the likes of a Fessenden.'

No sympathy in that quarter, he realized. Then could he speak to Hannah? She at least might advise him on how a sweet young maid was to be won. But no, Hannah was scarcely sixteen, and no one had come a-wooing yet to her. She could not help, and perhaps might even speak of it . . .

Then he must talk to Grandmother Mary.

She was out in the small shop's garden late that evening picking herbs. Her movements were deliberate

261

now, but her deft fingers did not hesitate over which sprigs to pick and which to leave.

He watched her unthinkingly as he talked; she hardly seemed aware of his voice, but he knew she was listening. She stood still once he had finished, and her eyes misted.

'Ah, Nicholas, this story is one I've heard before.'

'My father — ?' No one spoke of Robert in this house, and he liked the rare occasions when he could mention his father to Mary.

'Nay.' She looked away, uncomfortably, he thought. Her smile seemed forced as she went on, 'Thy father wooed thy mother away from home, mostly.' She dropped her eyes, apparently recalling the courtship. 'And your Uncle Isaac, too. I knew nothing of Rebecca until I came to Maidstone after your grandfather died.' She sighed. 'And a finer, sweeter wife he couldn't have chosen.'

Nicholas wanted to ask more about his parents, but she clearly desired to vouchsafe no more about their wooing. It seemed strange to him, all the same, that people never spoke of his mother the way they spoke of Rebecca. He looked down. But why was it strange? Hadn't he only a moment ago been thinking himself of his aunt's sweetness? And he had never received much affection from his mother — though it was just her way . . .

'Then, pray tell me who's been telling you tales like mine?'

His grandmother went back to her picking. The shears snipped, and the piles of lavender, mint, borage and fennel grew higher in her basket. 'You remind me through and through of your Uncle John. He was about your age, too, when he fell in love — '

Nicholas' face grew hot. 'In love, grand-dame? Did I say that?'

She laughed. Her gums were almost toothless now, but she still looked lovely, he thought. 'Nay, son. You didn't in so many words. But why'd you be talking of wooing if you be not in love, Nicholas? 'Tis a strange, wicked man that prates of marriage without love.'

He blinked. 'You loved my grandfather, then?' The old man had died soberly and quietly, a solemn event made more so by his own father's solemnity and grief. But Nicholas could not associate his grandmother with the drooling old man he remembered. Love? Was it possible?

Mary set down her basket and took him by the shoulders. Her hands were spotted with large brown freckles and twisted with age, but they were still strong. 'Yes, I loved him. It wasn't just a matter of convenience, you know, no matter what thy — what anyone said or thought. And he loved me, too. Loved me as much as thy uncle loved Jane. And still loves her, no doubt.'

'Then tell me, pray, how he wooed her.'

She laughed again. 'Oh, 'twas a curious wooing. Once he'd set his eyes on her, he was all fire but no resolve. How was he to get her from her uncle? A blackcoat in Canterbury he was, high and mighty, though he kept her poorly, John always said . . . but he hardly saw her before he'd made up his mind.' She looked up at him sharply. 'It was the Almighty's will, Nicholas. And you — have you prayed and sought God?'

He hung his head. She always asked the most difficult questions. But they were the questions he knew he had to answer: the right questions.

'No, I see thou hast not. Well-a-day — ' she sighed. ''Tis a hopeless case, I'd say. She a gentleborn maiden and thou a penniless orphan dependent upon thine uncle. You had best think no more of her until you get a trade and settle yourself — if she's not wed by then.'

He groaned at the simplicity of her summary. 'And in the meanwhile? How shall I see her? How shall she know I want to acquaint myself with her?'

'"Acquaint myself with her"? Oh, Nicholas, thou'rt a comical lad!'

He spread his hands with a shrug. 'But I know not what to say, how to — '

'Let's see now. Does she sew well?'

He frowned. 'Perhaps, though Adam thought — '

Mary was all business now. 'And does she speak wisely?'

'I hardly heard her voice, madam.'

263

'Not so good. And does she read?'

'Oh — !' he let out an angry exclamation. 'Oh, I do not know. It was just that she looked — in such a way — ' How could he explain?

She smiled. 'Your uncle John, again.'

'Pray, no more questions or comparisons!' he said in exasperation.

'No more questions, then. But I see no remedy, Nicholas. You must meet her again ere her father return to Goudhurst. It could all be vain fantasy — and her father's a Cavalier — '

He held up his hand. 'No more obstacles, pray, either. How shall I meet her?'

Mary considered. She turned the lavender slowly in her fingers. 'Her mother's ill, I heard your uncle say. I might make up some cordial for her and send her some of these herbs. By thee.'

'And my uncle?'

'He shall know of it, of course, and I think he will relent. He loves thee dearly; Sir George is his friend. And times are changing, when with no more kings, I suppose, a merchant's son may look upon a gentleman's daughter.'

The basket of herbs, however, was not enough, he decided, nor was the flask of cordial. He wanted to take Anna something of his own. It would be a sign between them. But what could he take her? He owned nothing except a share of the bed with his brother, and the clothes and boots he wore. All his father's remaining things had gone overboard in the storm with Thomas, and his mother had left little except her Bible and a house of spotless furniture that had all been sold to pay the last of the Fessenden debts to weavers, dyers, and fullers.

Leaving Mary out of doors in the fading light, he went within. Josiah was already asleep, but Rebecca was softly talking with Adam and Charlie below stairs. He passed them and mounted the stairs slowly. Then he remembered Culpeper's *Herbal*. Mary had presented it to his mother some years before, but the book had lain unused on an attic shelf. Reclaiming it after his mother's death, Mary still referred to it, though not often.

He ran heavily downstairs again. 'May I give her thy *Herbal*, Grandmother Mary?' The words came rushing out.

She did not answer immediately but came back into the house first. He lit a candle to show her way up the back steps. At last, she said, 'Thou'rt hasty, Nicholas. I doubt she'll accept it.' She sighed. 'But you may try. Take it, and welcome.'

'The master's to the sessions,' the maid assured him insolently. 'But his daughter's above stairs, I lay.'

He took a deep breath, resenting the girl's rude, suggestive grimaces. She tossed her head so that her bodice shook with the weight of her breasts, and he knew the display was intended to provoke him.

He looked away. 'Then tell her —' His voice sounded odd: tight, and lower than usual. 'Pray, ask her if she will receive me in the parlour where we sat yester afternoon.'

The girl eyed him wickedly and wiped her hands down the greasy sides of her skirt so that her hips showed plainly beneath the stained, coarse material. 'And what wilt'ou give me to do thy bidding?'

He stood up straight. 'A box in the ears if you won't, and a sprig of lavender if you will.'

Laughing, she turned to the stairs, and he crossed into the parlour. To his dismay, it was not empty. Two heavy gentlewomen sat gossiping in the corner. They rearranged their skirts when he came in, preened themselves slightly, but then went on with their loud discourse. *Perhaps*, he thought, *'tis as well we shall have older folk about.* Disappointment nagged, but he would make the best of it.

The women inclined their heads as Anna Tolhurst came in — a slight acknowledgment for the daughter of a gentleman.

Nicholas stood, bowing, only half aware that he was holding the basket so tightly that the dry rushes were squeaking against his palms.

'Pray do sit down, sir,' she said stiffly. Her voice was quiet, but a few tones lower than any he had heard in such a young woman. It was cool, like music, and her patched silk skirts rustled like faint waterfalls. With her came the scent of sandalwood and pomander; she was altogether lovely.

'I've come to bring — ' The words failed, and he began to stammer. 'That is, these herbs — and — I've brought a cordial — for — I mean, for your lady mother. And 'twas my grandmother that did send me.' Seated again, now opposite her, he leaned back, half laughing, glad to be shot of the speech he had rehearsed in his head all morning.

She was nodding, her eyes soft and yet amused, timid and delighted — all at once. He had a curious feeling that she had not heard one word he had said.

'For your mother,' he repeated stupidly.

'Aye, so you said. 'Tis very kind of you, Master Fessenden.'

He looked desperately at the basket and felt her eyes on his face. He was even more afraid than before. He searched for the right words and found none. 'My name is Nicholas,' he murmured at last.

'And mine is Anna.'

Still he clung onto the basket, not knowing how to proceed.

'May I see?' She was stretching her arms towards the basket, and under the soft material of her bodice he could see the gentle swell of her breasts and the curve of finely made shoulders. She seemed to be drawing and draining him as if he were a draught she drank with her eyes. He felt almost unbalanced.

'Of course — ' he managed. But then he remembered the *Herbal* and pulled it out. He passed her the basket. She was not looking at it any more, however, but at his face. Her cheeks were flushed and her eyes anxious.

'And there's this. I brought it for thee.' He heard the strange note in his voice again and the oddness of the word 'thee'. It was a word Isaac used to Rebecca, not one he himself had ever used to a woman.

'Oh, but I cannot accept . . . my father . . . ' Her face was pained again, and he was afraid he had offended her. He moved to the edge of his seat. Her face wore such an agonized expression that he wanted to make her smile again. From the other side of the room, the two women sent them frowning looks.

'Anna — I know not how to say it, sweetheart.' His voice and his body had begun to shake. 'But this is all I can give thee now. Will it please thee take it?' He was confused, overwhelmed by the love that took possession of him.

She leaned slightly towards him. He gave in to his impulses, fell forward onto his knees, and laid the book in her lap. She was shaking her head, speechless, her eyes watering. A wave of impressions flooded into his mind: that he was wrong to be wooing without consent, wrong to be alone with her without her father's knowledge, foolish to have chosen a maiden so far beyond him. And it was all in vain. She was accepting the book, but she was not accepting him. He had overstepped the bounds of courtesy and had disturbed her.

He stood up and backed away from her. He felt as he had felt as a child when reproved by Mary for disobedience.

'Forgive me, Anna.' His hand was on the door. 'I'll think on thee.'

He turned and went out. In the courtyard outside a crowd of unkempt men gathered for a cockfight. The cocks were restrained in baskets but were crowing loudly. He felt sick with loathing and disappointment.

3

GEORGE
Goudhurst, September 1658

This field was already ploughed for the barley sowing. The brown furrows lay as straight and even as links in chainmail or threads in linen. He whistled and sang as he stepped over them.

> *And when the dogs of war growl loud*
> *I'll quit the Weald and be a proud —*
> *A Cavilally man!*

The mild afternoon sunshine touched his shoulders, and he was glad to be alive. Cromwell — 'the Protector' they had called him, poor man — was dead, or so the Kentish news asserted, and England was weary of Puritan zeal. The rumour mills in Kent ground out the word that King Charles across the water would not tarry long now, and soon the county — the country — would be restored!

He sighed and hoisted his hop hook on his shoulder. Life was good. He had the estate almost back to order again, and Tolhurst Court was not as poor as it had been at the end of the war, now that the rents were coming to him instead of to the County Committee, and now that he had recovered all his losses from the heavy fines after the war. The hops were drying in the oasts; there had been no plague of damson-hop flies this year; and the hop burrs were big and fat with pollen. And not only the hops. Elizabeth was with child again.

This strange event had shaken them in the early spring. Eleanor, the youngest, was thirteen, and they had long ago ceased to expect more. Elizabeth was almost to the end of her child-bearing years now, and she had been ill for several years with a persistent flux.

268

"Tis like to be a canker, sir,' the physician had told him.

Then suddenly, this spring — when after a cold winter he had taken her to Tunbridge Wells for the waters — the flux had stopped as mysteriously as it had started. They had rejoiced and thanked God, but fear had followed fast on the heels of joy, as Elizabeth's body began to swell.

'The canker,' she had cried. "Tis the canker, George, after all.'

And looking at her face, then growing thinner, he had feared as much. But no, more joy awaited them, for now it was quite clear that the swelling of her belly was a living, moving child. When it had first quickened, early one morning in May, she had come running out into the courtyard weeping for joy, her red hair streaming down her back and all her reserve forgotten before the servants in the moment of her discovery.

He laughed aloud, thinking of it now, for Elizabeth was plump and rosy again. She was carrying this child more easily than any before: comfortable, cheerful, young again.

He began to hurry as he neared the kitchen garden. Anna was strolling indolently under the cherry trees, but he did not want to talk to her. Since Elizabeth had been with child, all his delight in his eldest daughter had been replaced by care for his wife. In return, Anna had withdrawn. She irritated him often, seeming to prefer the company of some of the servants — especially the two kitchen maids who tended the herb gardens — to that of her own sisters. But what of that? Soon she would be wed and would have a husband to wait on. He clicked his tongue impatiently. Yes, it was time she was wed.

He frowned and scratched his jaw. Ah, but there's the rub! Will she be wed? She had proved stubborn about a short betrothal to William Frittenden, the man they had chosen for her. She wanted to wait.

He looked away from Anna and could not even bring himself to bow or smile. But his other daughters rescued him as he mounted the steps to the courtyard. Henrietta,

269

Charlotte, and Eleanor had been playing at bowls, and a spaniel bitch was chasing and barking round their ankles in high excitement.

'Hush up Maria!' Charlotte scolded. She ran to her father. 'Oh, thou'rt dreadfully hot, Father. Take some water, pray.' She wrinkled her nose at him.

He wiped away the sweat on his forehead. 'I shall. I shall. What's ado, ladies?'

'We're playing at bowls, as you can rightly see for yourself,' Eleanor said pertly.

'No we're not, goose,' Henrietta murmured. 'We have ceased and were just a-going to send Matty for you. Our mother has need of you.'

His heart constricted. 'She's ill?' Even now he worried about her.

'Nay!' the girls began to giggle. 'She's sent for the midwife . . . thinks her time is come.'

His temper rose, and he heard the snap in his own voice: 'Oh, why did ye not tell me?'

His daughters stared back, wide-eyed and flushed with excitement. The spaniel stopped barking and sat down on the bricks with its tail swishing back and forth in the dust. But he could not be angry; the girls had all been longing for this day.

As he hurried to the scullery door, Henrietta caught his sleeve. 'Is there nothing we can do, Father?'

'The midwife's bidden?'

'Aye.'

'Then nothing — but tell Nancy to heat water quickly. And get thy oldest sister inside at once. Thy mother's well, I know, but — ' He did not bother to finish what he was saying.

Elizabeth was sitting in the great family bed upstairs where they had first lain together. A maid hovered in the doorway, wringing her hands in distress. George dismissed her with instructions to bring in the midwife as soon as the old woman arrived.

He leaned over the bed, kissed Elizabeth's forehead, and adjusted the bolsters. 'It's time, is it, already?'

She nodded. Her eyes were glittering. 'I'm certain 'tis a son. I've never felt so sure and strong ere this.'

He smoothed the folds of the loose linen gown around her shoulders and looked lovingly at the rounded curve of the baby pushing up the sheet. 'Son or daughter, it matters not, so you be well.'

'I'm well.' Her voice dropped lower, and he saw the feverish joy of motherhood that he had never expected to see on her face again.

'Then I'm content,' he said.

'Sit, husband, wilt'ou — whilst thou may? I'd like thee by me, till the midwife comes at least.'

He settled on the edge of the bed and took her hand. Every so often she held his harder, and he watched her face change as a pang gripped her body. But she did not yet cry out.

'Art sure, dear heart?' he asked uncertainly. 'You have had false pangs ere this — then nothing.'

Another pain crossed her body like a harrow turning up earth and twisting it over. There was no doubt this time.

'Yes,' she whispered, smiling drily as she saw his doubt melt away, 'Yes, I'm sure.'

'Then there is nothing — ?'

'I want to talk for now. 'Tis easier than the other babes, except when the pain passes me. I want to talk.'

'Then we'll talk. But rest, dearling, for what is to come.' He remembered Charlotte's birth in particular, though Eleanor's had been more recent. The child had seemed to tear Elizabeth's body in two and at birth was as red and resentful at being brought into the world as a fox-cub pulled unsuspecting from its lair. Red and angry — and leaving Elizabeth wracked with exhaustion. He did not want her so exhausted this time, and he said so. 'Thou must rest, dearling.'

'I know.' Another pang tightened its hold, and she moaned this time. But as soon as it had gone, she brightened. 'Then you talk. Talk to me of Anna's wedding.'

He shut his eyes for a second and almost leaned against Elizabeth before remembering her condition. 'Ah — Anna.' He opened his eyes again and frowned.

'You look so troubled, love.' Elizabeth touched his brow lightly.

'I am, for her sake. Anna and I — we've hardly been able to speak to each other in latter days.'

She looked at him sharply. 'That's unlike your Anna.' She always called her *Your Anna*. 'Why? Have you offended her?'

'Not that I know of. At first I thought 'twas just a fit of womanish temper, but it passes not away — grows worse, even.'

'I am dismayed I haven't observed — oh!' Her hand tightened on his again, and her face paled. She doubled over, her breath coming hard and ragged and her face prickling with sweat.

Sweat broke out on his own brow as he remembered Charlotte's birth again. He murmured in compassion but felt utterly helpless. ''Tis bad, is it?' he whispered a moment later when she flopped back on the bolster with her eyes shut.

She did not answer immediately, and when she did he saw that her lips were slightly cracked. 'I've a terrible thirst, George.'

Glad of an errand, he leaped up. Too quickly, for she opened startled eyes to him, wide with fright. As he had many times before with this wise and beautiful woman, he felt a clumsy fool. 'I'm sorry, love. I'll send Nancy for water. She's boiling water anyhow.' He stumbled over the doorframe and stood at the top of the stairs. 'Ho! Nancy!'

There was no answer. Instead he could hear the drone of a wasp in the window and the girls' voices from below stairs, giddy with joy. *Damme!* he thought angrily. *Can't they be still?*

He rushed headlong into the hall below and headlong into Anna. Her face was pink and her skirts were stained here and there with purplish-red splotches. In her hair was some leaf or other, and her hands were full of greenery. He opened his mouth to rebuke her for unseemliness, but then swallowed the rebuke. She of all his daughters would be most help with Elizabeth if the babe came untimely, before the midwife. He could not cross her now.

He plucked the leaf out of her hair and made himself smile. 'Anna, sweetheart, thy mother —' Her

272

blue eyes were soft, and he realized painfully that all the constraint between them was on his side, because of William Frittenden.

'I know — is in labour,' she said quietly.

He was flustered at the plainness of her words. What could she know of the pangs of childbed and the sufferings of women? 'Nancy's not about. I sent her off. Mayhap you'll wait on us a while?'

Her eyes lit up, and he saw a joy in her that had been quenched for months. 'I shall, Father. Pray forgive my graceless dress, but I knew my mother was brought to bed, and I was gathering leaves for her.'

'*Leaves*? Have you lost your senses?'

Anna laughed and dropped a curtsy. 'Nay. I've been getting raspberry leaves for her. And I need hot water and honey to make a cordial for her. And comfrey — '

'Raspberry leaves? Comfrey?' His head was dizzy with bewilderment. 'Well, you shall speak of it ere long . . . come, the women are in the scullery. Make haste, for I cannot leave your mother alone for long.' And he turned and ran back up the stairs, forgetting about the cold water.

He found Elizabeth bolt upright in the bed. She had flung back the sheet and torn off her gown. The bed was soaked, water dripping to the floor. He saw her in all her beautiful and terrible womanliness, and loved her as he had never loved before — loved her as fiercely as she loved this little being that was battering its way into the world through her body. Her face was intent, eyes wide open and fixed on the end of the bed. She neither saw nor heard him, nor could she speak. Her hands were like claws on the side of the bed, stiff and white as she crouched forward and dug her nails into the flock mattress. But for the moment she was not crying out. She had become somehow inhuman, yet altogether human.

Her body convulsed and shuddered as he stepped to the foot of the bed. Fear rose in him like a sickness. 'Oh, my dear Bessie! Whatever shall I do? How shall I help thee?' The sound of his panicked voice only frightened him more.

At last she seemed to hear. She looked at him as if from a long way off. 'The midwife,' she ground out from between clenched jaws. 'Oh, *fetch the midwife!'*

Then two things happened at once: the tension in her body eased for a moment, and she became plainly aware of his horror and fear. She bowed her head over her knees, drew them together, and tried to pull up the sheet, as if ashamed.

He reached forward quickly. 'Nay, do without it, if thou'rt better this way. Dost think I'm dismayed to see thee naked, dear heart?' He leaned against the post of the bed.

A ghost of a smile touched her lips. 'I know thou art, but — God help me — ' The pain seized her again, cutting off her answer. She bore down again.

He could see that something was different now, for her cries and groans had turned to roars, and her face was suffused with blood. He thought he had never seen her so bright and so alive, yet so aweful.

He came to the head of the bed and put his mouth against her ear and his arm around her back. He found himself wanting to shout and gasp with her. 'Lean hard on me, Bess. Lean hard. The babe is nigh coming.'

Nancy and Anna were in the room, suddenly — Nancy the old nursemaid who had waited on all the girls since their babyhood, and now pressed into service in the absence of a midwife; and Anna, who had never before seen childbed, now to see her mother naked on the bed, shouting in pity and joy to birth her child. He had not heard them enter, and lost all track of time, except that punctuated by the waves of tension in Elizabeth's body. She was falling asleep between them now, limp against him, eyes dazed and surprised when she woke after these brief intervals to push down again. He wondered if he was falling asleep himself, for the sun seemed to have lengthened the shadows a little.

Anna placed a cool cloth over Elizabeth's forehead and with him supported her each time she bore down. Nancy hobbled, muttering, around the bed, until at last Anna sent her out. 'Go, Nancy, pray — '

George saw the old woman's unhappiness, and her relief as well. But then Anna softened her words. 'Perhaps the midwife is tarrying, or Matty is waylaid.

274

I beg thee, send and see. This babe won't wait for anyone.'

He looked at Anna gratefully. Her face was just a few inches from his own, separated only by the red stream of Elizabeth's unbound hair and her hot, straining shoulders.

'Well said,' he whispered. 'Nancy's not a one for childbed, and never was.'

Anna did not smile back, but her eyes were steady, holding his, and saying, *All will be well, do not fear.* He drew courage from those steady eyes.

But then Anna moved abruptly, and he noticed that the tone of Elizabeth's cries had changed. The lapses between the waves of pain had grown longer, and she had relaxed.

Anna was facing her mother now, her hands on Elizabeth's feet. He was surprised at her bravery and sympathy; she seemed to know quite naturally what her mother needed.

'Push down, dear mother! I see the babe's crown.'

He almost let go of his wife's shoulders; he saw for the first time that he was faint-hearted and cowardly in comparison with a woman. Would the midwife *never* come?

Elizabeth was gasping, crying, laughing — all at once. Then with a final heaving, shuddering push, the baby was born, and she sank back against him. Anna's hands were out, swift and somehow knowing, gathering the wailing child into the cloths laid out in the wooden cradle beside the bed weeks before — gathering, and lifting the baby onto Elizabeth's distended belly.

He leaned over to see the baby's form, but she was too quick for him. He eased Elizabeth gently down and covered her legs.

'I have a brother,' Anna whispered. Tears began to pour down her face. 'Thou hast a son! Look, Father, oh, look, my lady mother!'

Elizabeth reached forward feebly and rested her arms on the baby's loosely covered body. Another thin, mewing cry splintered the room, and George's own breathing became uneven. He fell to his knees with his face pressed against Elizabeth's damp skin and wept for joy.

When he came fully to himself again, the midwife had come and was busying herself about the room giving directions to Elizabeth to suckle the babe, and to Nancy — now that the birth was over — to remove the sodden bedding. His son was properly swaddled now, and the midwife was going through her mysterious rites with all the haste and mumbling of an old village priest saying the mass. He stood up again.

The midwife looked at him suspiciously. 'Fie upon you, Squire Tolhurst, weeping like a woman by your new babby's bed. You've no place at a birthing, sir. Get you gone — you'll bring ill luck.'

Elizabeth raised her eyes from the baby's face: serene, madonna-like — all the lioness in her gone now. The child was suckling noisily at her breast, and he swelled with pride. 'Superstitious cant, Goody Medhurst,' Elizabeth said firmly. 'I'll have none of it here. But for my husband and my daughter, this babe would have had rough passage. I thank thee not for thy lateness.'

The old woman's face turned scarlet, and her cheeks puffed out like a toad's. 'Aye — ' she spat, 'Yon babe's faster on his little feet than I on mine in my dotage, I lay. But I'm here at your bidding now, am I not? And there's more yet adone.' She looked spitefully at Anna, who now stood apart with her hands clasped, watching hungrily, waiting to be of further service. George wished he could hold her, to thank her for her calm resolve, but he guessed she would spurn him now after his months of indifference . . .

'This lass 'ere, now, is she good for nothing but a-standing and a-gawping?'

For the second time that day he felt his temper rise. 'You're speaking to my eldest daughter. Hold your tongue, and do your work. She has a cordial — '

The old woman looked cunningly at Anna. 'A cordial, have you? And what be in't, pray?'

Anna came forward with an uncertain look at him to which he tried to respond with silent encouragement. ''Tis raspberry leaves and comfrey, ma'am. I read in Culpeper's 'tis the very thing.'

George saw the midwife's startled and grudging recognition. The old woman's face changed. 'Ah, you're wise, then, lass, after all. Aye, thy mother hath need of this.' She folded back the lower part of the sheet, and he saw with dismay that there were new blood stains on the fresh linens. 'See, there is still blood a-plenty.' Was there a glint of evil or triumph in her eyes because she was still needed? 'The suckling child should assuage it, yet — '

He looked anxiously at his wife, but she was completely absorbed. He prayed that she had not heard and pulled the covers back quickly. Then he drew the midwife aside into the window alcove for a moment. 'This bleeding,' he said, unsure of himself — hating her, yet needing her counsel, ' — all's not well?'

'She *will* bleed,' the old woman said laconically. 'They all bleed, as you would know, were husbands midwives, as you be not! And she *will* bleed.'

He took her shoulders to shake her in impotent fury, but she pushed him away; her arms were muscular and strong like none he had seen on a woman, and he was suddenly afraid. 'What do you mean?'

'The cordial will help. Fortunate for you your daughter's wise. But the blood is heavy. You were best to your knees, squire, and mayhap look for a wet-nurse.'

He returned to the bedside, shaking slightly. *No,* he thought slowly, *No, the woman has lied.* He looked at Elizabeth's face — pink, unaware, and happy — and at the baby's. *My son. My first son.* The hair was dark and wet, the crinkled face shut against the sudden light, but at ease in the warmth and comfort of his mother's milk. The child was well. The mother was well. *All would be well.*

He turned away. The voice inside him was a chant in the dark.

Anna followed him out into the upstairs corridor and put her hand lightly onto his shoulder. He looked into her face, then away again.

'How did you learn from Culpeper's *Herbal?*' His voice seemed to be swallowed in the stifling heat of roof timbers and narrow walls in the autumn

277

evening unmoving air, and he leaned exhausted against the wall.

''Twas a gift, my Father — ' She broke off.

'From whom?' he asked, thinking of her friends the serving maids, and wondering where maids had money nowadays for such extravagances.

'From — from the Fessendens.'.

He hardly registered surprise, but then the name penetrated, and Isaac's face came vividly before him.

Isaac, he thought. *Matty must go for Isaac. But why? What can Isaac do? No physician to stop the bleeding . . . All shall be well . . . Rebecca . . . has she not just on St Mary's day in harvest time gotten herself a child again? So I think I heard . . .* He struggled to remember. *And if the child be not alive . . . for she has lost many before . . .*

'Anna,' he said unsteadily, straightening his back again.

She looked back at him, and beads of moisture broke out on her upper lip. She was afraid, and he didn't understand why.

'Anna, before you speak to your sisters — and I want you to tell them, for I shall sit here and wait upon your mother — I want you to send Matty or Edmund to Maidstone this night. I shall have a letter for Isaac Fessenden, the tailor — did you not mention him ere this?' His mind was confused now. How had Isaac come into his thoughts? 'I may have need of Isaac — ' He stopped, frowning, almost broken with weariness. 'Or of his goodwife. I think — I think — she has kinsmen hereabouts and may not mind to come with him anyhow — ' He knew his mind was browsing and tried to tug it back with the reins of his will. 'So bring me a quill and a paper, and send Matty here.'

She heard him out, and he knew she was thinking — quick as her mother — about the meaning under the words. 'I shall, Father, but — '

He dropped onto a chest beside the stairs and leaned back on a tapestry Elizabeth had sewn in the early days of their marriage. 'But what, Anna?'

'Matty is old and slow, now. Can you not — ?'

'Then send Edmund. It matters not.' He stared at her, still pleased by her usefulness, but puzzled by her look of determination.

She swung round so that her skirts lifted, and he caught a glimpse of petticoats: lace and a slim ankle. Her face was transfigured with joy.

NICHOLAS

'You *shall* go with us, Nicholas,' Isaac said. 'I'll be glad of someone with me on the lonely way home.'

'And Adam? Should he not — ?' Nicholas grew uncomfortable, knowing he himself was his uncle's favourite (though unresented by the others) and not wanting their birthright.

'No, I cannot spare Adam — or Charlie — from the work. Thou'rt good with the donkey, too, and Rebecca's still not strong.'

In his mind's eye Nicholas saw his uncle in the cart with his arm around Rebecca: the strong and the sweet. He groaned inwardly. *I need my own.* 'Yes,' he said aloud. 'She needs thee. I'll gladly go with thee.'

One of Isaac's large hands suddenly came out and caught him by the sleeve. If his uncle's hands had not been accustomed to the ways of soft, yielding cloth, the garment would have torn, but Isaac was gentle. He looked up to see his uncle's eyes, dark and liquid as they looked into his own.

'It is good for my dear friend George,' he said slowly. 'I have long wanted to return the thanks I owe him. Now I can. And — I know — it is good for thee, also.' His face crinkled into laughter. 'Good, is't not?'

Nicholas felt himself redden. Since he had confessed his love of Anna to Isaac, his uncle had relented and even sometimes encouraged him by bringing news of her. But now he was speechless. He had not seen her for two years.

'I said, 'twill be to thy advantage, perhaps, to accompany us, Nicholas.'

'Aye.' He looked up, marvelling at Isaac's understanding, and moved. 'But how can I repay *you*, my uncle?'

Isaac abruptly let him go and turned away. His voice was harsh. 'There's naught to repay, Nicholas. 'Tis I who pay a debt — to thee.'

ANNA

A hush had fallen on the house today. Henrietta, Charlotte, and Eleanor kept to their chamber, bidden by Nancy, and fretted in the heat. Only she had been left to her own, and she wandered restlessly in and out of the house. She heard the murmur of her mother's and father's voices from time to time, from behind the shut door of their chamber, or the cry of the baby, so she knew all was well. But where was the rejoicing they should expect, and why had her father not sent to the church to have St Mary's bells rung in thanksgiving?

All the joy of yesterday had vanished in the chill breath of this morning's early fog as it rolled up the Weald and curled round the cherry trees. So what if Edmund had been sent for Isaac Fessenden and his wife? What good was that to her? It was Nicholas she wanted, but he would not come. And in the meanwhile something was oddly amiss above stairs, and no one would speak of it.

She must find out. She had held that child, seen his minuscule toes, fingers, and felt his flailing, crying, wet body next to hers for an instant before she had wrapped him. She had seen the strange little buds between his legs — buds that meant manhood: minute, frightening, beautiful . . . her *brother*.

She bit down on her lip, willing the child to live. Would he die? Was this the cause of the hush and secrecy?

She *must* find out.

She pressed urgently into the kitchen where the wenches were dressing fowl for dinner. Odd how the round of maids went on while their ladies bore sons in the chambers above . . . Martha would know . . .

The frightened girl, drawn from the kitchen into the courtyard, where they would not be overheard, began to blubber. 'He doesn't want thee frighted, lady. We maysn't tell any o' ye a word.'

'Martha, come,' she coaxed, hating the honey in her own voice, 'I'm not frightened like my foolish sisters. Was I not at the birthing?'

The girl stared stupidly. 'Truly, I don't know.'

'I was, so tell me, pray — '

Martha could not answer but led her with faltering steps to the outhouse where most of the household linens were purged. Piled inside on the flagged floor were bundles of bloodstained sheets.

The maid burst into tears.

Absently, Anna reached into her pocket, found a comfit for her, then sent her back to the kitchen. Alone, she stood and stared at the bedding.

She did not remain there for long. Instead she gathered her skirts and ran back into the house. Raspberry leaves and comfrey had failed. She must find something else! Oh, would that she herself had the knowledge of a Culpeper!

Book in hand, she returned to the courtyard. She could hear her sisters' voices in their chamber above the back kitchen, chattering like sparrows. They seemed as unaware of her relative freedom as she felt uninterested in their incarceration. Instead she leafed slowly through the book, her eyes staring blankly at the neat drawings of fumitory and foxglove, bittersweet and bryony.

Then she clapped it shut. There was no comfort in it. She must see if she could encourage her mother, instead, with ordinary cordials to make her cheerful. She could not stop the bleeding, perhaps, but she could at least cheer her.

Dropping the book into the deep pocket of her skirt, she went thoughtfully down the steps to the kitchen garden. She would collect fennel, St John's wort, and knapweed . . . she counted them off on her fingers. The weight of doubt and sorrow lifted slightly under the late morning sunlight as she began to gather what she needed.

A smell of drying hops came on the air from the oasts. She knew her father was pleased with the harvest and was glad, but she could think of nothing else for very long except the bloodied sheets. She looked around unhappily. Under the cherry and hazelnut trees the wavering beams of sunlight were hazy with motes of dust from the wheat harvest: everything was golden and still.

Everything except Anna Tolhurst, she thought, snapping off a twig violently.

She set the herbs aside and walked beyond the trees to the dovecotes. One hen was sunning itself — fat and sleek — at one of the tiny entrance holes. The rest — shy as ever — were somewhere secretly within. She heard the occasional flutter and soft calling. Above her the wild woodpigeons in the poplars that guarded the hop gardens were calling to their tame cousins below, but the doves remained. A cart rumbled somewhere down the lane.

She sat down under a poplar and let herself drift, neither hearing nor seeing anything clearly. The book in her pocket lay heavily against her thigh. She pressed her hand on it and felt the warmth of book and fabric under her palm. Then without moving her hand she shut her eyes. The book was the strong back of Nicholas Fessenden, hard and warm under her fingers. Her arms were round him, and his round her, pressing into her own back, pulling her close to him. And if she screwed her eyes tightly shut she could see — not her wooer, William Frittenden — but the face she had seen only twice; the face that was as stamped on her memory now as Culpeper's perfect drawings: his dark, searching eyes and small nose, his crinkling black hair cut short like a Roundhead's. It was his face that stopped her at every turn when her father spoke of marriage.

She turned her head and began to weep. The crying had been pent up too long, and it took her by surprise. Since no one could see her, she let the tears flow where they would, her hand moving slowly over the book he

282

had given her, and his face receding further into the abstraction of grief.

At last she opened her eyes.

The reality was shattering. She screamed and jumped to her feet.

The very face she had seen behind her tightly closed eyelids was leaning close to hers. Now, as she leaped up, she was almost as tall as the young man who faced her.

'Anna Tolhurst?' he seemed unsure, and she remembered her tear-stained face and wiped it quickly on the back of her hand. But she felt vulnerable, stripped before him because he had seen her crying, so she kept the back of her wrist over her mouth and just stared.

He stepped back, and she could see that he was afraid of offending her. 'It *is* Anna?'

She let her hand drop and pushed it into her pocket. There was the book, still hard and warm. 'Yes.' It was all she could say.

He laughed suddenly, his hair bobbing backwards and his teeth very white. 'Am I a ghost that you scream and stop your weeping to stare? Or am I just hatefully ugly? Pray tell me, if so, and I shall leave you.'

Ugly? She stared all the more, still speechless. *No, he was the fairest man she had ever looked upon!* 'No, no,' she said stupidly.

'Then what — ?' He frowned, but then seemed embarrassed. His eyes sought something else, and he pointed to the pocket that was now stretching the cloth of her gown. 'What — is this? Don't you know 'tis too heavy a thing for such fine stuff as your dress?'

She found herself smiling at his carefulness. 'Aye, but see what it is.' And she pulled out Culpeper's *Herbal*.

His face changed. The laughing youth was replaced by the ardent lover. 'So you do read it?'

'Read it?' Her voice was steady now, but faint. 'I read it daily. 'Tis never far from me, and I know it well.' She was answering unthinkingly now, her tongue moving without command while her mind sifted the questions. *Why had he come? How had he found her?* 'But, sir, how did you find me?'

He pushed his hands inside his jerkin with a slight swagger that she rather liked. 'I asked thy father's

283

maids.' He shrugged, and his eyes didn't leave her face. She saw that his face had matured and grown more serious, but that — by his closely barbered hair — he was still a Parliament's man. How could she tell him — directly — that she was glad to see him? Absently she noticed that the poplars had already dropped a few triangular yellow leaves at her feet. How could she tell him — ? She raised her eyes; he was still watching her, so that her heart began to hammer loudly and her voice sounded cracked. 'Why have you come?'

He did not answer with his voice but with his hands — stretching them out. His hands were large but finely boned.

She stepped back a pace but was angry with herself for doing so. However, once it was done, how was she to step forward again? 'My father sent for your uncle and his wife, but not for you, did he not?' she blurted at last.

His hands returned to his jerkin, but with slightly less assurance now. He breathed a heavy sigh. 'Aye, but Isaac had need of me. And so, I think, Anna Tolhurst, do you.' He looked at her so piercingly now that she began to tremble. 'But I do speak out of turn, I fear,' he went on, moving away. He leaned against the tree nearest the one where she had been sitting. 'For I hear you have another sweetheart. Perhaps I was mistaken, but I thought you had understood — '

'Understood what?' she begged. His bitter tone was unfamiliar.

'Never mind it . . . but is't true? If 'tis, I should go away and trouble you not.'

She sank down on the grass beside him on her knees. 'Nay, I'm sorry, Nicholas. Do not say so. I do not have a sweetheart.' She shook her head, now as earnest as he. 'But I *am* betrothed. My father — ' She averted her eyes. 'My father arranged it because he and my mother — ' She could not finish it: *had no son*. He would misunderstand her now. But the mention of her mother was her undoing, and she began to cry again.

'Then heaven forgive me.' He bent towards her as if to raise her up. 'May I not kiss thee, then, as a farewell?'

She did not think of hiding the tears this time. Let him think what he would! But she could not betray her family by letting him kiss her. She scrambled up quickly and brushed the dead leaves off her skirt. 'No,' she said sadly, 'no, I think not.' She made herself walk away.

His voice followed her, an edge of desperation in it. 'Then I should never think of thee more as a sweetheart?' He spread his hands, and all the remaining bravado had gone out of his voice and face. 'I do not know if I can bear that.'

The words cut into her. She turned. 'Your mind is free, Nicholas; your heart is free to think as you like.'

'And so is thine, Anna.'

'Then we shall be thinking the same,' she said softly.

Up in the courtyard, the spaniel began to bark, and Charlotte's loud voice called imperiously across the gardens. 'Where *is* she, Henrietta? Dost know? . . . *Anna!*'

Her sisters were evidently out of doors at last. She did not want to be found with Nicholas. 'I must go now,' she said quickly, turning away again.

He had reached her before she knew it. In the cushioned grass under the trees his footfalls made no noise, and he caught up with her before she had taken five steps. Seizing her shoulders, he pulled her gently round to face him, so that her eyes were on a level with his chin, but only a few inches away. 'Don't leave me like that, sweetheart, I beg thee.'

She tried to pull away, but it was a half-hearted attempt, and she saw that he knew it.

'Thy sisters — aye, I know,' he murmured. 'That's what thou'rt fretting about.'

She moved her shoulders slightly and looked straight into his eyes, seeing her own reflection in the dark pupils. He seemed to take her into himself, all of her, as she wanted to take him to herself.

Neither of them spoke for several moments. Then he let her shoulders go and slid one hand around her back, and with his other hand lifted her chin.

Is it so easy? she wondered — if there was time for wondering. *It's just as I thought of him.* She leaned towards him, slowly allowing him to draw her forward, slowly letting her mouth go up to his. Then he was kissing

285

her, and she was engulfed in the tide of her own blood as it rushed to her face and sent her heart hammering again. Her knees weakened. He smoothed her back with his hand and pressed close against her until she felt they had become one being.

But then she awoke. The excited barks of the spaniel came nearer, and behind the dog — her sisters.

She fought free of him, fear overcoming passion. 'I must go now, love.'

'Aye — go. But I shall see thee again. Rebecca is to stay a while.' His voice was strangely calm to her own frantic mind.

The spaniel suddenly leaped onto her skirts. She was strung so tight that she struck it down with a shout of anger. 'Away, foolish dog!'

The spaniel dropped its tail between its legs and cowered in the grass. Nicholas reached down to stroke it, glad — she thought — of the diversion. His face was flushed.

Hearing her own voice, she was stung by the sound of her own rage. She went forward to face the inevitable Charlotte, but although her back was now turned to Nicholas again, she was as aware of his hard, warm body against her own as if he still held her. No daydreams, these, and her heart sang out. She was loved by — and loved — this man of Kent.

4

GEORGE
Goudhurst, October 1658

This morning she had not spoken distinctly to him. She seemed able to hear him clearly enough, but her speech was slurred, and she was drifting now in and out of a deep sleep. It wasn't an easy sleep, but something heavy and drugged, as if the midwife had mixed too strong a syrup of poppy seeds for her. When she did awake it was usually only to loll about clumsily on the bolster. She had ceased asking for little Edward now, too; her mind seemed shadowed and confused. A few days ago she had asked him faintly for Charlotte, and he had sent for her, only to watch the poor child sent away again. *'Nay! That's not my baby! 'Tis a full-grown wench. Bring me my baby!'*

But her weeping entreaties had stopped the same day, and she seemed to have forgotten not only about Edward — who was now safely feeding in Rebecca's arms at the other end of the house — but also about their daughters. She wandered in and out of her childhood: one day she was a girl again, and the next day Livesey's men were sacking Tolhurst Court. And every day the blood flowed on, a thin, scarlet nightmare. Her life was seeping away.

He realized as he watched at her bedside that he had relied on her even more than he knew: her cool judgment, her quick mind, her ability to see to the heart of their trials. And now she was leaving him, slipping away as surely as the poplars were losing their leaves. Now he would have to decide everything, solve everything, dispose everything. He bowed his head. *I am too old to do these things without her.*

Then there was the matter of Anna's marriage. He would have to get the banns called. Yet, was there need for haste? He had Edward now, and — he smiled to himself — Edward was growing apace. He would not have to have the estate, what was left of it, settled upon Anna; he would have to go to Chancery and change his will . . . And she would marry well, certainly, but it was Edward who would come into the estate: a son, not a daughter.

He turned his eyes again on his wife's white face. Her eyes were closed and her breathing shallow. *How could he think of Edward, Anna, Frittenden, and the estate at such a time?* A choking sensation blocked his throat, and he was furious, suddenly, with the demand of death. *How could his own heart keep beating while her blood was trickling from her body?*

He moved the linens aside tenderly, willing the blood to be an illusion, an evil from which he might escape. But no: the same hideously familiar stain of fresh blood. *God's wounds! Would nothing assuage it?*

He pushed the covers back in place so roughly that Elizabeth's eyes opened. She made the words 'dear love' with her lips, then slept again. He cried out in despair and leaned his head against her. Though he could feel her ribs, she was still warm. *Dear God in heaven, let her live. Let her live.*

Unbidden, William Frittenden's face returned to his mind. If Elizabeth died, Anna would be beside herself with sorrow. Even when a horse or puppy died she grieved bitterly . . . but for her mother? Yes, she needed a man to comfort her.

Frittenden was courteous and well-bred. He played the lute and viol charmingly and attired himself in the satins and lace of Cromwell's sons-in-law now (curiously) the fashion again. Such refinements struck George as somewhat frivolous, but Frittenden was good-humoured and well-to-do. *Needs must,* he thought to himself. *And Anna must.*

Had he said it aloud? No one stirred. He kept his head where it was, still feeling the warm bed-linens against his brow, and thought of Anna. Somewhere in his mind a faint warning wriggled like a maggot on a hop bine. *What was it?*

Anna did not want Frittenden. Perhaps she wanted someone else. But who? He could not remember.

His mind strayed back to Edward again, curled in Rebecca's arms, and to Rebecca herself, growing plump on the sweetmeats and fruits of a countryman's autumn table, and resting from the demands of her own family. Edward had smiled at him today — or was it yesterday? Puzzled blue eyes clearing into a beatific twinkle, and the little mouth pursing, trembling into a gummy smile, then a chuckle. Edward . . . but there was a shadow standing behind Rebecca, falling over the face of his child.

Nicholas Fessenden. He did not like the youth and wished Isaac had not left him with Rebecca. Though like his uncle to look upon, Nicholas was too saturnine by half, glowering at him, serious like his father Robert — not to be trusted. He would send for Isaac to fetch the lad home. No, he did not need to. Nicholas could quite well go home by himself.

'Oh — George — '

His head went up, and he shook it, trying to think. Had he been dreaming?

Elizabeth's eyes were open wide now. She was straining forward. Quite clearly, she said, 'The butterfly is on her hair. See it?'

He frowned, afraid now. 'Yes,' he murmured, not understanding at all. Any words to comfort her.

'It will fly away.'

He squeezed her hand hard, nodding dumbly as she shut her eyes again.

NICHOLAS

Make thyself useful, Isaac had instructed him. But how?

He sat thoughtfully in the cramped room above the stables that he was sharing with one of the servants. That in itself did not trouble him; he had never slept alone since he was a child, and he was used to low ceilings and crowded spaces. Yet his aunt was housed in comfort; she was his only tie with home — or what he called home — but he could not see her. Her meals were taken to her in the nursery, he found out, by Nancy, and she either did not or could not ask to see him. He felt shut out, neglected. Tolhurst, courteous as long as Isaac had remained, had withdrawn and was churlish with him now.

Worse still, he had scarcely seen Anna since that first day out under the trees. He had no idea what she might be thinking or feeling, no idea how to find or approach her. From time to time the servants at table in the hall spoke of her and of Frittenden, her betrothed, but they were disinterested, and all the talk was of the mother, who was dying now. They did not speak of Rebecca, but he guessed she had won favour, for everyone said how fat and healthy the new babe was growing.

Anna he saw only in the distance as she walked with her younger sisters or occasionally at the high table at the end of the hall — when the family took their meals with the servants — but she seemed as distant as a princess, and he dared not go to her.

Tolhurst's servants stolidly refused all offers of help; he felt impotent as well as lonely. For the first few days he had perused the Tolhurst library, though there was little to his taste. But for Anna, he would gladly have gone home.

Following his thoughts first down one path and then down another, he at last decided he would risk trying to talk with Anna again. But whom could he trust? No one. All the servants stood steadfastly with their master.

He jumped up with a sudden resolve and found a quill and inkhorn.

> My Aunt Rebecca, he wrote carefully, I wish to go home, for I can do no good here. But first, I pray you, will you speak to Mistress Anna on my behalf? As you have ever loved mine uncle, so do I love this lady.

He set down the pen, and ink splattered everywhere. Despair seized him. *Rebecca cannot read!* And moreover, if she could, whatever could she say to Anna that he could not say quite as well himself? No, it was a foolish idea to put a note in the basket of food Nancy carried

to Rebecca from the hall. An utterly childish thought!
He must find some other means to put a stop to fantasy
and vain hope.

He banged the chamber door behind him and
clattered down the wooden stairs into the stableyard.
Edmund, the fellow who had ridden to Maidstone with
the plea for Isaac's help, was raking muck out of the
stable and shovelling it into a cart.

He hesitated. 'May I not help thee, Edmund?'
The fellow must be about ten years his senior, he
judged, and throughout the week had been sullen and
resentful of him.

He kept up his shovelling now, grunting with the
effort, not looking up. 'Aye, there's a shovel back
of the manger.' It was the most friendly word he
had given so far.

They worked side by side. Nicholas was unaccustomed to such drudgery and soon felt his back aching
and his arms trembling, but he went on, his teeth
clenched in resolve. He would not be the first to give up.

'Thou'rt a good worker, Master Fessenden,' Edmund
said at last. His face was streaked with sweat and
muck, but he was grinning, and Nicholas knew he'd
gained an ally.

He nodded breathlessly. 'And you — you're a
Hercules.'

Edmund looked back blankly. 'What?'

'Thou'rt as strong as can be — that's what I meant —
and quick, too.'

Now the lad looked embarrassed. 'Well-a-day, so
art thou.' He seemed to be sizing him up. Then, 'How
should you like to take the master's mare out in my
stead? I was late rising this morn and am behindhand
in my work. No 'arm'll come; she's gentle as a lamb,
but wants her head, and thou'rt a man with horses,
as I've heard.'

The length of this speech, as well as the contents,
took Nicholas completely by surprise. 'I don't know who
told thee tales of me. I doubt they spoke the truth.' He
frowned. 'Would you not let me do your work here while
you take the mare yourself?'

'Not I! Matty would have me in the stocks for't.'

291

'Nay!'

'He would, though.' Edmund stepped into the stable and came out with a bridle. 'Here, you've been looking peaky. A ride will be the thing. Take it.'

'But if I damage the mare?'

'You shan't.'

Nicholas straightened his back. 'No, I shan't.' He looked back into the stable. 'But what horse is that?' An unfamiliar animal was stalled there, and he heard the steady grinding of the horse's jaws and the rustle of hay.

'Oh — that? 'Tis young William Frittenden's beast. He's here a-courtin' our lady Anna.'

Something snapped in Nicholas' mind. He turned angrily. Would Anna betray him? *No*, reason argued, *no, for she has good as said she loves me*. He tightened his fists. *The lass is straitened by her father's wishes. Poor Anna!* Still, the thought of Frittenden's presence at Tolhurst Court made him desperate with jealousy.

He flung himself onto the horse's back so violently that she started, and Edmund shouted a warning. But now he needed a gallop as much as the horse did.

Within a few minutes he was out in the lane with the breeze in his face and the strong legs of the mare striding under him. He held her hard at first — she should know who was master — for he knew she was accustomed to a heavier weight on her back and might be skittish. At the gate he turned her away from the village and rode south-east along the lane.

He was reminded for a moment of errands for his father around Chilham, and of errands his father had done for his grandfather before that. And where was the Fessenden clan now? Poor, or dead. And where was he going? He knew not where. And what if, please God, Anna were free to wed him, how could he support a wife? How indeed! He was not even apprenticed, and now that Adam was of age and Charlie almost so, and both with sweethearts already, they would soon want their cousins out of the shop and out of the house . . .

The mare started at the sound of a squirrel chittering in a chestnut tree. Several nuts descended in front of them, and she shied. 'Go then!' he cried, and loosened the reins. The mare began to pant with excitement, and her hooves thudded and thundered into a gallop.

It was then that he knew what he must do. With the whole blue Weald spreading out before him under the faint mist of autumn, he knew what he must do.

He bent forward, gathered the reins closer, and laid his face to one side of the rising, falling, straining neck of the horse. The wind in his face and the flying strands of mane almost forced his eyes shut, but through the cracks between his eyelids he could see the windmills of Cranbrook in the distance, and he kept his eyes on them.

Cranbrook, Goudhurst, Maidstone, Chilham — all he had known as a boy and as a young man — must be left behind. He would take Josiah his brother and go to the New World. If they worked for their Uncle John, who wanted sons, he would have the means to send for Anna and to provide for her in the Bay Colony. Would she come? Could she leave her betrothed?

He turned the horse before reaching Cranbrook. Now that he had made up his mind what he wanted, he felt hopeful and carefree. If he could show himself worthy to Anna's father, all might be well, after all. He must simply give his heart's desire into God's hands and let it rest there.

He clattered into the stableyard and threw the reins over the mare's head as he slid off. She was lathered and trembling. In the stable he rubbed her down, covered her with a cloth, filled her manger with hay, and went to look for Edmund.

The place was deserted. He called up the stairs to the loft, and he called across the gardens. Edmund did not answer. There was no sound but the calling of the doves and pigeons and the wind in the poplars.

He rushed across the kitchen gardens. His eyes were down so that he would not miss his footing on the courtyard steps, so he saw the hem of her dress barely in time to avoid hurtling into her. *Anna.*

'Nicholas!'

He stood only a step or two below her. For a moment he forgot entirely about Frittenden. 'Oh, my dearest girl — ' His arms went straight out to her.

293

She drew back. 'Oh, no, thou canst not come nigh me. William is here. I should be — '

He looked properly at her face for the first time. It was red and swollen with weeping again. He backed away. She would never be his. His hands dropped to his sides, empty. 'Forgive me. I had forgot.'

'No, you don't understand. He is hateful and jealous. I have told him to go, but he will not. He badgers and pets me till I am beside myself, and my father encourages him. So I bade him go — ' she said again. 'But since he will not, I have left him standing.'

He reached up hesitantly and touched her cheek. 'There are always tears here, Anna. It isn't right.'

She wiped her face with a kerchief, and her voice was bitter. 'Those tears are not for William, for all that I despise him!' Her face crumpled, and she covered it with the kerchief.

'Anna — can we go aside? We shall be seen, and I would comfort thee, love.' Tenderness overcame him, and he took her free hand and led her back among the cherry trees. She was weeping loudly, trying to catch her breath. Behind a clump of hazel bushes he put his arms around her.

'I was looking for thee,' she began. 'I could not bear to stop in the house more.'

It did not matter now that he stank of the stable or that her face was distorted and raw. *She has looked for me!* 'Did he hurt thee?'

Her head tossed up. 'Aye, this morning, early, he did.' Her face reddened. 'Pinched my arm and — and put his hand — ' She stopped.

The rage came back again. 'I'll make him cry mercy if he — '

'No, Nicholas!' Her voice was steadier now. 'He'll not be touching me again. 'Tis not that man makes me weep so. My mother — my mother — ' Her head sank onto his shoulder.

A crowd of questions clamoured in his head. She had died? And how was he to console her when he knew not how men and women of the King's party consoled themselves in time of grief? But then he ceased trying — as he always did — to unravel the tangle. His love for her swept everything else aside, and he tightened his arms round her again.

'Thy mother?' he whispered, his mouth beside her ear.

She did not need to answer; the renewed sobs told him.

'Then God will comfort thee, dear Anna. And so shall I — come.' He stroked the hair from her forehead and lifted her face to his. He was surprised to see a slow smile breaking in her eyes. 'What?'

'Aye, I grieve for my mother.' She was struggling between tears and joy.

'Sorely, as you should.'

'But there is one good — one good come of it — God forgive me for thinking so, for my father will not.'

He was puzzled by the change in her. 'What, then?'

'I shall be able to give the "nay" to William now. We shall be in mourning, all of us, and 'tis not decent — Nicholas — thou wilt abide here?'

He was bewildered and half laughed, 'As long as thy father suffers me, and as long as my aunt — '

'Rebecca has no need of me. My father has told me he likes thee not, but will you stay?'

He looked down, misery descending like a shroud. 'How can I?'

'Your aunt — Rebecca — I've heard her say you have kin hereabouts.' The high colour returned to her face.

'Dear, sweet, Anna — yes — but — '

She was reaching towards him this time, and the tears had started again. 'Pray, I beg thee, do not go! But oh, I am wicked to be thinking thus when my mother lies above stairs, dead.'

Groaning, he bent and pressed his mouth slowly and gently against hers. For a few moments they clung to each other and sank down among the round yellow hazel leaves. He did not let her go but raised her so that she lay against his chest, out of the damp grass, with her face now against his neck. 'I love thee, Anna, as I never thought to love any woman on earth. I want thee for my only love, my wife, though I know I am not worthy.' The words came out in breathless fragments between kisses.

She said hotly, 'Oh, but you are worthy. Every bit and more worthy than — than — and I do love thee in return.'

He laughed to hear her indignation and began to kiss her again. They lost all account of time, knowing only kissing, comforting, and each other's warmth.

When he first became aware again, a flock of pigeons was whirring up in fright, a dog was barking.

Anna's father was standing over them, his face mottled with anger. He reached down and grabbed Anna by the arm. 'Get up, you slut! So this is why you've played so coy with William, is it?' He pushed her away from him so that she staggered backwards against a cherry tree and stood there panting.

Then he went for Nicholas. The first blow fell on his cheek. 'Get up! Lollylagging with my oldest girl when her mother's scarcely cold, would you?' And Tolhurst struck him again as he was rising.

Nicholas lifted his hands to defend himself, but Anna had begun to scream, and shame suddenly struck him harder than any man could.

He fell to his knees. 'I cry you mercy, sir,' he said. His body stiffened, ready for the next blow, but it did not come. Tolhurst had gone to Anna. He could hear him saying to her, 'Anna, sweet, pray come in with me, do.' The voice was conciliatory, wheedling, and Nicholas hated Tolhurst.

The older man took his daughter's hand firmly, then turned to Nicholas. 'You'll be gone by morning. I count your uncle my friend, and you even bear his likeness in your face, but you have brought disgrace on him. Trouble not my mourning household, nor my daughter, or you shall pay dearly.'

Anna was struggling. 'No!' she cried, 'No, my father. 'Tis *I* will pay dearly.' She was distraught now.

Nicholas watched Tolhurst turn to her and shake her. 'And so you shall, if you ever come nigh this lad again. Come with me.'

A dangerous look came into her eyes. 'If you command it. But I swear to you upon my soul that I shall never, never wed William.' She broke free and ran away through the trees, but her voice floated back. 'You have your son, now, remember.'

The last glimpse Nicholas had of her was the gleam of her red hair among the yellow leaves. He passed Tolhurst without a look and walked back to the stableyard. Bright sunshine washed down over his head, but he was mired in the blackness of despair.

5

ISAAC
Goudhurst, December 1658

Isaac had sat in the great hall of Tolhurst Court before
now and had not felt awed by it. This time it seemed
different. The harvest had been good; his friend was
prospering; and with Rebecca's continuing care young
Edward thrived. Yet the man sitting opposite him by the
fire was old and unhappy. Blessed with harvest, house,
a son, and lovely daughters, he nevertheless lacked the
one thing that Isaac had: a wife.

And although a fire roared up the chimney and
the bells of St Mary's were pealing in celebration of
Christmas Eve, the room lacked both warmth and music.
Outside the leaded window the sky hung dour and grey
over the bare hills. Isaac shivered and drew his stool
nearer to the blaze.

George, however, did not move. His head was bowed
and his back bent over; in one hand he cradled a mug
of sack. From Isaac's place on the other side of the
mantel, he could see the top of Tolhurst's head; it was
almost bald, threaded with white. Isaac watched him and
shared his dull pain.

Part of him wanted to see George as Nicholas had
seen him: bitter, obdurate, jealous of his daughters, but
although he could understand Nicholas' view, he had
known George too long to see him as anyone but the
gentle, unassuming squire of Goudhurst — now broken
by grief. And if his own wife had not already given three
months to the babe Edward (and promised another year,
at least, until the child was weaned), he would have felt,
because of Nicholas, as if he had betrayed his friend.

At last George's voice came, but it was muffled by the
loose jerkin against which his head had sunk. 'I suppose

I'm sorry for the lad — a mite.'

'Then — ?'

'No, Isaac,' George murmured, still not looking up. 'Come now, Master Tailor. How well does silk do, sewn together with frieze?' His hand moved idly to the coarse stuff of his jerkin. 'Shall the silk not tear?'

'Aye, thou know'st it will,' Isaac conceded cautiously. 'But you do Nicholas an injustice. He is no rough village simpleton. He has more booklearning than your village priests had, I shouldn't wonder, before Old Noll threw 'em out.'

'He's his father's boy: a Roundhead.'

Isaac leaned forward. It was no use saying, *Sit up, George Tolhurst, and harken to me,* for he would not. Yet he wished the older man would at least meet his eyes. 'George, yes, he's a Roundhead — if that means aught these days. The "Roundheads" — half of them are turned Cavalier, and this-way-that-way. I couldn't keep him in my house, or his brother, were they canting brethren of the kind you — we both — hate. He's but a lad.'

'Aye, an unformed lad.' George's voice was dry and unconvinced.

'Young as I was when I met Rebecca. Young as my brother John was with Jane — whom you never met — but none the worse for it.'

George looked up at last. 'Nay, 'tis not his age that I oppose, nor even, in truth, his politics. And were he thine own son, Isaac, I'd give her gladly to him.' He drank deeply of the sack and stared at the floorbeams again.

Isaac felt his throat tighten, and his next words came out choked with emotion. 'He's not mine own, but never a lad closer to me than Nicholas — and dearer than either of my own two sons — though I would never confess it to anyone.'

George shook his head. 'Thy brain is addled by the sack I gave thee.'

'Nay, I speak the truth.'

'But he was your *brother's* son, he that betrayed thee, betrayed Rebecca. The one I saw and never will forget that first day of May. He was a — '

Isaac held up his hand. 'I know what he was, well enough.' He dropped his voice. 'But I was his murderer. Thou sit'st with a murderer, George.' He shivered, and Robert's dying face rose up before him for an instant.

A tiny smile flickered round George's cracked lips. 'Nay, I sit with an honest gentleman.'

Isaac half laughed. 'A yeoman. A tailor. Phaw! Away with all the flattery.' He laid his broad hands palm down on his knees and studied them. 'George, I beg you, as you love your daughter, let her come to him! If 'tis a matter of money — '

'No! 'Tis *not* a matter of money. 'Tis his father, as I said. She's my eldest daughter, and though he's your eldest and dearest nephew, she shall *not* come to him.' He stood up, but his body shook, and he had to lean on the mantel for support. 'This is my last word on't, Isaac. Say no more, I pray thee . . . Come, thy wife is languishing for thee, I've no doubt.' His voice softened. 'Go and see her. An old man needs his solitude by the fire.'

Isaac stood, too, facing George. Neither man spoke for several moments. Then Isaac put out his hand to George's shoulder. 'Bless thee, good squire,' he said.

He went out through the arched doorway into the hall and to the door of the parlour, where he knew the womenfolk were sitting, for he could hear their voices. He recognized one from among the others: low, musical, full of joy: very like her mother's.

'Oh, Edward! What a poppet! Rebecca, let me have him a while, pray.' That was Anna.

Then Rebecca's: soft, more fluting: 'Pray do, mistress. I believe I heard the cart but a few minutes ago. Isaac may be here to see me.' She would be blushing.

All the girls laughed softly; then the wooden door came open and closed again, just as he approached to knock. Rebecca hesitated on the threshold, then flew into his arms. He held her, rocking her to and fro. 'My dear love, oh, how I have longed for thee.'

'Come, then,' she whispered.

And he led her above stairs to the small, warm room they had given her beside the nursery, where a cradle, now empty, stood beside the bed.

NICHOLAS
Maidstone and Chatham, 1659

He had never doubted that he would see Anna again.
But God — he thought — must have another design
for his life. When Isaac had finished speaking with him,
he went out into the back of the inn where the Fessenden
donkey was stabled and spent an hour furiously combing
and brushing the animal's coat. All the while it stood
patiently still, eyes glazing and mouth slavering with
delight at all the attention. At the end he thumped it
on the rump, bolted the stall, and went back home as if
nothing had changed.

But everything had changed.

In the summer, Isaac had advised, he should set sail
with Josiah for the Bay Colony — but without Anna.
As Isaac had told him Tolhurst's words, his soft brown
eyes sad with sympathy, he had urged Nicholas not to
give up hope.

'If she loves thee, as thou say'st, then it will not be
for naught. Set thyself up with brother John and see if
Anna's father doesn't relent when he hears how great a
merchant thou hast become.'

But words like these did not comfort him at all. What
if their ship were blown off course by an early gale and
he never reached Boston Harbour? What if John fell ill
and could not teach his trade to him? What if — ?

Then a soft inner voice calmed him. *Trust also in him,
and he shall bring it to pass. This is the way; walk ye in it.*
He must simply abandon himself — and Anna too — to
the Providence of God.

In this way he went on stolidly with preparations
for the voyage. Everything took longer and cost more
than he expected, and in the end they were delayed in
their departure until the early autumn, as he and Josiah
had to find journeymen's labour to pay their way. He
thought of Anna often, and dreamed of her, but she was
usually at the back of his mind: a lovely room to sit in or
scene to contemplate when he had moments alone.

Rebecca was released from her service in Goudhurst
upon Edward's first birthday, and carried home to

Maidstone in the coach by Edmund. The little boy was fat and cheery and had weaned himself, she said. She now glowed with health, and in reflection of her, Isaac too seemed renewed. In payment for her nursing, the whole family now ate well and had goods in store.

Nicholas pressed her for news of Anna. She would give little.

'Is she wed?'

'Nay, indeed not!' Rebecca laughed.

'Betrothed, then?'

'I hear she is.'

'To the same man as before?' His teeth clenched as he thought of it. 'And does she know I go to the New World and would take her there . . . ?'

'Truly, Nicholas, thou must not set thy heart on her, love.'

Sighing, he had left her to her sewing. After that he had wrestled with God until he found a measure of peace again.

They were to sail from Chatham. Isaac would make a festival day of it: his cousins, his sister Hannah, and all of Isaac's family would journey over Boxley Hill to the docks, Isaac said, and see the great ship sail in full furl down the estuary. Only Mary, too old now to make such a journey, would stay behind to mind the shop.

Josiah was filled with excitement, babbling and laughing all the way. For himself, there was only a dull ache about the parting, and an increasing, deadening certainty that he might never see Anna again. This he tried to push from his heart as the family made the slow journey northwards. Hannah, Rebecca, and Isaac rode in the creaking cart with their bundles of clothes and a small hamper of books; Adam, Charlie, and Josiah strode close behind. Meanwhile he himself walked at the donkey's head exchanging an occasional word with his uncle and an occasional glance with Hannah, whose soft eyes were full of understanding. But most of the way he kept a loose hold of the bridle, stared at the chalky road under their feet, and thought bitterly of the man who was opposing his dearest wish.

Crossing the Pilgrims' Way they passed under the tangled trees and over the peaty ground of Boxley

Woods, then emerged again at the top of the hill into open farmland. After the comparative dimness of the early-morning light under the trees, the mist rising over the napped stubble of the golden fields was almost unbearably white. But then a breeze sprang up, the fog blew away, the donkey pricked its ears and quickened pace, and Isaac and Rebecca began to sing an old sheep-shearing ballad.

> We'll pipe and we'll sing, love
> We'll dance in a ring, love,
> When each lad takes his lass
> All on the green grass,
> And it's oh — to plough,
> When the fat oxen graze low,
> And the lads and their lasses
> Do sheep-shearing go.

Their voices — hers sweet and high, his deep and somewhat out of tune — were merry in spite of the song's sad cadences, and he turned briefly to look at them. Isaac: forty-five now, in the peak of his strength — not a grey hair among the black curls, his eyes bright, his face broad and honest. Ah, no wonder everyone loved him! Rebecca: diminutive beside him, yet with a strength of her own since she had nursed little Edward Tolhurst; her cheeks pink in the freshening wind. Again, no wonder she was loved! Even on the verge of becoming an old woman by many people's reckoning, she was still lovely. And yet — he checked himself gently — Rebecca had been the daughter, so he had heard, of a fiery preacher, and here she was singing pagan songs! What was it, then, about both his uncle and his aunt that he loved so much? They acknowledged God, though not in his parents' ways. They helped each other and gave to others: to Tolhurst, to himself, to Josiah, Hannah, and Mary . . . though not as the godly folk would have done it.

Unaware of what he was doing, he stopped on the track. The donkey tossed impatiently and wrenched its head from his grasp. Surprised, he went on. *Not as the godly folk would have done it . . .* and his mother's face came before him: her carefulness over detail, her insistence on obedience, however harsh, her watchfulness over the family purse. Was there perhaps a lack of generosity in her? If so, he had never knowingly thought that way about her.

He threw another look over his shoulder at his uncle. That was it! Isaac had always reminded him in his stature of a Goliath, but in his nature of a David: dignified, almost kingly, but with the spontaneous gaiety and generosity of spirit of the David who had danced his way into Jerusalem. He was indeed a king of Kent: lordly but lowly, poor, but giving all he had.

Nicholas turned his face back to the north. Yes, Isaac was a good man. Would John — the elderly uncle he had never seen — be as kind?

They passed down through Canny Fields and uphill into Rome Lane. The lane was flanked by more farms and a few cottages, until at last they reached the near end of the High Street, marked by the Little Crown Inn. A farmer driving sheep and cows to the public stocks blocked their way, so they moved more slowly now. Nicholas could see over the crowded heads of the bleating sheep and plodding cattle to the posting-house. A tide-coach stood outside ready for its journey, and in the High Street there was an air of business and prosperity.

Chatham was foreign to Nicholas: neither a mannerly Wealden village with the grace and beauty of Chilham or Goudhurst, nor the bustling, bricked market-place of Maidstone — spacious and established. It was something quite different: a naval town just come up from a wattle-hut village: noisy, squalid, in the making as a place of shipbuilding. Carpenters', ropemakers', and ironsmiths' shops lined the thoroughfare, and everywhere hammers clanged on anvils and the smell of hot tar hung in the air. Chatham, some said, provided such safe anchorage that it might one day be more useful to their naval vessels than London.

Looking around as they went further along the High Street, he doubted it. Not that he had seen London yet, nor ever would, if he went to the other side of the ocean; but that Chatham seemed like a grovelling, snivelling serving man. In the New World, so he had heard and read, there was freedom and space. But here was an old world of dirt and degradation even where there was supposedly hope for the future in daring naval enterprise. Aye, it was just as well he was leaving England. He smiled quietly to himself, then laughed aloud. *A grovelling, snivelling serving man!* What a fantasy! What a foolish, proud conceit! He had read too much of Tolhurst's Cavalier poetry broadsides, perhaps, to be thinking in that way of a town he did not know.

'Beyond that church — yonder,' Isaac called to him. 'Follow down the hill. Hold the beast hard, now, Nicholas, as it's steep, thou'lt find.'

Underfoot the cobbles became more slippery and uneven, and strange smells, rank and putrid, oozed up from the gutters and — Nicholas suspected — from the docks, too. He found that he had to look down to see where he was stepping to avoid leading the donkey into the slimy ditches on either side of the street. Their progress was slower than ever.

'Are you sure, Isaac, that you want the donkey down this-a-way?' he shouted back.

'Aye, go on, son. Adam, give thy cousin a hand. Charlie, Josiah, hold ye on to the cart lest we all tip out.'

Rebecca's voice floated unhappily over all the commotion. 'Could we not walk, love, and leave the cart at an hostelry?'

'Nay, we haven't enough to pay for such a thing, sweetheart, as thou should'st know.' Isaac was gathering the reins tighter, his face intent.

'Please,' Hannah begged, 'let me walk with my brother!'

Nicholas heard her voice and grieved for her. *Poor Hannah!* He wished she could go with them, but she would be safer with his uncle and aunt. He would miss her.

He signalled to Adam, and they steadied the donkey, waiting until Hannah, assisted by Charlie, had climbed down. Nicholas felt her small hand press into his free hand as she came to walk beside him.

'Thank you, Nicholas.'

'Thou'rt welcome, but won't you foul your petticoats?' He tugged the donkey forward again and noted with disgust a pair of dead rats in the gutter.

'Never mind if I do, silly.'

He looked at her quizzically. Her voice was light, but he knew she was making a brave face of it and that she was as sorry to part from him as he was to lose her.

'Hannah — ?'

'What?' She turned her pale face upwards to search his.

He knew he had sounded far too serious, and that she was too young to bear the weight of his own sorrow. All the same, he knew she would understand. 'Wilt'ou do something for me, Hannah?'

'I'll try. Yes, indeed, I shall do anything that you ask.' Her voice was pert, but unsteady.

He squeezed her hand. 'If any word should come from Goudhurst . . . from the maid there that I love . . . wilt thou find a way to send word, my sister?'

She returned his enquiring gaze with wide, frightened eyes. 'But our uncle is to do that. Thou know'st I cannot write more than a word or two. Or Grandmother Mary shall send — '

'No, no!' He gave her hand a little shake. 'Isaac and our grand-dame I believe I can count on, but if anything should befall . . . can I count upon thee as well?' He was speaking softly, his face close to his sister's so that Adam might not hear.

Hannah's eyelashes went down. 'Thou may'st, dear Nicholas.' Her voice was wistful. 'Ah, would that I had met this maid of thine!'

He warmed to their conversation, hardly noticing that the wharves and the sluggish waters of the Medway at ebbtide lay not far below them now. 'Thou shalt meet her, Hannah, of a surety.' He wished he could believe it, himself.

She was pouting slightly. 'But thou shalt never meet my sweetheart, I fear.'

He threw back his head and chuckled. 'Thine, little one?'

'"Little one"? Old, wise brother, I'm barely littler than thee.'

'And big enough to have a dozen sweethearts. But somehow, pretty sister, I doubt — '

She sighed. "Tis true. I do not have one.'

'God has a husband for thee, Hannah.'

She smiled shyly. 'I hope he has.'

'And a wife for me, too,' he added, still picturing the red hair among the hazel leaves and the face of the woman he had not seen for a year but had loved for three.

ISAAC

The ship was laden already with provisions. She nevertheless rode high in the water, a stately vessel with four masts and seven sails, now furled, and pennants of gold fluttering from the mast-heads. The brass cannons on the forecastle and main decks gleamed in the sunlight, and on the ship's prow the figure of a white horse leaped forward towards the mouth of the river. That horse would ride the waves all the way to Charlestown and into the Charles River of which Isaac's brother had written. She would carry Nicholas and Josiah away for ever.

The master had rung the last bells; the seamen were swarming on the ropes; and the ship would sail as the tide rose. On the wharf Isaac and Rebecca put their arms round the two boys, wept over them, then bade them go.

Shouldering a hamper, while Josiah clutched their bundle, Nicholas looked over his left shoulder at the ship. 'It will wait long enough,' he said in the calm voice Isaac loved and always associated with him, 'for us to say a prayer together.'

Isaac saw him glance at his sister, for Hannah was crying. He nudged Rebecca, and she put her arm round the girl. Then he took off his hat, feeling awkward, suddenly. 'Go on, Adam, Charlie,' he said uneasily, and his two sons bowed their heads and pulled off their own hats.

Nicholas' voice came softly against the noise of whirring cables and clanging bells. 'Father of heaven,' he was

307

saying, 'we commend ourselves to thee upon the deep. And we commend to thee our beloved sister Hannah, our cousins Adam and Charles.' The voice was wavering now, thick with sorrow. 'I pray thee, keep my aunt and uncle and all their dear ones unto thyself . . .'

Isaac held his breath, his eyes shut. His nephew had stopped, as if he could say no more. He heard with surprise his own voice continuing for Nicholas: 'And keep thy servants Nicholas and Josiah safe. May thine eye, Lord, be ever upon John and Jane also, and upon the maid Anna . . .' He hesitated. 'And upon her father also . . .'

'Amen,' Josiah answered fervently.

'Amen,' the others replied, more slowly.

He straightened his back, donned his cap, and gripped Nicholas' shoulders for the last time. He felt hot, suddenly, with the heavy heat of early autumn hanging in the fetid dampness of the dockyards, and he longed to be on the open uplands again, away from Chatham and the stinking Medway. 'Go now, nephews,' he murmured.

They all stood watching as Nicholas and Josiah mounted the gangway. Wavelets were slapping noisily against the gunwales as the tide began to flow, and above the ship a few gulls circled or dived for debris on the incoming water while the sails were unfurled for the voyage. Josiah turned once to wave, but Nicholas never looked back.

Heavy-hearted, Isaac lifted Rebecca and Hannah into the cart again. He felt empty and sad without Nicholas to lead them back the way they had come, but he knew Hannah felt the loss even more deeply. She seemed light as a bolt of muslin, compared with his newly plump wife. He noticed as he seated Hannah that her face was bright pink as well as unhappy, and as she arranged her skirts, he caught sight of a small red welt on her ankle. He looked away quickly; she would be embarrassed if she found him looking at her ankles, and anyway she had complained of no discomfort.

Thinking no more of the women, he gave the reins to Adam, and with Charlie turned the donkey back uphill towards the church. It would be night before

308

they reached home again, and hunger gnawed at his stomach. The bright day seemed suddenly forlorn and overcast. The shop would seem cheerless when they returned; the excitement of this festival day had all evaporated.

His back to the wharves, he saw no more the fluttering pennants and leaping fair horse. Instead, everything they passed seemed foul. Chatham smelled and looked close and evil. The donkey's ears were laid back against its neck, and the poor beast was panting, its eyes bulging and its back wet with sweat.

'We must find a clean watering trough,' he called back to Rebecca.

'I thought I did see a well by the church,' she answered.

'Aye — I believe you are right. And I'm a-hungered; are ye not, too?' He could hear Hannah crying quietly from the cart, but he did not want to look back and shame her, so he kept his eyes on the church. 'The lass is, for sure.'

Rebecca said, 'I'm forgetting, Isaac, but I brought some apples, and Hannah baked some pasties for us all. Will't please thee stop?'

Isaac laughed, glad of her thoughtfulness. His head had been so full of Nicholas, Josiah, and Hannah's sorrow that he had not given a thought to food for the donkey, or even for himself. He wiped his upper lip and his cheeks with a sleeve. 'Aye, but let's get to the church first.'

At the top of the hill he cranked the iron handle of the churchyard pump. The water came in a fast, cold rush. Then he filled the tankard he usually kept on his belt for a journey, and they passed it round, gasping with pleasure and relief. He saw no need to use the well water; winching up the bucket would take more time than he wanted to spare at the moment.

In the short shadow of St Mary's they sat still and ate the pasties. A few seamen swaggered past, eyed Rebecca and Hannah, then noticed Isaac and glanced elsewhere. The women, he observed, did not even look up from their food, though they could hardly fail to notice the sailors, reeking of tar, ale, and sweat.

A rat crept out from behind a tombstone, frisked its tail, and vanished into a hole. Another, or perhaps the same one, came out of the same hole a few moments later, crouched down, and dropped dead where it had just stood. Isaac shuddered. Chatham was indeed an unwholesome place.

'Come, dearlings,' he said, 'let's away home now.'

They set out along the street again and were soon in the open air of the Downs farmlands.

ANNA
Goudhurst, October 1659

She waited until the house was quite still and dark, then sat up with her arms round her knees and watched the moon rising slowly over the thin mist outside. No word had come from Nicholas in answer to the messages she had sent with Rebecca, but she knew without doubt that he still loved her. *If only I had gone to Maidstone with Rebecca,* she thought over and over again, *I might have hidden without . . .* Without what? At this hour of night her thoughts were unformed and desperate. Surely Nicholas knew that they could not wait longer? William was arriving on the morrow to claim her; the year of mourning for her mother was over now by several weeks, and she could refuse her father no further.

She was trapped. In the year since her mother had died, her father had become more and more a stranger. He wept openly for Elizabeth, ignored even her brother Edward, and spent most of his time out of doors with the labourers. It was harvest-time, true, but he had become slovenly about the house and allowed his new steward to behave just as carelessly. He minded not if they brought dung, straw, and mud into the hall on their boots, or if the spaniels leaped onto the table to eat the food off his trencher. He drank too much sack and snored shamelessly over the table. He made no pretense of keeping Sundays or praying in his private chapel. He was unhinged. He had become a stranger: a crazed stranger — but a stranger with power over her future.

Last night, driven to despair, she had bowed to him and agreed he could ask the incumbent to arrange the marriage to William. He would not wait any more, especially now that Henrietta and Charlotte both had wooers. He wanted to see her wed first — he had said on one of his clearer days — as was proper for a gentlewoman in the county. Her fate was sealed unless she could find an escape.

She saw no way but to flee to Nicholas. There was a risk in that, certainly, for the uncle was her father's friend. But surely Isaac was a merciful man and would spare her if she cast herself on his mercy and told him that her father was beside himself now? All she had heard of Isaac from Rebecca convinced her he would be kind.

She had laid her plans shrewdly, trusting no one. A few days before, she had thought of asking help from Martha, one of the serving maids, or from Edmund, who had liked Nicholas. But she could neither take them with her nor leave them to face her father if he were crazed or in his cups. No, she had decided, it was better to fend for herself.

The previous night, soon after the discourse about William, she had lain awake as long as she had tonight. Then she had crept out of her chamber, down the back stairs, past the privy and into the kitchen to where she knew her father had long ago hidden gold in an unused pot. All the way along the passage, down the stairs and back again, she had been frightened by the sound of her own breathing, by the creaking boards of the stairs, and tonight it was the same. Last night, nevertheless, she had achieved her errand; and she would tonight, as well.

Shivering, she took off her shift, poured water from the ewer that stood ready for the morning, splashed her face, and bound her hair tightly in an old kerchief of her mother's. She caught a glimpse of her naked body — white and unreal by moonlight — in the glass that hung by the window.

What if he does not want me as his wife? In the dim light of her chamber, she felt her face grow hot. *What if I am*

311

deceived, and he does not even want me as his love? Should I make him a potion of mint and vinegar, or of onion and dog's mercury? She shook her head sternly. No — such thoughts were devilish; she needed no false props. He loved her, wanted her as his wife, and would protect her. Still shivering, she pulled on her oldest petticoat, then hooked her bodice and dress.

In her bride chest she found a stout pair of pattens and a heavy cloak of her mother's. Then she took out the bundle of clothes and small bag of gold that she had hidden under the bed. Inside them she wrapped her prayer book, Culpeper's *Herbal,* and some scraps she had saved from the table. The gold she tied inside her dress where it could not be seen, all except a few smaller coins that she put in a little purse at her waist.

She stood still for a moment in the middle of the room that she had been entitled, as the eldest, to keep to herself all her life. She had once loved the room's privacy and cosiness. Now it felt like a prison, and she was not going to change one prison for another in the bed of William Frittenden. She shuddered. He was gracious, a skilled horseman, and he was wealthy. But his insipid smiles and elaborate courtesies left her cold. She would never be his wife: so she had vowed a year ago, and so she intended now.

A woman walking alone by day would attract attention, she had decided, and these bright, full-moonlit nights were clear and beautiful to walk in. She knew the way as far as Marden at least, and after that — she supposed she might find a carter who would carry her further north. It would not take her above a day to reach Maidstone.

She took a last glance in the glass. Her eyes were far too bright, dancing at her from her pale face. She would be safer, perhaps, if she streaked her face and hands with dust like a poor travelling woman going from one farm to another for the harvesting.

Outside she wet her hands in the dewy grass, rubbed them with a little earth, and smeared her face. Then, pulling the cloak tightly round her, she trudged out of the gateway of Tolhurst Court and turned up the village street. She did not look back. No one passed her. An owl

312

dropped silently out of the church tower and swooped past her into a grove of yellowing horse chestnuts — so close that she heard the whir of its feathers and felt the downrush from its wings.

In places the road led through coppices and under trees, where the moonlight was feeble. In other places it dipped down into misty hollows and she had to take off her pattens to ford the stream in her path. But she went on steadily, exulting every time the path led her uphill so that she could see the dark countryside spreading out before her under the wide sky.

Marden was hushed and shuttered, except the inn, where there were lights and the sound of revelry. She hurried past and on into the countryside. The land was more open beyond Marden: farms and orchards on either side, and clumps of chestnut, beech, and ash by the roadside. The soft breathing of cattle and the strong smell of sheep under the apple trees hung in the damp air.

She stole an apple from a tree near the road, then continued. Her spirits rose high as she thought of seeing Nicholas; each time he entered her mind, her heart quickened and a smile came to her lips.

At a crossing in the road she hesitated, unsure of her way. There were milestones either side, but in the scarce light she could not read them. The moon was setting, the sky that peculiar shade of indigo that suggests dawn is not far off, and she wondered if she should wait and ask for the help of another traveller before going on. But she had seen no one and dared not cast herself on the first knave who passed. The night seemed darker now than before.

There was a stile in the hedgerow beside her; she climbed over it, careful not to tear her petticoats. In the field ahead of her she could make out against the darkness the vague outline of a hut or shed: a shepherd's hut no doubt. She went forward carefully, glad of the pattens in the wet grass, until she could see clearly the white weatherboards on the side of the hut. Even though its low roof had long ago collapsed on one side, she thought it would afford shelter until daylight, and it seemed deserted.

313

The hut stank of sheep dung and old, worm-eaten fleeces, but it was dry. When her eyes became accustomed to the gloom inside, she could see spindly grass pushing up here and there on the earth floor. A small creature scuttled across the floor to gather the crumbs from her loaf as she broke pieces off it. She felt dusty, dirty, and a little afraid, but by now she was too tired to dwell for long on how she felt. Wrapped in the cloak, and with her head on her bundle, she soon fell asleep.

When she awoke, a broad beam of sunlight was falling over her from the broken roof. One wall of the hut was apparently being wrenched off, and a man's face was peering in on her in surprise. She was utterly bewildered.

'Well I never, maidy! Tut! Stir thyself, and get up out of my barn. Fie, shame on thee!' He was an old man, a shepherd, with broken teeth and a crabbed, leathery face.

Shocked into wakefulness, she pulled the cloak around her more securely and opened her mouth to scream.

'Fie! Out on thee!' the shepherd shouted angrily. But then his voice softened, and he went on irritably, 'I mean no harm.' The wall swung wider now, and she saw it was not a wall after all, but another door. 'And I trust you meant none, neither, in my barn, indeed.'

She shut her mouth and breathed out loudly. The man was just a foolish shepherd, an old labourer like her father's man, Matty. No wonder he was surprised to see her. Awkwardly she sat up. 'Forgive me, sir, I meant no harm, either. Tell me what o' clock is't?'

'Why, 'tis broad afternoon, lass.'

She groaned and jumped up.

'What art thou? A lass, or a lady? For you do speak like a lady.'

'I — I'm a lady's maid, but I lost my way last night and came in here to bed.' She bit her lip. *I have never lied before that I can remember*, she thought.

The shepherd put his hands on his hips and twisted his face grotesquely. 'A likely tale, but never mind.'

She pulled her things together, her mind working. 'Barn' he had said. But surely this was only a hut?

314

Should she offer to pay him for her night's lodging, or would that only arouse suspicion? And could it truly be the afternoon? Then she must be on the road quickly, or her father might come looking for her.

She came and stood beside him at the door, and he stepped aside for her. She blinked in amazement to see that the door led into a huge, dark-beamed barn that she had not even been able to see the night before. The same, strong smell of sheep . . . and her night's lodging had only been a lean-to on the side of the barn.

'Why dost start and stare so, maidy?' the shepherd laughed. 'Ain't you never seed a shearing barn afore?'

Eager to be gone before she betrayed herself, she pulled up her hood and lowered her eyes. Perhaps the damage was done: he would have seen her face clearly as she was waking — but she had to do what she could. He must not remember her; she must not say anything out of the ordinary.

'Nay, I'm not from these parts,' she muttered.

'Whither bound, then, maidy? Haste, now, for I've a hundred sheep from the staple this very day to drive into my fold.'

His tone told her that he was proud of his purchase. 'Aye, God speed to you, then. I did not mean to trespass . . . Can you show me the way to Maidstone?'

The shepherd looked curiously at her, then pointed up the lane. 'That-a-way. Walk 'til you come to Linton. 'Tis not so far. And you'd best wash your face there, as you be a lady's maid, for you're fair besmirched from this place — not fitten for a lass of your breeding.' He clicked his tongue indignantly. 'What'd your father say if he saw you thus?'

Her heart leaped into her throat and her head felt light for a moment, but looking at the old shepherd's face again, she could see that the question was fanciful: he did not know her father, of course, but was himself probably the father of daughters. The question required no answer in any event, and she scrambled over the gate and off on the path he had shown her.

By the time she reached Linton, hunger gripped her and the bundle felt heavier every step she took up the long Linton Hill. Carters, shepherds, and an occasional

315

post messenger passed her, but all seemed to be going towards the coast, away from Maidstone. She decided to stop at the Bull Inn and buy a pennyworth of bread and ale, as any other traveller might do.

No one paid her any attention at first, and she kept her hood up deliberately. Sitting in the corner of the parlour, she listened to snatches of the discourse to discover a fellow traveller who might bring her the rest of the way to the town. Though it was long past the noon hour and far too early for most country people to sup, the inn was crowded and noisy.

''Tis them prisoners they've been sending down from the pesty Fleet in London, I reckon,' one man said.

'Nay, 'tis those filthy soldiers from York, I warrant thee. They've brought 'un with 'em.'

'It makes no sense . . . not since thirty years — '

'Nay, 'tis Maidstone itself.'

'Aye, venomous, scurvy place it is.'

Anna's heart contracted uneasily. What sedition was being planned here? Why would the men of Linton speak so harshly of their fellows in Maidstone? There was so much she did not understand! Never had she heard men talk this way of the town where Nicholas lived and where she had gone sometimes for the assizes and petty sessions, with her father. She bit hard into the bread, kept her eyes down, and listened intently.

'Nay,' a softer voice argued. ''Tis a fine market town, and the half o' ye never set foot in't! 'Tis Chatham that's to blame, and the whoreson seamen there.'

'Chatham? Where's that?' jeered a fat man. 'We've never heerd of Chatham.' All the men laughed.

The soft-voiced man directed his words towards her corner, suddenly, and she knew without looking up that she would have to answer. 'Yon maiden there — she's heard of Chatham, I lay.' The voice was wooing, smooth as silk, and she shrank inside.

'By name only,' she murmured.

'What's that? Speak up, lass.'

'By name only,' she repeated.

'Pretty voice,' he wheedled.

She did not look up.

316

'Let her alone, Martin,' the innkeeper shouted. 'What wert thou saying about Chatham, anyhow?'

The parlour became hushed so that all Anna could hear was the sound of her own quiet chewing on the coarse bread that now tasted like wool to her, and the slurping of the men over their ale.

''Tis where the plague's a-come from,' the man called Martin declared. 'I'll wager any man.'

'Can't prove it either way,' another argued.

Anna barely heard what followed. *Plague! In Maidstone?* Fear clutched her round the neck so that she grabbed her bundle and rushed out of the low doorway and was immediately sick in the road. Shaken, she sat on a stool by the door and tried to take slow, deep breaths. *Plague, plague . . .* The word would not cease clamouring in her ears.

Someone was standing beside her, a man with torn, dusty breeches. She would not look up but remained hunched over, waiting for doom to strike. It would be Martin, that man who had singled her out.

'What ails thee, lass? A-breeding, art thou?' The voice was different: rough, but not unkind, and someone was holding out a tankard of cold water to her. The hand was dusted with some fine, white stuff. Flour? Perhaps he was a baker . . .

She took the water without sitting upright, but kept her free hand firmly round her bundle. 'Thankee, no.' She sipped, spat, and sipped again. The joy of the moonlit night before had disappeared into the terror of harsh October daylight. She was lost between the hated world of her father in Goudhurst and the unfamiliar — now threatening — world of Nicholas in Maidstone.

'Thou'rt bound for Maidstone?'

She was not sure whether to answer.

'If you be, and you mind not the wares of a fuller's cart, I can take you there.'

At last she looked up. The speaker was grey-haired, his forehead lined, and his face drawn with pity for her. She nodded gratefully. 'Aye, and I can pay you, too.'

'No need for that. Come, let's be gone before the wolves come out.' He gestured to the inn with his

317

thumb, and she could not help smiling a little. 'I have sacks to leave in Loose, then on to Maidstone by tonight. Will it serve?'

They jolted along under the trees and up the lane to Loose. The fuller's donkey was slow and lazy, but the fuller himself was kind and companionable. 'Don't fret about the plague, lassie,' he said, when he at last set her down at the Market Cross. 'Just mind where you stay and what you drink. You know where you're bound?'

She hesitated. Even this dear man might unwittingly betray her. Then she remembered where she had first met Nicholas. 'Aye, to meet my master at the sign of the Cock.' She hated lying to the fuller, but she could trust no one . . .

The fuller frowned, and she wondered if she had blundered. 'Well, have a care then, love.'

She waved and turned away. Though she had been to Maidstone many times with her father as a child and knew her way quite well, she did not want to go where there might be pestilence, and she did not even know exactly where the Fessendens lived. She trod carefully but quickly. Darkness was falling again and a band of thick mist was rising from the Medway. *Nicholas, I shall soon be with thee, Nicholas love.*

A tall man with a muffled face banged heavily into her so that her bundle fell heavily to the road and spilt open like an over-ripe plum. She cried out indignantly, then something in his posture and voice struck her as familiar.

'Forgive me, ma'am. I was in haste.' He stooped to retrieve her belongings, then dropped them as if burned. 'Oh, I cannot — '

She stared at him fearfully. 'Whatever is the matter?' She now bent down herself to pull the bundle together again. The books were still safe, she saw with relief.

''Tis the pestilence,' he said, backing away. 'All my womenfolk have the plague . . . pray forgive me.'

She reeled as she heard the deep, clear voice. The words meant nothing to her. *Isaac. Isaac Fessenden. My father's friend. Nicholas' uncle* . . . Trembling, she said aloud, 'Sir, are you not Isaac, the tailor?'

318

He was still backing away. The cowl round his neck and face had slipped slightly, however, and she could see the man's dark, curling hair beneath. His likeness to Nicholas made her hungry with longing.

'What do you want of me?' She heard the fear in his voice this time. He did not know her.

She pushed back her hood and shook out her hair so that he gasped in recognition. 'I have come to see you, to find Nicholas.'

His hands went together as if he was begging for his life. 'Oh, mistress, but you don't understand. Did you not hear what I said? You cannot bide in this place. My household is all shut up lest we spread the plague. I myself — ' He dropped his voice, but it was ragged with emotion, 'I myself should not be abroad, but I must fetch Doctor Cox or Doctor Bennet . . . Rebecca is so ill . . . you cannot bide here.'

Her heart constricted with dread. 'Oh, I had no notion!' her hands flew to her mouth. 'And Nicholas — is he well or ill?'

Isaac's eyes were glazed with pain. 'I pray you, let me go for this doctor. Spare me — '

She grabbed his sleeve, but he shook her off and started to run. Was he afraid to answer her? 'Wait — I have gold. Will that fetch the surgeon faster?'

But he had left her standing, a gold coin foolishly in her outstretched hand.

She swung round looking helplessly for guidance and hope. She went naturally the way she knew: past the upper and lower court houses, past the Shambles — where the market was held — and down to the Rose and Crown. Just behind the Rose and Crown was another inn where her father had sometimes stayed during the assizes. The innkeeper there might remember her and tell her where to find the tailor's house. But as she dragged herself wearily to the inn door, she became aware again of how dirty she was with mud and chalky fulling-dust. The innkeeper would laugh if she said she was Anna Tolhurst.

She waited by the door, leaning against the door-frame in utter exhaustion. A serving maid came out, eyed her coldly, and was about to slam the door shut again, when Anna pushed the gold coin into the girl's hand and closed her fingers on it. 'Gold for thee,' she said hurriedly, 'if thou'lt tell me where Isaac Fessenden's shop is.'

The maid looked cunningly at her as if she was a simpleton. 'Mill Lane,' she snapped, and she snatched her hand out of Anna's to close the door.

Anna ran back up towards the market-place. She did not care now about mud or footpads or plague — or anything on earth. Her pattens clattered and slithered on the cobbles until she found the top of Mill Lane and slowed to look at the signs above the doors. *Cablewright . . . Smith . . . Baker . . . Mason . . . Tailor.*

The door was barred fast from within. But weren't they expecting Isaac's return?

She beat it with her fists. Her bundle fell to the doorstep, and she heard herself crying.

Bolts and bars were moved, and a young man whose face she did not know opened the door a hand's breadth. As the door moved, a smell of sulphur or some other foul smoke came out on the air. Her disappointment, however, was more bitter than the sulphur.

"Tis I — Anna Tolhurst — is not Nicholas here?'

'We have the plague.'

The word was becoming familiar, no longer so terrible, somehow, now that she was near him. 'I know, I saw Isaac.'

'My father? You'd best go away.' He began to close the door again.

She jammed her foot into the crack so that she winced as the door hit her. 'I beg you — tell me — is Nicholas here?'

'Nicholas?' The young man sounded doltish and slow. 'My cousin? Or do you want Doctor Bennet — that is Nicholas, too?'

'Oh, your cousin! Please, please — '

'He's gone. Last week. What do you want? Who are you?'

'I told you! Anna Tolhurst.'

His face registered recognition for the first time. 'Are you not of Goudhurst and Squire Tolhurst's house? What are you to Nicholas?'

She withdrew her foot painfully. 'I'd thought to be his wife, one day, and cousin to you.'

She leaned against the wall outside and wept.

6

ISAAC
Maidstone, Autumn 1659

Isaac found her on the doorstep when he returned. The
shop door was still barred, as he had bidden Adam to bar
it — and the Tolhurst girl was huddled over a bundle of
clothes outside.

He could not be angry with her for long (and it was
anger born of fear, not directed towards the girl) for
he remembered the flash of red-gold hair as she had
pulled back her hood, and for a moment he saw her with
Nicholas' eyes.

'Poor lass,' he murmured, bending over her. 'But
what am I to do with you? We're sick of the plague . . .
several households nearby are likewise, and this is no
place for you.' Then he remembered Rebecca tossing
feverishly upstairs, and panic seized him again. 'And
my wife — the doctors are both ill themselves. Neither
one can leave his bed . . .' Scarcely aware of what he
was saying or doing, he stood above her clenching and
unclenching his hands.

She looked up, and he saw that her face was smeared
and marked by runnels of tears. She was shaking her
head in dumb misery.

'I must look to my wife, maiden, do you understand?
Have you enough money to find a safe house to
lodge in?' The words came out unthinkingly, and he
immediately regretted them. But what was he to do? He
could offer no hospitality, not even to the daughter of
his dearest friend. Yet how could a squire's daughter, a
lovely one at that, put up at a hostelry by herself and not
be molested by the men of the town? 'Have you — ?'

She stood up suddenly. She was much taller than
Rebecca and looked taller still by the tilt of her chin

and the straightness of her bearing. 'Yes.' Her face cleared slightly. She seemed ashamed of her stricken appearance. 'Yes, I have gold. But I cannot use it.' Her hands went together in supplication. 'I beg you, let me lodge with Nicholas' kin. I'll cause you no trouble and will see food on your — '

'*Food*? You're mad! Moonstruck!' He stared at her and lifted his hand to bring Adam to the door.

She caught his hand in her own, and he was surprised at the strength in her hands and in her voice. 'No, not just food on your table,' she burst out, 'but physic as well. I know something of healing. Please, please let me in — '

He shook her hand away but made no further attempt to raise Adam by knocking just yet. 'Let you in to your death, Mistress? Nay, your father is my friend.'

She was still shaking her head, and tears started out of her eyes. 'Rebecca did not tell you? You're *nothing* to my father. Nor am I. Nor is even little Edward, the babe your wife nursed so tenderly as her own . . . He is crazed, he is beside himself . . . we are nothing to him now.'

The words penetrated to him, and his shoulders slumped forward. He felt hot all of a sudden, too, and wrenched the clouts away from his face and neck. Tiredness came over him like a wave, and he leaned heavily on the doorpost. Her voice was continuing: that low, bewitching voice he remembered in her mother; the same voice that had captivated his nephew.

'I shall look to Rebecca, sir, I assure you.' She was pulling something out of her bundle and waving a book under his nose, but his head had begun to swim, and he had no strength left to argue.

Without lifting his head, he said, 'Come in, then. At your peril. No one can leave this house again until the angel of death has passed over it. Neither can you.'

She did not answer immediately. Then her voice seemed to come from a long way off. 'But I must gather herbs.'

He did not hear much more. The shop doorway, the girl's face, the dark lane — all rushed in a dizzy whirlpool round him. He felt his grip on the doorpost loosen. His vision darkened, and he sank down under thundering waters.

When he awoke again, it was only for a few moments. He was aware of burning pains in his back and pressure under his arm and in his groin. He was in his bed, alone, and the room was smoky with a strong smell he could not recognize. Blinding light poured in through the window; it pierced him like arrows; he turned his head. *Rebecca?*

He struggled to sit up, but his head pounded as with a thousand fulling mallets. His body seemed disjointed, floating like an old, unravelled garment on a foul pond. The smoke cleared for an instant, and the face of a woman who was not Rebecca blocked out the swords of light that were slicing into his eyes.

'Oh, shut the curtains,' he moaned.

'You must drink this water. 'Tis sweet and cool.'

How did she know his throat was burning? He floated away again, this time under the water. It was stagnant, thick and green, yet it roared in his ears like a tumultuous waterfall. The roaring grew and grew, and he was fighting for his life in the raging filth around him.

He opened his eyes again and saw his own arms and legs flailing in the darkness. A stranger was standing beside him with a candle in her hand. The flame seemed to burn his eyes, and he shut them. A woman's voice came to him, and he opened his eyes again. The woman and the candle had moved, the candle now at the foot of the bed where it would not hurt him. But then the woman came and stood beside him, her hair unbound and beautiful in the faint light. She was stretching out her hand to pull up the covers.

'You must be covered,' she said gently.

'But — I am hot — ' He felt ashamed of his nakedness before this woman, but his body was burning, and his mouth was swollen and tasted foul. 'I am hot. Tell Rebecca — tell her to bring me a drink.'

Then her hand was under his head, cool and strong, raising it up, and a phial of something sweet and thick was at his lips. 'Drink it,' she commanded.

He could not remember whether he had drunk it, but when he opened his eyes again, there was twilight in the room and the phial was beside him, now empty. The same woman — he remembered her face now, though not her name — was standing in the corner of the small room with her back to him. He heard the sound of water poured out: not the black waters of nightmare, now, but fresh, real water.

She turned around, a jug in her hand. 'I must wash you, Isaac Fessenden, and salve your sores.'

'Who are you? Where is Rebecca?'

'Rebecca is with your mother Mary. Remember? Both were ill.'

'And they are well?'

She did not hesitate. 'They are well. But I am here in their stead — your physician, if you will . . . I must wash you.' She caught her lower lip under her teeth as she squeezed out a strip of clean linen.

'I'll do it myself, woman.' He shook his head, but the motion made the room dip round him again, and he retched into the flock bedding.

'I have washed you before, Isaac.' She pulled away the fouled bedding and rolled back the sheet.

He did not dare move. The water was lukewarm on his tight, burning skin, and her hands were light but sure. He looked down, ashamed again, though he did not know why: *Thou hast the longest, strongest, kindest body of any man on earth,* Rebecca always said. But now it looked swollen in places, flaccid in others, and dark lumps marked his groin.

He let his head go back with a moan. So the pestilence had come to him, as well. He screwed his eyes shut.

'I must lance these, you know,' the same woman's voice said. 'Or the venom will consume you.'

Floating on the hideous pond of his half-dreams again, he no longer cared. 'Do as you will,' he mumbled.

She raised his arms first. He opened his eyes to see her face only inches from his own, her eyes narrowed with concentration on the ugly mass under his arm. 'You will feel pain,' she murmured, and he heard her swallow.

He did not trouble to answer her, and she went on, 'I have a salve of cuckoo-pint and ground ivy. You will *not* die, Isaac.' He felt the knife probing, then a release of pressure, followed by a hot plaster that stung and soothed him at once. He moaned again.

Her voice was triumphant, half on the verge of laughter. 'There, now the others.'

'What is it to you?' His teeth had begun to chatter violently. Then the black tide came up again and carried him away. He was swallowed in it, rolled over and over in the wet darkness like Jonah in the belly of the great fish. In the sea of sickness that enclosed him and that he enclosed, he heard a bell ringing over and over again, and a wild voice crying, 'Bring out your dead.' He was carried out on the clang of the bell and the surge of the waves, and he had died.

Later, when he woke again, it was full daylight, and the room was empty. He heard the voices of Adam and Charlie below stairs, and the low, musical voice of the strange woman answering them. He remembered the hideous black lumps, but he felt no pressure now, and the fever had left him. *I have not died, after all.*

He tried to sit up but was still too weak. He waited, but no one came, so he eased the bedding back cautiously and looked down at his body again. There were neat poultices in his groin, and his legs looked thin as sticks, his belly hollow so that his ribs stuck out like the timbers of a half-built ship in Chatham dockyard.

Chatham . . . His mind was clearing now. How long had he lain ill? Three separate pictures formed themselves in his mind: the red mark on Hannah's leg; the dead rats in the gutter . . . and the sad resolute face of young Nicholas as he left for the New World.

Then he remembered the strange woman below stairs and knew who she was at last. The plague bell rang outside again, and a cart rumbled up the lane. 'Bring out your dead!'

He did not know whether to weep for himself or for the woman.

JOHN
Cambridge, The New World, January 1660

Five years of waiting, hoping, and praying had brought a
double reward: a fair wind at Christmasstide had carried
not one of his nephews, but two. The Almighty had
not blessed him with sons — unless he counted poor
Nathaniel — but both his brothers had been generously
endowed, and now both Nicholas and Josiah had come
to him. Steady in the faith, eager to work and to
learn, they were turning his old age into a time of
peace and joy.

Jane, inconsolable after Nathaniel's ugly death, now
moved more swiftly about the house. Even on these
mornings of deep frost and falsely bright winter skies
she sang as she stirred the fire.

His mind was full of plans now: plans for the work of
the tannery and the gloving business, and plans for his
two nephews. Nicholas, the stronger of the two boys, was
learning the trade more quickly than his brother, but
Josiah was clever with the glovemaking itself and kindly
with the customers. To Nicholas he therefore entrusted
the oversight of the tanning yard, the account-keeping
in the shop, and the trading with Indians and trappers
who came seasonally to sell to him. To Josiah he
entrusted the day-to-day management of the shop and
the glove work.

Both lads already thrived in their labours, but John
was puzzled by Nicholas. Sometimes on the Sabbath as
they sat cosily by the fire and Jane read aloud to them all,
he fancied that Nicholas' eyes wandered away, and the
boy's chiselled face became melancholy and remote. He
thought he remembered in Robert's face such moments
of withdrawal, though Nicholas generally reminded him
far more of young Isaac than of Robert — but this
sadness puzzled him.

*How old is the lad? . . . Aye, going on twenty-four, and still
not wed!* John had come to see all men's trials in terms
of their need of womenfolk. *A man's not a man without a
woman beside him* had become his most favoured saying
to fellow selectmen and other Cambridge freemen.

Jane only smiled when he said as much to her. 'So thou'd make a married man of him when he's scarce set foot on the new land, would you?' She bent to blow out the candle by their bed.

'Aye, I would.' John pulled the quilts around his shoulders and enfolded Jane in his arms as she came to lie beside him. Before they came up she had warmed the bed with hot bricks from the fireplace.

'Josiah's as likely to need a wife himself, is he not?' she asked, laughing a little.

'I suppose so, though he never casts an eye on the maids as our Nicholas does.'

'Nicholas plays the lecher?' In the dark, her voice was loud with surprise.

'Hush! Nay, I never said so. But he looks hungry, ne'ertheless, poor lad. Think now of the young women of our fellowship. Is there a proper maid for him, not betrothed and goodly enough to look upon?'

Beside him, Jane lay silent, but he knew by her quick breathing that she was still wide awake and thinking carefully. At last, she said, 'Aye, there *is* such a lass.'

He squeezed her. 'Say on.'

'I'm thinking of John Cheney's girl.'

'What? Margaret? Oh, she's but a thin hop-pole of a girl. And far too young for Nicholas.'

'Dost think so? She's of age, I'm sure. And John, dear, you've not been looking at the lasses lately, that's quite clear, for Margaret's as sturdy as I am.'

He ran his hands over her breasts and belly under the coarse material of her shift. 'Then she'll do,' he teased. '"Sturdy"? What a word, sweetheart! You be not "sturdy" —'

'And thou art shameless.' She pushed him gently away. 'Give o'er.'

'Not while I have a sturdy wife.'

Her arms held him at a distance. 'Wait, we're speaking of Nicholas, not of ourselves. And though he wants a wife, he wants his sister, also.'

'His sister?'

'Aye, have you not heard him speak of Hannah? She sounds to be an honest maiden. Could we not bring her hither, too, to be with her brethren? She must be lonely without them.'

He considered. Sons he had always wanted. The responsibility of a daughter: that might be another matter. 'Aye, she must be lonely. I'm sure Isaac's good to her, but he's not quite of our persuasion nowadays, and mayhap she feels neglected at times. And if God gives us the means to bring her across the sea, why not? But Jane, Nicholas wants a wife more . . . ' He lay quiet for a moment, then, 'Shall I broach the idea with him?'

She hesitated again. 'He's not straightforward, like Josiah. I don't mean he's devious, but thou'lt need to be tender with him. I shouldn't wonder if he'd been crossed in love.'

He clicked his tongue impatiently. 'Oh, trust a woman to dream up such a thought! Very well, you speak to him, then.'

'Good,' she exclaimed. 'I shall, my love.'

He gathered her into his arms again and pushed away the shift. 'Will she be as good to him, think you, as you are to me?' he whispered.

Her answer came more slowly this time. 'I hope so, John.'

She touched his face in the dark. 'Poor lad, I hope so.'

Jane would have spoken to Nicholas the next morning, had not a letter come in by sea. A messenger had carried it up at dawn from the harbour, since it was marked *For John Fessenden, on Eliot Street, most pressing.* Jane brought the letter straight to the table where John, Nicholas and Josiah were breaking their fast with a bowl of hot cornmeal.

'Best open this, husband,' she murmured.

The arrival of any letter was cause enough for surprise. Nicholas' spoon rattled into the trencher. ''Tis my uncle's hand. I pray nothing be amiss.'

John looked across the table at Nicholas' inquiring face, silently wishing the boy less earnest. Jane was more understanding, he thought, for she came and stood with one hand on the shoulder of each of his nephews.

'He probably sends to see that ye be safe arrived,' she said gently.

He broke the seal quickly and scanned the letter. As he did so, the cornmeal rose into his gorge again, and he felt the sweat start out of his face.

Nicholas rose to his feet and leaned over the table, but Josiah's face was passive. 'Is it our sister?' Nicholas asked. 'Has aught befallen Hannah?'

John shook his head slowly, but his mind had gone numb. 'Nay. Hannah hath been — she hath been ill.' He stumbled over the words; they would not come right. 'But she is well, and she has come, that is — will come to us ere long, at the summer's end, God willing.'

The blood leaped into Nicholas' face. 'Oh, but that is good news indeed!'

John reached for his beaver. On cold mornings he wore it even indoors, and now he pulled it off roughly. 'Aye, good news. But there is more, and ye must both brace thyselves like men.'

Nicholas flinched. 'Is it Anna, then?'

'*Nay!*' His voice was sharper than he had intended. 'Nay,' he repeated, more softly. 'I told thee, she is well.'

'Uncle John,' Josiah broke in, 'he means *Anna,* not Hannah. Anna is his beloved.'

Jane caught John's eye, but he was upset now, and he looked again at the letter. 'There *is* an Anna mentioned, I see, but I know not — I confess, I am befuddled and thought he meant thy sister, but listen, and wait.' He took a deep breath. 'Mary, our good stepmother, and thy grandmother, has been taken to the Lord. And Rebecca, Isaac's sweet wife — ' He heard the quaver of his own voice and felt tears prick hot against his eyelids. 'Rebecca, also. Of the *plague.*' His teeth ground together so that the last words came out harshly.

Except for the sharp intake of Jane's breath and the hissing of the firewood, the room was silent.

One of Nicholas' hands clamped onto his wrist, and the other whipped the letter from his hand. 'Forgive me — !'

John watched him scan the letter frantically, his lips moving slightly. Then Nicholas turned to Josiah. 'Our sister lived through the plague. Our cousins somehow escaped it.' His voice was bitter. 'Isaac cared for them all, until Anna, my Anna, came. Now she, too, is at the door of death.'

John watched the interchange without fully understanding. Josiah's arm went round his brother's shoulders, and the two turned to each other and wept. '*My Anna . . . now she is at the door of death.*'

'Who is this girl, this Anna?' Jane asked softly. She had not moved from where she stood, and the three figures were now locked together in sorrow.

John retrieved the letter from Nicholas' hand to look at the date. *Ye 10nth Octobre* was scrawled below Isaac's enormous signature. And now more than three months had passed.

Nicholas raised his head to Jane. 'I forbore to tell ye of her as I had so little hope. And now I have none.'

John could not answer. What if he had lost Jane at the same time in their young lives?

At last, Jane said, 'The Almighty *is* merciful, Nicholas. He knoweth all things, and all things are in his hand. He will bring Hannah to us, I believe, and you can console each other.' Her voice was unsteady, but John marvelled at her discernment. 'I know not of thy Anna, but if it has pleased him to take her unto himself, she is indeed at rest now.'

Nicholas stood up abruptly and pulled on his worsted surcoat, wool cap, and thick mittens. Then he went out.

John got up to follow but sank down again on the bench. Nicholas was not Nathaniel to go running to the ordinary for comfort.

'Let him be, my Uncle John,' Josiah said after a moment. 'He has loved that maid for many months now, and hoped — in spite of all he said — to have her to his wife one day.'

John nodded. 'Aye, I can see that.' He pushed the letter across the table and sighed. Though he had loved Mary, her death did not disturb his own settled life. It was Isaac's life that was shattered; it was Nicholas' life that was shattered.

John wrote to his brother:

> On a drizzling morn this month, our nephew Nicholas was married to Margaret Cheney of Cambridge. Reverend Thomas Shepard did perform the ceremony, with Josiah and me to witness. Margaret is a chaste maid. They will live a godly and sober life, so rest you that we have done all we can for our brother Robert's children. Our greetings to Hannah, whom we hope to welcome to this house in the fall, should she set sail when you receive this paper. We shall hope to find as good a wife to Josiah and husband to Hannah, so please God.
>
> Brother, we grieve for thee and thy dear Rebecca. Of the maid Anna I know not what to say, save that Nicholas has grieved full sore for her, but wants a bride, so is wed. May God rest that poor maid. God save thee, dear my brother Isaac.

He signed and dated the letter, *March 1660, John Fessenden*, then decided to add a postscript:

> Isaac: I have taken thought to another matter. If there be naught to keep thee in England now, would you not come hither, bringing our niece Hannah with you?

ISAAC
Maidstone, Summer 1660

He had become quite used to Anna's ways now, since she had recovered. She had made herself indispensable to him, driven, no doubt, by a false sense of debt for her lodging: a 'safe' lodging that had almost cost them their lives. She polished, scrubbed, and washed more vigorously than any woman he had known or heard of, and there was no more sickness in the house after the plague, even when the fierce spring fevers in Maidstone carried off many other families.

But Anna could not stay for ever. Adam and Charlie were bringing brides to their beds later in the summer; the rooms above the shop would be crowded again, and summer was the best time for journeying.

They heard nothing from Anna's father, and they rarely spoke of him now. Whenever his name was mentioned, shadows crossed Anna's eyes, and at the time of the assizes and petty sessions she kept closely indoors. He knew that all she wanted was to escape Kent and go to Nicholas again.

It troubled him to discover that he was delaying in arranging the young woman's passage. He grieved deeply for Rebecca, but Anna was unwittingly filling her place at home. He had resented her at first. *Nicholas' sweetheart. George's daughter* — she meant little to him, except as someone belonging to other men. *But she has healed me. I owe her my life.*

More and more, her delicate skin (had he not seen her entire, when she was ill?), her mass of angel-like hair and her laughing eyes — entered his dreams. On mornings after such dreams he was abrupt with her as she spoke happily about Nicholas and of the coming voyage. But when he spoke harshly, she only pricked herself and bloodied the sewing so that he grew all the more irritated.

It was not as a seamstress that she filled Rebecca's place, then, for she would never sew well, he thought. No, she was 'all things to all men' — that's what his father would have said. She was sister to Adam and Charlie: prodding Adam out of his dull discourse, teasing Charlie when he ranted about the delights of his sweetheart, doctoring them with physic when they were low, comforting him when he cried for Rebecca . . . She was, he suddenly realized, exactly what Mary had been to his father.

But that, he thought, entailed more than he could contemplate . . . *Nicholas' sweetheart,* he told himself. *I must find another wife.*

The end of May brought word from London and Kent that the King would return at last from France.

'We should go and see the King ride in,' Charlie insisted one afternoon when they were shutting up the shop for the day.

The smell of finely seasoned mutton drifted in at the back door of the shop. *She's made a meal fit for a king again,* he thought, forgetting — as they all had — that he himself had taught her how to prepare food. She cooked it now with as much discrimination as she made cordials and poultices. Even the most commonplace of foods set his mouth watering.

'My father, I said we should go over to Barham to see the King,' Charlie persisted, hands on hips.

Isaac saw himself at the same age: black, curling hair bouncing as he spoke, brown eyes shining. Is that how Rebecca had seen him, fallen in love with him? *I'm wool-gathering.*

'Charlie, I'm sorry, I was thinking of thy mother.'

The boy's face had schooled itself to seriousness. How could he expect his sons to understand his muddled feelings about Rebecca, about Anna . . .

'Dost not think 'twould be a fine thing to see the King, my father?'

'Yes, 'twould indeed.' He gripped himself, concentrating. 'Let's think now — I was but a lad when the last king came to the throne . . . but I believe thy uncles went to see him ride in . . . ' He met Charlie's eyes. 'Aye, 'twould be good to see him for ourselves.' He laughed suddenly, unexpectedly. 'And it would be good for the King to see us, too, do you not suppose?'

Charlie, mystified perhaps by the sudden change from reflection to merriment, smiled back absently, and they went back to the kitchen.

The outer doors stood open, and warm air breathed in from outside. Remembering the plague of last autumn, Isaac silently gave thanks for the blessing of open doors and windows, for the freedom they had with the passing of the pestilence to go in and out as they pleased.

Anna stood by the fire in a patched apron of Rebecca's. She was tasting the meat, and steam curled up around her pink face. She looked young and beautiful, and Isaac felt again a surge of resentment that he must

334

give this girl to Nicholas — even to Nicholas, whom he loved. He wanted to touch her flushed cheek with his fingers. He wanted to kiss her.

She left off stirring and crossed the room close to him, but not looking at him. She was quick like that, not patient (unless someone were ill), nor timid like Rebecca. Now she was reaching up to the dresser, and she pulled down a folded note from behind an upturned milk pitcher. Her voice jolted him uncomfortably.

'There's a letter, Isaac, from someone . . .' Her face was red now, right to the roots of her hair. 'I think from Nicholas, or from thy brother — does it say when they expect us?' She threw an eager look across at Hannah, who was separating curds and whey on the other side of the room, and whose face was equally bright.

'Oh, open it, do!' Hannah pleaded.

He broke the seal and glanced at the writing with a heavy heart. Now they must go at last. They had never complained of the waiting; he had marvelled at that, but now they could wait no longer.

> *Our nephew Nicholas was married to Margaret Cheney
> . . . Brother, we grieve for thee . . . Of the maid
> Anna I know not what to say . . . would you not
> come hither? . . .*

His eye jumped from phrase to phrase but could make no sense of the letter. ''Tis from John,' he muttered, not looking up.

He read it again, more slowly, and his hand began to shake. 'Hannah.' He swallowed hard. 'Thy brothers expect thee forthwith. I shall see to it tomorrow.'

He was aware, suddenly, that Anna was standing close to him. Her breathing was quick and uneven, and his eyes travelled reluctantly from the letter to her clasped hands and to her face.

'And me? Do they not know that I shall journey with her?' Her eyes were wide and frightened. He hated to see that look of fear in them. She was not a woman to be afraid.

'No.' Did she know how difficult that word had been?

Her hands fell to her sides. 'Then — how so, Isaac?' Her face was hurt and puzzled now.

335

'My brother, and Nicholas — all of them — they believe thou didst die of the pestilence, my — '

Her face flamed, and she threw out her arms. 'But I didn't!' she shouted. 'I am alive!' She began to laugh wildly and spun round the room.

He leaned forward and dropped his head into his hands. The rough paper of the note scratched his cheek. His joy was her destruction, and he could not look her in the face.

'Anna,' he said at last, and she stopped her dancing. 'Anna, my dear love, Nicholas — Nicholas is wed to another.'

Hannah was due to sail from Dover, since after his experience with Chatham the year before, Isaac had decided to arrange her voyage from another port. She was to travel with an elderly cobbler and his family, neighbours from Mill Lane, but no one else would accompany her.

He presumed Anna would not want to go with them to Dover. She had spoken vaguely of finding employ with an apothecary in London, but otherwise had said very little since John's letter arrived. So they had left her to herself, Hannah tiptoeing in and out of the chamber the two women shared in the attic; and though he heard her weeping many times, she spurned all offers of comfort.

On the morning of Hannah's departure from Maidstone, however, he found her dry-eyed in the kitchen at dawn — just as she had been in the past — making broth. He sat at table, saying nothing, watching her as she moved about. He was familiar with every curve and line of her body now, and he ached to hold her, as much for himself as to comfort her. She would have none of him, of course.

At last, he ventured, 'Anna, art sure thou'lt not with us towards Dover? I believe Hannah would be sorry if didst not go, though I — ' He let his voice die. It would be foolish to say that he would understand if she did not choose to go.

She turned her blue eyes on him. 'I meant to go, Isaac, all along. 'Tis painful — that's all.' She shrugged.

'But 'tis painful for thee, also, to see the last of thy kin save two sons go away for ever.' Her voice was hollow, as if she was reciting what someone else had asked her to say, or lines she had rehearsed for a pageant.

With his eyes he drank in the pale skin of her neck that showed above the partlett, the tilted roundness of her breasts, the slenderness of her waist — she was too thin now, he thought — and he was struck speechless.

She caught his wandering eyes and began to stammer. 'I said, I shall go. But then I must —' She turned away and began to stir the broth again, her hand moving in quick circles. 'I feel I'm here on sufferance. 'Tis time I were gone.' Her shoulders were taut, and he could not see her face.

He stood up uncertainly. 'Thou'rt *not* here on sufferance, Anna,' he grated. 'Thou art my —'

'I know — "my dearest friend's daughter".' Her voice was bitter, even lower than usual.

He waved his hand helplessly. He could not say what he wanted to say. It was futile to speak of it at all. He sat down again. 'We may well see the King on his way if we make a good start.' He would begin on a new tack, he decided, and he tried to sound matter-of-fact.

She was ladling broth so hastily into the bowls that some of it spilled hissing into the fire. 'Aye, so Charlie tells me.' She sounded steadier again.

He rose to lift the broth onto the tables. Hannah's eyes were sparkling. 'Aye, there's the King coming, and I'm a-going t'other way.'

Isaac was glad of her interruption. 'Foolish king! He should make thee his queen, Hannah, then we'd keep thee in England.'

Hannah laughed. 'Nay, I'd keep *ye*. Take all the gold of Parliament and give it to the people. His poor Majesty shall have none anyhow.'

Charlie came down the back stairs. 'Hush, cousin,' he shouted. 'What a way for a woman to talk! What would you know? And I thought thou wast a Roundhead, anyway, like thy —'

Isaac caught his eye, and Charlie swallowed the last words, but Hannah seemed to notice nothing amiss. 'I was, ere I came here. 'Tis listening to thee and my uncle

337

that's changed me. Now I'd love to see the King as dearly as Anna would — wouldn't you, Anna?'

Charlie scoffed, 'Fine Puritan thou'lt make in Boston!'

Anna smiled faintly. 'Oh, she'll regain her senses there,' she murmured.

Isaac breathed a sigh of relief to see them sparring as usual, but Anna would still not meet his eyes.

The Dover road was lined with timber merchants, shepherds, fullers, and travellers like themselves. The heat shimmered up from the chalky track as it had done thirty-five years before on Barham Down when King Charles I had picnicked there on his own way from Dover to Canterbury; as it had shimmered thirty-five years before when on one side of the hill John and Robert Fessenden and on the other George Tolhurst had watched the new king ride to be crowned in Canterbury.

Dover, Canterbury and all the towns in between made holiday of the day. The road was decked with flowers and banners; musicians brayed on horns and trumpets; and men dressed in liveries, chains, velvet, and cloth of gold marched to and fro.

In the crush of people, Charlie, Adam, and Hannah had for now drifted away with the cobbler and his wife. Isaac watched the spectacle without feeling he was part of it. The splendour could not touch him as long as there was a banner of silence between himself and Anna. He was aware only that she was near, aware — though he did not dare look straight at her — that her eyes were fixed forward on the road. She might have been blinkered.

But suddenly he no longer minded what she thought or did not think of him. He looked at her directly. The sunlight drew a circlet of copper round her hair; her back was straight and unafraid. *This is the woman who has nursed me back to life. This is the woman who thought she lived for Nicholas, but now is dead in her heart because, save God, she has no one. And this is the woman, young though she be, that I want as my wife.* Slowly, so slowly that he scarcely felt his own movement, he put out his arm toward her. She did

338

not move — he hardly expected her to move — and her eyes did not shift. He hesitated, but then, remembering the great crowd around them, grew bold again. His hand reached her waist and touched her.

Her head turned, her face questioning, surprised.

'Anna?'

She nodded almost imperceptibly.

'Wilt thou come hither, then?' He did not move his hand or force her, but she seemed to understand.

'Isaac — '

The people around them had begun to shout, but he did not notice, his eyes watching her mouth say his name. 'Anna, I love thee. I know I am but a tailor — ' He spread his hands, letting go of her again.

A small blue butterfly had settled on her hair and sat there basking in her warmth and in the sunlight falling on them both. She smiled suddenly, as if she had heard the words before, but her eyes were warm, and she came nearer.

He fitted his arm round her waist again and drew her close, as he had wanted to. The noise of his heart obscured all other noise around them. They looked at each other, and Anna rested her head against his arm.

Then they both turned their eyes toward the road. A cavalcade was riding past: proud stallions and grey mares stamping and tossing, bridles ringing. The tall, dark-wigged new king passed only a few feet from where they stood. He waved an enormous plumed hat, and Isaac found himself calculating ridiculously the length of felt that had been used, and the size of the peacock from which the feathers had been plucked.

'We want to keep a free Parliament!' some rogues shouted from the crowd.

A sardonic grin twisted the King's face, and he reined in his horse almost in front of Isaac and Anna. The crowd fell silent in embarrassment.

'Pray be quiet,' Charles Stuart said clearly. His voice was clipped like a Frenchman's. 'And ye shall have both King and Parliament.' He laughed and waved his hat again. 'Ride on.'

Isaac threw back his head and laughed with him.

HISTORICAL NOTE

Home on holiday in England in 1974 from America, I discovered that my husband's ancestors and mine had lived near each other — some of them in the same Kentish village — in the seventeenth century. A book written by one of Jim's relatives — *The Fessenden Family in America* — gave us a few clues. Others were supplied by my mother's family, and soon we found ourselves trying to read parish records and churchyard tombstones. History led to speculation as I realized that the Fessendens had been Puritans and (I surmised) the Tolhursts had been King's men.

Sons and Brothers tells a story of three generations of Fessendens and two generations of Tolhursts. The lives of its characters are rooted in history, but this is not a history book. I have changed history only where I had to for the purposes of the story, though of course I have embroidered history, too, and have inevitably looked at it through my own particular set of prejudices.

The places mentioned, and many of the minor characters (Sir Dudley Digges and Mainy on the Royalist side, and Sandys, Livesey, and Weldon on the Parliamentarian/County Committee side) are as true to life as I can make them, relying on county records and Civil War accounts both contemporary and modern. The daily life of Kentish gentlemen and yeomen — their homes, their way of conversing, their songs, their dependence on cloth and hops — these were all real, and I have tried to reproduce them here faithfully.

But as I have said, this is story, not history. Hence I have changed somewhat the birthdates and names of the Fessenden family (Robert's wife, for example, was Mary, not Patience, but since his stepmother's name was Mary, I preferred to avoid the confusion). The desecration of Canterbury Cathedral actually took place over two successive summers — 1642 and 1643 — but, again, I have compressed the events into one to avoid too much repetition. Similarly, the plague struck Maidstone severely in the 1630s, but did not return until 1666, not 1659 as in my story. But since there was indeed severe sickness in Goudhurst in the late 1650s, I simply transposed this to the county town. Correspondence between a gentleman and Samuel Pepys in 1665 documents what *did* happen in Maidstone during the terrible plague years.

When I was researching this book, many people in Kent were surprised there was anything to write about the Civil War. Surely nothing happened *here*, they said. Nothing could be further from the truth. The Kentish tradition of rebellion asserted itself quite vigorously during that century — first in protests against the imposition of heavy royal taxes, then against the demands of Parliament. And no government — regal or Roundhead — could afford to ignore the strategic importance of Kent, standing as it does between France and the rest of Britain. Kent had to be silenced! Rebellions of the 1640s and 1650s were often ill-planned; to the modern eye they seem somehow quaint (as in the case of the Canterbury Christmas riots of 1647) or foolhardy (as in the case of the Battle of Maidstone in June 1648, when the King's rebels ended with their backs to the wall of St Faith's churchyard or hunted down in the nearby hop gardens). But whatever else may be said about Kent's history at the time, it cannot be said to lack colour!

NIGHTFALL

Christopher Bryan

Brilliant young astronomer Professor Charles Brown is in possession of dangerous information. Bound by the Official Secrets Act, yet driven by an inner compulsion to tell the truth, he wrestles with his conscience.

To tell the world would unleash untold panic. But to give no warning . . . ?

Nightfall is the spine-chilling sequel to Christopher Bryan's first thriller, *Night of the Wolf*.

ISBN 0 7459 1003 3

NIGHT OF THE WOLF

Christopher Bryan

'He was beginning to feel that more had been involved in the life and death of Nikos Kakoyannis than a mad old man meeting an untimely end.'

Chief Inspector David Adam's suspicions were justified.
This case was to draw him into an investigation of the works of darkness, of unholy ambition and the ruthless pursuit of power.

'*Night of the Wolf* grips the reader from the first page and never lets go for a moment.'
Sheldon Vanauken

ISBN 0 85648 446 6

THE DRAGON KING TRILOGY

BOOK 1: IN THE HALL OF THE DRAGON KING

Stephen Lawhead

Quentin, a young acolyte serving in the temple of Ariel, is
thrust into the centre of a conflict in which the life of the king
and the future of the realm of Mensandor hang in the balance.
Drawn into the web of intrigue spawned by the Necromancer
Nimrood, Quentin, with the aid of friends loyal to the Dragon
King, embarks on a dangerous quest.

ISBN 0 85648 859 3

BOOK 2: THE WARLORDS OF NIN

Stephen Lawhead

Mensandor is once more in desperate straits. The Wolf Star
grows nightly greater and more threatening as the power of
Nin increases and black terror reigns. It is Quentin, once
again, who holds the kingdom's destiny in his hands. Hope
lies in the forging of a sword — Zhalighkeer, the Shining
One. But the secret source of lanathil, the living metal from
which it must be made, is long since lost.

ISBN 0 85648 874 7

BOOK 3: THE SWORD AND THE FLAME

Stephen Lawhead

Quentin now reigns as the Dragon King, and is faced with the bitterest onslaught of all — the insidious attack of evil from within himself. As a young acolyte in the temple of Ariel he set out gladly on a journey which was to take him away from the old gods to a life-giving encounter with the Most High. Now it is not simply his own life, or the kingdom, which hangs in the balance. Nimrood holds Quentin's son hostage. The Dragon King has lost his sword — Zhalighkeer, the Shining One — and he has lost his way. Will he also betray his vow to the Most High?

ISBN 0 85648 875 5

DREAM THIEF

Stephen Lawhead

'The dreams had been at Spence again. He could feel their lingering presence like a dimly remembered whisper. They were unsettling in a vague sort of way — haunting. There was a word that seemed to fit. He felt haunted.'

Dr Spencer Reston, sleep scientist on space station Gotham, has become a vital link in a cosmic group masterminded by a mysterious creature known as the Dream Thief.

ISBN 0 85648 838 0

EMPYRION ONE: The Search for Fierra

Stephen Lawhead

Cynetics, the largest corporation on Earth, has sent Orion Treet to its first space colony located on the planet Empyrion, ten light years away from Earth. His mission is to observe and write about what he sees at the colony for the Chairman. When he arrives with three other explorers, he discovers a world that has progressed three thousand years from the time it was first colonized. Before Treet realizes it, he finds his comrades and himself enmeshed in a conflict between the two civilizations that have developed there.

The Search for Fierra shows the effects on people when a culture institutionalizes its dark side. A fast-paced adventure story, and thoughtful examination of human culture, the book both intrigues and entertains.

ISBN 0 7459 1110 2

EMPYRION TWO: The Siege of Dome

Stephen Lawhead

'Treet listened to the tension in the voices; heard the fear
creeping in. It was as if an unseen hand had closed around
the group, slowly crushing out hope.

　　He was on his feet.

　　"Listen to me. What you feel is the ancient mindless fear
that paralyzes and consumes, that destroys first the will and
then the heart." His voice rose to a shout. "You think to pull
down a dictator, but the danger is greater than you suspect.
We have a world to save."'

Empyrion Two brings the SF epic thriller begun in *The Search
for Fierra* to a world-shaking climax.

ISBN 0 7459 1148 X

THE PENDRAGON CYCLE

BOOK 1: TALIESIN

Stephen Lawhead

Taliesin is the first book of the Pendragon Cycle: a magnificent epic set against the backcloth of Roman Britain and the legends of Arthur and Atlantis.

'I will weep no more for the lost, asleep in their water graves. The voices of the departed speak: Tell our story, they say. It is worthy to be told. And so I take my pen and write . . .'

So begins the tragedy of lost Atlantis, extinguished for ever in a hideous paroxysm of earth and sea. Out of the holocaust, three crippled ships emerge to bear King Avallach and his daughter to the cloud-bound isle of Ynys Prydein.

Here is another world, where Celtic chieftains struggle for survival in the twilight of Rome's power. One heroic figure towers over all, the Prince Taliesin, in whom is the sum of human greatness — grandeur and grace, meekness and majesty, beauty and truth.

This is a tale that spans two worlds, a vision that sings in the heart, and a love that spawns the miracle of Merlin . . . Arthur . . . and a destiny that is more than a kingdom.

ISBN 0 7459 1309 1

A selection of top titles from LION PUBLISHING

THE SHADOWED BED Jack Clemo	£3.95 ☐
NIGHTFALL Christopher Bryan	£1.95 ☐
NIGHT OF THE WOLF Christopher Bryan	£1.95 ☐
IN THE HALL OF THE	
DRAGON KING Stephen Lawhead	£2.99 ☐
THE WARLORDS OF NIN Stephen Lawhead	£2.95 ☐
THE SWORD AND THE	
FLAME Stephen Lawhead	£2.95 ☐
DREAM THIEF Stephen Lawhead	£2.50 ☐
EMPYRION I Stephen Lawhead	£2.95 ☐
EMPYRION II Stephen Lawhead	£2.95 ☐
TALIESIN Stephen Lawhead	£2.99 ☐

All Lion paperbacks are available from your local bookshop or newsagent, or can be ordered direct from the address below. Just tick the titles you want and fill in the form.

Name (Block letters)...

Address..

....

Write to Lion Publishing, Cash Sales Department, PO Box 11, Falmouth, Cornwall TR10 9EN, England.

Please enclose a cheque or postal order to the value of the cover price plus:

UK: 60p for the first book, 25p for the second book and 15p for each additional book ordered to a maximum charge of £1.90.

OVERSEAS: £1.25 for the first book, 75p for the second book plus 28p per copy for each additional book.

BFPO: 60p for the first book, 25p for the second book plus 15p per copy for the next seven books, thereafter 9p per book.

Lion Publishing reserves the right to show on covers and charge new retail prices which may differ from those previously advertised in the text or elsewhere, and to increase postal rates in accordance with the Post Office.